THE
INNER CIRCLE

THE
INNER CIRCLE

T. Coraghessan Boyle

VIKING

VIKING
Published by the Penguin Group
Penguin Group (USA) Inc., 375 Hudson Street, New York, New York 10014, U.S.A.
Penguin Books Ltd, 80 Strand, London WC2R 0RL, England
Penguin Books Australia Ltd, 250 Camberwell Road, Camberwell, Victoria 3124, Australia
Penguin Books Canada Ltd, 10 Alcorn Avenue, Toronto, Ontario, Canada M4V 3B2
Penguin Books India (P) Ltd, 11 Community Centre, Panchsheel Park, New Delhi–110 017, India
Penguin Group (NZ), Cnr Airborne and Rosedale Roads, Albany, Auckland 1310, New Zealand
Penguin Books (South Africa) (Pty) Ltd, 24 Sturdee Avenue, Rosebank, Johannesburg 2196, South Africa

Penguin Books Ltd, Registered Offices: 80 Strand, London WC2R 0RL, England

First published in 2004 by Viking Penguin, a member of Penguin Group (USA) Inc.

10 9 8 7 6 5 4 3 2 1

Copyright © T. Coraghessan Boyle, 2004
All rights reserved

PUBLISHER'S NOTE
This is a work of fiction. Names, characters, places, and incidents either are the product of the author's imagination or are used fictitiously, and any resemblance to actual persons, living or dead, business establishments, events, or locales is entirely coincidental.

LIBRARY OF CONGRESS CATALOGING-IN-PUBLICATION DATA

Boyle, T. Coraghessan.
    The inner circle / T. Coraghessan Boyle.
      p.   cm.
    ISBN 0-670-03344-8
      1. Kinsey, Alfred C. (Alfred Charles), 1894–1956—Friends and associates—Fiction.   2. Kinsey, Alfred C.
(Alfred Charles), 1894–1956—Fiction.   3. Sex—Research—Fiction.   4. Sexologists—Fiction.   I. Title.

PS3552.O932I56 2004
813'.54—dc22   2003069462

Printed in the United States of America

Designed by Carla Bolte • Set in Minion

Without limiting the rights under copyright reserved above, no part of this publication may be reproduced, stored in or introduced into a retrieval system, or transmitted, in any form or by any means (electronic, mechanical, photocopying, recording, or otherwise), without the prior written permission of both the copyright owner and the above publisher of this book.

The scanning, uploading, and distribution of this book via the Internet or via any other means without the permission of the publisher is illegal and punishable by law. Please purchase only authorized electronic editions and do not participate in or encourage electronic piracy of copyrightable materials. Your support of the author's rights is appreciated.

For Robert Coover, *mi apreciadísimo maestro*

AUTHOR'S NOTE

This is a work of fiction, and all characters and situations have been invented, with the exception of the historical figures of Alfred C. Kinsey and his wife, Clara Bracken (McMillen) Kinsey. I am indebted to Dr. Kinsey's biographers—Cornelia Christenson, Jonathan Gathorne-Hardy, James H. Jones and Wardell B. Pomeroy—for much of the factual material delineating the details of their lives. In addition, I would like to thank Jenny Bass and Shawn C. Wilson of the Kinsey Institute for their help and generosity.

Eternity was in our lips and eyes,
Bliss in our brows' bent. . . .

—William Shakespeare, *Antony and Cleopatra*

Some sort of non-penile stimulation of the female genitalia is
almost universal among the lower mammals, where, however,
the lack of prehensile hands places the burden of activity on
the nose and mouth of the male.

—Alfred C. Kinsey, *Sexual Behavior in the Human Female*

THE

INNER CIRCLE

PROLOGUE

Bloomington, Indiana

August 25, 1956

Looking back on it now, I don't think I was ever actually "sex shy" (to use one of Prok's pet phrases), but I'll admit I was pretty naïve when I first came to him, not to mention hopelessly dull and conventional. I don't know what he saw in me, really—or perhaps I do. If you'll forgive me a moment of vanity, my wife, Iris, claims I was something of a heart-throb on campus, though I would have been the last to know of it be-cause I wasn't dating and had always been uncomfortable with the sort of small talk that leads up to the casual inquiry about after-class plans or what you might or might not be doing on Saturday after the game. I had a pretty fair physique in those days, with a matching set of fullback's shoulders and a thirty-inch waist (I was first string on my high school team till I suffered a concussion midway through my junior season and my mother put a premature end to my career), and unlike most men at college, I was conscientious about keeping myself in trim—I still am— but that's neither here nor there. To complete the portrait, because al-ready I've managed to get myself out on a limb here, I was blessed with what Iris calls "sensitive" eyes, whatever that might mean, and a thatch of wheat-colored hair with a natural curl that defeated any cream or po-made I'd ever come across. As for sex, I was eager but inexperienced, and shy in the usual way—unsure of myself and just about as un-informed as anyone you could imagine.

In fact, the first time I developed anything more than a theoretical grasp of what coitus involved—the mechanics of the act, that is—was during my senior year at IU, in the fall of 1939, when I found myself sitting in a lecture hall jammed to the rafters with silent, dry-mouthed students of both sexes as Prok's color slides played hugely across the screen. I was there at the instigation of a girl named Laura Feeney, one of the campus femmes fatales who never seemed to go anywhere without an arm looped through some letterman's. Laura had the reputation of being "fast," though I can assure you I was never the beneficiary of her sexual largesse (if, in fact, the rumors were true: as I was later to learn, the most provocative-looking women often have the most repressed sex lives, and vice versa). I remember being distinctly flattered when she stopped me in the corridor one day during fall registration, took hold of my arm at the muscle and pecked a kiss on my cheek.

"Oh, hi, John," she breathed, "I was just thinking about you. How was your summer?"

My summer had been spent back home in Michigan City, stocking shelves and bagging groceries, and if I had five minutes to myself my mother had me pruning the trees, reshingling the roof and pulling weeds in the vegetable garden. I was lonely, bored to tears, masturbating twice a day in my attic room that was like a sweatbox in a penal institution. My only relief derived from books. I came under the spell of John Donne and Andrew Marvell that summer, and I reread Sir Philip Sidney's *Astrophel and Stella* three times in preparation for an English literature course I was looking forward to in the fall. But I couldn't tell Laura Feeney all this—or any of it. She would have thought me a washout. Which I was. So I just shrugged and said, "All right, I guess."

Voices reverberated in the stairwell, boomed in the corners and fled all the way down the corridor to where the registration tables had been set up in the gymnasium. "Yeah," Laura said, and her smile went cold a moment, "I know how you feel. With me it was work, work, work—my father owns a lunch counter in Fort Wayne, did you know that?"

I didn't know. I shook my head and felt a whole shining loop of my hair fall loose, though I must have used half a bottle of crème oil on it. I was wearing one of the stiff new Arrow shirts my grandmother had sent me from Chicago and a glen-plaid tie I think I wore to class every day that year in the hope of making a good impression, my briefcase was in one hand, a stack of library books in the other. As I've said, the gift of small talk eluded me. I think I said something like, "Fort Wayne, huh?"

In any event, it didn't matter what I said, because she let her turquoise eyes go wide (she was a redhead, or a strawberry blonde, actually, with skin so white you'd think it had never seen the sun), gave my muscle a squeeze and lowered her voice. "Listen," she said, "I just wanted to know if you'd mind getting engaged to me—"

Her words hung there between us, closing out everything else—the chatter of the group of freshmen materializing suddenly from the men's room, the sound of an automobile horn out on the street—and I can only imagine the look I must have given her in response. This was long before Prok taught me to tuck all the loose strands of my emotions behind a mask of impassivity, and everything I was thinking routinely rushed to my face along with the blood that settled in my cheeks like a barometer of confusion.

"John, you're not blushing, are you?"

"No," I said, "not at all. I'm just—"

She held my eyes, enjoying the moment. "Just what?"

I shrugged. "We were out in the sun—yesterday it was, yesterday afternoon. Moving furniture. So, I guess, well—"

Someone brushed by me, an undergraduate who looked vaguely familiar—had he been in my psych class last year?—and then she let the other shoe drop. "I mean, just for the semester. For pretend." She looked away and her hair rose and fell in an ebbing wave. When she turned back to me, she lifted her face till it was like a satellite of my own, pale and glowing in the infusion of light from the windows at the end of the corridor. "You know," she said, "for the marriage course?"

That was the moment it all began, though I didn't realize it at the time—how could I? How could I have foreseen that a shallow, manipulative girl I hardly knew would be the motive force that was to lead me to Prok and Mac, Corcoran, Rutledge, to the desk at which I'm now sitting, trying to get as much of this out as I can before the world goes to pieces? I said, "Yes." I said, "Yes, all right," and Laura Feeney smiled and before I knew it I was on my way to becoming an initiate in the science of sex, abandoning the ideal for the actual, the dream of Stella ("True, that true beauty virtue is indeed") for anatomy, physiology and an intimate knowledge of the Bartholin's glands and the labia minora. All of it—all the years of research, the thousands of miles traveled, the histories taken, the delving and rooting and pioneering—spun out like thread from an infinite spool held in the milk-white palm of Laura Feeney on an otherwise ordinary morning in the autumn of 1939.

But I don't want to make too much of it—we all have our defining moments. And I don't mean to keep you in the dark here either. The "marriage course" to which Laura Feeney was referring—Marriage and the Family, properly—was being offered by Professor Kinsey of the Zoology Department and half a dozen of his colleagues from other disciplines, and it was the sensation of the campus. The course was open only to faculty and staff, students who were married or engaged, and seniors of both sexes. There were eleven lectures in all, five of them covering the sociological, psychological, economic, legal and religious facets of marriage, these to be delivered by faculty outside of the Zoology Department, and they were to prove to be informative enough, I suppose, and necessary, but if truth be told they were nothing more than window dressing for the six unexpurgated lectures (with audio-visual aids) Prok was scheduled to give on the physiology of intramarital relations.

Word was out on campus, and I suspect there were any number of junior girls like Laura Feeney shopping at the five-and-dime for rhinestone rings—maybe even sophomores and freshmen too. My guess is that Laura's lettermen were engaged to their fall sports, and, by extension, their coaches, and so she cast me in the role of prospective bridegroom. I didn't mind. I would say she wasn't my type, but then all women are every man's type, under the right circumstances. She was popular, she was pretty, and if for an hour or two a week people took her to be mine, so much the better. To this point, I'd been immersed in my studies—I made dean's list five out of the first six semesters—and I barely knew any girls, either on campus or back at home, and to have her there at my side as other couples strolled by and the late-blooming sun ladled syrup over the trees and the apparent world stood still for whole minutes at a time was like no feeling I'd ever had. Was it love? I don't know. It was certainly something, and it stirred me—I could always hope, couldn't I?

At any rate, as I say, word was out, and the lecture hall was full to overflowing when we got there the first day. I remember being surprised at the number of younger faculty crowding the front rows with their prim and upright wives and how many of them I didn't recognize. There was a sprinkling of older faculty too, looking lost and even vaguely queasy, and their presence was a real puzzle—you would have thought people in their forties and fifties with grown children should be acquainted with the basic facts of life, but there they were. ("Maybe they need a refresher course," Laura said with half a grin and very much sotto voce, and even that, even the barest mention of what those couples must have done in private—or once have done—made me go hot all over.) But of course the real multitude was composed of students—there must have been three hundred or more of us there, crowded in shoulder to shoulder, all waiting to be scandalized, to hear the forbidden words spoken aloud and see the very act itself depicted in living color.

Dr. Hoenig, the Dean of Women, had been stationed at the door as we filed in, ready to pounce on anyone who wasn't on her list of registered students. She was a short, top-heavy woman in a dowdy dress and a gray cloche hat that seemed like an extension of her pinned-up hair, and though she must have been in her forties then she seemed to us as ancient and vigilant as the Sphinx, her spectacles shining as she bent to check names against the list and scrutinize the ring fingers of all the girls who claimed to be engaged. We passed muster, and sat through the preliminary lectures, biding our time until Dr. Kinsey took the stage. We'd seen him at the outset—he'd electrified us all in his introductory lecture by claiming that there were no abnormalities when it came to sex, save for abstinence, celibacy and delayed marriage—but then he'd been succeeded by a doctor from the medical school whose voice was perfectly pitched to the frequency of sleep, and then a Methodist minister and a pinched little man from the Psychology Department who spoke ad nauseam on Freud's *Three Essays on the Theory of Sexuality.*

It was raining, I remember, on the day we'd all been waiting for—the day of the slide presentation—and as Laura Feeney and I stepped into the anteroom with the mob of other students divesting themselves of umbrellas and slickers, I was struck by the deep working odor of all that massed and anointed flesh. Laura must have noticed it too, because the minute she ducked demurely past Dean Hoenig, she wrinkled up her nose and whispered, "Smells like somebody let all the tomcats loose."

I didn't know what to say to that, so I gave her a faint smile—it wouldn't do at all to look as if I were enjoying myself, because this was education, after all, this was science, and every face had been ironed sober—and allowed my right hand to rest lightly at her waist as I guided her through the crush and into the semi-darkened hall. We were fifteen minutes early, but already all the aisle seats had been taken and we had to edge awkwardly through a picket of folded knees, book bags and umbrellas to reach the middle of one of the back rows. Laura settled in, shook out her hair, waved to thirty or forty people I didn't recognize, then bent forward over her compact and stealthily reapplied her lipstick. She came up compressing her lips and giving me the sort of look she might have reserved for a little brother or maybe the family dog—she was a junior from Fort Wayne and I was a senior from Michigan City and no matter how much I wanted to believe otherwise there was nothing, absolutely nothing, between us.

I gazed down the row. Nearly all the girls were glancing round them with shining eyes while the men fumbled with loose-leaf binders and worried over the nubs of their pencils. A man from my rooming house—Dick Martone—happened to glance up then and our eyes met briefly. Both of us looked away, but not before I could read his excitement. Here we were—he wedged in between two other senior men, I with Laura Feeney preening at my side—about to see and engage what we'd been hungering after for the better part of our lives. I can't begin to describe the *frisson* that ran through that hall, communicated from seat to seat, elbow to elbow, through the whole yearning mass of us. Over the course of the past weeks we'd been instructed in the history and customs of marriage, heard about the emotions evoked, the legal ramifications of the nuptial bond and even the anatomy of the structures involved in reproduction, heard the words "penis," "nipple," "vagina" and "clitoris" spoken aloud in mixed company, and now we were going to see for ourselves. I could feel the blood pounding in my extremities.

Then the side door swung open and Dr. Kinsey was there, striding purposefully to the podium. Though a moment before he'd been slogging across campus in galoshes and southwester, you would have thought he'd just stepped out of a sunlit meadow, the sheaf of his bristling flat-topped pompadour standing upright from the crown of his head as if it had been pressed from a mold, his dark suit, white shirt and bow tie impeccable, his face relaxed and youthful. He was in his mid-forties then, a looming tall presence with an oversized head, curiously narrowed shoulders and a slight stoop—the result of the rickets he'd suffered as a child—and he never wasted a motion or a single minute of anybody's time either. The anticipatory murmur fell off abruptly as he stepped up to the lectern and raised his head to look out on the audience. Silence. Absolute. We all became aware of the sound of the rain then, a steady sizzle like static in the background.

"Today we shall discuss the physiology of sexual response and orgasm in the human animal," he began, without preliminary, without notes, and as his equable, matter-of-fact tones penetrated the audience, I could feel Laura Feeney go tense beside me. I stole a glance at her. Her face was rapt, her white blouse glowing in the dimness of the lecture hall as if it were the single radiant point in the concave sweep of the audience. She was wearing knee socks and a pleated skirt that pulled tight to reveal the swell of the long muscles of her thighs. Her perfume took hold of me like a vise.

Professor Kinsey—Prok—went on, with the help of the overhead projector, to document how the penis enlarges through vasocongestion and at orgasm releases between two and five million spermatozoa,

9

depending on the individual, and then turned his attention to the female reproductive organs. He talked at length about vaginal secretions and their function in easing intromission of the penis, spoke of the corresponding importance of the cervical secretions, which, in some cases, may serve to loosen the mucous plug that ordinarily lies in the opening—the *os*—of the cervix, and can prevent fertilization by blocking movement of the sperm into the uterus and subsequently the Fallopian tubes. We bowed our heads, scribbled furiously in our notebooks. Laura Feeney swelled beside me till she was the size of one of the balloons they floated overhead during the Macy's parade. Everyone in the place was breathing as one.

And then, abruptly, the first of the slides appeared, a full-color, close-up photograph of an erect, circumcised phallus, followed by a shot of the moist and glistening vagina awaiting it. "The vagina must be spread open as the erect male organ penetrates," Dr. Kinsey went on, as the next slide dominated the screen behind him, "and thus the female has employed two fingers to this end. You will observe that the clitoris is stimulated at this point, thus providing the erotic stimulation necessary for the completion of the act on the part of the female." There was more—a very detailed and mechanical account of the various positions the human animal employs in engaging in coitus, as well as techniques of foreplay—and a teaser (as if we needed one) for the next lecture, which was to focus on fertilization and (here the whispers broke out) how to circumvent it.

I heard it all. I even took notes, though afterward I could make no sense of them. Once the slides appeared I lost all consciousness of the moment (and I can't overemphasize the jolt they gave me, the immediate and intensely physical sensation that was like nothing so much as plunging into a cold stream or being slapped across the face—here it was, here it was at long last!). I might have been sitting there upright in the chair, Laura Feeney swelling at my side, and I drew breath and blinked my eyes and the blood circulated through my veins, but for all intents and purposes I wasn't there at all.

Afterward—and I can't for the life of me recall how the lecture concluded—people collected their things in silence and moved up the

aisles in a somber processional. There was none of the jostling and joking you would normally expect from a mob of undergraduates set loose
after an hour's confinement. Instead, the crowd shuffled forward list-
lessly, shoulders slumped, eyes averted, for all the world like refugees es-
caping some disaster. I couldn't look at Laura Feeney. I couldn't guide
her with a hand to her waist either—I was on fire, aflame, and I was
afraid the merest touch would incinerate her. I studied the back of her
head, her hair, her shoulders, as we made our way through the crowd
toward the smell of the rain beyond the big flung-open doors at the end
of the hallway. We were delayed a moment on the doorstep, a traffic jam
there on the landing as the rain lashed down and people squared their
hats and fumbled with umbrellas, and then I had my own umbrella
open and Laura and I were down the steps and out into the rain.

We must have gone a hundred yards, the trees flailing in the wind, the
umbrella streaming, before I found something to say. "Do you—would
you like to take a walk? Or do you need to, perhaps—because I could
take you back to the dorm if that's what you—"

Her face was drawn and bloodless and she walked stiffly beside me,
avoiding body contact as much as was possible under the circumstances. She stopped suddenly and I stopped too, awkwardly struggling
to keep the crown of the umbrella above her. "A walk?" she repeated. "In
this? You've got the wrong species here, I'm afraid—I'm a *human animal*, not a duck." And then we were laughing, both of us, and it was all
right.

"Well, how about a cup of coffee then—and maybe a piece of, I don't
know, pie? Or a drink?" I hesitated. The rain glistened in her hair and
her eyes were bright. "I could use a stiff one after that. I was—what I
mean is, I never—"

She touched my arm at the elbow and her smile suddenly bloomed
and then faded just as quickly. "No," she said, and her voice had gone
soft, "me either."

I took her to a tavern crowded with undergraduates seeking a respite
from the weather, and the first thing she did when we settled into a
booth by the window was twist the rhinestone band off her finger and
secrete it in the inside compartment of her purse. Then she unpinned

her hat, patted down her hair and turned away from me to reapply her lipstick. I hadn't thought past the moment, and once we agreed on where we were going, we hadn't talked much either, the rain providing background music on the timpani of the umbrella and plucking the strings of the ragged trees as if that were all the distraction we could bear. Now, as I braced my elbows on the table and leaned toward her to ask what she wanted to drink, I realized that this was something very like a date and blessed my luck because I had two and a half dollars left in my wallet after paying out room and board from my scant weekly paycheck (I was working at the university library then, pushing a broom and reshelving books five evenings a week). "Oh, I don't know," she said, and I could see she wasn't quite herself yet. "What are you having?"

"Bourbon. And a beer chaser."

She made a moue of her lips.

"I can get you a soft drink, if you prefer—ginger ale, maybe?"

"A Tom Collins," she said, "I'll have a Tom Collins," and her eyes began to sweep the room.

The lower legs and cuffs of my trousers were wet and my socks squished in my shoes as I rose to make my way to the bar. The place was close and steaming, shoulders and elbows looming up everywhere, the sawdust on the floor darkly compacted by the impressions of a hundred wet heels. When I got back to the table with our drinks, there was another couple sitting opposite Laura, the girl in a green velvet hat that brought out the color of her eyes, the man in a wet overcoat buttoned up over his collar and the knot of his tie. He had a long nose with a bump in it and two little pincushion eyes set too close together. I don't remember his name—or hers either, not at this remove. Call them Sally and Bill, for the purposes of this account, and identify them as fellow students in the marriage course, sweethearts certainly—worlds more than Laura and I were to each other—though not yet actually engaged.

Laura made the introductions. I nodded and said I was pleased to meet them both.

Bill had a pitcher of beer in front of him, the carbonation rising up from its depths in a rich, golden display, and I watched in silence as he tucked his tongue in the corner of his mouth and meticulously poured out half a glass for Sally and a full one for himself. The golden liquid swirled in the glass and the head rose and steadied before composing itself in a perfect white disc. "You look like you've done that before," I said.

"You bet I have," he replied, then lifted his glass and grinned. "A toast," he proposed. He waited till we'd raised our glasses. "To Professor Kinsey!" he cried. "Who else?"

This was greeted with a snicker from the booth behind us, but we laughed—all four of us—as a way of defeating our embarrassment. There was one thing only on our minds, one subject we all were burning to talk of, and though Bill had alluded to it, we weren't quite comfortable with it yet. We were silent a moment, studying the faces of the people shuffling damply through the door. "I like your ring, Sally," Laura said finally. "Was it terribly expensive?"

And then they were both giggling and Bill and I were laughing along with them, laughing immoderately, laughing for the sheer joy and release of it. I could feel the bourbon settling in my stomach and sending out feelers to the distant tendrils of my nerves, and my face shone and so did theirs. We were in on a secret together, the four of us—we'd put one over on Dean Hoenig—and we'd just gone through a rite of initiation in a darkened hall in the biology building. It took a minute. Bill lit a cigarette. The girls searched each other's eyes. "Jeez," Bill said finally, "did you ever in your life see anything like that?"

"I thought I was going to die," Sally said. She threw a glance at me, then studied the pattern of wet rings her beer glass had made on the table. "If my mother—" she began, but couldn't finish the thought.

"God," Laura snorted, making a drawn-out bleat of it, "my mother would've gone through the roof." She'd lit a cigarette too, and it smoldered now in the ashtray, the white of the paper flecked red from the touch of her lips. She picked it up distractedly, took a quick puff, exhaled. "Because we never, in my family, I mean never, discussed, you know, where little boys and girls come from."

Sally raised a confidential hand to her mouth. "They call him 'Dr. Sex,' did you know that?"

"Who does?" I felt as if I were floating above the table, all my tethers cut and the ground fast fading below me. This was heady stuff, naughty, wicked, like when a child first learns the verboten words Dr. Kinsey had pronounced so distinctly and disinterestedly for us just an hour before.

Sally raised her eyebrows till they met the brim of her hat. "People. Around campus."

"Not to mention town," Bill put in. He dropped his voice. "He makes you do interviews, you know. About your sex life"—he laughed—"or lack of it."

"I would hate that," Sally said. "It's so . . . *personal*. And it's not as if he's a medical doctor. Or a minister even."

I felt overheated suddenly, though the place was as dank as the dripping alley out back. "*Histories*," I said, surprising myself. "Case histories. He's explained all that—how else are we going to know what people—"

"The human animal, you mean," Laura said.

"—what people do when they, when they mate, if we don't look at it scientifically? And frankly, I don't know about you, but I applaud what Kinsey's doing, and if it's shocking, I think we should ask ourselves why, because isn't a, a . . . a *function* as universal as reproductive behavior just as logical a cause for study as the circulation of the blood or the way the cornea works or any other medical knowledge we've accumulated over the centuries?" It might have been the bourbon talking, but there I was defending Prok before I ever even knew him.

"Yes, but," Bill said, and we all leaned into the table and talked till our glasses were empty, and then we filled them and emptied them again, the rain tracing patterns in the dirt of the window, then the window going dark and the tide of undergraduates ebbing and flowing as people went home to dinner and their books. It was seven o'clock. I was out of money. My head throbbed but I'd never been so excited in my life. When Bill and Sally excused themselves and shrugged out the door and into the wafting dampness of the night, I lingered a moment, half-drunk, and put an arm round Laura's shoulders. "So we're still engaged, aren't we?" I murmured.

Her smile spread softly from her lips to her eyes. She plucked the maraschino cherry from her glass and rotated it between her fingers before gently pressing it into my mouth. "Sure," she said.

"Then shouldn't we—or don't we have an obligation, to, to—"

"Sure," she said, and she leaned forward and gave me a kiss, a kiss that was sweetened by the syrup of the cherry and the smell of her perfume and the proximity of her body that was warm now and languid. It was a long kiss, the longest I'd ever experienced, and it was deepened and complicated by what we'd seen up there on the screen in the lecture hall, by the visual memory of those corresponding organs designed for sensory gratification and the reproduction of the species, mutually receptive, self-lubricated, cohesive and natural. I came up for air encouraged, emboldened, and though there was nothing between us and we both knew it, I whispered, "Come home with me."

The look of Laura's face transformed suddenly. Her eyes sharpened and her features came into focus as if I'd never really seen them before, as if this wasn't the girl I'd just kissed in a moment of sweet oblivion. We were both absolutely still, our breath commingling, hands poised at the edge of the table as if we didn't know what to do with them, till she turned away from me and began to gather up her purse, her raincoat, her hat. I became aware of the voices at the bar then, someone singing in a creaking baritone, the hiss of a newly tapped keg. "I don't know what you're thinking, John," she said, and I was getting to my feet now too, rattled suddenly, flushing red for all I knew. "I'm not that kind of a girl."

But let me step back a moment, because I don't want to get off on the wrong foot—this isn't about me, this is about Prok, and Prok is dead, and I'm sitting here in my study, the key turned in the lock, the sorry tepid remains of a Zombie cocktail at my elbow, trying to talk into this machine and sort out my thoughts while Iris paces up and down the hall in her heels, stopping on every third revolution to rattle the doorknob and remind me in a muffled shout that we're going to be late. Late for what, I'd like to know. Late for tramping through the funeral home with a mob of newspaper reporters and the rest of the curiosity seekers?

15

Late to show our support? Or dedication? Is it going to do Mac any good? Or the children? Or Corcoran, Rutledge, or even my own son, John Jr., who locked himself in his room at the top of the stairs two hours ago because he's had enough of death and sorrow and mourning, because unlike the ghouls and the carrion sniffers and all the rest he hasn't the faintest desire to look on the empty husk of greatness? The corpse, that is. The mortal remains. Prok in his casket, propped up like a wax effigy, drained and flushed and pumped full of formaldehyde, the man who had no illusions, the scientist, the empiricist, the evolutionist, Prok. Prok is dead, is dead, is dead, and nothing else matters.

"John, goddamn you, will you open this door?" Iris is abusing the doorknob, she's pounding with a balled-up fist at the oak panels of the door I myself stripped and varnished. And who took us to look at this house, who loaned us the money for it? Who gave us everything we have?

"Okay, okay!" I shout, and then I'm up from the desk, forcing down the dregs of the joyless drink and shuffling across the carpet to twist the key in the lock and fling open the door.

Iris is there, her face blotted with anger, with exasperation, stalking into the room in her black dress, her black stockings and heels, the hat and the veil. My wife. Thirty-six years old, the mother of my son, as slim and dark and wide-eyed and beautiful as the day I met her. And angry. Deeply, intensely angry. "What are you doing?" she demands, crowding into me, her hands windmilling in my face. "Don't you realize we're twenty minutes late *already*?" And then, catching sight of the glass in my hand: "Are you drinking? At two o'clock in the afternoon? Jesus, you make me sick. He wasn't God, you know."

I'm feeling hollow, a cane with all the pith gnawed out of it. I don't need prodding, don't need anything but to be left alone. "Easy for you to say."

I don't know what I expect, the baring of the talons, the first superficial swipes of the marital row that has been going on here now for the past fifteen years, and then the rending of the deeper wounds, the ones that fester. I'm ready for it, ready to fight and throw it all back at her, be-

16

cause she's wrong and we both know it, but she surprises me. Her hands go to her hips, then drop to her side, and I watch her take the time to compose her face. "No, John," she says finally, and she puts all the bruising power of the years into the sad low hopeless cadence of her voice, "it's not easy. It's never been easy. You know what I wish?"

I won't answer, won't give her the satisfaction.

"I wish I'd never met him, never heard of him. I wish he'd never been born."

I can hear our son moving around in his room overhead, the dull reverberation of his feet like distant thunder. Iris's jaw is set, her shoulders thrown back in full martial display, and she's already dismissed me, moving toward the door now in her brisk chopping strides. "Get your tie on," she snaps over her shoulder, and she's gone. But no. She's back suddenly, on the rebound, her head framed in the doorway, her eyes slicing from me to the tape recorder and back again. "And shut that damn thing off, will you?"

PART I

BIOLOGY HALL

1

For all my bravado that day at the tavern, I have to admit I had my qualms about the interview, and I know this must sound ridiculous coming from me, since I've contributed materially to the project to a degree exceeded only by Corcoran and Prok himself, and ultimately wound up conducting some two thousand interviews on my own, but if the truth be known, I was scared. Or perhaps "intimidated" would be a better word. You have to understand that back then sex and sexuality simply weren't discussed—anywhere, in any forum—and certainly not in a public lecture hall on a college campus. Marriage courses had begun to spring up at other colleges and universities around the country, most pointedly in response to the VD scare of the thirties, but they were bland and euphemistic, and as far as counseling was concerned, as far as a frank face-to-face discussion of pathologies and predilections, there was nothing available to the average person aside from the banalities of the local minister or priest.

And so, as Dr. Kinsey reiterated in his concluding lecture, he was undertaking a groundbreaking research project to describe and quantify human sexual behavior as a way of uncovering what had been so long hidden behind a veil of taboo, superstition and religious prohibition, so as to provide data for those in need of them. And he was appealing to us—the prurient, feverish, sweaty-palmed undergraduates of the audience—to help him. He had just concluded his overview of the course, summarizing his comments on individual variation, as well as his remarks on birth control (adding, almost as an afterthought, that if condoms lacked the natural lubrication provided in the male by secretions from the Cowper's glands, saliva could be used as an effective succedaneum), and he stood there before us, his face animated, his hands folded on the lectern in front of him.

"I appeal to you all," he said, after a momentary pause, "to come forward and give me your individual histories, as they are absolutely vital to our understanding of human sexuality." The light was dim and uniform, the hall overheated, a faint smell of dust and floor wax lingering in the air. Outside, the first snow of the season was briefly whitening the ground, but we might as well have been in a sealed vault for all it mattered. People squirmed in their seats. The young woman in front of me glanced furtively at her watch.

"Why, we know more about the sex life of *Drosophila melanogaster*—the fruit fly—than we know of the commonest everyday practices of our own species," he went on, his voice steady, his eyes fixed on the audience, "more of an insect's ways than of the activities that go on in the bedrooms of this country, on living room sofas and in the rear seats of automobiles for that matter, the very activities through the agency of which each of us is present here in this room today. Does that make scientific sense? Is it in the least rational or defensible?"

Laura was seated beside me, keeping up the pretext, though in the course of the semester she'd fallen hard for a member of the basketball team by the name of Jim Willard and had twice been caught in his company by Dean Hoenig, who had a fine eye for the temperature gradient of campus romances. Both times Laura had managed to wriggle out of it—Jim was a friend of the family, a cousin actually, second cousin, that is, and she was just taking it upon herself to help him with his studies, seeing that basketball consumed so much of his time—but Dean Hoenig was on to us. She'd bristled visibly as we came in the door together and made what I thought was a wholly inappropriate remark about wedding bells, and I was still fuming over it midway through the lecture. At any rate, Laura was by my side, her head bent to her notebook in the further pretext of taking notes, when in fact she was doodling, sketching elongated figures in dresses and furs and elaborate feathered hats and at least one palpitating heart transfixed by the errant arrow.

What Dr. Kinsey wanted from us—what he was appealing for now—was our one-hundred-percent cooperation in arranging private sessions with him to give up our sex histories. For the sake of science. All disclosures to be recorded in code and to remain strictly confidential—in fact, no one but he knew the key to this code he'd devised, and thus no one could ever possibly put a name to a given history. "And I must stress the importance of one-hundred-percent cooperation," he added, gesturing with a stiff swipe of his hand, "because anything short of that compromises our statistical reliability. If we are to take histories only from those who seek us out, we will have a very inaccurate picture indeed of the society at large, but if we can document one-hundred-percent groups—all the college students present in this lecture hall, for instance, all the young men in a given fraternity house, the membership of the Elks' Club, women's auxiliaries, the incarcerees at the State Penal Farm in Putnamville—then we are getting an accurate, top-to-bottom picture." He paused to run his gaze over the entire audience, left to right, back to front. A stillness descended on us. Laura lifted her head.

"Very well," he said finally. "In the service of this end, I will be scheduling appointments directly after termination of this lecture."

Because of our ruse, Laura and I were scheduled consecutively, as future husband and wife, though Laura's use for me had by this time expired and she pointedly avoided me as she strolled around campus in the towering company of Jim Willard, who, at six feet one and one hundred ninety pounds, provided stability under the boards for our basketball team. We went separately to Biology Hall on a bitter, wind-scoured December afternoon, the husks of leaves chasing across a dead scrub of lawn, the trees stripped and forlorn, and everybody on campus sniffling with the same cold. Laura had been scheduled first, and as the interviews in those days averaged just over an hour, there really wasn't much point in my escorting her there. Still, I'd got cold feet the night before and when I ran into her and Willard on the steps of the library I'd argued that we should nonetheless show up together for appearances' sake—I didn't mind, I'd bring my books and study while she was in Kinsey's office—but she was shaking her head before I'd even got the words out. "You're very sweet, John," she said, "and I appreciate your concern, I really do—but the semester's nearly over. What can they do to us?"

Willard was hovering in the background, giving me the sort of look he usually reserved for tip-offs at center court.

"Besides," she said, showing her teeth in a tight little smile, "people do fall out of love, don't they? Even Dean Hoenig has to be realistic—she can't expect *every* engagement to last."

I didn't want to concede the point. I was feeling something I'd never felt before, and I couldn't have defined it, not then, not with the powers available to me and the person I then was, but can I say that her face was a small miracle in the light spilling from the high, arching windows, that I remembered the kiss in the tavern, the feel of her stirring beside me in the lecture hall? Can I say that, and then let it rest?

"What about disciplinary action?" I said.

She let out a curt laugh. "Disciplinary action? Are you kidding?" She looked to Willard and back again. "I don't care two snaps for all the disciplinary action in the world."

And so I went alone to Biology Hall, following the faint lingering traces of her perfume, the collar of my overcoat turned up against the wind, a load of books tucked under one arm. The building, like most on campus, was made of local limestone. It rose up out of the black grasp of the trees like a degraded temple, the sky behind it all but rinsed of light, and I couldn't help thinking how different it had looked in September when it was cushioned in foliage. As I came up the path, leaves grating underfoot, I felt a sudden sharp stab of apprehension. I didn't know Prok yet—or I knew him only as a distant and formal presence on the podium—and I was afraid of what he might think of me. You see, it wasn't only the subterfuge with Laura that cast a shadow over things, but my history itself. I was deeply ashamed of it, ashamed of who I was and what I'd done, and I'd never broached the subject of sex with anyone, not my closest friends, not the school counselor or even the uncle (Robert, my father's youngest brother) who did his best to take my dead father's place till the wandering bug got him and he disappeared too.

I was turning it over in my mind, wondering what sort of things Dr. Kinsey would want to know and whether I could dare equivocate—or lie, outright lie—when the outside door swung open and Laura emerged. She was wearing a dark, belted coat, white socks and saddle shoes, her lower legs bare against the cold, and she looked small and fragile in the lee of the building and the big weighted slab of the door. A gust came up and both her hands went automatically to her hat, and if she hadn't glanced up in that instant and seen me there, I don't know if I wouldn't have just turned heel and vanished. But she did glance up. And she gave me a curious look, as if she couldn't quite place me—or was somehow seeing me out of context. I had no choice but to continue along the path and up the stone steps, and now she gave me a rueful smile. "Your turn, huh?" she said.

She was poised on the landing, holding the door for me. "What did he ask?" I puffed, taking the steps two at a time. The corridor behind her was deserted. I saw the dull gleam of linoleum tile, the lights set at intervals, the dark stairwell opening like a mouth at the far end.

"Oh, I don't know," she said, her breath streaming in the cold, "everything."

"Did he ask about, about us?"

"Uh-uh. Frankly, I don't think he cares one way or the other. He's—he really believes in what he's doing, and he wants people to . . . open up, I guess you'd say. It's all about the research, about getting at the real truth of things, and the way he does it—I mean, it's not what you'd think. It's not embarrassing, not at all. You'll see. He just puts you at ease."

I didn't know what to say to this. She was right there beside me, so close I could smell the faint aroma of her mint toothpaste, which was all mixed up with her perfume and the scent of the shampoo she'd used on her hair. Her face was open and her lips parted, but her eyes looked beyond me, as if she expected Jim Willard—or Prok himself—to issue from the line of trees across the street. She simply stared, as if she'd just woken up—or been hypnotized by one of the charlatans at the county fair. The wind was at the back of my neck and I could feel the heated air of the building like the breath of some beast on my face. "He doesn't hypnotize you, does he?"

Her back was propped against the door and she gave me a long, slow look of appraisal. "No, John," she said, patronizing me now, "no, he doesn't hypnotize you. But listen"—she reached up to tuck one last flowing curl under her hat—"I never really got to thank you for what you've done—a lot of the boys I know wouldn't have been caught dead in that course—and it was really white of you. So, thanks. Really."

"Sure," I mumbled, "my pleasure," and then she let the door go and I caught it with one hand and slipped into the building as she retreated down the steps.

Dr. Kinsey's office was at the end of the corridor on the second floor. My appointment was the last of the day, and the halls that had been thrumming with students an hour ago were deserted now. The staff had gone home too, all the offices and classrooms darkened up and down the length of the building—even the janitor was apparently busy elsewhere. I paused at the water fountain—my throat had gone dry—and then continued down the hallway, my footsteps echoing like gunshots in the empty innards of the building. There was a small anteroom, windowless and drab, and beyond it, the softly lit confines of the office itself. The door stood open and I could see two crammed metal bookcases reaching all the way to the ceiling, and then the blond flash of what I took to be Kinsey's head bent over a desk in a nimbus of yellow light. I hesitated a moment, then rapped my knuckles on the doorframe.

He swung his head out away from the desk so he could get a clear view of the doorway, then immediately sprang to his feet. "Milk?" he called, rushing to me with his hand extended and a look of transport on his face, as if I were the single person in all the world he was most happy to see. "John Milk?"

I took his hand and nodded, fumbling through the usual gestures of greeting. "It's a pleasure," I might have said, but so softly I doubt if he would have heard me.

"Good of you to come," he pronounced, still squeezing my hand. We stood there in the doorway a moment, and I was conscious of his height—he was six feet tall at least—and of his sheer physical presence, thinking he would have made a match for Jim Willard if he were so in-

26

clined. "But please come in," he said, releasing my hand and guiding me into the office, where he indicated the chair stationed on the near side of his desk. "Milk," he was saying, as I settled in the chair and he in turn eased himself back behind the desk, "is that of German derivation—originally, that is?"

"Yes, we were Milch in the old country, but my grandfather changed it."

"Too overtly Teutonic, eh? Of course there's nothing hardier than good Anglo-German stock—except maybe the Scots. We're Scots in my family, you know, though I suppose you surmised that from the surname . . . Care for a cigarette?"

On the desk before me, spread out like an offering, were fresh packs of cigarettes in four different brands, as well as an ashtray and lighter. I didn't know then how much Prok detested smoking—he thought it should be banned in all public places, and no doubt in most private ones as well—nor that he provided the cigarettes despite himself, in addition to soft drinks, coffee, tea and, in the appropriate venues, alcohol, all in an effort to make the interviewing process more congenial. What he wanted above all else was to gain the sort of intimacy that yields up confidences, and he had a true genius for it—for putting people at ease and bringing them out. Absent it, the project would never have gotten off the ground.

At any rate, I selected the brand I liked best but couldn't really afford, lit up and took a deep, palliative pull and let the gentle pulse of the nicotine calm me. All the while Prok was beaming at me, the kindliest, friendliest man in the world, and you would have thought from his expression that he'd invented cigarettes himself and owned a controlling interest in the Pall Mall company. "I hope you've enjoyed the marriage course," he was saying, "and that any misconceptions you and your fiancée may have had—charming girl, by the way, lovely, very lovely—have been cleared up . . ."

I looked away from him—a mistake, as it was one of his cardinal rules to engage the subject at all times in direct eye contact, as the first indicator of veracity. I said something noncommittal. Or rather mumbled something both noncommittal and non-audible.

"Don't be afraid, Milk, there's no one here going to bite you—or sit in judgment either, and I'm well aware that any number of ingenious undergraduates are forming, let us say, *convenient* attachments in order to satisfy Dean Hoenig and the other self-appointed moral guardians of the campus and community."

I tapped my cigarette in the ashtray, studying the perfect cylinder of pale ash that dropped from it, then looked him in the eye. I felt my face flush in an instant, the old exposure. "I'm sorry, sir," I said.

He waved an impatient hand. "Nothing to be sorry for, Milk, nothing at all. I'm interested in getting information out to people who need it, and if it were up to me and me alone, there would be no prohibitions of any kind on the course. But tell me about yourself—you're how old?"

"Twenty-one."

"Birth date?"

"October second, 1918."

"Are you a native of Indiana, born here, that is?"

"Michigan City."

"And your parents?"

"My mother teaches elementary school back at home. My father's dead. He was killed in an accident on the lake—or, actually, no one really knows what went wrong. There was—they weren't able to recover the body."

Prok never took his eyes from mine, but he was making notations on a single sheet of paper that lay on the desk before him. Without my knowing it, the interview had already begun, but he paused now to express his sympathy. He asked how old I was at the time of my father's death—I was nine, not quite out of school for the summer, and my father had gone mad for sailing, sanding and varnishing the boat all winter and into the spring, and now it had been launched and all I could think of was the long irradiated days ahead when we would coast unencumbered over the chop like the God who made the water and the son who came to walk on it—and then he said that he too had had to make do without a father's guidance, at least once he went to college and broke free of a stifling paternal influence. His father had seen him as an

28

engineer—could I imagine that?—but he himself had preferred biology. Biology was his passion. And he made a casual gesture to the cramped office behind him, and the great standing racks of insects pinned in trays. "Did you know," he added, "that I've identified sixteen new species of gall wasp?" And he let out a chuckle. "If it was up to my father they'd be unknown today." His eyes were shining. "Poor things."

Our conversation—it was just that—had developed its own logic and rhythm. It was uncanny. The longer we spoke, and it was almost like speaking with your inner self or confiding in the family doctor behind closed doors, the more he seemed to know what I was thinking and feeling. And it wasn't simply that he was a master at what he was doing, but that you felt he really and truly sympathized, that when your heart was breaking, so was his.

Which brings us to the real content of the interview: my sex history. We talked for perhaps fifteen minutes before the first question insinuated itself, as casually as if it were no more charged than a reflection on one's parents or upbringing. We'd been talking about my playmates when I was a boy, and I was lost in nostalgic recollection, faces and places and names drifting like gauze through my brain, when Dr. Kinsey, in his softest, most dispassionate tones, asked, "How old were you when you first became aware of the anatomical differences between girls and boys?"

"I don't know. Early on, I suppose. Five? Six?"

"Was there nudity in your home when you were a child? On the part of your parents or yourself?"

I took a moment, trying to recollect. "No," I said, "no, I don't think so."

"Did your parents make you put your clothes on when you appeared naked?"

"Yes. But again, this would have been at a very early age, probably two or three. Or no, later. There was one incident—I must have been five, five at least, because it was before we'd moved to the house on Cherry Street—a hot day, bathing with my mother at the lake, and I came out of the water and removed my wet trunks. She was angry with me, and I remember I couldn't understand why."

"Were you reprimanded then?"

"Yes."

"Physically?"

"I must have been. Not the first time, though."

"What were the other occasions?"

Each question followed logically from the one previous, and they were very much rapid-fire: as soon as Prok got and recorded his response, he was on to the next, and yet you never felt as if you were being interrogated, but rather were part of an ongoing conversation focused on the most fascinating subject in the world: yourself. And the questions were always formulated so as to achieve the most precise—and unambiguous—answer. So it was not "Have you ever masturbated?" but rather "When did you first masturbate?" and "How old were you when you first saw the naked genitalia of your own sex? Of the opposite sex?" All the while, as the interviewee progressed in recollected age, so too did the questions delve ever more deeply into his sexual practices, going from the relatively innocuous data-based queries ("How old were you when you first began to sprout pubic hair?") and calculations of your height, weight and handedness, to "When did you first experience coitus?"

My nose was dripping—I too had contracted the cold that held the campus in its thrall—and I was on my fourth cigarette and entirely unaware of where or even who I was by the time this last question came up. Dr. Kinsey studied my reaction, my face, his eyes locked on mine, his pencil poised over the sheet of paper. *It's all right,* he seemed to say, *whatever it is, it's all right. You can confide in me.* And further: *You must confide in me.*

I hesitated, and that hesitation told him everything. "Never," I said. "Or, that is, not yet, I mean."

Unbeknownst to me, there were a series of questions—twelve of them, to be exact—that gave an indication of one's predilection toward same-sex behavior, or, as Prok liked to call it so as not to alarm or prejudice anyone, the H-history. It was at this point that he shifted in his chair and cleared his voice. "Backtracking now," he said, "you were how old when you first saw the naked genitalia of a person of your own sex?"

I gave him the answer, which he quickly checked against my previous response.

"And when did you first see another individual's erect penis?"

I gave him the answer.

And then the questions proceeded in what we would come to call our "steamroller" fashion, one hard on the heels of the next. "When did you first touch the genitals of a person of your own sex? When did you first bring to orgasm a person of your own sex? When was the first time you brought a person of your own sex to orgasm orally?"

I looked away and he broke off the interview a moment. There was a silence. I became aware of the bells tolling six on the clock tower across campus. "Milk," he said, "John—let me remind you that there is nothing, nothing whatever, to be ashamed of. There is no sexual act between consenting parties that is in any way qualitatively different from any other, no matter what the prevailing ethos of a given society may be. If it will interest you to know, my own sex history was very much similar to yours when I was your age—and even later."

But perhaps this would be a judicious time to bring up the 0–6 scale Prok devised to measure an individual's sexual preferences—a scale that seeks to chart the entire range of human sexual proclivities, from the purely opposite-sex context (0) to the purely homosexual (6). You see, Prok believed—and I've come to believe too—that man in a state of nature is pansexual, and that only the strictures of society, especially societies under the dominion of the Judeo-Christian and Mohammedan codes, prevent people from expressing their needs and desires openly, and that thus, whole legions suffer from various sexual maladjustments. But I get ahead of myself.

That day, in that room, with a handkerchief pressed to my dripping nose and Prok's presence guiding me, I began to know myself in a way I'd never thought possible. What I'd seen as a source of shame became usual—Prok himself had had similar experiences as a boy and had masturbated continually—and if I could say I rated perhaps a 1 or 2 on the

0–6 scale, then that was something, something momentous. And I hungered for experience, like anyone else, that was all. I'd been awkward with girls, terrified of them—I'd placed them on a pedestal and never saw them as sexual beings just like me, who had the same needs and desires as I, and that it had been perfectly natural to experiment with the only partners available to me, with boys, because as Prok says, we all need outlets. Or perhaps I didn't realize all this on that late afternoon in Prok's office, but I did think of Laura Feeney sitting there before me—in the very chair—and how Prok would have asked her at what age she began to masturbate and when she'd first seen the naked genitalia of the opposite sex, and when she'd first seen the phallus erect and first brought the opposite sex to orgasm, and I felt like Columbus spying land on the horizon.

The clock on the tower was tolling the quarter hour, for six forty-five, by the time we were finished and Dr. Kinsey leaned across the desk to hand me a penny postcard addressed to himself—Dr. Alfred C. Kinsey, Professor of Zoology, Biology Hall, University of Indiana. "Just here, you see," he was saying, "I will need four basic measurements, please."

"Yes," I said, taking the card in what seemed like a trance—and no, he hadn't hypnotized me, not in the conventional sense, but he might as well have.

"Very well, then. We will need you, when you arrive at home, to measure first the circumference and then the length, from the base of the abdomen out, of the flaccid penis, and then, when you're properly stimulated, the circumference and length while erect. And, oh, yes, if you would just note the angle of curvature as well . . ."

THE WIND PERCHED in the trees that night, gathering force for a run down into Kentucky, and by nine o'clock it was flinging compact little pellets of sleet against the window of the attic room I shared with a fellow senior, Paul Sehorn, in Mrs. Elsa Lorber's rooming house on Kirkwood Avenue. This was an old house, aching in its bones and not at all shy about voicing its complaints, especially at night. It had been built in the 1870s and was solid enough, I suppose, even after a generation of undergraduates had given it the sort of hard use that had brought down any number of other houses of its era. Unfortunately, it was insulated about as thoroughly as an orange crate and the balky antiquated coal furnace never seemed to elevate the temperature much above the zone of the distinctly uncomfortable. The winter previous, I'd woken one morning to find a crust of ice interposed between my lips and the water in the glass I'd left out on the night table, and for a month thereafter Paul referred to me as Nanook.

There was a desk in one corner, dominated by the secondhand Olympia typewriter my mother gave me when I went off to college and an old Philco radio I'd salvaged after my grandmother had given up on it. Against the facing wall, beside the door, was an armoire that stank regally of naphtha, and we shared its limited space, our shirts, trousers and suits (we each had one, mine in glen plaid, to match my tie, Paul's a hand-me-down blue serge that showed a good three inches of cuff at the wrist) hanging side by side on a dozen scuffed wooden hangers. Other than that, it was shoes under the bed, overcoats downstairs on the hooks reserved for them in the vestibule, personal items laid out on our matching bureaus and books neatly aligned on a cheap pine bookcase I'd found at a rummage sale (four shelves, equally divided, eighteen inches per shelf for me, eighteen inches for Paul). The bathroom was across the hall.

Most nights, Paul and I tuned in the radio (we limited ourselves to two serials, and then it was swing out of Cincinnati, as soft and fuzzed with distance as a whisper), propped ourselves up in our beds and studied till our fingers went numb from the cold. Tonight, though, Paul was out on a date and I had the room to myself, though it was hardly peaceful, what with the unending stamp and furor of the other undergraduate men in the house and the long disquisitions on everything from the existence of God to the Nazi push for lebensraum that seemed always to take place outside the bathroom door. By ten, the sleet had changed to snow.

I lay there beneath the comforter on my bed, trying to read—as I remember, I had an exam the following day—but I didn't get very far. The branches of the elm out back kept scraping at the house as if something were trying to crawl up the side of the building to escape the storm and the reception on the radio was so bad I had to get up and switch it off. I rubbed a circle in the frost and peered out the window. The world was dense and blurred, the streetlights pinched down to nothing, no sound but the wind and the intermittent rasp of the snow thrust up against the pane. I felt small and boxed-in. Felt restless. Bored.

I thought of Dr. Kinsey then—if truth be told, I hadn't really thought of much else all evening, even at dinner—and crossed the room to my desk for what must have been the twentieth time to examine the postcard he'd given me. I let a hand drop to my trousers, a pressure there, and began massaging myself absently through a layer of gabardine. And how *would* I measure it? I didn't have a ruler, but I could easily have gone down the hall and borrowed one from Bob Hickenlooper, the architectural whiz—if anyone would have one, he would—and yet I still wasn't sold on the idea. It was vaguely obscene, ridiculous even. Measuring your own penis? But there was more to it than that, of course—and I'm sure you've anticipated me here—what if I didn't measure up? What if I was, well, *smaller,* than other men? What then? Would I add an inch or two so as not to disappoint the distinguished scientist eagerly waiting to tabulate the results? Of course, I had little idea what the average length of the male penis was—but then wasn't that the whole concept of the enterprise to begin with? What had Kinsey's lecture on individual variation been but an attempt to make us all feel a bit more secure with regard to such things as breast size and penis length and the like?

Yes, I told myself, yes, certainly I'll do the measurements and see to it that I'm as accurate and honest as possible. But, of course, in thinking about it, imagining the cold butt of some architectural student's T square pressed to my penis, I found I had an erection. It was then (and please don't mistake my meaning here) that I thought of Mrs. Lorber. She sat in the parlor downstairs each evening, listening to her own radio and knitting, and I knew she had a tape measure in her sewing basket, a soft and supple one, made of finger-burnished cloth, the very sort of thing you might imagine yourself using in a private scientific endeavor akin to the one I was contemplating.

All right. Fine. Before I could think I was thumping down the three flights of loose-jointed stairs, ignoring a shout from Tom Tomalin to come play a hand of pinochle and an off-color greeting from Ben Webber, all two hundred and forty-five pounds of him, who was laboring up to his room on the second floor. Out of breath, and with my excitement barely contained, I paused outside the open parlor door and tapped gently at the doorframe. Mrs. Lorber was seated in her favorite armchair, working at a ball of butterscotch-colored yarn, a cat sprawled in her lap. She didn't glance up, though she knew I was there—she knew everything that went on in the house, every least stir and breath of her charges, and she'd positioned her chair so as to give her a strategic view of the entry hall and stairway in the event that anyone might be so foolish as to attempt to smuggle contraband into his room. (Mrs. Lorber was in her mid-sixties then, a big-shouldered ventricose old lady with a succession of chins and a focused, predatory look: alcoholic beverages, foods that required heating and, especially, women were strictly interdicted.)

"Uh, excuse me, Mrs. Lorber?" I murmured.

She fixed her gaze on me, and I expected her to smile or at least nod in recognition, but her face showed nothing.

"I just wondered, if I could, uh—if I could borrow your, uh, tape measure. For just a minute. I'll bring it right back, I promise."

She let out a sigh compounded of all the little inconveniences, crises and mounting disasters undergraduates had inflicted on her over the years, and then, without a word, leaned down to her right and began fishing through her sewing basket. "Here," she said finally, coming up with the tape measure as I crossed the room to her, "but just make sure you return it."

Leaning over her, I caught a smell of the liniment she rubbed on her legs each night and of the warm, yeasty air trapped beneath her skirts. The cat looked up at me blankly. "Yes," I said, her cool, dry fingers coming into contact with mine as I took the tape measure from her, "I will. It'll just be a minute and I'll be right back with it, I promise."

I was nearly out of the room when she stopped me. "But what on earth would you need to measure, John? What is it, curtains? Because I sincerely hope you two haven't damaged—"

"It's a, uh, project. For my literature class."

"Literature? What, lines of poetry? The number of feet per line in 'Don Juan'? Hmm?" She let out a laugh. "Now there was a poem—is that part of the syllabus still? Or, no, of course it must be. Lord Byron, eh? Now there was a poet."

"Yes," I agreed, "but you'll have to, I mean, I have to—"

"Go, go," she said, making a shooing motion with both hands. "No need to waste your time on an old woman when you've got *measuring* to do."

I trudged back up the stairs, the tape measure burning like a hot coal in my pocket. I felt guilty, dirty, all the worse for the lie and the use to which I was going to put my landlady's blameless instrument, and I kept thinking of her handling the thing and holding it up to a scarf she was knitting for a favorite niece or granddaughter. Maybe I should just return it to her, I thought, right now, before it's been desecrated. I could slip out in the morning and purchase one of my own—a tape measure was a practical thing to have, after all, because you never knew when you'd be called upon to measure something, like bookshelves, for instance. My feet hit the stairs like hammers. The storm whispered at the windowpanes.

By the time I got back to the room, I found that my enthusiasm for Dr. Kinsey's little statistical exercise had worn thin, but I loosened my belt and dropped my trousers dutifully, unscrolling Mrs. Lorber's tape measure to record my now-flaccid dimensions. But the thing was, as soon as I laid the measure against my penis I began to grow hard again and couldn't get an accurate measurement; before I knew it, I was stroking myself and trying to summon the look of Laura Feeney as she sat beside me in the semi-darkness of the lecture hall while the slide projector clicked and clicked again and we all held our breath. And then I was seeing a girl from the front row of my literature class, a girl with puffed lips and violet eyes and calves that caressed each other under the desk until I wanted to faint from the friction of it, and finally there was just a woman, featureless, anonymous, with her breasts thrust out and nipples hard and her cunt—that was what I wanted to call it, her cunt—just exactly like the one on the screen.

I was up early the next morning, the light through the window trembling on the sloped ceiling above the bed—it was a paler light than we'd been used to, bluer, like the aqueous glow at the bottom of a swimming pool, and I was filled with the anticipation that comes with the first good snow of the season. The storm had passed on, but outside the sky was a polished silver, a big, upended tureen of a sky, flurries trailing down like an afterthought. I didn't wake Paul. He'd come in late—long after I'd gone to bed—and I didn't want to disturb him, not so much out of any consideration for his beauty rest, but because I wasn't in the mood for company. I wanted to tramp the streets, see the world transformed—just enjoy it, all to myself—before heading over to the Commons for breakfast and a final look at my notes for the exam.

There was a foot and a half of snow, maybe more—it was hard to say because the wind had piled it up in drifts against the fences and buildings. None of the walks had been cleared yet, people's automobiles sat drifted over at the curb and the birds dipped in perplexity from the black field of the evergreens along the street to the sealed white envelope of the ground. Lights gleamed dully from the depths of the houses. I smelled bacon, woodsmoke, the clean, dense perfume of the new air swept down out of the north.

It wasn't yet seven, and hardly anyone was stirring on campus. Those who were out moved silently across the quad, huddled figures excised from a dream and patched in here where they didn't belong, and there were no more than ten students in the Commons where normally there would have been a hundred—even the staff was reduced to a single ill-defined woman who served out the food mechanically and then moved to the cash register through crashing waves of silence to record the sale. I took a table by the window and sat there staring out over my books and into the trees along the creek, idly stirring sugar into a cup of coffee. It was one of those quiet, absorbing moments when the world slows to a standstill and all its inherent possibilities become manifest. Magic. The magic moment—isn't that what they call it in the love songs?

She was speaking to me before I became aware of her—"Hello, John; *hello*, I said"—and when I did look up I didn't recognize her at first. She was in a winter coat and hat, the black silk of her hair tugged down like an arras on either side of her face, her eyes lit from within as if there were twin filaments behind them and a battery secreted under her clothes. It was seven a.m.—or no, not even—and she was wearing mascara, the better to show off the color of those eyes, which managed to be both blue and green at the same time, like the sea off the port of Havana where the onshore waters meld with the pelagic and the white prow of your boat drifts placidly from one world to another and everything dissolves in a dream. "Don't you recognize me?"

She was unfastening the snap at her collar, working at her hat, her hair, the scarf wrapped twice round her throat. Everything was suddenly in motion again, as if a film had just been rethreaded through the projector, her books sliding onto the tabletop beside mine, the coat open to reveal her dress and the way it conformed to her, and then the chair beside me pulling out and the girl—who *was* she?—perching at the edge of it. And then it came to me. "You're Iris," I said.

She was giving me her full-lipped smile, the smile that borrows some of the juice from her eyes and runs off the same hidden power source. "Iris McAuliffe, Tommy's little sister. But you knew that."

"I did, yes. Of course I did. My mother—I mean, she, and then I saw you around campus, of course—"

"I hear you're engaged."

I didn't know what to say to this—I certainly wouldn't want it getting back to my mother in any way, shape or form—so I dipped my head and took a sip of coffee.

Iris's smile faded. "She's very pretty," she murmured. "Laura Feeney."

"Yes," I said, my gaze fixed on the cup. "But I'm not really—we're not . . ." I looked up at her. Off on the periphery of my vision the woman at the cash register rang up a coffee and cruller as if she were moving underwater, and I saw the balding head and narrow shoulders of my literature professor, his coat dusted with snow. "That is, it was a pretense, you know. For the marriage course."

I watched her grapple with this ever so briefly before the smile came back. "You mean, you—faked it? Just to—? God," she said, and she let her posture go, slouching back in the seat, all limbs and jangling, nervous hands, "I hear it was really *dirty* . . ."

2

I TOOK EXAMS, wrote papers ("Duality in John Donne's Love Poems"; "Malinowski's Melanesia"), took a bus home to Michigan City for Christmas break and gave my mother a set of bath oils and scented soaps carved in the shape of fishes and mermaids. Some of my old high school friends came round—Tommy McAuliffe, in particular, who was now assistant manager at the grocery—and what a surprise that he'd thought to bring his kid sister Iris along, and did I know that she was a sophomore at IU now? There she was, standing on the doorstep beside him, and though I barely knew her I began to appreciate that here was the kind of girl who understood what she wanted and always got it—always, no matter what. I told Tommy I'd just seen her on campus—on the day of the snowfall, wasn't it?—while she looked on with her big ever-widening sea-struck eyes as if she'd forgotten all about it. We ate pfefferneuse cookies in front of the fireplace and sneaked drinks of brandy every time my mother went back out to the kitchen to check on her pies. Just before New Year's I thought of asking Iris to the pictures or maybe to go skating—on a date, that is—but I never got around to it. Then I was back at school and the days closed down on the bleak dark kernel of mid-January.

One night I was at the library, reshelving books in the second-floor stacks, when I glanced up at the aisle directly across from me and there was Prok—Dr. Kinsey—down on one knee, scanning the titles on the bottom shelf. He was a tumult of motion, grasping the spine of one book or another and at the same time shoving it back in place, all the while scooting back and forth on the fulcrum of his knee. It was strange to see him there—or not strange so much as unexpected—and I froze up for a moment. I didn't know what to do—should I say hello, ignore him, grab an armload of books and duck round the corner? Even if I did say hello, would he remember me? He had hundreds of students, and though he'd conducted private interviews—like mine—with all of them, or practically all of them, how could he be expected to recall any one individual? I watched him out of the corner of my eye. He seemed to be muttering to himself—was it a call number he was repeating?—and then he found what he was looking for, slipped it from the shelf and sprang to his feet, all in one motion. That was when he brought his eyes forward and saw me there.

It took a moment. I watched his neutral expression broaden into recognition, and then he came down the aisle and extended his hand. "Milk," he said, "well, hello. Good to see you."

"Hello, sir. I'm—I didn't think you'd remember me, what with all your, well, students—"

"Don't be foolish. Of course I remember you. John Milk, out of Michigan City, born October two, nineteen eighteen." He gave me a smile, one of his patented ones, pulling his lip back from his upper teeth and letting the two vertical laugh lines tug at his jowls so that his whole face opened up in a kind of riotous glee. "Five foot ten, one hundred eighty pounds. But you haven't lost any weight, have you?"

"Hardly," I said, my smile a weak imitation of his, and I was thinking of those other measurements, the ones I'd inscribed on a postcard and sent him in the mail. And beyond that, my secrets, and my shame, and all it implied. "My mother's cooking, you know. Over the holidays."

"Yes," he said, "yes, yes, of course. Nothing like a mother's cooking, eh?" He was still smiling, smiling even wider now, if that was possible. "Or a mother's love, for that matter."

I had to agree. I nodded my head in affirmation, and then the moment detached itself and hung there, lit from above with the faint gilding of the electric lights. I became aware of the muted stirring of library patrons among the stacks, a book dropped somewhere, a whisper.

"You're working here, I presume?"

I told him I was, though they'd cut my hours recently and I could barely make ends meet. "Reshelving, mostly. Once we close the doors, I sweep up, empty the wastebaskets, make sure everything's in order."

He was standing there watching me, rocking up off the balls of his feet and back again. I couldn't help glancing at the title of the book: *Sexual Life in Ancient Greece,* by Hans Licht. "Late nights, eh? Isn't that a bit tough on your studies?"

I shrugged. "We all do the best we can."

He was silent a moment, as if he were deciding something, his eyes all the while fixed on mine. "Do you know, Milk—John," he said softly, almost musingly, "I have a garden out at my place. Mrs. Kinsey and I do. Clara, that is. In season, it's the pride of Bloomington, a regular botanical garden on two and a half fertile acres—I grow daylilies, irises, we're planning a lily pond. You should see it, you really should."

I wasn't following him. I'd been keeping late hours and I was pretty well exhausted. For lack of a better option, I gave him my fawning student look.

"What I mean is, I've been thinking for some time of hiring somebody to help me with it—of course, it's nothing but husks and frozen earth at this juncture—but in the spring, well, that's when we'll really bring it to life. And until then—and beyond that, in addition, as well— we're going to need some help in the biology library. What do you say?"

A week later I was working in Biology Hall, with expanded hours and no late nights. The biology collection was considerably smaller than that of the main library and the patronage proportionately reduced in size, so that I found I had more time to myself at work, time I could apply fruitfully to my own studies (and to be honest, to daydreaming—I spent a disproportionate amount of time that semester staring out into the intermediate distance, as if all the answers I needed in life were written there in a very cramped and faint script). I didn't see much of Prok—he kept to himself for the most part, in his office on the second floor—and as the sex survey was then in its incipient stages, he didn't yet need anyone to help him with the interviewing or tabulating of results. He was, as you no doubt know, one of the world's leading authorities on Cynipids—gall wasps—and he was still at that time busy collecting galls from oak trees all over the country, employing his assistants (three undergraduate women) exclusively in helping to record his measurements of individual wasps and mount them in the Schmitt boxes reserved for them. Taxonomy—that was his forte, both as an entomologist and a compiler of human sexual practices.

At any rate, the job was something of a plum for me, and for the first week or two I snapped out of the funk that seemed to have descended on me, exhilarated by the free nights and the extra change in my pocket. I went bowling with Paul and his girlfriend Betsy, and then insisted on treating them to cheeseburgers and I don't know how many pitchers of beer after Paul took me aside and told me they wanted me to be the first to know they were engaged to be married. The jukebox played "Oh, Johnny" over and over, Betsy kept saying, "You're next, John-Johnny-John, you're next," and I barely flinched when Laura Feeney and Jim Willard sauntered in and took a booth in the back. We stayed up late that night, Paul and I, pouring out water glasses of bourbon smuggled upstairs right under Mrs. Lorber's nose, and though I overslept the next morning, I woke feeling glad for Paul and hopeful for myself.

Unfortunately, the mood didn't last. It struck me that my roommate—a man of my own age and inclinations—was going to be married and that he already had a job lined up with his father's feed-distribution company, while I had to look at myself in the mirror every morning and admit I had no idea what was to become of me. I was at loose ends, as most seniors are, I suppose, worrying over my course work and facing June graduation without a single notion of what I was going to do in life—or even what I was going to do for gainful employment. All I knew was that I'd rather be sent to Devil's Island as underassistant to the assistant chef in the soup kitchen than go back to Michigan City and another summer with my mother. And as if that weren't enough, looming over it all was the prospect of war in Europe and talk of conscription.

So I was feeling blue, the weather going from bad to worse, Paul always off with Betsy somewhere till I'd begun to forget what he looked like, and the books on the library cart growing progressively heavier (I felt like a bibliographic Sisyphus, the task unending, each shelved volume replaced by another and yet another). And then two things happened. The first had to do with Iris, as you might have guessed. Though

43

she was an English major, like me, she showed up at the biology library one afternoon in desperate need of information on the life cycle of the *Plasmodium* parasite for a required introductory course in biology she was taking from Professor Kinsey himself. "We have to cite at least three scientific journals," she told me, still breathless from her dash across campus in the face of a steady wind, "and I have to write it all up by tomorrow, for class."

I'd been filling out catalogue cards for the new arrivals when she came up to the desk and took me by surprise. Before I could even think to smile, a hand went to my hair, smoothing it down where the rebellious curl was forever dangling. "I'd be—sure," I said. "I'm not really—it's the librarian you want, Mr. Elster, but I could—I'll do my best, certainly." And then I found my smile. "For you, of course."

Her voice went soft. "I wouldn't want to be any trouble—I'm sure you have better things to do. But if you could just point me in the right direction—"

I got to my feet and shot a glance across the room to where Elster sat at his own desk, partly obscured by a varnished deal partition. He was a short, thin, embittered little man, not yet out of his twenties, and, as he was quick to remind me, it wasn't my job to take queries or assist the patrons—that was his function, and he guarded it jealously. For the moment, however, he seemed oblivious, absorbed in paperwork—or one of the crossword puzzles he was forever fussing over. When I responded, my voice was soft too—this *was* a library, after all, and there was no reason to draw attention to ourselves. "Current issues of the journals are alphabetized along the back wall, but what you'll want are the indexes, and they're—well, why don't I just get them for you?"

She was smiling up at me as if I'd already found the relevant citations, written them up for her and submitted the paper all on my own, and her eyes twitched and roved over my face in a way we would later identify as one of the subliminal signals of availability (readiness to engage in sexual activities, that is, in kissing, petting, genital manipulation and coitus), though at the time I could only think I must have something caught between my teeth or that my hair needed another dose of

Wildroot. "Have you heard from your mother?" she asked, abruptly changing the subject.

"Yes," I said. "Or, no. I mean, why do you ask, has something—?"

"Oh, no, no," she said, "no. I just wanted to know how she was doing, because I never did get to thank her for that lovely afternoon and her hospitality. And yours. We had a really memorable time, Tommy and I."

"They were terrific cookies," I said stupidly. "My grandmother's recipe, actually. They're a family tradition."

For a moment I thought she wasn't going to respond and I stood there self-consciously at the desk, fumbling in my mind for the key to the next level of small talk—her mother, shouldn't I ask about her mother, though I barely knew her?—but then she said something so softly I didn't quite catch it.

"What?"

"They were, I said." I must have looked puzzled, because she added, "The cookies. I was agreeing with you."

I floundered over this for a minute—as I told you, I wasn't much with regard to small talk, not unless I had a couple of drinks in me, anyway—and then she let out a giggle and I joined her, my eyes flicking nervously to Elster's desk and back. "Well," I said finally, "why don't you find a seat and I'll, well—the indexes . . ."

She settled herself at one of the big yellow-oak tables, laying out her purse, her book bag, her gloves, coat and hat as if they were on display at a rummage sale, and I brought her the journal indexes that might have been most promising, then retreated to my work at the main desk. The room was warm—overheated, actually—and smelled, as most libraries do, of dust and floor wax and the furtive bodily odors of the patrons. A shaft of winter sunlight colored the wall behind her. It was very still. I tried to focus on what I was doing, writing out the entries in my neatest block printing, but I kept looking up at her, amazed at the vitality she brought to that sterile atmosphere. She was wearing a long skirt, dark stockings, a tight wool sweater that showed off her contours and complemented her eyes, and I watched her head dip and rise over her work—first the journal, then her notebook, and back again—as if she

45

were some exotic wild creature dipping water from a stream in a pastoral tale.

But she wasn't wild, not at all—she was as domestic as they come. And, as she later admitted, she'd brought herself to the library that day for the express purpose of reminding me that she was still alive and viable, that she had lips that could be kissed and hands that yearned to be held. In truth, she'd already written up her notes on the nasty little parasites that cause malaria—already had everything she needed—and was there at the desk with her hair shining and her head dipping and rising for my delectation alone. She had, as my mother knew long before I did, set her cap for me, and she was determined to allow me to discover that fact in my own groping way. Before she went home we had another little chat and I'd somehow managed to ask her out for Saturday evening to attend a student production of a popular Broadway play.

The other thing that happened involved Prok, and I suppose it was emblematic of all that was to unfold between us—that is, between Prok and me on the one hand, and me and Iris on the other. It was the same week Iris had come to the library—perhaps even the same day; I can't really remember now. I was just leaving work when I heard someone call out my name and turned to see Prok coming down the steps at the front of the building. "Milk, hold up a minute, will you?" he called, and then he was at my side, peeling off one glove to take my hand in his. "So how is it, then? The new position suitable?"

"Yes," I said, "I'm very much—it's interesting." My words hung in the air as if no one had spoken them. I felt for my cigarettes inside my jacket pocket, then realized I must have left them back at my desk.

"But let's walk," he said. "You going my way?"

"I live over on Kirkwood."

"Ah. Well. Wrong direction, then. But indulge me—a young fellow like you ought to be able to stand a two-block detour I would expect, no?"

And then we were walking—in the direction of his house on First Street—the campus trees arrayed around us like statuary, lights riding high in the windows of the big pale buildings under a darkening sky.

The air was tense with the cold, stretched thin over the skin of the evening, but it felt good to be out in it after the confinement of the library. There were patches of ice in the street. Trashcans stood at the curb. Prok was just slightly ahead of me, chopping along in his usual two-for-one stride (for Prok everything was competitive, even walking) and speaking over his shoulder so that his words came to me wrapped in an envelope of frozen carbon dioxide.

"I was just remarking to Clara what an interesting person you are and how much you impressed me, and she said, 'Well, why not have him over for dinner, then?' and I thought that would be just fine because I expect you don't get all that much home cooking, do you? You know, as we were saying the other week, the mother's touch?"

"No," I said, "you're absolutely right. It's either the Commons or the diner, I'm afraid." I was aglow with the compliment—*I'd impressed him*—and the words came easily.

"Plenty of grease and gristle to fuel those expanding brain cells." He'd swung his big head round to smile at me.

"And of course we're not allowed to cook for ourselves—"

"Rooming house, eh?"

I nodded. We were on one of the side streets now, across from the university. There was very little traffic.

"Well," he said, pulling up short and swinging round on me, "so how about it? Shall we say Saturday, six p.m.?"

I must have hesitated, because he added, in a different tone altogether, almost as if he were preparing to build a case, "If you're not doing anything, of course. You don't have any plans, do you? For Saturday?"

I looked off down the deserted street, then came back to him. "No," I said. "Not really."

PROK'S HOUSE WAS an easy walk from campus, but in those days it was considered somewhat off the beaten path, as First Street and the neighborhood around it hadn't yet been developed to the extent it now is. I had the impression of the odd sprawling house bracketed by tall black spikes of forest, and somewhere in the near distance there was the sound of a brook. Though there were no streetlights this far out, the glow of the stars and a three-quarters moon was enough to guide me past the occasional dark hump of an automobile drawn up alongside the curb, and each of the houses I passed seemed to have a lamp burning in every window. I was running a bit late because I'd spent the better part of an hour deciding on what to bring the hostess—an arrangement of dried flowers and pinecones that seemed to have been sprayed with white concrete in which were set some sort of piebald bird feathers, a bottle of bonded Kentucky bourbon, or a cheese that caught my eye in the grocery window. I'd settled on the cheese finally—the dried flowers were too risky, since I didn't know a thing about botany and I'd be entering the domain of experts, and I passed over the bourbon because I didn't know how Prok felt about the consumption of alcoholic beverages, though I suspected he was opposed to it both as a waste of time and inimical to one's health.

When I did get there, at quarter past six and out of breath, I had to stop and recheck the address. I'd always been shy of social gatherings, afraid that I was in the wrong place or that I'd got the date confused or that the hosts wouldn't recognize me or had forgotten they'd invited me to begin with. It was foolish, I know, but I'd even felt that way with my childhood friends in Michigan City, standing on a playmate's doorstep with a catcher's mitt or a basketball as I'd done a thousand times before and suddenly filled with the conviction that they'd turn me away, say something sharp and wounding, run me off like a stray dog. It didn't help matters that I was out of my depth with this middle-aged professor and his wife (whoever she might turn out to be, I was terrified of her and what she might think of me, and in a state approaching panic over the thought of the other guests, who, for all I knew, might range from the town mayor to my literature professor and the president of the university). What would I say to them? What would I do?

So why then had I accepted the invitation in the first place? I can't say, really. It was like that moment with Laura Feeney in the hall outside registration, a moment that seems to present itself as offering up a choice but is in actuality a confluence of circumstances that pins you to a course of action as decisively as Prok pins his Cynipids to the mounting board. Fate, I guess you would call it, though I wouldn't want to give the impression that I'm making any sort of metaphysical or mystical connection here—I haven't got a mystical bone in my body, not after spending the last sixteen years with Prok. I made my choice. I said yes, as I was to say yes to so many other invitations Prok would offer me, whether I wanted to or not. Again, looking back on it, I could see that Prok was a father figure to a young man whose own father was long dead and gone, and that he was powerful and persuasive—no one ever said no to Prok—but it went beyond that too. I was flattered by him. He'd chosen me—he was *impressed* by me—and I broke my first date with Iris to be there on that Saturday night in February.

But I had to recheck the address because the house was so—what better word for it?—unusual. From the street, in the grip of the night, it looked like a gingerbread house, something out of a fairy tale, the haunt of the necromancer or the sprite. The brick path wound circuitously through clumps of vegetation (Prok's horticultural credo: "The orthogonal line is the recourse of the city planner, the curvilinear the gardener's delight"), and though you could see that there was an order to it and that it did indeed lead to the front door, the effect was deceptively natural. As for the house, it glowed with windows and featured a stepped, shingled roof and walls constructed of odd-shaped bricks (seconds Prok had bought for a song) with great dabs of mortar leaking over them like icing on a sagging cake. This was the house of a scientist? I couldn't believe it. I was certain I'd got the address wrong—misheard it, transposed the numbers—but by this time I was standing on the doorstep, and I was late, so there was nothing else to do but tuck the cheese under my arm (it was a Stilton and it must have weighed ten pounds), steel myself and lift the brass knocker.

A woman answered the door—or rather a *female*, as Prok would have it. She was tiny, childlike, with hair even blacker than Iris's and cut short in a bob that left her ears exposed. She had a beautiful smile, natural and unaffected, and she was training it on me even as she pulled the door back with a slim white hand.

"I was—I've come— Does Professor Kinsey live here? By any chance?"

"I'm Clara," she said, already accepting the cheese. "And you must be John. But here, come on in, Prok's just finishing up some things and he'll be with us in a moment."

She led me inside, into the living room, which was as unconventional as the exterior of the house. The walls were painted black (or, as I was later to learn, stained with tea, which Prok felt would preserve them more effectively than paint) and the furniture, rustic and homemade, was of bent hickory, similarly painted black. There was a stand-up piano against one wall (also black), several bookcases full of records, and a gramophone. Lamps were placed about the room, softening the corners, and a fire burned in the open hearth. There was no sign of other guests.

"Mrs. Kinsey, I have to tell you I'm so sorry to have been, well, late— I'm not normally—but, I, uh, had some trouble finding the place, and I, uh—"

"Nonsense," she said. "We don't stand on ceremony here, John—we'll eat when we're hungry, so don't you worry yourself. And please, call me Clara. Or better yet, Mac." Her voice was breathy and hesitant, each syllable pulling back from the next with a gentle adhesion, as if words were like candy, like taffy, lingering reluctantly on her lips. She was forty-one years old, the mother of three, and no beauty, but she was fascinating, utterly, and from that moment forward she had me in her thrall.

We were standing in the middle of the room on what appeared to be a homemade rug. I must have been studying it unconsciously because Mac (her nickname, an abbreviation of her maiden name, McMillen, just as Prok was the short version of Professor K.) remarked, "Lovely, isn't it? My husband's handiwork."

I said something inane in reply, along the lines that he was a very talented man.

Mac let out a little laugh. I wondered where the children were, where the other guests were, and at the same time secretly prayed there would be none. "But listen to me—I haven't asked if you would like something to drink?"

I would. I wanted a bourbon, a good stiff one, to bring back the feeling in my fingers and toes and unfasten my tongue from the roof of my mouth. "Oh," I said, "I don't know. Anything. Water maybe?"

At that moment, as if on cue (but that's a cliché: he was there all along, observing from the hallway, I'm sure of it), Prok appeared with an enameled tray in his hand, and on it a selection of liqueurs and three miniature long-stemmed glasses.

"Milk," he cried, "glad you could make it, and welcome, welcome." He set the tray down on a low black table in front of the hearth and motioned for me to take a seat. "I see you've already met Mac, and what's this—a cheese?—ah, splendid. Perhaps Mac would do the honors, and some crackers, please, dear, crackers would be nice. And now," turning back to me, "you'll have a glass of spirits?"

I accepted one of the little glasses—about a thimbleful—while Prok expatiated on the properties of the various liqueurs on the tray, remarking how a colleague traveling in Italy had brought him back this one and how that one had come highly recommended by Professor Simmonds of the History Department, and I really didn't have to say much in response. I sipped at the drink—it smelled powerfully of some herb I couldn't quite place and had the consistency and cloying sweetness of molasses—all the while realizing that my initial surmise was correct: Professor Kinsey didn't know the first thing about drinking. We were talking about the marriage course—my impressions of it—when Mac slipped back into the room with another tray, this one featuring my Stilton in the center of an array of saltine crackers.

"Just dissecting the marriage course," he said, giving her a look I couldn't fathom, and it occurred to me then that he must have taken her sex history as well—she must have been among the first—and the thought of that, of the husband quizzing the wife, gave me a strange rush of feeling. He was a master of the interview, as I knew from experience and would have reemphasized for me again and again as the years went by, and there was no dodging him—he could tell in an instant if the subject was hedging, almost as if he were hooked up to him like a human lie detector. She would have had to tell him everything, and he would know her secrets, as he knew mine. I saw, with a sudden thrill, the

51

power of that knowledge. To give up your history was to give up your soul, and to possess it was the ultimate aggrandizement, like the cannibal growing ever greater with the subsumed spirit of each of his successive victims.

At dinner, the conversation was exclusively of sex. Prok went on about his project, how he could develop a taxonomy of human sexual behavior in the way he was able to classify wasps according to variations within the species. We were eating a stew of some sort—goulash, Prok called it—which he'd prepared himself. He served milk rather than beer or wine, pouring it out of a glass pitcher and making one of his rare stabs at wit ("Care for some milk, *Milk?*"), and there were just the three of us at table. The children had apparently been fed earlier, so that, as Prok put it, "We can get to know one another without having to divide our attention," and every time Prok drew a breath, which was rarely, Mac put in her two cents on the subject. And that surprised me, because she was every bit as informed as he—and every bit as capable of dropping terms like "cunnilingus" and "fellatio" into the dinner conversation.

For my part, I luxuriated in the attention. I'd never thought of myself as anything other than ordinary, even when I made A's in my course work or managed to score a touchdown on a broken play in a high school football game, and here were two vibrant, intelligent, worldly people—two adults—soliciting my opinions and treating me as an equal. It was heady, and I felt I never wanted to leave that table or that sofa by the fireplace where we settled in after dinner with bowls of vanilla ice cream while Prok lectured in his high tireless voice and Mac knitted with perfect articulation. Nine o'clock came and went, and then ten. Mac disappeared at one point to be sure the children were in bed (two girls of fourteen and sixteen, and a boy of eleven), and there was an awkward moment during which I expressed my concern over the lateness of the hour, but Prok dismissed me with a wave. Far from being exhausted, he shifted into a higher gear.

He poked at the fire, then eased himself down on the floor with the cloth braids he was fashioning into a new rug ("Very economical, Milk—you should take it up. Any discards, old clothes, sheets and the like, plus strips of muslin dyed in whatever color you prefer, and you'd be surprised how durable such a rug can be. Why this one, the one beneath me here? I wove this as an assistant professor in our quaint little rental back in 1921, our first home, in fact, after we were married") and in the quiet broken only by the snap and hiss of the fire, he opened up to me all his hopes and aspirations for the project. Ten thousand interviews, that was what he wanted—at a minimum—and the interviews had to be conducted face-to-face to assure accuracy, unlike the printed questionnaires or subjective analyses previous researchers had favored. Only then could *we* (he was already including the young neophyte before him) have the data to drive down the hidebound superstitions that had ruined so many lives. Take masturbation, for instance. Did I know that reputable people—doctors, ministers and the like—had actually promoted the egregious notion that masturbation leads to insanity?

He turned to me, his spectacles giving back twin images of the fire eating at a split oak log so that the reflection dissolved into his eyes. "Why, masturbation is the most natural and harmless outlet the species has acquired for release of sexual tension. It is purely positive, a veritable benefit to the species and to the society at large, and any minister worth his salt should be delivering sermons on that subject, believe me. Just think, Milk, just think of all the harm done by sexual repression and the guilt normal healthy adolescents are meant needlessly to feel—" I must have colored at this point, thinking of our last interview, because he changed tack suddenly and asked me point-blank if I wouldn't help him by contributing to the project.

"Well, yes, I mean—certainly, I would be—" I fumbled, trying to recover myself. "But what could I do, in any material way, that is—?"

"Very simple," he said, shifting his legs on the rug. "Just poll the men in your rooming house—you say there are fourteen of them in addition to yourself?"

"That's right," I said. "Yes. Fourteen."

"Just poll them and convince them to come on into my office to give up their histories—you've got a potential one-hundred-percent group, there, John, do you realize that?"

I wasn't the sort who fraternized easily—I think I've made that much clear here—and the prospect was daunting, but I found myself nodding my head in assent, because, as I say, you just didn't say no to Prok.

And yet, even as I sat there conspiring with him like a favored son, somewhere in the back of my mind, obscured for the moment, was a dull but persistent sense of guilt over Iris. You see, it wasn't simply my indecision over the cheese that had made me late that evening, but the fact that I'd left Iris—or the Iris situation, I should say—to the last minute. I don't know why that was—I'm not a procrastinator, or not normally, else I wouldn't have accomplished what I had at school or would come to achieve in later years with Prok—but every time I thought of phoning Iris my heart began to pound so violently I was afraid I was having a seizure, until finally I realized I had to see her in person, if only to explain myself and try to patch things as best I could. I did want to go out with her, very much so—I'd begun to think about her at odd moments, picturing her the way she was that day in the library or that afternoon at my mother's, swinging her legs beneath the chair like a little girl, gesticulating to make a point, her eyes boiling up like cataracts over any issue at all, over parasites or poetry or the plight of the Lithuanians— but the longer I put off breaking our date the worse it was.

Finally it was Saturday, and I still hadn't mounted the courage to see her. I woke to a burst of Paul's blunt, ratcheting snores and a gray scrim of ice on the window, thinking Iris, thinking I had to go to her dorm right that minute and ask her to breakfast so I could look into her eyes over fried eggs and muffins and coffee and tell her I'd take her out the following Saturday, without fail, that I was looking forward to it, that there was nothing I'd rather do (and maybe, since I'd already bought the tickets for tonight she might want to go with a friend?), but that she had to understand, and I was sorry, more than sorry—distraught—and could she ever forgive me? But I didn't go to her dorm. It was too early. Seven. It was only seven, or just past, and she wouldn't be up for hours, or so I told myself. Instead, I took my books to breakfast alone at the Commons and read the first six stanzas of Milton's "Il Penseroso" over and over till I couldn't take it anymore ("Hence vain deluding Joys, / The brood of Folly without father bred," et cetera), pushed myself up from the table and slammed out the door before I knew what I was doing.

The clock tower was ringing eight; the cold leached through the soles of my shoes. One of Laura Feeney's discarded lettermen, vastly overfed and with feet like snowshoes, limped past me on his way to the gym, even as I cut through a patch of woods and made diagonally across a dead brown strip of lawn for Iris's dorm. Inside, there was a smell of artificial fragrance, as if I'd somehow been transposed to the Coty counter at Marshall Field's, and the resident assistant—a girl of twenty with bad skin and a limp blond pageboy—looked up at me as if I'd come to ravish every coed on the premises. "Hello," I said, moving briskly across the room and trying to keep my head of steam up, because it was now or never, "I was wondering if, by any chance, well, if Iris McAuliffe is in. If she's up yet, I mean."

She gave me a stricken look, her features reduced to the essentials.

"I'm John," I said. "John Milk. Would you tell her John Milk is here? Please?"

"She's not in."

"What do mean she's not in? At eight o'clock in the morning? On a Saturday?"

But the RA wasn't forthcoming. She simply repeated herself in a long, drawn-out sigh of exasperation, as if I'd spent every morning of my life in the reception hall of the girls' dorm, pestering her: "She's not in."

I looked to the door at the far end of the lounge, the one that gave onto the inner sanctum beyond, and at that moment it swung open and two girls emerged, buttoning up their coats and adjusting their hats for the plunge through the outer doors and into the concrete clasp of the morning. They gave me a look of amusement—what man in his right mind would be calling for a girl at this hour?—and passed out of doors in a flurry of giggles. "All right, then," I said, taking the coward's way out, "can I leave her a note?"

But now I was with Prok, in front of the fire, agreeing to take my first unambiguous step on the road to a career in sex research, and who would have guessed? Who even knew there was such a thing? Ask a boy what he wants to be and he'll answer cowboy, fireman, detective. Ask an undergraduate and he'll say he intends to go into the law or medicine or that he wants to teach or study business or engineering. But no one chooses sex research.

I watched Prok work at his rag rug, pulling tight a six-inch strand of cloth, then interweaving it with another, the whole business spread now like a skirt over his sprawled legs. He was talking about his H-histories, how he'd been to the penal farm at Putnamville on his own and begun taking histories among the prisoners—"And they are very extensive histories, Milk, make no doubt about it"—and how one man in particular had offered to introduce him into the homosexual underworld of Chicago, and how significant that was, as H-histories were every bit as vital to assessing the larger picture as heterosexual histories, as I, no doubt, could appreciate. And then he paused a moment to offer a clarification, his eyes seeking mine and holding to them with that unwavering gaze he must have mastered by staring down his own image in the mirror for whole hours at a time. His voice softened, dropped. "That is, John, I believe you, of all people, should be especially attuned to the issue—"

I might have colored. I don't know. But I do remember his embrace that night as he stood at the door thanking me for coming, thanking me for the cheese and my insights and offering all sorts of Prok-advice and admonishments about the cold, the icy streets, incompetent drivers and the like. "Goodnight, Milk," he said, and took me in his arms and pressed me to him so that I could feel the ripple and contraction of his muscles and the warmth of him and breathe in the scent of his hair oil, his musk, the hot sweet invitation of his breath.

He let me go. The door pulled shut. I walked off into the darkness.

3

"So, PAUL, PLEASE, you're going to have to reiterate it for me, because I must be missing something here. You're opposed to science, is that it? To data collection? Honestly, I just don't get it."

We were in our room, waiting to go over to dinner, the day shutting down around the last pale fissures of a lusterless sun. It was cold. And not only outside: Mrs. Lorber must have had the furnace running on fumes. Paul—and I realize I haven't yet described him, and you'll forgive me, I hope, because I'm a novice at this—Paul was lying diagonally across his unmade bed, his head propped against the wall behind him, a comforter drawn up to his chin. He was almost a full year older than I and he wore a very thin, obsessively manicured mustache of the Ronald Colman variety, but his natural hair color was so pale and rinsed-out that you could barely detect it, even close up. His eyes were blue, but again, so weak a shade as to be almost transparent. He had two ears, a nose, a mouth, a chin—and a pair of thin colorless lips that always seemed to be clamping down on something, due, I think, to a congenital overbite. What else? His parents were English, from Yorkshire, he loved chess, Lucky Strikes and *The Lone Ranger,* and, of course, Betsy. With whom he'd gone all the way, though they were yet to be married— or rather, with whom he went all the way all the time. How did I know? He'd described it to me—coitus with Betsy—in the kind of detail that would have gratified Prok, if only I could get him to sit for an interview.

I would stay awake nights waiting for him to come home so we could lie smoking in the dark while he went on in his soft hoarse tones about how he'd maneuvered her against the wall in the hallway of the campus heating plant or pinned her beneath him on the backseat of a borrowed car, the heater going full, and how willing she was, how hot, how she only wore skirts now and no underwear, just to facilitate things, and how they longed to be married so they could do it in a bed, with sheets and blankets and no worries of the police or the night watchman or anybody else . . .

"But why should I?" he said. "Why should I waste an hour and a half—or what, two hours?—on some stranger I've never met and might not even like? What's in it for me?"

"Science," I said. "The advancement of knowledge. Did you ever stop to consider that if there were more men like Dr. Kinsey maybe you wouldn't have to sneak in and out of the heating plant with your fiancée, because premarital sexual relations would be sanctioned, even encouraged?"

He was silent a moment. The window had gone gray and I got up to switch on the lamp before wrapping myself in a blanket and easing back down on my bed. Shadows infested the corners. I could see my breath hanging atomized in the air. "I don't know," he said, "it's too personal."

"Too personal?" I couldn't believe what I was hearing. "How can you say that to me, of all people, when you give me a running description of everything you and Betsy do seven nights of the week, whether I want to hear it or not—"

"Aah," he said, and his hand rose and fell like a pulsing vein beneath the skin of the comforter, "you're just a sad sack. You don't even know where it goes, do you? You can't imagine, for all your marriage course, how sweet it is, how hot and sweet, and I guess I'm going to have to help you find it the first time, huh, with what's her name, *Iris*?"

"Screw you, Paul. I resent that. I do. Just because you got lucky with Betsy, found somebody, I mean, that doesn't—"

"Okay," he said, "all right. Keep your pants on. I'll do it. Okay? You happy now?"

It took me a moment, the breath congealing under my nose, the blanket drawn tight at my throat. "Yes," I said finally, and I tried to sound mollified, above it all, but he'd hurt me, he had—I was inexperienced and I knew it, but was that a crime? Did he have to rub it in? Didn't he think I wanted love—love *and* sex—as much as anybody else?

He was thinking. He kicked absently at the fringe of the comforter to better wrap it round his stocking feet. Two fingers licked over the shadow of his mustache. "So where do I go? Are you signing people up, or what?"

I was up off the bed and at the desk now, the blanket trailing across the floor, notebook in hand. "I've got his schedule right here," I said.

BEFORE THE MONTH was out, I was promoted from library underling to special assistant to Dr. Alfred C. Kinsey, Professor of Zoology, and when I chanced to pass Elster in the hallway or on the steps of the biology building, he looked right through me as if I didn't exist. I suppose there must have been some resentment among a faction of the biology majors as well—I had no training whatever in the field, aside from the introductory course I'd taken from Professor Eigenmann in my second year, and here I'd been rewarded with what might be considered one of the department's plum positions—but what Prok was looking for above all was someone to whom he could relate, someone who could share in his enthusiasm for the inchoate project that would ultimately produce the two seminal works in the history of sex research. That person could have been anyone, regardless of discipline. That it was I, that I was elected to be the first of Prok's inner circle, is something for which I will be forever grateful. And proud. To this day, I thank Laura Feeney for it.

At any rate, Prok installed me at a desk in the back corner of the office, where I was wedged between towering gunmetal-gray bookcases and enjoyed a forward view of the windows, which were piled high with galls wrapped in mesh sacks to contain any insects that might hatch from them, and these galls might have been collected in the Sierra Madre Oriental or Prescott, Arizona, or even in the Appenines or the rugged hills outside Hokkaido (interested parties were sending Prok samples from all over the world). There was an indefinable smell to the office, not unpleasant, exactly, but *curious,* arising from and connected only to that constructed and confined space on the second floor of Biology Hall. The wasps had something to do with it, of course, but a gall—this is the woody excrescence found on oaks and rose bushes, the growth of which is promoted by the larvae of the wasps living within it—really has a bit of a pleasant smell, a smell of bark and tannin, I suppose. (Break one from a tree next time you're out in the woods and hold it to your nose a moment and you'll see what I mean.) And the wasps themselves had no discernible odor, so far as I could detect. There were the lingering traces of the cigarette smoke Prok's subjects exhaled in dense blue clouds as they gave up their histories, and the smell of Prok himself—bristling and spanked clean; he was a great one for the cold plunge each morning and almost obsessive about soap. Finally, into the mix went the perfume of the three female assistants, who shared the desk with me and rotated shifts round my schedule, plus the usual odors of a working office: ink, pencil shavings, the machine oil of the typewriters and (in this case) the chemical used to discourage a minute species of beetle that routinely wreaks havoc on entomological collections round the world.

On my first day, Prok helped me settle in and gave me my initial lessons in deciphering his secret code and translating the results to his files. He was very precise, a model of efficiency, and if his longhand was somewhat artistic, full of flourishes and great slashing loops, his printing, like mine, was an almost mechanical marshaling of block letters so uniform it might be mistaken at a glance for typescript. Looking over my shoulder, rocking from foot to foot, his energy barely contained, he would cluck over my writing, seize my hand impatiently or snatch the paper out of my hands and ball it up as a reject. This went on for hours that first day, he pacing back and forth from his own desk to mine, until finally, when he felt I'd got the hang of it, he eased one haunch down on the corner of my desk and said, "You know, Milk, you're really doing quite well. And I have to confess that I'm pleased."

I looked up at him and murmured something in reply, trying to indicate my pleasure for the praise but at the same time not sound too obsequious—Prok may have been firmly in charge, always in charge, a born leader, but he never demanded obsequiousness, no matter what you might have heard from other sources.

A moment slipped by. Then he said, "You've noticed the galls, of course."

He moved easily up off the corner of the desk, went to the bookcase and lifted down a massive, bulbous, many-faceted thing that looked like the preserved head of some extinct beast, then laid it on the wooden surface before me. "Biggest known gall extant," he said. "Twelve chambers, fifteen point nine ounces. Collected it myself in the Appalachians."

We both admired it a moment, and then he encouraged me to run my hands over the craggy pocked surface of the thing—"Nothing to be afraid of, it's simply the expression of a particularly vigorous colony of *Cynipidae*. But then you probably don't know the first thing about Cynipids, do you? Unless, perhaps, Professor Eigenmann touched on them in the introductory course?" He was smiling now. Grinning, actually. This last was a joke, both on me—how could I have remembered?—and his colleague, who would have had to cover all of life on earth, from the paramecium to the horsetail to the giant sequoia and *Homo sapiens*, in the course of a semester and could hardly have devoted more than a single breath to the gall wasp, if that.

I grinned back at him, not quite knowing what was expected of me. "I know that they're wasps," I said. "And that they're relatively small compared to the ones that would be flying around out there if it were summer now."

"This is a parasitic insect, exquisitely adapted," he said, looking down almost lovingly on the gall. "An all-but-sedentary species, flightless and living out its entire life cycle in a single gall on a single tree. Perhaps, once in a great while, the adults will emerge and crawl overland to another tree fifty or a hundred feet away, and that is the compass of their independence and the extent of their range, which makes them such an interesting study—you see, I have been able to trace the origins of a given species simply by following its geographic trail and noting variations in inherited characteristics."

He began pacing again, stopping only to pluck off his glasses and gaze out the window a moment, before coming back to the desk to gently remove the exemplary gall and carefully replace it atop the bookcase. "But I'm afraid I have some bad news for you"—he was grinning; this was another joke in infancy—"they do tend to have a rather limited sex life. Unfortunately—for them, that is—males are very rare indeed in Cynipid society, most species reproducing through parthenogenesis. You do recall parthenogenesis from Professor Eigenmann's course, don't you?"

Another grin. His face dodged at mine and then away again. "Don't think I bring up the subject of my Cynipids just to hear myself talk, and, yes, yes, I can see that questioning look in your eye, don't try to hide it— *What in God's name is Kinsey up to now,* you're thinking, no? But there's a method to my madness. What I'm trying to say is, your presence here is the hallmark of a new era: as of Monday, I will be reducing the hours of my three female assistants in your favor, Milk. I've gone as far as I can with the gall wasp, and now, with your help and the prospect of adequate funding from the Rockefeller Foundation and the National Research Council, we are going to focus on one thing and one thing only, and I do think you know what that is . . ."

THAT YEAR MARCH came in like a lamb and went out like a lamb too, and I found myself doing double duty in Prok's office and his garden alike. The mild weather seemed to invigorate him (as if a man of his almost superhuman energy needed invigoration), getting him out of doors as much as possible on weekends and particularly on Sundays. He'd had a strict Methodist upbringing that caused him all sorts of adolescent torment with regard to his natural urges, and once he'd discovered science and applied a phylogenetic approach to human behavior, he became rabidly a-religious and made a point of working his garden while the rest of Bloomington was at church. By the end of the month it was warm enough so that he was able to work bare-chested and in shorts, and he encouraged me to do the same. Eventually, as the days warmed into late spring and summer, we would both habitually work as near to naked as was decently possible—but I'm getting ahead of myself here.

I remember that month distinctly as a time when I felt at peace with myself in a way I hadn't for a long while, if ever. There was the constant attention of Prok, his gentle prodding, his instruction, the feeling of mutuality as we sat in silence, bent over our desks, the sense of getting in on the ground floor of something revolutionary and exciting. There were nature hikes—he and Mac took me and the children to Lake Monroe, Bluespring Caverns, Clear Creek, for rambles in the patchwork of fields and forest out back of their house, Prok all the while lecturing on the geology of the soil, on the weeds and wildflowers that had begun to spring up in the clearings or the first of the migratory birds to reappear—and I remember too the enveloping peace of the dinner table and the hearth. It felt good to be with them, good just to be there. Mac simply took to preparing an extra portion any time I was working in the garden or we returned from one of our rambles, and the more I protested that I was putting them out, that I didn't want to be a pest or nuisance, the more the two of them went out of their way to reassure me. It got to the point where I was spending more time at the Kinseys' than at Mrs. Lorber's, and Paul, who'd been the rock of my world for the past three years—my dearest and closest friend on campus—began to joke that the only time he saw me anymore was when I was asleep. He had Betsy, I had Prok and Mac. It was only inevitable that we should grow apart.

It was around this time that I did something of which I'm not particularly proud, but which should be reported here, just to set the record straight. Or rather keep it straight. After all, what is the point of this exercise—of this remembrance of things past—if I'm not going to be absolutely candid? I have nothing to hide. I'm a different person now than I was when I stepped into that marriage course, and I wouldn't change anything that's happened, not for the world.

At any rate, I was an apt pupil—I've always been good with puzzles and ciphers—and I learned Prok's code in record time. Within two or three weeks I had it memorized. One afternoon—it was midweek and Prok had driven up to Indianapolis to address the faculty of a private school on the subject of the sexual outlets available to adolescents, and, not coincidentally, to collect as many histories as he could, of both staff and student body—I found myself alone in the office, transcribing coded histories from Prok's notation sheets to a larger format for the files so that we could calculate the incidence of various behaviors for statistical analysis (in Prok's system, a single encrypted sheet contained as much as twenty pages of information; eventually, of course, this information would have to be collated, at first by hand, and then, after we got our Hollerith tabulating machine, on punch cards). Initially, the work seemed exciting—the subject was sex, after all—but on this day, with these histories, which were of undergraduate men not much different from the one-hundred-percent group I'd managed to get him from my rooming house, it was pretty pedestrian. There had been some (limited) experimentation with other boys and farm animals, furtive masturbation, little coital experience but a good dose of petting, deep kissing and (again limited) forays into oral-genital contact. My hand ached from clutching the pen. My fingertips were stained with ink. I stifled a yawn.

I don't know what came over me or how the idea even sprang into my head, but I found myself looking through Prok's desk for the secondary code, the one that gave the key to the identities of all the individuals in his files—a code he was distinctly chary of sharing with me or anyone else, for security's sake. If his subjects weren't absolutely assured of anonymity, the vast majority of them would never have given up their histories in the first place. Security was the cornerstone of the project—then, as it is now. But when I actually had that code in my hand, I couldn't help noticing certain correspondences with the interview code (imagine a kind of reinvented shorthand, conflating abbreviations, scientific symbols and the markers of the stenographer's code into a new sort of encryption), and once I hit on those correspondences I couldn't help my mind from leaping ahead. In brief, it took me less than an hour to break the secondary code, and when I had it, when I held the key to all the files in my hand, I couldn't help using it. I couldn't. I just couldn't resist.

In later years, when Prok was the single most recognized person in this country outside of the president himself, when he appeared on the cover of *Time* magazine and the press couldn't get enough of him, the most frequent question put to him concerned his own sex life, and he would invariably answer that he had contributed his history to the project as so many thousands of others had and that it would remain anonymous just as theirs would. That, of course, was true, and only we of the inner circle came to know the details of that sex life firsthand—we were sworn to secrecy, because the fabric of all of our lives would have unraveled if any of it got out—but on that sleepy afternoon with an overactive sun poking through the blinds and big droning flies sailing obliviously over the racks of preserved wasps, Dr. Kinsey's was the first file I went to, and after his, it was Mac's.

I stood there at the filing cabinet, my breath coming in shallow gulps, the manila folder spread open before me. Every other second I stole a glance over my shoulder, ready to slip the file back in place at the first hint of a sound from the outer office. I was keyed up, yes, but riveted too. Here was Prok's history, right here in my hand, his deepest nature revealed in the most elemental way: he had my history, and now I had his, and it was unlike anything I'd anticipated.

As a boy Prok had been even more awkward and shy than I, not at all interested in organized athletics or social activities of any kind, and to compensate for a system weakened by early bouts with rickets, typhoid and rheumatic fever, he took to nature, hiking and exploring obsessively till he'd built himself into the fit and vigorous man I knew (though he never lost his pronounced stoop, a result of double curvature of the spine). He was an Eagle Scout. He masturbated compulsively. His father was a religious moralist. Until he was well into his twenties—older than I—he never had a mature and satisfying sexual experience, and that came only after his marriage to Clara.

And here was where his history got interesting. Though the honeymoon involved a long and arduous early-summer hiking trip through the White Mountains during which he and his bride were forced together in the close proximity of their tent each night, the marriage wasn't consummated till some months on. The delay, as I was later to learn, was a result both of their inexperience and a slight physiological impediment with regard to Clara's hymen, which was unusually thick (added to the fact that Prok's penis was a good deal larger than normal). I pictured their mutual embarrassment, their prudery, their lack of knowledge or insight, envisioned them kissing and stroking and wrestling in their sleeping bags and tents, on the cots in the summer camp where they served as counselors in July and August of that year, and then back at home in their first rental in Bloomington, nothing gained but frustration. After three months of marriage, sex still remained a mystery for them—it wasn't until a surgical procedure relieved Mac's discomfiture that they were finally able to achieve coitus. Prok was twenty-eight at the time.

Knowing this—uncovering it in the way an Egyptologist might have decrypted the hieroglyphs telling of the life and habits of some ancient pharaoh—gave me a strange rush of sensation. On the one hand, I couldn't help thinking of my mentor as somewhat diminished—here he was preaching sexual liberation, at least privately—and he'd been as much a prisoner of antiquated mores, of shyness, ignorance and his own inability to act, as I was. And yet, on the other, his history gave me hope and a kind of eerie confidence that my own sexual confusion would eventually resolve itself.

There was more. His H-history, which began with adolescent alliances, as mine had, became increasingly complex. The zoology professor, the distinguished scientist with a star beside his name in *American Men of Science*, the middle-aged father of three and happily married entomologist with the no-nonsense manner, was moving higher up the 0–6 scale, having initiated relations with several of his graduate students in the course of their long field trips and ultimately experiencing an intense and very close relationship with a male student not much older than I. And how do you suppose that made me feel? And Mac, what of her?

My blood was racing and I suppose if anyone had looked in on me in the office that day they would have seen the color in my face. I riffled through the pages, all greedy eyes and trembling fingers, then slipped Prok's folder back into the cabinet and took up Mac's. Her history was more extensive than I would have guessed, and as the symbols gave themselves up to me I couldn't help picturing her naked, her hands, her lips, the way she walked, the cloying catch in her voice. I was aroused, I admit it, and I was already up from the desk and searching through the files for Laura Feeney's history, for Paul's and the Kinseys' children's, when I caught myself. What was I doing? This was voyeuristic, it was wrong, a violation of the trust Prok had invested in me, and here I was throwing it all over just to satisfy the tawdriest kind of curiosity. Suddenly—it was dark now, the lamps softly glowing, the galls shadowy and surreal—I felt ashamed, as deeply ashamed as I'd ever felt in my life. I could barely breathe until I'd put the files back and replaced the code under lock and key in the drawer, all the while listening for footsteps in the hall. I switched off the lights. Locked up. And when I slunk off into the corridor, I turned up my collar and averted my face like a criminal.

The next day Prok was back, a volcano of energy, whistling a Hugo Wolf song under his breath, bustling about the office in a running pantomime of quick, jerky movements, up from his desk and back again, a glance into one of the Schmitt boxes, then the files, a cursory check of a two-years'-dormant gall that had suddenly begun to hatch out and then a shout from the microscope—"A new genus, here, Milk, I believe, a new genus altogether!" When I'd first come in he gave me half a moment to settle myself and then, with a grin, he laid a compact folder on my desk. "Eighteen histories," he said, showing his teeth. "And thirty-six more promised. I was up till two in the morning just to record them."

"Wonderful news," I said, sharing the grin with him.

"Any difficulties while I was away?"

I fought to keep my face straight. *Don't shift your eyes*, I told myself, *don't*. "No," I said, shifting my eyes, "no, everything was fine."

He was looking at me curiously. I opened the folder in the hope of distracting him, but it didn't work. Actually, I don't think there was ever a person born on this earth more attuned to the nuances of human behavior than Prok, no one more sensitive to facial expression and what we've come to call body language—he was a bloodhound of the emotions, and he never missed a thing. "Everything?" he prodded.

I wanted to confess in that moment, but I didn't. I murmured something in the affirmative, and, further to distract him, said, "Do you want me to transcribe these right away?"

He seemed absent, and didn't answer immediately. He was always young-looking for his age—in those days people routinely took him for five to ten years younger than he actually was—but I saw the lines in his face then, the first faint tracings of the finished composition he would take to his grave with him. But he must be exhausted, I thought, pushing himself to collect his histories, driving all that way in his rattling old Nash, up late, up early, nobody to help him. "You know," he said after a moment, and it was almost as if he were reading my mind, "I've been thinking how convenient it would be—how essential—for me to train another interviewer, someone I could trust to collect the data along with me, a person who might not necessarily have any scientific training but who could immerse himself in the technique I've developed and apply it rigorously. A quick study, John. Somebody like you." A pause. "What do you say?"

I was so taken by surprise—and so consumed with guilt over my invasion of the files—that I fumbled this one badly. "I—well, of course," I began. "Well, certainly, you know, I would—and I *do* have to graduate yet . . ."

"English," he said, and the noun came off his tongue like something distasteful, something chewed over and spat out again. "I never quite understood the application of that—as a field, that is."

"I don't know." I shrugged. He was watching me still, watching me with a preternatural intentness. "I thought I might like to maybe teach. Someday, I mean."

He sighed. For all his qualities, patience wasn't one of them. Nor did he take disappointment well. "Just think about it, John, that's all I ask. No need to decide right this minute—let's talk over dinner, and we are expecting you tonight, six sharp, that is, unless you have other plans?"

"Sex research? Are you nuts?"

Paul was stretched across his bed as if he'd been washed up there by a tide just recently receded. He was chewing gum and idly bouncing a tennis ball up off the racquet propped on his chest. Half a dozen books were scattered across the floor, face-down, another kind of flotsam. I didn't feel like explaining it to him—he wouldn't have understood anyway.

"At least it's a job," I said, pulling the sweater up over my head as carefully as I could so as not to disarrange my hair. I was changing for the Kinseys (they didn't stand on ceremony, as Mac had said—behind closed doors they were even what might have been considered bohemian—but I felt that a dinner invitation, no matter how frequent or informal, required a jacket and tie, and I still feel that way).

Paul let the ball dribble off the racquet and fall to the floor, where it took three or four reduced hops and disappeared under my desk. "But the sort of questions he asks—it's embarrassing. You're not going to—?" he caught himself, then saw it in my face. "You are, aren't you?"

I was knotting my tie in the mirror, studying my eyes, the way the hair clung slick to the sides of my head. "You didn't seem to have any objections at the time, if I recall—you said, in fact, that you found the experience unique. Wasn't that the word you used, 'unique'?"

"Look, John, I might be all wet about this, but don't you think it takes kind of an *unusual* sort of person to be poking into people's dirty underwear all the time?"

I gave him a look that projected from the mirror all the way across the room, and there he was, diminished on the bed, diminished and growing smaller by the moment. I didn't say anything.

"I wouldn't want to call the professor an odd duck or a pervert or anything, but don't you realize everyone's going to think of you that way? And what about your mother? You think she's going to approve— as a career choice, I mean?"

"I've told you a thousand times," I said, slipping into my jacket now, "it's science, research, just like anything else. Like Lister discovering antiseptic or what's his name with the mold on the bread. Why shouldn't we know as much as we possibly can about everything the human animal does?" I was at the door now, on my way out, but I paused to give him his chance to reply.

"The human animal? You sound just like him, John, you realize that? That's what he says. But what about human beings, made in the image of God? What about us? What about the soul?"

I was irritated suddenly. "There is no God. And no soul either. You know what's wrong with you?"

He never moved from the bed, never even lifted his head. "No, but I guess you're going to tell me."

"You just have a narrow mind, that's all," I informed him, and I let the door punctuate the truth of it on my way out.

Mrs. Lorber nodded to me from her post in the rocking chair and I gave her a strained smile in return, and then I was out in the street, the pussy willows at the corner in bloom, the tight pale buds firing on the trees, a warm breeze coming up out of the south freighted with the promise of the season to come. My eyes followed a trim dark girl as I crossed Atwater in front of the campus, her legs bare and thrilling as she receded down the avenue of trees, and I thought of Iris. I hadn't seen her in over a month, since I'd stood her up, that is, and I felt bad about it—and, of course, the longer I put off facing her the worse it was.

A car rolled slowly up the street, so slowly I thought the driver meant to pull up to the curb and park. He was an old man, his face drawn and anxious, and he gripped the wheel as if he were afraid someone was about to snatch it away from him. I watched him a moment, long enough to see a pair of bicyclists overtake him, and he never looked right or left or gave any sign he noticed them or anything else, and I found myself daydreaming about getting a car of my own someday and just taking off up over the hills and out of town until the road spooled out beneath me and I could be anywhere. Students drifted by in both directions. A pair of boxer dogs sat on their haunches and regarded me steadily from behind a picket fence.

As I turned onto First, I encountered a couple just ahead of me, the girl leaning into the man till they were a single entity, strolling along on four synchronized limbs, and I crossed to the far side of the street to avoid having to overtake them; seeing them there, seeing the way they made each other complete, made me think of Iris again. What I'd done was inexcusable, and I told myself I was going to call her the very next

70

day—just steel myself and do it—and if she told me to get lost, drop dead, dry up and blow away, well, at least the situation would be resolved. And there was no denying I deserved it.

So I walked. And if I noticed the various operations of nature in its season of renewal—if I smelled the scent of the forsythias or watched the birds ascend to the trees with bits of straw or twig clamped transversely in their beaks—I don't know if I really remarked them, at least not consciously. It was spring, that was all, and I was on First Street, going to the Kinseys'. For dinner.

Prok himself met me at the door. He was dressed in his gardening shorts and nothing else, his legs lean and muscled, his bare toes gripping the long polished boards of the sweet-gum floor. His hair, as always, looked as if it had been freshly barbered. "Ah, Milk," he said, ushering me in, "I've just been spreading a little humus on the irises—and the lilies too. Couldn't resist it, the weather's so agreeable."

He put on a short-sleeved shirt for dinner, but no shoes and no socks. Mac too was dressed more informally than she'd been on any of the previous occasions I'd come to dinner, in her own pair of shorts and a pale blue cotton blouse that showed off her throat and the delicate line of her clavicle. She seemed to have cut her hair as well, and it was as short now—nearly, that is—as a man's. I felt a bit foolish in my coat and tie, but both Prok and Mac reassured me: they were just rushing the season a bit, that was all.

After dinner the children dispersed, and Prok, Mac and I sat in the front room awhile, chatting. Prok was at his rug, Mac at her knitting. Prok had been talking excitedly about the premature return of some sort of bird—I forget which—and how it portended an early summer, when he broke off abruptly and turned to me. "Milk," he said, "John. Have you thought about what I said this afternoon?"

Mac's needles flashed. She was studying me out of her soft brown eyes, a maternal smile fixed at the corners of her lips.

I told him—told *them*—that I had. "It would be, well," I said, "an honor. And I want to say how much, that is—that you can be so generous to a young man, a student, who, uh—"

"Good," Prok said, in his honeyed tones, "very good. We'll see about

71

increasing your hours, then, and as soon as the semester is out, you'll come on with me full-time. Salary to continue as current. And of course we'll be working together in the garden as well."

The evening went on in that vein—a congratulatory vein, in a relaxed and amiable atmosphere—until Mac excused herself and Prok and I were left alone. I had no qualms about the work he was offering—it was important, exciting, noble even—and I was deeply grateful to have been offered steady employment at a time when the global situation was anything but settled, yet I did have one reservation. Or rather scruple, I suppose I should say. I didn't feel right about what I'd done in the office behind his back. Here he was, going out of his way to make something of me, to invest in me and my future in the most concrete way, and I had let him down, cheated him, betrayed his trust in me. He was talking about the school in Indianapolis—the Porter School, it was called—describing some of the details of the more intriguing histories, especially of two of the male faculty, who were hiding their extensive H-histories from the administration and the community too, when I interrupted him.

"Professor Kinsey," I said. "Prok. Listen, I, well, I must tell you something."

He stopped what he was doing—his long nimble fingers arrested on the fringe of the making rug—to focus his gaze on me. "Yes," he said. "What is it, Milk?"

There seemed to be a ringing in my ears, some sort of tocsin repeating itself there, and I must have raised my voice to be heard over it. "I have a confession to make."

For once, Prok had nothing to say. He receded into his interview mode, all ears.

"Well, I—when you were away I broke the code. The secondary code, that is. I—I'm afraid I went through your desk."

His first response was disbelief. "Impossible," he said.

I held his gaze unflinchingly, the bells ringing in my ears, his eyes fading in and out of focus till they were like twin blue planets floating in the ether. "I looked up only two histories, that's all, and I know it's unforgivable but I just couldn't help myself . . ."

One word only: "Whose?"

Something flew at the window then, beating toward the light of the lamp, a bat, I suppose, or a bird disoriented in the shadows of the fallen night. There was a dull thump of wings against the glass, and then it was gone. "Yours," I said, the voice strangled in my throat. "And Mac's."

He let me dangle a moment, then said, "You broke the code?"

"Yes," I murmured.

"I never imagined anyone could break my code, even if they did somehow get access to it. You realize I'll now have to devise a new one?"

"Yes."

"And that it will have to be infinitely more complex?"

I said nothing, thinking of the work it would entail, the waste of his irretrievable time, my own idle curiosity and how I'd set back the project before I'd even had a chance to contribute to it. I was angry with myself. And ashamed.

Prok got up, crossed to the mantel and spent a moment rearranging the framed photos there. I studied him from the rear, the long tapering range of him, the narrowed shoulders, the bristle of hair. He went next to the window, peered out into the darkness, then came back across the room and settled on the sofa before reaching up to flick off the lamp. Shadows stole out to enclose the room, the only light emanating from a lamp in the hallway. "So," he said finally, "you know my history, then? But here"—patting the place beside him on the sofa—"come here and sit."

I obeyed. I got up from the chair and eased in beside him on the sofa.

He put his arm round my shoulder then and drew me to him so that our faces were no more than six inches apart. "You shouldn't have pried, John," he whispered. "Shouldn't have. But I tell you one thing, it was good of you to confess."

"I'm sorry," I said.

"Demonstrates character. You realize that, don't you?" He gave my shoulder a fraternal squeeze. "You're a fine young man, John, and I appreciate your candor, I do."

And then something strange happened, the last thing I would have

73

expected under the circumstances—he kissed me. Leaned in, closed his eyes and kissed me. Some period of time passed during which neither of us spoke, then he took me by the hand and led me up the stairs to the spare room in the attic, and I remember a Ping-Pong table there, children's things, a fishing rod, an old sewing machine—and a bed. I didn't go home that night, not until very late.

4

Iris was taking a Shakespeare course that semester in the same building where I was sitting in on Professor Ellis's Modern British Poetry. I didn't realize it at the time because I hadn't yet got around to contacting her, though I'd meant to, so it was something of a surprise to run into her in the corridor one afternoon. As I remember it, the day was dismal, hanging like lint in the windows, the linoleum slick with wet, the whole world giving off a reek of mold and ferment. Rain had fallen steadily for the past week and there was more in the forecast. I was thinking nothing, umbrella, notebook and poetry text tucked under one arm, dripping hat in the other, making my desultory way through the mob of students in the corridor. Perhaps I was dreaming. Perhaps that was it.

She was on me before I could prepare myself, right there in front of me, two sets of shoulders parting, a girl in a yellow mackintosh grinning and ducking out of the way, somebody calling out something. Iris. There she was. We both pulled up short. "Hi," she said, and her smile was an education in itself.

"Yes," I said, "hi."

Her eyes seemed to drain all the available light out of the corridor, and there was nothing I could do but stare into them, fascinated. She seemed to have done something to her hair too, or maybe it was just wet. What was she wearing? A sweater six sizes too big for her, woolen skirt, ankle socks, saddle shoes. "You have Ellis this period?"

"Modern British," I said. "Poetry, that is. But listen, I never—did you get my note?"

She gave me a quizzical look.

"You know, that day—when we were supposed to go to the play? I left the tickets, and you know, a note, with the girl at the desk. The RA. I just wondered if you, well, if you got them."

Two streams of students were making their way round us as we stood there like posts in the dank hallway. There was a buzz of talk, I saw Professor Ellis at the far end of the corridor, a hundred pairs of shoes squealed on the wet linoleum. "Please, John," she said, her mouth drawn down to nothing, a slash, a telltale crack in the porcelain shell of her shining, martyred face, "not here. This isn't the place."

I just stared at her, mortified. An overwhelming sense of guilt and loss, of a doomed and inextricable culpability, began to drum at the taut skin of me, and, yes, the back of my neck went cold and the hair prickled on my scalp. "At least hear me out," I said.

"You want to talk? All right. Fine. I'd be interested to hear what you have to say, I really would." Her face was bled of color now, and she held herself absolutely rigid. "Four o'clock," she said, her voice struggling for the right tone, "at Webster's. You can't miss me. I'll be the girl at the back table, sitting all by herself."

I had to ask Prok to shift my hours that day, and I can't say that he was overjoyed about it—anything that interfered with work was antithetical to his project, and so, by extension, to him—but I managed to get to Webster's Drugstore before she did, and when she came through the door in her rain hat and made a show of shaking out her umbrella and throwing back her hair to mask whatever she was feeling, I was there. I told her I was glad she could come and then I told her how much I liked her and how sorry I was for what had happened, and my explanation probably ran to several paragraphs, but suffice it to say that I did adduce Prok and the importance of cultivating him for the sake of my job and future prospects.

She listened dispassionately, let me go deeper and deeper until at some arbitrary point her face lit with a smile and she said, "I took a friend. To the play, I mean. And it was one of the most enjoyable things I've done since I got here freshman year."

"Oh," I said, "well, I, in that case—"

"Don't you want to ask his name?"

We were drinking tea and fighting the impulse to dunk our powdered donuts into the little ceramic cups set out on the saucers in front of us. I didn't drink tea. I didn't particularly like tea. But I was drinking tea because that was what she had ordered with a look at the waitress—and then at me—that made tea seem exotic, the ultimate choice of those in the know. I'd just raised the cup to my lips, and now I put it down again. I tried to be casual. "*His* name?" I said. "Why, do I know him?"

She shook her head, her hair catching the light through the window. "I don't think so. He's a senior, though. In architecture. Bob Hickenlooper?"

What can I say? Hickenlooper's face rose up before me, a conventionally handsome face, the face of one of the most popular men on campus, one who had a reputation for chasing anything that tottered by on a pair of heels—or in flats, for that matter—and he was a brain too, with a great and staggering future ahead of him. Jealousy seized me. My hair—the loop of it that never seemed to want to stay where it belonged—fell across my forehead and I had an impulse to reach up and tear it out of my scalp with a single furious jerk. "He's—he lives in my rooming house," I said, making my voice as cold and small as I could.

She was enjoying herself now—that much was evident from the glint in her eyes and the way she shifted in her seat to get a better look at me. I watched her lower her head and purse her lips for a long slow sip of tea. "But enough of me," she said, "what about you? I hear you've been promoted."

"Yes, I—"

"Sex research, right?"

I nodded, a hundred thoughts warring in my brain, not the least of which was how she would have known: Through Hickenlooper? Paul? Her mother? But how could her mother know if mine didn't? I wanted to change the subject, wanted to ask her out to the pictures for Saturday night, right then and there—and I did, but not before she said, "How did ever you get *that*?"

THE WEATHER WARMED. Prok and I spent more and more time in the garden, hauling rocks for edges and borders, spading up the earth, pushing wheelbarrows of shredded bark and chicken manure back and

77

forth, trimming, cutting, pruning. We divided and transplanted endless clumps of lilies of all varieties, and irises—irises were his passion, and he'd collected over two hundred and fifty varieties of them and was forever trading and selling bulbs by post all across the country. We also planted trees—fruit trees, ornamentals, saplings we dug out of hollows in the hills—and all sorts of native plants, poke, goldenrod, snakeroot, wild aster, Queen Anne's lace, which had a surprising cumulative effect, setting off the splendor of the flowerbeds and giving the whole property a sylvan air, as if it were the product of nature rather than man. While we worked, Prok talked of one thing only—sex—and particularly of the H-histories he was collecting not only in Chicago and Indianapolis now, but in New York as well. He was moved almost to tears by the accounts of sex offenders he'd interviewed in prison, people incarcerated for common acts that happened to run afoul of the antiquated laws of record and who were prosecuted almost arbitrarily, like the South Bend man jailed for having received oral sex from his wife (or rather ex-wife, and on her report), or the many homosexual couples ferreted out and exposed by vindictive spouses, parents, small-town police. Coitus out of wedlock was universally banned, masturbation illegal, sodomy a felony in most states. "You know," he told me, and he told me more than once, making his case, already preparing the next lecture in his head, "it's utterly absurd. It's got to the point where if all the sex laws on the books were rigorously prosecuted, some eighty-five percent of the adult populace would be behind bars."

I told him that I agreed with him. That I couldn't agree more. That my life would have been a thousand times better if it weren't for all the prohibitions placed on me from the time I knew what the equipment between my legs was for.

He smiled, put an arm round me. "I know, I know," he said, "I'm preaching to the converted."

I began to see more of Iris during this period—I took her to the pictures and we went for walks or met for study dates at the library—though with finals coming up, graduation looming and the time I was required to devote to the project, not to mention the garden, our relationship progressed by fits and starts. By this time both Prok and I were stripped down to the barest essentials while working out of doors, and both of us developed such deep tans you might have mistaken us for a pair of Italian laborers. Prok wasn't a nudist, not officially (he was far too self-sufficient to join any group or movement), but he was often naked or as close to naked as he could reasonably be given the circumstances, because to his mind nudity was an expression of the most natural and relaxed state of the human animal—the very same agencies of social control that had proscribed certain sex acts dictated that people should wear clothing, whereas any number of societies outside the ken of the Judeo-Christian tradition did perfectly well without it, or with very little of it. "The Trobriand Islanders, for instance, Milk, think of the Trobriand Islanders. Or the Samoans." To emphasize his point with the neighbors and any uninformed pedestrians who might happen by, Prok ultimately reduced his gardening costume to a kind of flesh-colored jockstrap and a single shoe, which he wore on the right foot, for digging. I followed suit, of course, because this was what was expected of me, and I always did what was expected. (It was a question of loyalty, that was all, of an ethic central to my training, my upbringing—my very nature, I guess—though Iris in later years could be savage on the subject.)

What happened next—it was just before graduation in June—surprised even me, and I was the initiator of it. All this talk of sex, of how natural and uncomplicated it was and would and should be if only society would loosen its strictures, got me thinking about my own situation and the outlets (Prok's term) available to me. I was young, healthy, and the exercise and the sun and the feel and smell of the soil had me practically bursting with lust. I was hot, never hotter, frustrated, angry. I wanted Iris, wanted Laura Feeney, wanted anyone, but I didn't know where to begin. On the other hand, Prok and I continued to have *encounters* (but how he would have hated the euphemism—sex, we had sex), though, as I say, my H-history was limited and if I were a 1 or at best a 2 on the 0–6 scale, that would describe the extent of my inclination in that direction, and so I began in my hesitant way to broach the subject of heterosexual relations with him. But let me draw back a moment, because I remember the day clearly and need to set the scene here.

It was a Sunday morning, and we'd got to work early in the garden, church bells tolling in the distance, people strolling by on their way to services, the air dense with heat and humidity, the promise of a late-afternoon shower brooding over the hills. The garden was open—each Sunday Prok posted a hand-lettered sign to that effect so that people could have a chance to tour the property and listen to him lecture on each variety of flower and plant, its classification, its near relatives, its preferences with regard to soil, light and watering. Prok liked nothing better than to show off what he'd accomplished horticulturally, and again, this derived as much from his competitive instincts (nobody's lilies could ever hope to match his) as anything else. We were working on a massive clump of daylilies in one of the beds in the front yard, both of us down on all fours, when Prok glanced up and said, "Why, look, isn't that Dean Hoenig? And who's that with her? I'll bet—yes, I'll bet that would be her mother, come to visit all the way from Cleveland. Hadn't somebody mentioned that her mother was visiting?"

Prok had risen to his knees, a tight smile on his lips. I looked up to see the Dean of Women, dressed for church, making her way along the walk past the house, talking animatedly with a stooped, open-faced old woman in a hat like an inverted wedding cake. I knew that the dean had just recently moved into a house two doors up from Prok's, but beyond that I knew little or nothing of the faculty and really didn't have an answer for him. "I don't know," I said. "I haven't heard anything."

The smile broadened. He was watching them in the way of predator and prey, and I saw that they didn't have a chance, the old woman moving with such deliberation she was practically standing still. "It occurs to me," Prok said, his voice rich with subversive joy, "that the garden is open, is it not?"

I didn't give back the smile. I wanted nothing to do with the dean. I might have been under Prok's protection, but still I couldn't help shrinking inside every time I saw her, guilty, guilty as charged, and the irony was I'd never got more than that single kiss out of Laura Feeney despite all the squirming the situation had caused me.

Prok caught them at the gate. "Dean Hoenig, Sarah!" he called, darting out onto the walk in his jockstrap and single flopping shoe. The dean gave him a look of bewilderment, while her mother, who couldn't have stood more than four feet ten in her heels, visibly started. But Prok would have none of it. He was the smoothest, courtliest, most perfect gentleman in the entire state of Indiana, and he'd happened to see the ladies passing—"On your way home from church, I take it?"—and felt he just had to awaken them to the delights of his garden and offer them the rare privilege of a personal guided tour. "And who might this charming lady be?" he inquired, turning to the old woman with a bow. "Your mother, I presume?"

The dean—compact, busty, tough as a drill sergeant—was at a loss. She was always in command, overseeing her charges and ruling the dorms with an iron hand, but the situation was clearly out of her control. "Yes, this is my mother, Leonora. Mother, Professor Kinsey of the Zoology Department."

Prok took the old lady's hand and gave it a squeeze. There was a sheen of sweat on his chest, the long muscles and veins of his arms stood out in work-hardened definition, his lower abdomen bristled with pale blond hairs that were beginning to turn gray. He loomed over the old woman like a naked troglodyte, all flesh and presence, and yet what she heard coming from his mouth was the language of culture and civility. "I understand you're from Cleveland?"

The old lady's eyes had retreated into her head. She could barely croak out an answer in the affirmative.

"A jewel of a city," Prok said, idly scratching at the axillary hair under his left arm. "First-rate museum. Absolutely. Not to mention your symphony orchestra—I do envy you that, Mrs. Hoenig. But, please, don't let's stand out here in the street, come and let me show you my pride and joy—you do like lilies, don't you?"

The dean's mother nodded in a numb way, then shot a helpless look at her daughter. Dean Hoenig was wearing a tight smile, and it wasn't a welcoming smile, not at all. "I'm afraid we must be going, Professor Kinsey, though I do thank you for thinking of us—"

Prok cut her off. "Don't be ridiculous," he said, taking the old lady by the arm and steering her toward the gate, "it's no imposition at all, my pleasure, in fact, and how often does your mother get to see a botanical wonder like this and at a time when it's looking its very best too, I might add? Isn't that right, Mrs. Hoenig?"

The dean's mother didn't have an opportunity to express an opinion one way or the other because that was when she caught sight of me standing there in front of the hydrangeas, all but naked myself. (Prok had lectured me on what he saw as my excessive modesty, and I'd gradually come round to his way of thinking—though my gardening attire wasn't as minimal as his, I was at the time wearing nothing but a kind of dun loincloth he'd fashioned for me and a pair of earth-stained tennis shoes, sans socks.) She jerked back as if an electric current had just passed through her, but Prok held firm and guided her up the path to me, the dean following grudgingly behind. "Mrs. Hoenig," he was saying, "I'd like to introduce my assistant, John Milk. Milk, Mrs. Hoenig. And I think you know the dean . . ."

Even as I took the old lady's hand in my own and gave it a gentle shake, I could feel the dean's eyes probing me. She was out of her element here, already defeated—she was going to see the garden with her mother and listen to Prok's nonstop monologue and in the process learn something about the natural condition of the human animal whether she liked it or not—but she couldn't help making a thrust at me. "Yes, certainly," she said. "From the marriage course. But I guess you're waiting till after graduation to tie the knot, is that it, John?"

I was learning. From Prok. From the master himself. And I didn't flinch, didn't drop my eyes or let my face give me away. "Not really," I said. "Not actually, that is."

The old lady let out an exclamation over the bearded irises, a kind of long, attenuated coo, and Prok encouraged her, delighted, but before the dean could come back at me, he looked over his shoulder and said, "He's met someone else, isn't that right, Milk?"

What could I do but nod?

After the women left, laden with cut flowers, Prok and I finished up the chore that had been interrupted out front and then put in a good solid hour of pick and shovel work in the backyard (Prok was then constructing the lily pond, and there was plenty of hard labor involved in digging out rocks and hauling and spreading the dirt we removed). Just after noon, Mac came out with sandwiches and soft drinks and the three of us sat on the ground contemplating the contours of the hole and chatting. She was barefooted and dressed in the khaki shorts and blouse she wore as a camp counselor and troop leader for the Girl Scouts. I noticed that she'd parted her hair on the left, swept it across her brow and pinned it in place with a barrette over her right ear. I don't know what it was, but on this particular afternoon she was as gay and lighthearted as I'd ever seen her. She drew up her legs and rocked back against them as she ate and laughed and broke in on Prok's running monologue to make one point or another, and though she was in her early forties then, she seemed insouciant and girlish, not at all what you would expect from a housewife and mother.

What did we talk about over lunch that afternoon? I don't know. The pond, most likely, its depth and dimensions, the plantings Prok was planning for it, pickerelweed, irises of course, with their feet right in the water, and what did we think of *Sarracenia purpurea* for the transitional zone? I found myself stealing glimpses of Mac, of her legs, her ankles, the place where her tanned thighs vanished into the crotch of her shorts. That was what prompted it, I suppose, what made me dare something I would have been incapable of even a few weeks earlier, but as I say, my education was rapidly advancing. Here it is: when Mac gathered up the plates and Prok and I had watched her saunter across the lawn and disappear into the rear of the house, I turned to him. "Prok, I hope you won't, well, take this in the wrong way," I began, "but I've been thinking—with regard to my education and my needs too—about what we were talking of yesterday, my need for a female outlet, that is?"

He was in the act of pushing himself up, already anxious to get back to work. "Yes," he said, "yes, what of it?"

"Well, you see, I was wondering how you would feel about, well, about Mac—?"

He looked puzzled. "Mac?"

"Yes," I said, and I looked him right in the eye, apt pupil that I was, "Mac."

It took him a moment. "You mean, you want to—with *Mac*?"

You can say what you will about him—and everybody has an opinion, it seems—but Prok was no hypocrite. He preached sexual liberation for men and women both and he lived what he preached. A wan smile came to his lips and his eyes sparked with amusement, as if the joke were on him, then he laid down the shovel and told me he'd put the proposition to his wife that night, and that if she consented, I had his blessing.

As it turned out, Mac was as surprised as her husband, surprised but flattered too, and when I came to work in the garden the following weekend I found that she was alone in the house. I was out back, knee-deep in the crater Prok and I had excavated, wondering where he was— had he slept late? (an impossibility in itself; even when his heart was failing him in his late fifties he never slept more than four or five hours a night)—when I became aware of the susurrus of bare feet in the grass and looked up to see Mac standing there before me, a soft shy smile pressed to her lips. "Hello, John," she said, her eyes shining, that cloying catch in her voice, "I just came out to tell you that Prok has taken the children to Lake Monroe for the day. To do a bit of hiking and collect galls. He said—"

It felt as if the chambers of my heart had been wedged shut. I was having trouble breathing. The sun was a palpable thing, a weight on my shoulders I could barely sustain. I thought I might lose consciousness, and maybe I did, for just an instant, swaying there on my feet while the earth spun out of control beneath me.

"He said you really didn't have to work today. Not if you didn't want to."

Again, i want to be frank here—if Prok taught me anything, he taught me that. Euphemism is the resort of the inauthentic, the timid, the sex shy. I don't deal in euphemism and I believe in telling it like it is. Or as it is. To put it simply: I became intoxicated with Mac. She was my first, the woman who relieved me of my virginity, or to put it in the crudest possible terms, just to get it out, to express it in the way our lower-level subjects would in countless interviews—in the vernacular that so often gets to the truth so much more powerfully than the loftiest circumlocution—she was my first lay. There, I've said it. And if Iris should ever listen to this once events have played themselves out—or transcribe it for a book, and that's what it should be: a book—I have nothing to hide. She knows my sex history. She's known it from the beginning, just as I've known hers.

But on that June day in the garden with the flowers in riot and the air so soft and sustaining it was like a scented bath, with the faerie house looming behind us and the dense drugged stillness of the morning insulating us from the world, Mac reached out her hand to me and I took it. She didn't say a word. Just tugged gently till she conveyed what she wanted and I came up out of the dirt and let her lead me to a place at the back of the yard where the trees closed us in. There was a blanket there, spread out on the grass, and the sight of it made me surge with excitement: she'd planned out everything in advance, thought of me, wanted me, and here was the proof of it.

"Here," she said, "sit," and I obeyed her, my breath coming shallow and quick as she stood above me and unbuttoned her blouse, stepped out of her shorts, and with a slow graceful dip of her body, knelt down beside me and let her hands flow over my chest and abdomen, all the while exerting the gentlest soothing pressure on the strung-tight cords of my shoulders and upper arms, until finally I was resting on my elbows, then my back, and I could feel her fingers at the sash of the loincloth. The moment seemed to last forever, then the cloth slipped free and I felt her take hold of me in the one place that mattered. I knew what I was doing. I'd seen the slides, transcribed the histories. And I'd taken Professor Keating's classics course and I knew *Oedipus Rex* and *Oedipus at Colonus* and I knew that Prok was the old king and I was the son and Mac the mother. My eyes were open. I was no victim. And this was sex—not love, but sex—and I came to it as if I'd been doing it all my life.

5

I GRADUATED THE following Saturday.

My mother—and more on her in a moment—drove all the way down from Michigan City with Tommy McAuliffe and my Aunt Marjorie in Tommy's Dodge (we'd never had a car; it was a luxury, according to my mother, that we just couldn't afford, hence I'd never learned to drive, not till Prok took it upon himself to teach me later that summer). This was in June of 1940, and events in Europe—the evacuation at Dunkirk and the imminent fall of France—overshadowed what must have been one of the glummest graduation celebrations in IU history. Everybody was unsettled, and not just the seniors going out into the world. Conscription was a virtual certainty now. All the undergraduate men would be affected.

But I was graduating—magna cum laude, no less—and my mother was going to make an occasion of it, Hitler or no Hitler. She'd booked rooms for herself and my aunt a full year in advance so as to outmaneuver the other parents, the ones who might not be quite so astute or forward-looking, and Tommy was going to sleep on a cot in the room I shared with Paul Sehorn, everything arranged on the up-and-up with Mrs. Lorber beforehand. Now, as to my mother. I feel I should give her her due here, though one could argue that her role is hardly central to Prok's story, and yet I find it difficult to talk about her (she's alive and well, as of this testimonial, still teaching elementary school in Michigan City and not yet sixty). Hers was—is—a character formed by circumstance, and by circumstance, I mean, specifically, having to raise a son on her own during the Depression, widowed at thirty and with her parents nearly a thousand miles away and unable (and unwilling) to help. She was frugal, precise, as efficient and predictable as a machine, and nothing anyone had ever done or could ever do was quite up to her standard. But that sounds harsh and I don't mean to be harsh—she gave me clothing, food, opportunity, and if her emotional self went into retreat after my father disappeared, then certainly I'm not in any position to blame her. Nor is anyone else for that matter. She absorbed her sorrow, drank it up like a sponge, and then hardened with it till she calcified. But that's not right either. She's my mother and I love her unconditionally, in the way any son loves his mother. That goes without saying. Perhaps a physical description, perhaps I'd better stick to that.

My mother was taller than average—five foot seven—and she played intramural basketball when she was in high school, loved swimming and hiking and gossip. She was of Dutch descent—her maiden name was van der Post—and she had a natural wave to her hair, which was an amalgam of red and brown that in summer went to gold on the ends. She had a dramatic figure (I'm aware of this, in retrospect, not so much from observation—you just don't think of your mother in that way—but because she was proud of it, forever dispensing the information that so-and-so had complimented her legs or made some reference to the way her sweaters fit her like a model's and how she ought to have a screen test in Hollywood), but if she had any sexual outlets after my father's death, she was careful to conceal them from me, and I wouldn't mention the subject here at all but for what transpired between her and Prok. And for the sake of inclusivity, of course.

In any case, I was watching at the window that Friday afternoon when Tommy's Dodge pulled up to the curb in a flash of reflected sunlight and my mother and Aunt Marjorie got out, looked round them as if they'd been delivered to the Amazon instead of Bloomington, Indiana, and adjusted their hats a moment before mounting the front steps of the rooming house. I could have met them at the door, but I held back a moment, and I don't really know why. This was a time of celebration, of joy—for once I had the prospect of being spoiled a bit; there would be a nice dinner certainly, oysters, celery sticks with blue-cheese filling, steak served up medium rare on unchipped plates against a field of linen so white it could have been manufactured that very morning—

but I just stood there at the window and never made a move to go downstairs till I heard her voice in the hallway. I don't know what she was saying—greeting Mrs. Lorber no doubt, making some sort of animadversion on the state of the roads or Tommy's driving, or the weather: Wasn't it hot?—but the tone of it took hold of me and I went downstairs to her cold embrace, the dutiful son, John, her boy John.

The three women stood there in the vestibule, turned slightly toward the staircase, as if posing for a group portrait, which I suppose you might call *Awaiting His Footsteps in a Time of Quiet Jubilation* or *Who Will Save the Day?* "Mother," I said, taking the steps one at a time, slowly, with dignity, no bounding or undergraduate hijinks here, "welcome. And Aunt Marjorie—thanks so much. And Mrs. Lorber—have you met Mrs. Lorber?"

My mother embraced me in her stiff, formal way, but her eyes told me she was proud of me and pleased too. She was about to say something to that effect—or at least I assumed she was—when Tommy came rocketing up the steps from the street and burst through the door to wrap me up in a bear hug. "Hello, professor!" he shouted, spinning me around like some oversized package he was about to raffle off. "You know it don't mean a thing if it ain't got that swing!" Everyone smiled as if he'd lost his mind. Which he had. A moment later, when we were alone up in the room, he showed me the agency of his temporary derangement: a flask of whiskey convenient to the inside pocket of a sports coat. He handed it to me and I automatically took a long burning swallow, and when I tried to pass it back to him, he wouldn't take it. "Look at the initials on it," he said, sinking into Paul's bed as if his legs would no longer hold him.

Reproduced there, in filigree, were the initials JAM, for John Anthony Milk. "These are *my* initials," I said stupidly.

Tommy regarded me out of eyes that ran down the depths of two long tunnels. He'd listened to my mother and aunt for hours on end and who could blame him for being on the far side of sober? "You bet," he said.

There were five of us at dinner that night—my mother, my aunt, Tommy, Iris and myself. The restaurant was on the ground floor of a downtown hotel (not the one where my aunt and mother were staying, which was much more modest), and it had the reputation of being Bloomington's best, at least in that sleepy, provincial era before the war. There were potted palms to shield the tables from one another, the maitre d' was decked out in his best approximation of a tuxedo and had managed to paste his hair so tightly to his scalp it was like a black bathing cap with a part drawn down the side of it, and the menu ran from onion soup au gratin to grilled veal chops, whitefish and, of course, beef in all its incarnations. We all started out with shrimp cocktails, the shrimp perched prettily up off individual goblets of ice, and Tommy and I ordered beers while the ladies had a round of gin fizzes. I was feeling elated. Not only was I the center of attention—this was a fete for me, and because I was an adult now, a college graduate who'd achieved something in his own right, it had none of the constraint of the regimented birthday parties my mother used to arrange right up until the time I left high school for the university—but there was the flask to consider too. Its contents had gone a long way toward fueling my enthusiasm. Was I tipsy? I don't know. But I saw things with a kind of blinding clarity, as if the world had suddenly been illuminated, as if I'd been living in two dimensions all my life, in a black-and-white picture, and now there were three and everything came in Technicolor. Iris, for instance.

She sat across the table from me, her shoulders bared in a strapless organdy gown—blue, a soft cool pastel blue, with a tiny matching hat pinned atop the sweeping shadow of her hair—and I saw that she'd plucked her eyebrows and redrawn them in two perfect black arches that led the way to her eyes. To this point we hadn't said much to each other, she absorbed with my mother and aunt, Tommy and I reliving old times with a series of sniggers and arm cuffs and all the rest of the adolescent apparatus that still imprisoned us in boyhood though we would have been mortified if anyone had taken us for anything less than men. My mother said, "We have to intervene. There's no choice to it now. God forbid my son should have to go—I don't have to tell you he's the only thing I have left in this world—but we can't afford to divorce ourselves from the rest of humanity, we just can't, not anymore."

"That's what they want you to believe," Iris said, setting down her fork. She'd ordered the fish, and the white flakes of it gleamed on the tines against an amber puddle of sauce on her plate. "Why should we get drawn in? Forgive me—I know Holland's been occupied—but it's happened before, hasn't it? War after war?"

Tommy was in the middle of a reminiscence about a prank he'd pulled off after a football game against our biggest rival, and he was mistaken in thinking that I'd been part of it, but he was so wrapped up in the memory that I didn't want to disabuse him. But now he looked at his sister as if he couldn't believe what he'd just heard. "Oh, come on, sis, are you kidding me? France'll be gone in a week, two at the most, and then Hitler can pound England till there's nothing left but rubble, and you really think he'll be satisfied with that? You think he'll send a box of chocolates to Roosevelt and kiss and make up?"

"Exactly," my mother said, and her chin was set. "It might take him years to get here—a decade even, who knows? But the world is smaller than you might think, Iris, and nobody is safe as long as that madman is in it. Did you see him in the newsreel last week? The goose-step. Aren't you sick to death of the goose-step?"

"You don't understand. It's not our war," Iris said. "It has nothing to do with us. Why should our boys die for some crumbling empire, for, for— John," she said, turning to me, "what do you think?"

What I thought was that the celebration had gone sour. What I thought was that Iris looked like the prettiest thing I'd ever seen in my life, her eyes lit with indignation, her mouth puckered, the whitefish at her command. I tried on a grin. "I don't know," I murmured, "but personally? I don't want to die."

I was trying for levity, trying to take us all someplace else and expunge the strutting dictator from my celebratory dinner, but no one laughed. They just looked at me—even Aunt Marjorie, the mildest person I've ever known—as if I'd admitted to fraud or child rape or murder. War. We were in the grip of war, and there was no shaking it off.

It was Iris who came to my rescue. She'd taken a moment to slip the fork between her lips and masticate her fish and a sliver of green bean.

"That's my point," she said, still chewing. "I don't want to die either. Nobody does."

My mother waved a hand in dismissal. "You're too young yet. You don't understand. There's a larger picture here, and a larger issue—"

"Hey," Tommy said, as if he were awakening from a nap, "anybody want another beer—or cocktail?"

We walked my mother and Aunt Marjorie back to their hotel, then went out for a nightcap, just the three of us, and finally took Iris back to the dorm just before curfew. A dozen couples were sitting around the lounge gazing into each other's eyes. One of the girls had a conspicuous grass stain on her skirt—a stripe of vivid green against a beige that was almost white—and a guy I vaguely recognized was on the sofa with his girl, leaning in so close he looked as if he'd been glued to her. Her feet were on the floor, though—that was the rule—and so were his. The RA—the same blonde with the limp hair—had her head buried in a book.

Tommy had slowed down considerably as the evening wore on, and now, as we crossed the lounge to a semi-private spot against the far wall, behind the RA's desk, he wasn't so much walking as lurching. Iris's arm was linked in mine. We stood there bunched against the wall a moment, while Tommy struggled to light a cigarette—he dropped the cigarette twice to the carpet, then dropped the matches. "Listen," he said, straightening up and squinting round the room as if he'd never seen men and women necking before, "I've got to—it's hot in here, isn't it? Listen, I've got to go find a lavatory somewhere, all right?"

We watched him pull one foot and then the other up off the carpet, moving as if the solid floor had suddenly been converted to a trampoline, and then he was out the door, a smell of the scented night air trailing behind him. "Good old Tommy," I said, for lack of anything better to say. "He must be a swell brother. You're really lucky, you know that?"

Iris was drawn into herself, leaning back against the wall, her shoulders narrowed as if she were cold. She was watching me closely. Her arms—lovely arms, beautiful arms, the shapeliest, most perfectly formed arms I'd ever seen—were folded across her breasts, but she dropped them now to her sides, as if she were opening herself up to me. We had kissed here before, in this very spot, just out of sight of the RA, but the kisses had been constrained and proper, or as proper as they could be given the fact that we were pressed up against the wall in a place where the lamplight was dimmest and our tongues had just begun to discover a new function altogether. She didn't believe in petting or premarital sex of any kind, raised a Catholic and haunted by it, diminished by what had been imposed on her and helpless to escape it. "You don't mind, do you?" she'd whispered one night, her breath hot on my face, the taste of her on my lips. "No," I'd said, "no, I don't mind."

But now—tonight, on my big night, the night before the graduation ceremony and all the uncertainty it implied—she took hold of me and pressed her body to mine so that I could feel her breasts go soft against my chest. Her voice was so low it was barely audible. "Kiss me," she whispered.

THE CEREMONY WENT off as planned, the speeches sufficiently inspiring, the weather cooperating, President Wells exercising his handshake and handing over the diplomas one after another as a gentle breeze came down out of Illinois to animate our robes and tug ever so gently at the girls' hairdos. Afterward, there was a private reception at Prok's— he'd insisted, he wouldn't take no for an answer, it was the least he could do for a young man who'd done so much for him—and we got to glory among the flowers and sample Mac's punch and Prok's liqueurs. My mother didn't really hit it off with Mac, which wasn't unusual for her— she'd always worn her reserve like a suit of armor and had never really warmed to people, not till she'd mixed with them four or five times, and even then there was no guarantee—but there was something deeper and more complex involved here, and I'd probably cite Freud at this juncture but for the fact that Prok so rigorously educated me against him.

Prok, though, was a different story—she seemed to take to him right away. Of course, he went out of his way to make my mother feel comfortable, zeroing right in on her and giving her an extended tour of the garden, all the while soliciting her opinion on the dahlias or the heliotropes—or the azaleas that just seemed to thrive in the most acidic conditions he could provide, and had she tried coffee grounds? Coffee grounds were one of the most convenient and effective ways of changing the pH factor of the soil, at least as far as Prok had been able to discover. Of course you had to be mindful of chlorosis, but that could be cured by the addition of iron chelate to the soil, well worked in, needless to say . . .

I watched them draw slowly away from the main body of the party, my mother balancing a tiny liqueur glass in one gloved hand, the sun glancing off the crown of her hat and making a glowing transparency of the single long trailing feather, Prok nodding and gesticulating as he guided her down the path. He was dressed formally, in what we (that is, Corcoran, Rutledge and I) came to regard as his uniform: dark suit, white shirt, crisply knotted bow tie in a two-color geometric pattern. I could see that he was a bit on edge because of having to give up a day's work, first for the academic convocation at the graduation ceremony and now for this little gathering, but to the uneducated eye he seemed as relaxed and charming as an antebellum plantation owner showing off his holdings. The children were playing an extended game of croquet, while Iris, Tommy and I sat under a tree with my Aunt Marjorie and Mac, who'd kicked off her shoes and was forever dashing back and forth from the house with a tray of canapés or the persimmon tarts she'd baked herself that morning in my honor.

We were talking of everything but the war, because the war was happening someplace else, far across the sea, and this was our day— Tommy's, Iris's and mine—and there was no reason to let the darkness intrude. My aunt, never a loquacious woman, not unless she was gossiping with her sister-in-law, sat in a wicker chair with her ankles crossed and smiled a faraway smile, thinking perhaps of her husband, who'd been killed at Ipres in the first war. Mac, when she was with us, held forth charmingly on any number of subjects, including the Girl Scouts, knitting—Aunt Marjorie perked up a bit here—and, of course, sex research. It was all very relaxed.

At one point, just as the children ended their game with a shout of triumph from one of the girls, Iris pushed herself up off the lawn, patting down her dress as if she'd been lying there in the grass since it first sprouted. "Why don't we play?" she said. "You, me and Tommy. Come on."

If I hesitated (and I might have, lulled by her presence—and Mac's—as well as the golden fluid issuing from the flask on command), she wouldn't hear of it.

"Come on," she repeated. "Are you afraid I'm going to beat you or something?" She was wearing a summer dress that left her arms bare, and she stretched, then brought her heels together and made a muscle with her right arm. "Because you ought to be. I'll have you know I was croquet champion of the entire neighborhood."

"When you were nine maybe," Tommy said, but he was already getting up from the grass himself.

We played a languid game out on the lawn, the sun holding steady overhead, Iris chasing down our balls and hammering them into the flowerbeds whenever she had the chance. There were gales of laughter. The flask circulated. I don't think I'd ever been happier, but for one thing—the look Prok gave us when he emerged with my mother from the rear of the property. His face was stripped naked for just a moment, his mouth screwed up in a kind of pout of disdain, and I wondered what sin we were committing, what transgression, until it came to me: Prok hated games of any sort. Games were nonproductive. Games were, by definition, a waste of time—a pastime, that is, which was the same thing. Only work had any validity for him, and he never understood when we (again, Corcoran, Rutledge and I) spent even a moment's time engaged in any activity that didn't directly serve the project. We might have spent twelve hours in a single day taking sex histories and then come back to the hotel to relax with the radio and a game of cards, and Prok would insist that we should be reading and studying the literature so as to better perform our function and advance the research.

There was one time—and I'm jumping ahead here eight or ten years—when Prok, Corcoran and I had been on a research trip to take histories in Florida. We'd driven down from Indiana so Prok could address a group of college administrators who were holding a series of seminars in Miami, and we'd put in five intense days of recording histories from the moment we'd finished breakfast right on through to ten and eleven at night. On the final day, the day before we were to drive back to Indiana and the perennial ice of winter, we finished up by eight in the evening, and on a lark Corcoran and I pulled in at a miniature golf course. Corcoran—he was the ultimate extrovert, sunny, glad-handing, an obsessive serial sexual adventurer—was at the wheel because Prok was busy beside him with a flashlight and the sheaf of interviews we'd just concluded. "Say," he cried out suddenly, "John—do you see that, up ahead there on the left?"

I was in back. I leaned forward over the seat and saw what he was talking about—a glittering playland of lights leaching out into the Florida night, and a sign superimposed above them: TEETER'S MINIA-TURE GOLF.

"Time for a little rest and relaxation?" he asked, already swinging the wheel wide as Prok glanced up distractedly from the papers in his lap.

There was an anti-authoritarian streak in Corcoran, a boyish playfulness Prok tolerated in a way he wouldn't have in anybody else, and I wakened to it in that moment. *Why not?* I thought. *Why not get out from under the whip, if only for an hour?* "Sure, yes," I said, "that would be—that would hit the spot. And I've never, and we *are* going back tomorrow . . ."

And before Prok could protest, it was a fait accompli, the car pulled up snug to the admission booth in the gravel lot, Corcoran and I paying for our tickets and selecting our clubs while the palms rustled in a breeze that was as warm as the breath of the furnace back at home. We must have played for two hours or more, feeling lighthearted and a bit silly, feeling like boys who despite the frivolity of the situation had always been in competition with one another and fought to win no matter how inconsequential the victory might have been. (As I recall, for the record, I wound up beating him that night, if only just narrowly.) But Prok. Prok tried to be good-natured about it, yet he was beside himself. He couldn't understand it. Couldn't imagine why grown men would behave like adolescents, why they would dissipate precious time that could be devoted to the project, to work, to the accretion of knowledge and the advancement of culture, and all in the name of a vapid amusement. He paced. He hectored us from behind the fence. "Corcoran," he called, and his voice was a sorry bleat of remonstrance. "Corcoran. Milk. You're holding up the project!"

But on the day of my graduation, I didn't yet know of Prok's uncompromising view of what he considered frivolous pursuits—or at least not to the extent I one day would—and the look he gave us over an innocent game of croquet gave me pause. I tried to parse that look. Tried to decipher what it portended—was the celebration over? Had my mother said something to him—or he to her—that would have changed the complexion of the day? Did my mother know about Prok and me—or Mac and me—and had she said something?

As it turned out, it was none of the above, just Prok being Prok. And we finished our game and went back to the shady spot on the lawn and Prok retired to the house a moment and came back with a gift for my mother—an especially convoluted but bred-out gall he'd shellacked as an objet d'art—and when she thanked him I saw the hint of a mutuality there and I didn't know how I felt about it. There was something complicit between them, and I realized in that moment that it had nothing to do with me: Prok, I guessed, had been talking up the project and had convinced her, as he convinced practically everyone he ran across, to give up her history. My mother's history. She would sit with him for two hours the next day, or maybe even that evening, and answer the three hundred and fifty questions about her masturbatory habits and how often she brought herself to orgasm and what men she'd slept with since my father died.

Everything gets a bit hazy here, and I don't know if what happened next was a direct result of this or not—again, that would take a psychiatrist to iron out, and Prok hated psychiatrists—but I do know that I excused myself from the group gathered on the lawn, left Iris there, and my mother too, and went up the winding path for the house, where I knew Mac was preparing something, a light snack, she'd said, for all us. I went in without knocking, an honored guest by this point, almost a member of the family. The children were nowhere to be seen. Everything was still. The furniture seemed to recede into the depths of the room, shadowy and skeletal, the records canted on the shelves as if awaiting the hand to bring them to life. Distantly, from all the way across the yard, I heard the buzz of voices.

I found Mac in the kitchen, at the counter, her back to me. She was barefooted still, but she'd put an apron on over her dress and I could see where it was tied just above the swell of her hips. Do I have to tell you how much I needed her in that moment, how much a disciple of the master I'd become? I came up behind her—and she knew I was there, she was waiting for me—and pressed myself to her so she could feel the hardness of me against the softness of her buttocks, and I reached both hands round to embrace her breasts. The sweetest thing: she turned her head to kiss me, to give me the excitation of her tongue and underscore the reciprocity of the moment. And then—and then we were down on the kitchen floor, pawing at each other's clothes. No children appeared. No one intruded. And I had coitus with her there in a quick wild spate of thrusting and licking and biting that must have taken no more than three minutes beginning to end, and then I zippered up and went back out across the lawn to Iris and my mother.

6

Ever since the fall of 1938, when Prok inaugurated the marriage course, there had been whispers on campus and in the community too, and the whispers grew to a rumble of distaste and then outrage as the summer of 1940 gave way to autumn and a coalition of forces gathered against him. If I'd wondered at the number of faculty—and especially older faculty—attending the session of the course Laura and I had taken together, now I began to understand: these were spies, hostile witnesses, the drones of convention and antiquated morality who wanted to keep the world in darkness as far as sex was concerned. They weren't there to be educated—they were there to bring Prok down.

Foremost among them was Dr. Thurman B. Rice of the Indiana State Health Board and the IU medical faculty. Rice had himself taught a precursor to Prok's course in the early thirties—"a hygiene course," he called it—and it had been one of the running jokes of the campus, an exercise in innuendo, misinformation and Victorian nice-nellyism. Apparently, he'd sat through the lecture in which Prok showed his infamous slides, and protested, in writing, to President Wells, the Board of Trustees and Prok himself that the pictures were so graphic as to have stimulated even him—a man thirty years married, who had given the subject "real objective study"—and that, as a result, he feared for the student body. What if some innocent coed were to be so stimulated and wind up engaging in sexual intercourse, becoming pregnant and having to be sent home as damaged goods? What then?

He was joined by the rest of his colleagues on the medical faculty, who as one felt that Professor Kinsey was appropriating to himself what was essentially a medical function: how could he presume to interview and advise students of both sexes on physiological matters—behind closed doors, nonetheless—when he had no medical training himself? Add to this the unanimous outcry of the town's pastors, a cascade of letters from distraught Hoosier mothers who had heard rumors that this *professor* was instructing their daughters in the various methods of birth control and asking them to measure their own clitorises, and the undying enmity of Dean Hoenig, who would never forgive Prok that display in the garden and what she deemed his overzealous pursuit of the histories of some of the more reticent undergraduate women under her aegis, and you can well imagine that a public lynching was in the cards.

I was crossing campus on a dead-calm, slow-roasting morning at the beginning of September, on my way to work, thinking of nothing more significant than what I was going to do about dinner, when all of this—the rumors, the rancor, the anti-Prok sentiment boiling up out of the cauldron of the community—came home to me in an immediate way. Laura Feeney, a senior now and even prettier and fuller of figure than I'd remembered, was coming toward me along the path by the brook, a text clutched to her breasts (between which dangled a chain decorated with a class ring presumably belonging to Jim Willard). When she glanced up and recognized me, a change came over her face and she stopped in midstride and just stood there motionless until I closed the distance between us. "Laura," I said, awkward suddenly—awkward again—"hello."

It took her a moment. "John," she murmured, something tentative in the tone of her voice, as if she were trying the name out to see if it fit. "Oh, hello. So nice to see you." A pause. "And how was your summer?"

We could have been having the same conversation we'd had a year ago, except that this time I hadn't gone home to the crucifixion of boredom that was Michigan City and the attic room in my mother's house, because I was out in the world now, working a full-time job, and I'd stayed on at Mrs. Lorber's, though Paul Sehorn was gone and I would soon have a new roommate—that is, if anyone answered Mrs. Lorber's ad. I watched her face through the formalized exchange of ritualistic chitchat—she was a master at it, or rather, a mistress—and then I got bold and commented on the chain round her neck. "I see you're wearing Jim Willard's class ring."

"What? Oh, this?" (An excuse to brush her own breasts and lift the ring to eye level.) She let out a laugh that was meant to be self-deprecating, but managed only to be flirtatious. My interest piqued. "You're not going to believe this, but I've traded in one Willard for another." Again, the laugh. "You know Willard Polk?"

I hesitated.

"Co-captain of the football team? He's my steady. We're planning to get engaged come Christmas." She idly rotated the toe of one shoe and I couldn't help stealing a glance at her ankles and legs. "Jim and I? We just didn't seem to see eye to eye anymore, that's all. But now"—and here she gave me the full power of her smile—"now I'm in love. Really. Truly. This is it. For life." Another pause. Her face contracted round her mouth. Her eyes narrowed. "But what about you? If I hear right, you're actually *working* with Dr. Kinsey now?"

I nodded, tried for a smile.

"Our old professor," she said. "Dr. Sex." She was still playing with the ring, but now she let it drop between her breasts again. "I hear that you're conducting sex interviews yourself now, isn't that true?"

I was an entirely different person from what I was a year ago, sexually experienced, out in the world, conversant with every sexual practice in the book, but still I couldn't stop the blood rushing to my cheeks. "Only men," I said. "Undergraduate men. Because, you see, well, they're the least elaborate, if you know what I mean?"

"Oh?" The flirtation had come back into her voice. "But what about the girls? Aren't they even less—*elaborate*? All those vestal virgins in the dorms? Will you be interviewing them too, or will this be the kind of survey that just tells us what beasts men are—as if we didn't already know, right, John?"

So I was blushing. I'd had intercourse with Mac, I'd missed Iris all summer with an ache so deep and inconsolable it was as if some essential part had been cut out of my body, and as I stood there willing the blood to drain from my cheeks, I wanted—why not say it?—to *fuck*

Laura Feeney, no matter how many Willards she had. I saw her naked. Saw her without the dress and the little hat and the shoes, saw her breasts bared and her nipples erect with excitement. Laura Feeney, Laura Feeney: no other girl but you. That's what I told her with my eyes and she saw it, saw the change in me, and actually took one step back— that is, shifted her weight and ever so minutely extended the distance between us. "No," I said, and I was leering, I suppose, I admit it, "no, I'll be doing women too. Prok promised me. But not here. Not on campus."

A lift of the eyebrows. "*Prok?*"

"Professor Kinsey. That's what we, what I—"

"I hear they're going to fire him."

That was the moment when all the birdsong and the trickle of the brook and the backfiring of an automobile in the faculty parking lot were suddenly cued out as if at the upstroke of a conductor's baton. I didn't know what to say. I couldn't have been more surprised—or shocked, shocked is a better word—if she'd told me the Nazis were marching on Muncie. "They can't do that," I said finally, "he's a starred scientist. He's got tenure."

"The marriage course is finished. You know what they're calling it? They're calling it a smut session. 'That smut session,' that's what they say." She was watching my face for a reaction. "President Wells himself is going to fire him—for, I don't know, *moral turpitude.* That's what I hear, anyway."

THE FOLLOWING MORNING, before the sun was up, Prok and I climbed into the Nash (I don't recall the model or even the year of the thing, though he'd bought it used in 1928 and as far as I could see it seemed to be held together principally with C-clamps and rust), and headed off for West Lafayette, where he'd been invited to lecture to a combined group of sociology classes at Purdue University. Along the way, we were planning on stopping in Crawfordsville to pick up the remaining interviews we hadn't managed to squeeze in when Prok had lectured at DePauw the previous week. And, of course, we were looking forward to taking the histories of the cohort that would attend the evening's lecture, having budgeted the next three days to those. Lunch would be on four wheels, tepid water out of a jug I'd set on the floorboards behind the seat and a few handfuls of the trail mix (raisins, nuts, sunflower seeds and the odd nugget of chocolate) Prok consumed for lunch every day of his life, whether he was ensconced in the Astor Hotel on Times Square, wandering the withered foothills of the Sierra Madre in search of galls or sitting behind his desk in Biology Hall.

There was no radio in the car, but it didn't really matter, as Prok provided all the entertainment himself, talking without pause from the minute I slid into the seat beside him in the uncertain light of dawn to the moment we disembarked in Crawfordsville, and then continuing without missing a beat till we arrived, in late afternoon, in West Lafayette. He talked about sex. About the project. About the need to collect more lower-level histories, more black histories, more histories from cabbies and colliers and steam-shovel operators—for balance, that is, because undergraduate interviews, as invaluable as they might be, only supplied a portion of the picture. If we passed a cow standing by the roadside, he went on about milk production and the leanness of the drought years. He talked of the topography, of riverine and lacustrine ecology, of mushroom hunting—had I ever tasted fresh-picked morels, lightly breaded and fried? I didn't feel at a loss, not a bit. I let him talk. It was all part of my education.

We were coming up on the White River just outside Spencer when the sun rose behind us and spilled across the water, laminating everything in copper. A great blue heron stood out in relief against the mist rising off the surface, the cornfields caught fire, pear and apple trees emerged from the gloom, heavy with luminescent fruit. The surface of the road was wet with dew and as the sun touched it vapor rose there too until it fell away from the rush of the tires and fanned out over the rails of the bridge like a storm in the making. That was the moment that I chose to disburden myself of the unsettling information Laura Feeney had pressed on me and which I'd been turning over in my head now for the better part of the last twenty-four hours. "Prok," I said, interrupting him in the middle of a story I'd heard twice before about a subject at the state work farm pulling out his penis in the middle of the interview and laying it on the table for measurement, "is it true that, well, I've heard rumors that pressure is being put on you again—more than you've revealed to me, that is—regarding the marriage course. They're not going to, well, *fire* you, are they?"

A low spear of sun transfixed the interior of the car and illuminated Prok's face from the lips down, as if he were wearing a beard of light. He gave me a dour look, head slightly canted, eyes showing white. "And where, exactly, did you get that notion?"

"I—well, Laura Feeney. Laura Feeney told me yesterday morning. You know, the girl I took the marriage course with?"

"With whom."

"Yes, right—the girl with whom."

The planks of the bridge rattled under the wheels and I saw the heron stiffen and protract its wings. Prok's eyes were fixed on the road. He was silent a moment, then murmured, "I suppose Miss Feeney had an audience with President Wells himself? Or was it the Board of Trustees?"

"You're making light of it, Prok, and that's not right. I'm just, well, I'm concerned, that's all, and there *are* rumors, you can't deny that—"

He let out a sigh. Gave me a glance of commiseration, then turned back to the road. "I feel like Galileo," he said, "if you want to know the truth. Hounded and oppressed and denied the basic right of scientific investigation, simply because some cleric or some dried-up old maid like Dean Hoenig or a has-been like Thurmond Rice feels threatened by the facts. They can't face reality, and that's the long and short of it."

My heart sank. So it was true. I stared out the window on the fierce geometry of the cornfields, the engine moaning beneath my feet, the world slipping by.

"They're going to offer me an ultimatum: drop the marriage course or give up the research, one or the other."

"But you can't—that would be like an admission that sex *is* dirty, that they were right all along—"

Another sigh. The hooded look. His hands were claws on the wheel. "You see, the problem is with doing the course and the interviews combined, not to mention the advisement on sexual matters that has been so much a natural concomitant of the information we dispense—"

He shifted down as the car hurtled through a pothole, rising up off its springs and slamming down again with a shudder, and then he laid a hand on my knee. "It's the research they're after. They just can't abide the idea of our getting impressionable young things behind closed doors, because you never know what might happen." He gave my knee a squeeze. "Isn't that right, John?"

We were on a tight schedule, but we were fortunate that day because the DePauw subjects all appeared on time, delivered up their information and went back about their business so that we could go about ours. Trail mix and aqua pura in the car, Prok dodging farm wagons, overladen trucks and the odd cow, a long running trailer of intensely green fields alternating with flagrant forests and shadowy bottoms, and we were there, arrived safe and sound in West Lafayette three quarters of an hour before the lecture was scheduled to begin.

I don't remember much of the hotel, though I should, because that trip was a real watershed for me, but all the hundreds of towns and hotels and motor courts we've visited over the years seem to have produced a generic impression. It was a brick building from the last century, most likely, in need of sandblasting and paint, and it was, as likely or not, located on the main street near the courthouse. There would have been shade trees, a dog curled up on the sidewalk out front, cars parked on the diagonal. The building itself would be three stories, with a separate entrance for the restaurant and bar. We doubled up on the room, to save money—Prok was a prodigy of thrift—just as we would triple and quadruple up in later years, when we added Corcoran and finally Rutledge to the team.

As for the lecture. Did Prok need anything? No, he was fine. He stood bare-chested in the bathroom, shaving before the mirror, then he changed his shirt, knotted his bow tie, slipped into his jacket and went off at a brisk gait for the university, his host, Professor McBride of the Sociology Department, struggling to keep pace. I brought up the rear.

When we arrived, the auditorium was already full (the word was spreading, even in those early days, and if the combined sociology classes could boast sixty students among them, there must have been three hundred of the idle and curious there as well, hoping for a bit of titillation). As usual, Prok spoke ex tempore, without notes, and, as usual, he cast a spell over the audience from the first words out of his mouth to the last. (The subject might have been premarital sex, the psychology of sexual repression, the function of adolescent outlets, the history of sex research or the frequency of masturbation in the comparison of males and females of a given age group—it didn't really matter to Prok; all speeches were one speech. And I should say here too that he had a particular gift for delivery that never resorted to tricks or theatrical gestures, his voice clear and distinct and largely unmodulated, every inch the man of science expatiating on a subject of deep interest to all humanity. He was no Marc Antony or even a Brutus, but he got the job done as no one else could have.)

And again, as usual, a whole mob of potential subjects came forward to volunteer their histories at the conclusion of the lecture and Prok and I sat side by side at a long table set up behind the lectern and scheduled them. Dinner? I don't remember if we did eat that night—it might have been sandwiches sent up to the room—but we both started right in on taking histories as soon as the lecture hall had cleared and we'd had a chance to get back to the hotel. Prok conducted his interviews in our room and I was accommodated with a private conference room located just behind the restaurant. It must have been past midnight by the time I was finished (three undergraduate men, sociology students out to earn extra credit with Professor McBride in coming forward as volunteers, the expected responses, nothing I hadn't heard before), and I remember sinking into an armchair in the lobby, a watered-down drink at my side, watching the hands crawl round the clock as Prok conducted his final interview of the night.

Afterward, we compared notes as we got ready for bed, and that was when we discovered a discrepancy in the schedule for the following morning: we had inadvertently scheduled two females for the same hour, rather than one female and one male. Which meant we were either going to have to cancel or I would be forced to record my first female history, a step Prok to this point hadn't deemed me qualified to take. He looked up from the schedule, shook his head slowly, then rose from the sofa and padded into the bathroom to see to his dental prophylaxis (he was a great one for maintaining his teeth in good condition, a hygienic habit that allowed him to take the full set to his grave with him). "I don't know, Milk," he said, raising his voice to be heard over the sound of running water, "but I do hate to cancel. It's inefficient, for one thing. And it could cost us data, for another. No. There's nothing to do but go through with it."

A moment later he was back in the room, hovering over me, fully clothed, which in itself was odd because the moment we were done for the day he usually stripped to the skin and encouraged me to do the same. (Yes, we were alone together a great deal on these trips, and we continued to have sexual relations, though my education—and my predilections—were taking me in the opposite direction. I revered Prok—I revere him still—but gradually I was growing away from him in this one regard and toward Mac, toward Iris, toward the coeds in their loose sweaters and tight skirts who drifted across the campus like antelope on the plain. No matter: I enjoyed being with Prok—I felt privileged to be with him—and I looked forward to these trips because they took me away from the tedium of my desk and the constriction of small-town life and enabled me to see and absorb something of the larger world, of Indiana certainly, but eventually of Chicago and New York, San Francisco and Havana too.) "We're going to have to accelerate your training," he said, and there was no trace of levity to his tone.

I was exhausted. The travel, the skimped meals, the force of concentration required to record five histories in a single day—all of it combined to sap me as surely as if I'd spent the day at hard labor, chained to a convict and breaking up rock with a mallet. "We are?" I echoed.

"The interview for women requires, I would think, a little more finesse than the men's, especially the ones you've been conducting with undergraduates near to your own age, where you appear as a sort of fraternity colleague or perhaps an older brother. No, I am aware of how you feel in these matters, with regard to women, that is, and Mac and I have discussed it thoroughly"—he let that hang a moment—"and I wonder if you're capable of being absolutely disinterested and professional."

I made some noises to the effect that I was.

He was watching me carefully. Still standing over me, still in shirt and bow tie. "You'll forgive me, Milk, but your emotions too often show in your face, and we can't have that the first time a woman—*this* woman tomorrow morning—tells you of something you may tend to find stimulating."

I fought to keep my face rigid—and pale. "I think, well, if you'll give me the chance, I'm sure I can, that is—"

He wound up drilling me for two hours that night. First I was the woman, then he was, then vice versa and vice versa again. The questions came in spate, his eyes on me like whips, like cold pans of water first thing in the morning, intractable and unforgiving. He was exacting, demanding, hypercritical, and if I missed a beat he fed me hot coffee till my nerves were so jangled I don't think I slept at all that night. But Prok did. I lay there awake in the darkness, thinking of a thousand things, but mainly of Iris, whom I hadn't seen all summer though we'd written each other nearly every day. She was due back on campus the day after tomorrow, and I was thinking of her as the shadows softened and the first furtive wakening sounds of the street drifted in through the window and Prok puffed and blew and slept the sleep of the righteous.

In the morning, over breakfast in the room, Prok quizzed me again. I lifted a forkful of egg and toast to my mouth, put it down again, answered a question and took a quick sip of coffee. I nearly rebelled—didn't he have any confidence in me after all this time?—but I let him have his way, despite the fact that there was no essential difference in the way the male and female interviews were conducted, except that the sequence and type of the questions were specific to one sex or the other, as for example with the female you asked about the onset of menarche and the age at which breast development first appeared and so on. It wasn't my competency Prok was questioning, it was my age and experience, or lack of it. He kept saying, "Milk, Milk, I wish you were twenty years older. And married. Married with children. How many children do you want, John—shall we make it three?"

I was downstairs in the conference room ten minutes before the scheduled appointment, which was at nine. Before a subject arrived, we would routinely record the basic data—the date, the number of the interview (for our files), the sex of the subject and the source of the history (that is, through what agency the subject had come to us, and in this case, of course, it was as a direct result of Prok's solicitation after the sociology lecture). I didn't know what to expect. We'd scheduled some twenty-eight interviews for the next three days and many more than that for our return trip the following week, and I had no way of connecting the names on the schedule sheet with any individual, though I'd sat there and registered them the night before. The woman I was to interview—and I'm going to assign her a fictitious name here, for confidentiality's sake—was a young faculty wife of twenty-five, as yet childless. Mrs. Foshay. Let's call her Mrs. Foshay.

There was a knock at the door. I was seated in an armchair by a dormant fireplace, the schedule sheet and Mrs. Foshay's folder spread out on a coffee table before me. The other chair—mahogany, red plush, standard Edwardian hotel fare—was positioned directly across from mine. "Come in," I said, rising to greet her even as the door swung open.

In the doorway, peering into the room as if she'd somehow fetched up in the wrong place, was a very pretty young woman dressed in the height of fashion—dressed as if she'd just stepped out of a nightclub on Forty-second Street after an evening of dinner, dancing and champagne. She gave me a hesitant smile. "Oh, hello," she said, "I wasn't sure if I was in the right place—"

I'd crossed the room to her and now I took her hand and gave it a curt, professional shake. "It's really, well, really kind of you to come—and important, important too—because every history, no matter how extensive, or, or, unextensive—nonextensive, I mean—contributes to the whole in a way that, that—"

Her smile opened up suddenly, a dazzling full-lipped smile that made whole flocks of birds take off and career round my stomach. "Oh, it's my pleasure," she murmured as I motioned to the chair and watched her settle into it, "anything for science, hey?"

I offered her a cigarette—she chose a Lucky—lit it for her and wished it were nine in the evening rather than nine in the morning so we could both have a drink. A drink would have gone a long way toward calming my case of nerves.

"Good," I said, poised over the interview sheet, pencil in hand. "So, Mrs. Foshay, perhaps you'd like to tell me something of yourself—"

"Alice, call me Alice."

"Yes, *Alice.* You've lived here long, here in West Lafayette, I mean?"

The small talk, designed, as I've said, to put the subject at ease, consumed perhaps five minutes and then my brain froze up. I couldn't help noticing how Mrs. Foshay's breasts filled out the material of her blouse—filled it to the point of strain—and how silken her legs looked in a pair of sheer stockings. A moment of silence passed like a freight train. "All right, then," I said, "so. And you lived in Trenton, you say, until what age?"

I did manage to get into the rhythm of things as we moved along through the factual data (number of brothers, sisters, twin status, sorority membership, frequency of attending motion pictures, et cetera) keeping it in a simple question-response mode, and even the early sequential questions about onset of puberty came off well, but I'm afraid I broke down a bit when we got to the more sensitive areas. "When did you first begin to masturbate?" I asked, lighting a cigarette myself.

"I must have been eleven," she said, drawing at her Lucky. "Or maybe it was twelve." She threw her head back and exhaled, no more concerned than if she were at the hairdresser's or conferring with a girlfriend on the telephone. "We were living in Newark still, and I remember the curtains—my mother had made them for me when I was a child, very colorful, decorated with little figures out of nursery rhymes, Mother Goose, that sort of thing. My sister Jean—she's a year older than I—she showed me the technique."

I set down the cigarette, made a notation in the proper square. "Yes? And what was that technique?"

She tried to look away, but I held onto her with my eyes. I didn't blink. Didn't move.

"Well, you might find this odd or maybe hard to believe . . ."

"No," I said, and my voice was so pinched I could barely get it out, "no, not at all—there is no activity we haven't recorded, and certainly, as Prok—*Dr. Kinsey,* that is—outlined in the lecture last night, we make no judgments . . ."

She seemed encouraged. She patted her hair, which was piled up and pinned at the crown in a roll, with the bangs brushed into an exaggerated pompadour, reminiscent of the way Dolly Dawn used to wear her hair, and most people I think will remember her from George Hall's band ("It's a Sin to Tell a Lie" should ring a bell, or, at the very least, "Yellow Basket"). "Well," she said, "I'm double-jointed. So's Jean. And my brother Charlie."

"Yes?" I said, pencil poised.

"We—Jean and I—would get up on the bed, side by side, and do a kind of back flip, you know, the sort of things acrobats do at the circus? Only we would hold it there and then, well, because of being double-jointed, we would lick ourselves."

The term that came into my head was "auto-cunnilingus." Prok hadn't yet devised a box or code for that one, so I made a spontaneous notation. I was probably blushing. Certainly I was hard.

We forged on.

Was this her first marriage? Yes. Had she experienced deep kissing prior to the time she was married? Yes. Had she experienced petting? Yes. Had she fondled the male genitalia, experienced mouth-to-genital contact, engaged in coitus? Yes, yes and yes. How many partners had she had, excluding her husband? Somewhere, she guessed, around twenty. "Twenty?" I repeated, trying to keep my voice neutral. She couldn't say, really, it might have been a few less or even as many as twenty-five, and her eyes went dreamy a moment as she tried to recollect. And what about orgasm: When was the first time she was aware of having experienced an orgasm? Had she been able to bring herself to orgasm through masturbation, petting, intercourse? When had she most recently experienced an orgasm?

And here was where I found myself in deep water again, because I asked this conventionally pretty and very likely pampered professor's wife, this elegant blond jewel of a woman dressed in impeccable taste, the next question in the sequence, that is: "How many orgasms do you experience on average?"

She was on her fifth cigarette, and if she'd been relaxed from the outset, now she was as warm and enthusiastic as any individual I'd yet interviewed. She looked at me. Gave a little smile. I had been continuously—and unprofessionally—hard for the better part of two hours now. "Oh, I would guess maybe ten or twelve."

My face must have shown my surprise, because few even of our highest-rating individuals would have approached that numerical category. "Per week?" I asked. And then, stupidly, "Or is that a monthly approximation?"

Now it was her turn to blush, just the faintest reddening of the flesh under both cheekbones and around the flanges of her nostrils. "Oh, no," she said. "No. I'm afraid that would be *daily*."

IF IRIS WAS at all miffed that I wasn't there to greet her and Tommy and help drag her steamer trunk up three flights of stairs at the women's dorm, she didn't show it. Prok and I returned to Bloomington early on the morning of the fourth day, as planned—he still had his teaching schedule to work around in those days—and I went straight to the office to transcribe the coded sheets and add incrementally to our burgeoning data on human sexual behavior, and I should say that this was always exciting, in the way, I suppose, of a hunter returning from a successful expedition with his bag limit of the usual birds and perhaps a few of the exotic as well. (Further to the above interview, incidentally: please don't think that all the interviewees had such a rich and extensive sex life as that young faculty wife. Much more typical, of the females especially, was a record of sexual repression, guilt and limited experience, both in number of partners and activities. I should add too, just to close out the anecdote, that the moment the door shut behind her—Mrs. Foshay—I couldn't help relieving the pressure in my groin, though if Prok had heard of it he would have skinned me alive—professionalism, professionalism was the key word, at least on the surface. At least in the beginning. I came to orgasm in record time, the stale room still redolent with her perfume and the heat of her presence, and I barely had time to mop up with my handkerchief and tuck myself away before the next knock came at the door and the acne-stippled face of a nineteen-year-old sociology student, who wouldn't have recognized the female genitalia if they'd been displayed for him on a gynecologist's examining table, appeared in the doorway. He gave me a steady look, then said—or rather, croaked—"Am I in the right place?")

But Iris. Immediately after work I rushed across campus to the dorm. Earlier, when it looked as if Prok and I wouldn't be finished till seven or so, I'd left a telephone message with the RA to the effect that I would come straight from work and take her to dinner (Iris, that is, not the RA), so she should hold off eating. And, though it was the RA I was talking with and so couldn't really express much of what I was feeling, I added that I was looking forward to seeing her. After such a long time, that is. Very much. Very much so.

I got there at quarter past seven, but Iris kept me waiting. I don't know what she was doing—making me suffer just a bit on general principles, taking extra care with her dress and makeup so as to reinforce the impression she would make on me, falling back on the prerogative of women, as the pursued, to do whatever they damned well pleased—but I found myself jumping up from the sofa every other minute and pacing round the lounge, much to the dismay of the RA, who was at least putting on a show of reading from the book spread out on the desk before her. I was keyed up, and I couldn't really say why. Perhaps it was the anticipation—nearly three months apart, the exchange of letters and snapshots, the protestations of love on both sides—which was only to be expected. I couldn't say that I'd been lonely over the summer, not exactly, not with Mac and Prok and the long hours I'd put in both traveling and at my desk, but I guess I did use the letters as an opportunity of opening up to her my hopes and aspirations (and fears; I was in line to receive my draft notice, as was practically every other man on campus), and that made the moment of our reunion all the more significant. And fraught. I'd quoted love poems to her as well—"Now while the dark about our loves is strewn,/Light of my dark, blood of my heart, O come!"—and now I would have to make good on all of that. And so would she. But did she care for me still? Had she found someone else? Was I worthy of her?

It was nearly eight, and at least thirty women had come down the stairs and passed through the portals of the inner sanctum to meet and embrace their dates and go off to the pictures or the skating rink or the backseat of the car, when Iris finally appeared. I'd been pacing, and I was at the far end of the lounge, my back to the room, when I heard the faint wheeze of the door pulling back against the pneumatic device that kept it closed. I jerked round and there she was. Can I state the obvious? She was very beautiful, and beyond beautiful: she was special, one in a million, because I'd been writing to her and thinking of her all summer, because she was Iris McAuliffe and she was mine if I wanted her. I knew that then, knew it in the minute I saw her. This was love. This was it.

But how did she look? She'd curled her hair so that it hung in a succession of intricate lapping waves at her shoulders and framed the locket at her throat, the locket I'd given her, and whose picture was in that locket? Her dress—blue, sleeveless, cut to the knee—was new, purchased for the occasion, and her eyes, always her focal point, seemed to leap across the room at me (an illusion, I later realized, that was enhanced by the skillful application of mascara, eye shadow and rouge). She seemed smaller, darker, prettier than I'd remembered. I just stood there, helpless, and watched her as she crossed the carpet to me and let me hold her and kiss her.

"You're back," she said.

"Yes. And so are you. Did I miss Tommy?"

She nodded. "He had work, so he was only here for the day. He was disappointed, but he knew you were—where were you again?"

"Purdue. And DePauw."

"He knew you were working." The RA had fixed her eyes on us as if she had the power to look right through the layers of our clothing and our skin to reduce and examine our bones and even the marrow within. "He sends his regards."

I felt bad for a moment, a sudden little stab of regret penetrating and then withdrawing like the blade of a knife, and I knew I should have been there for her—for her and Tommy too—but I dismissed it. There was nothing I could have done. Prok's schedule had been set months in advance and I was powerless to alter it. "I wish I'd been here," I said, glancing over my shoulder at the RA (not the limp blonde, but a new girl, heavyset, with a dead-white face and hair piled up like detritus on her head). The RA dropped her eyes. I turned back to Iris—Iris, whose hand I seemed to be holding—and said, "But you must be famished. How about a nice steak?"

Now that I was settled—or as settled as a man who was awaiting his draft notice in uncertain times could ever expect to be—there was no real impediment to my seeing Iris as often as I wanted. I no longer had to attend classes, take exams or write papers, and my hours with Prok were relatively stable, if far in excess of the standard forty-hour work-week. Our only problem was the travel—I was out on the road with Prok for three to four days every other week, and that pace was soon to accelerate—but Iris and I were able to adjust, because we wanted to. If before we were dating casually, feeling each other out, no hurry, no pressure or commitment, now things were different, radically different. We went everywhere together—we met for meals, attended concerts, went dancing, hiking, skating, sat in the lounge in the evenings, side by side, so close we were breathing as one, Iris working at her studies and I poring over Magnus Hirschfeld and Robert Latou Dickinson to keep up with the literature in the field. It got to the point where I felt hollow if she wasn't there, as if I had no inner being or essence without her. When she was in class or I was at work or sitting in some second-class hotel staring into the eyes of an overfed undergraduate who was obsessed with Rita Hayworth or masturbated too much, I thought of Iris, only Iris.

The fall passed into winter and winter stretched across the holidays and into the New Year (we went home together, on the bus, to our respective families in Michigan City, and everything seemed new-made and cheerful, despite the fact that Tommy had been drafted into the United States Army and the Nazis, the Fascists and the Imperial Japanese were moving relentlessly forward on all fronts). We came back to the sunless gloom of January, the campus burdened with snow and afflicted with the kind of winds that made hats and scarves superfluous. I'd registered for the draft too, as required by law, along with all the other twenty-one to thirty-five-year-old men, but my number hadn't come up and so we picked up where we'd left off, spending every minute outside of work or school in each other's company. All was well. We were happy. I wrote Paul Sehorn long, chatty letters and found myself whistling as I strode across the barrens to the women's dorm each evening after work (where I couldn't resist joking with the RA, who had become as familiar and innocuous as a doting grandmother, though she couldn't have been more than twenty).

There was one essential problem, though, and I'm sure you've anticipated me here. Sex. Sex was the problem. Even if Iris was willing, and to this point I wasn't at all certain that she was, given her background and her virginity, there was absolutely no place we could go to put it to a trial. The year before, when I'd propositioned Laura Feeney in a headlong rush of sexual derangement, it was only bravado talking: I couldn't have brought her home unless Mrs. Lorber had coincidentally died of a stroke in the very moment of my asking. And even if I could somehow have sneaked Iris through a second-story window in the middle of the night, there was my new roommate to consider (a senior from a remote hamlet by the name of Ezra Vorhees, whose sensibilities and personal hygienic habits were, shall we say, rustic, to put it mildly). It was frustrating. Iris and I would neck for hours in the lounge or the library till I was in pain—actual physical pain, from what undergraduates termed "blue balls" and Prok defined as an excess buildup of seminal fluids in

115

the testicles and vas deferens—and then I would have to go back to my room and relieve myself under the blankets while my roommate pretended to be asleep. Whenever I could, I went to Mac, but I didn't feel good about it, not anymore.

Prok was the one who came up with the solution. As I say, he'd taught me to drive that summer, and now, as I explained my situation to him, he demonstrated just how generous he was—and how much he was willing to go out of his way for me. I remember broaching the subject to him on one of our collecting trips (this time to Gary and a particular Negro neighborhood there, and more on that later), and his turning to me with a smile and saying, "Yes, it's about time, Milk. You do need another outlet, as we all do. Why not this? Take the Nash. Take it any time you like."

"But I wouldn't want to inconvenience you—or Mac."

"No inconvenience at all—we never use the car at night anyway. In fact, what I'll do is simply leave the key under that loose brick we never got around to repairing last summer—you know, out back in the low wall round the persimmon tree? You know the one I mean?"

And so, for the first time in my life I had an automobile to do with as I liked, though of course I would have to be especially cautious since it represented the project's single biggest nonhuman asset, and where would we have been without it? At any rate, when we got back from the trip I went straight to Iris—I caught her in the quad as she was going between classes—and informed her I'd be picking her up in style that night.

"In style?" she said. She gave me a knowing smile. The wind lifted the brim of her hat and then set it fluttering like a bird's wing.

"That's right," I said. "Your own limousine, at your service, mademoiselle."

"Kinsey's car," she said. "The bug buggy. The wasp wagon."

"I'm taking you out of town. To a roadhouse. To celebrate."

"I don't know," she said. "*Kinsey's* car?"

"It's better than nothing." I felt as if I'd been transposed to one of Shakespeare's comedies, trading quips with Rosalind or Beatrice in the forest of Arden or a sunny piazza in Messina. Only this was Indiana and it was winter and Iris was letting me dangle. Just for fun.

"Do you know any roadhouses? Have you ever been to one?"

"Sure," I lied. "Sure, dozens of times."

"And then what?" she asked, fixing me with a teasing look.

"We eat, drink and make merry."

"And then?"

"And then," I said, leaning into her, the wind tearing at my collar, a flurry of students hurrying by with pale numb faces, "then afterwards we can drive off into some quiet, dark lane and, well, and have some *real* privacy."

Despite everything, despite all the thought I'd put into getting Iris alone in a private setting, not to mention the fantasies I'd indulged, I was all nerves that night. The roadhouse was anything but romantic, a smoky, ill-lit den ranged round with leering, drunken faces that offered up the kind of cuisine that gave Hoosier cooking a bad name. I had a bowl of what purported to be beef stew with at least half an inch of melted tallow floating atop it and a packet of stale saltines to help soak it up. Iris pushed something called a Salisbury steak around her plate until finally she gave up and mashed the peas that accompanied it into a kind of paste and ate that on the crumbling saltines. We each had two beers.

I was watching her over the second one, trying to gauge her mood. I'd made a number of passing references to what I hoped the evening would bring, and she'd seemed amenable, or at least resigned. "Hurry up and finish that beer," I said.

She gave me a smoldering look—or maybe that was just my imagination; more likely its intention was satiric. She did love to clown. "Oh, and why? Have you got something planned for the rest of the evening? There's a meeting of the Backgammon Club on campus, you know. And there's a group sing at the Presbyterian church. Do you feel like a good sing, John—wouldn't that be swell?"

My hand found her knee beneath the table. "You know what I want," I said.

"No," she said, all innocence. "Whatever could that be?"

The night was cold—arctic, in fact—and the Nash's heater didn't really amount to much. I'd heard of a couple who'd kept the car running inside the garage (it was the girl's father's car, three in the morning, her parents asleep upstairs in the house) and wound up asphyxiating themselves, only to be discovered half-undressed and rigid as ice sculptures the next morning, and I was aware of the dangers. Still, we *were* outside and the wind—the implacable, unrelenting, stern and disapproving wind—would at least fan the exhaust away from the cab, and, more important, the backseat. For a long while we sat there in front, necking and watching the stars, and then something seemed to give in her, a sense of release, as if all the old strictures and prohibitions had suddenly fallen away. She let me pull open her jacket, and then her blouse, and after a moment I tugged her brassiere down so that her breasts fell free and I began to stimulate them orally. She responded and that encouraged me. I was petting her now, petting her furiously, kissing her deeply, massaging her bare breasts and working the nipples between my fingertips, absolutely aflame, when I murmured, "Shall we—the backseat, I mean?"

She didn't say anything, so I took that for a yes, and after an awkward moment we were over the seat and into the back, my body stretched full atop hers, the engine eructating beneath us, the heater fighting down the onslaught of the cold. I was thinking of Mac, thinking of our first time in the garden and how receptive she was, how natural and pleasurable and easy it had been, when suddenly Iris clamped her legs together on the fulcrum of my right hand.

"What's the matter?" I asked.

Her face was faint and ghostly in the light of the stars that seeped in through the trees. I smelled the heat of her, her breath commingled with mine, the perfume she'd dabbed behind her ears that was all but dissipated now. "You don't think I'm going to go all the way, do you?"

I was stretched out atop her. My trousers were down at my knees. She'd had her hand on my penis and her tongue in my mouth. Suddenly I became eloquent. "Yes, of course," I said. "You know it's the most natural thing in the world, and it's only convention—superstition, priests, ministers, bogeymen—that keeps people from expressing themselves to the full. Sexually, I mean. Come on, Iris. Come on, it's nothing. You'll like it, you will."

She was silent. She hadn't moved. Her face was inches from mine, floating there in the dark of the car like a husked shell on a midnight sea.

"You know what we're discovering?" I whispered.

"No," she whispered back. "What?"

"Well, that premarital sex is actually beneficial, that people who have it—premarital sex, that is—are much better, well, *adjusted* than those who don't. And it carries over into their married sex life as well. They're happier, Iris. Happier. And that's the long and short of it, I swear."

She was silent again. I could feel myself shrinking, the blood ticking along the length of the shaft and ever so slowly draining away. The wind buffeted the car and we both tensed a moment, and then it passed, and the silence deepened. "Premarital," she murmured after a moment. "*Pre*," she said, holding it a beat, and then releasing it, "*marital.* Isn't that what you said, John?"

"Yes," I said, eager now, not quite taking her point. "*Premarital.* Sex before, well, marriage."

Another silence, but I could feel the change coming over her, communicated along the length of her body, through the nerve endings of her skin, directly to mine. She was grinning, I knew it, though it was too dark to read her face. "So," she said, "I take it you're proposing to me, then?"

In the end, President Wells did deliver the ultimatum Prok had been expecting, but Prok surprised him and the Board of Trustees too. They had assumed he'd choose the marriage course over the research, the teaching to which he'd devoted himself and at which he'd excelled for the past twenty years rather than what they must have seen as a new and perhaps passing enthusiasm, but they didn't know him very well. It hurt him, it outraged him, it made him more determined than ever to overturn the cant and hypocrisy of the guardians of the status quo, of the Rices, the Hoenigs and all the rest, but he gave up the marriage course— eventually gave up teaching across the board—in order to pursue the new and great goal of his life. Soon, very soon, the Institute for Sex Research would be born and the inner circle would expand by three.

7

"So it's iris—the lucky girl, that is?"

Prok was at his desk, bent over his papers in a cone of light. The windows looked as if they'd been soldered over, the corridor was in shadow and the dull weight of a steady drizzle seemed to have put the entire campus into hibernation. It was our lunch hour and we were eating at our desks, as we did most days, Prok dining on his trail mix while I made the best of a disintegrating tuna sandwich from the Commons, and I'd just told him the good news, though I'd been bursting with it since I got in that morning. (If you're wondering why I'd hesitated, it was because Prok had been even more than usually absorbed in his work all morning and I couldn't seem to find an opportunity—he hated to be interrupted—and, if truth be told, I was uncertain how he would take the news. Yes, he'd wanted me to marry, but that was in the abstract, on another temporal plane altogether, and this was in the here and now. I knew his first thought would be for the project and how my altered status would affect it.)

"Well," he said, looking distracted as he shuffled through his papers in search of something he'd momentarily misplaced—but that was a ruse, a ruse so he could buy time to sort out his thoughts—"she's an attractive girl, there's no doubt of that. And intelligent. Intelligent too." Another moment trundled by, the wheels turning in his brain with a creak and groan I could hear all the way across the room, and then it was done. "But what am I thinking?" he shouted, and suddenly he was on his feet and striding to my desk, his hand outstretched and his face lit with the wide-angle grin he used to such effect when it suited him. "Congratulations, John. Really. This is the best news I've heard all week."

I took his hand and gave him what must have been a shy but self-satisfied smile. "I'm glad, I'm really—because I didn't know, well, how you'd feel—" I was saying, but he cut me off, already racing on ahead of me.

"When did you say the date was?"

"Well, that is, I didn't. But we were thinking we'd like to, well, as soon as possible. March. Iris thought March would be—"

He was shaking his head. "That'll never do. Not March. The garden, as you of all people should know, is barely worthy of the name in March. No, it will have to be May, no question about it."

"The garden?"

He was looking directly at me—staring into my eyes—but I don't think he was seeing me at all. He was seeing sunshine and flowers, Iris in a trailing satin gown, the justice of the peace in his ceremonial robes, the deep cerulean arc of the sky overhead. "Yes, of course. I'm offering it to you—my gift, John. And think of it, in May the irises will be at their best—irises for Iris. What could be better?"

I told him it was all right with me—I thanked him lavishly, in fact—but that Iris had already called her mother and that certain undeniable forces had been set in motion, so that I wasn't sure if we *could* postpone it at this juncture. He didn't seem to hear me. "We'll have Mac do something special," he said. "A persimmon wedding cake, how about that? And I'll make up the nuptial supper, cold meats and that sort of thing, and a goulash—and champagne, of course we'll have to have champagne . . ." He trailed off and seemed to become aware of me again, as if I'd ducked out of the room and left a standing effigy behind and had just now returned to inhabit its shell. "But Iris," he said, "your intended—the sexual adjustment was satisfactory, I take it?"

I stood there in the gloom of the office, the desk between us, a numb smile adhering to my lips. I nodded.

He was grinning even more intensely now, shifting from foot to foot, squaring his shoulders and rubbing his hands as if to warm them. "Yes," he said, "yes. Nothing like the automobile for a modern-day aphrodisiac, eh? You see what I've been telling you all along, how fulfilled young couples across America would be, all those frustrated undergraduates out there, the lovesick high school faction, couples too poor to marry"—his arm swept the campus and the rooftops of the town beyond—"if only they could have the privacy and freedom from prejudice to express their sexual needs when and how they choose. Of course, John," and his eyes took hold of mine, "I hope you're not confusing the coital experience with the sort of commitment needed to build and sustain a marriage . . . Or Iris. She does know that sex is—or can, and in many cases should be—independent of marriage? That she doesn't have to marry the first—" And here he stopped himself, leaving the rest unspoken.

I was about to reassure him, to tell him that we loved each other and had been dating, as he well knew, for some time now, and that our sexual adjustment was just fine, thank you, more than adequate—terrific, even—and that we knew perfectly well what we were doing, but again he cut me off.

"But this is great news! To have you *married*, Milk—don't you see what this will do for the project? You won't be—and you'll forgive me—so wet behind the ears, or appear to be, at any rate. A married man conducting interviews has got to inspire more confidence, especially in older subjects, and females, of course, than a bachelor. Don't you think?"

And here I could answer him with confidence even as the image of Mrs. Foshay fought to crowd everything else out of my brain. "That goes without saying, Prok, and I *have* been listening, believe me, on all those occasions when you kept wishing I was older and more, well, experienced—"

"Good, good," he said, "good," and he'd turned to go back to his desk when he swung round on me with an afterthought. "Iris," he said. "Do we have her history?"

OVER THE COURSE of the next two months, Prok was in increasing demand as a lecturer, and we began, of necessity, to step up our travel schedule. Word had gotten around. It seemed that every civic group, private school and university in a five-hundred-mile radius wanted him to appear, and at this stage, Prok never turned down an invitation. Nor did he charge a fee, even going so far as to pay traveling expenses out of his own pocket, though his first fledgling grants from the National Research Council and the Rockefeller Foundation helped cover him here—as they did with my salary as his first full-time employee. The routine was the same as always—Prok would find himself in a hall somewhere, the crowd already gathered, and he would lecture with his usual frankness on previously taboo subjects and then ask for volunteers—friends of the research, he'd begun to call them—to step forward and have their histories taken. When we weren't in his office, working out our tabulations, curves and correlation charts, we were off on the road, collecting data, because, as Prok said, over and over, you could never have enough data.

And how did I feel about all this? I was excited, of course, and I was infused with Prok's enthusiasm—I believed in the project with every ounce of my being, and I still do—but the timing was a bit awkward, as you can imagine. Iris and I had just become engaged. We treasured each other's company. We'd begun to enjoy each other sexually (though both of us were still fighting our inhibitions and it wasn't at all the same as it was with Mac). I wanted to be with her, to stroll arm in arm round Bloomington and poke through the secondhand shops, looking for dishware, rugs and the like, pricing furniture for the household we hoped to set up come June—and we needed to find an apartment we could afford within our limited means, and that was going to take some time and footwork too. But instead I was sitting up in second-rate hotels till one and two in the morning, utterly exhausted, trying to squeeze as many histories as possible into each working day. I was drinking and smoking too much. My ears rang, my head ached, my eyes felt molten, and nothing, not even the details of the most arcane sexual practices, could arouse me from my torpor—not coprophilia, incest or sex with barnyard animals. I just nodded, held the subject's eyes, and made my notations on the position sheet.

We must have collected some two hundred histories during this period, really driving ourselves, but thus far the research was skewed by the fact that the majority of our histories were predominantly upper-level—that is, from college students and professionals. We'd begun to branch out, as I've mentioned, and we did make trips to collect histories among the denizens of the homosexual underground in Indianapolis and Chicago, as well as at least one prison and the state work farm where Prok had made so many of his most valuable contacts—and one contact invariably gave rise to another, and another, ad infinitum, so that now we were determined to pursue as many of these lower-level histories as we could. What we lacked above all were black histories, and so we decided to mount a second expedition to Gary, Indiana, and the aforementioned Negro neighborhood there.

We left Bloomington on a drizzly Saturday morning in mid-April (we were still working around Prok's teaching schedule then—though the marriage course was dead, he was nonetheless committed to his biology classes, one of which met at eight o'clock on Saturday mornings, a cruel hour for any undergraduate to have to bend over a dissecting pan or distinguish between mono- and dicotyledons). We drove straight through, going as fast as the roads, the Nash and the state police would abide, arriving just after dark. We had an indifferent meal at a poorly lit diner, and sat there over coffee and pie as the drizzle solidified into a gray intermittent rain that wasn't going to make our work—outdoor work, on the streets—any easier. Prok looked grim. He kept checking his watch, as if that could somehow stop the rain and accelerate the coming of the hour at which we were to meet our contact. He had good reason to be anxious. Our first expedition to Gary, in the deep-freeze of February, had been a failure. We'd spent endless hours circling one block after another, peering hopefully through the windshield any time a figure appeared on the deserted streets, but Prok's contact failed to show up, and we didn't get a single history. Neither of us mentioned it now. We just finished our coffee, shrugged into our rain gear and climbed back into the car, heading six blocks south, into the Negro neighborhood.

Prok parked on a side street around the corner from a bar called Shorty's Paradise, in a neighborhood of modest storefronts (HAIR-DRESSER, SANDWICHES MADE TO ORDER, BUTCHER SHOP) with walkup apartments above them and the smokestacks of the factories looming up in the near distance like the battlements of a degraded castle. The street was littered with sodden newspaper, bottles, discarded food wrappers. Rain streaked the windshield and painted a sheen of reflected light on the pavement. There was no sign of life. We got out of the car and the doors slammed behind us like a cannonade.

My first surprise came when we turned the corner—the street outside Shorty's Paradise was thronged with people despite the rain, a whole mob spilling from the open door of the saloon and fanning out in both directions under the tattered awning. But these were black people, exclusively black, and I have to confess that I'd never to this point had much contact with Negroes, aside from the occasional pleasantry— "Nice day, isn't it?"—I exchanged with the odd maid or cook who came into the market where I'd worked summers. There was music drifting out the open door, a gaggle of voices, the smell of tobacco, marijuana, alcohol. I didn't know what to do. I hesitated.

But Prok. Prok was the second surprise. Though he detested bars, cigarettes and, especially, what he termed the "jungle beat" of popular music, he strode right past the crowd and though the front door as if he'd been going there every Saturday night of his life. He was dressed, as always, in his dark suit, white shirt and bow tie, over which he'd casually slung a yellow rain slicker that seemed always to hitch up in back as if it had been sewn together from two mismatching bolts of oilcloth. I was dressed in a dark suit and tie as well, though my overcoat—a thing my grandmother had picked out for me—was gray with black flecks and hung to my ankles. I could feel the hair prickling under the band of my hat, ready to spring loose the minute I stepped inside. I ducked my head and followed Prok through the door.

A long, trailing mahogany-topped bar dominated the place, and it was packed shoulder-to-shoulder with chattering people, all of whom glanced up as we stepped through the door, then turned away as if they hadn't seen us at all. The jukebox was playing "Minnie the Moocher" at a dynamic volume and everyone in the place seemed to be shouting to be heard above it. Prok went straight to the bar, elbowed his way in and immediately started up a conversation with a towering man in an electric-blue double-breasted suit. And this was the third thing, the oddest of all: Prok began to speak in dialect. I was stunned. As you may know, Prok was a real stickler for standard English, and he wasn't at all shy about correcting grammatical mistakes—he could be brutally sarcastic about it too—but here he was, switching to the vernacular like a ventriloquist. The conversation went something like this:

"Evenin', friend," Prok said, fastening on the man with the blue talons of his eyes. "I'm lookin' for Rufus Morganfeld. You know him?"

The man in the electric-blue suit took his time, regarding Prok from eyes drawn down to slits. He had a cigarette in one hand, a not-quite-empty glass in the other. "You the law?"

"Uh-uh."

"What then? Sellin' Bibles?"

"Who I am is Doctor Alfred C. Kinsey, Professor of Zoology at Indiana University, and Rufus—brother Rufus—say he gone meet me here."

"That's somethin'," the man said softly. "Doctor, huh? What, you come to cure my hemorrhoids?"

Prok's face never changed. No one laughed. "You wouldn't be needin' a cocktail there by any chance, would you?" he asked.

There was a long interval, Prok remaining absolutely motionless, his eyes never wavering, and then the man in the blue suit let a smile creep out of the furrows at the corners of his mouth. "Crown Royal and soda," he said.

The drink was ordered, the drink came, the drink was handed over. By this time Prok was deep in conversation with the man in the blue suit and a group of four or five others who were nearest him at the bar, and Rufus Morganfeld himself—our contact, who had been down at the other end of the bar to this point, waiting to see how things sorted out—came up and introduced himself. Prok greeted him warmly, and I thought he was going to offer Rufus a drink as well, but instead he shook hands all around, took Rufus in one arm and me in the other and shepherded us out into the street. Immediately Prok went back to being Prok, as there was no need to coddle Rufus, whom he'd met at the work farm, whose history he'd recorded and who was being paid fifty cents for every history he helped us collect among the prostitutes who worked the neighborhood. (I should say that Prok was intensely interested in prostitutes, at least in the beginning, because their experience was so much wider than most—this was before we actually got to observe them at work—but ultimately, they weren't as useful as you might imagine in regard to the physiology of various sex acts because of their propensity to counterfeit response.)

At any rate, with Rufus as our Virgil, we were able to track down the prostitutes (it was a slow night for them in any case, because of the rain, and they tended to bunch up in a few locales), and begin to record their histories. At first they tended to be skeptical—"Oh, yeah, honey, for one greenback dollar you just gone *talk*"—but Prok on the scent of histories was not to be denied and they quickly came round to the view that this was strictly on the up-and-up, pure science, and that we valued them not only as a resource but as human beings too, and this was another facet of Prok's genius—or his compassion, rather. He genuinely cared. And he had no prejudices whatever—either racial or sexual. It didn't matter to him if you were colored, Italian or Japanese, if you engaged in anal sex or liked to masturbate on your mother's wedding photo—you were a human animal, and you were a source of data.

The problem we encountered, however, was that since there were no adequate hotels nearby, we were at a loss for a private venue in which to conduct the interviews. We did have the car, but only one of us could interview in the Nash and the necessity was to conduct our interviews simultaneously. We were standing there on the street corner, the rain coming down harder now, in a forlorn little group—two prostitutes no older than I, Prok, Rufus and myself—when Rufus came up with the solution. "I got a room," he said, "two blocks over. Nothin' fancy, but it's got a electric light, a bed and a armchair, if that'll do—"

In the end Prok decided to take the Nash himself and leave me to the relative comfort of Rufus's room, reasoning that I was still the amateur and didn't need any additional impediments—such as cold, rain and inadequate lighting—put in my way. It was a noble gesture, or a practical one, I suppose, but either way, it was destined to backfire on him. I took my girl—and I call her a girl because she was just eighteen, with a pair of slanted cinnamon eyes and skin the color of the chocolate milk they mix up at Bornemann's Dairy back at home—up to Rufus's sitting room at the end of a hallway on the third floor of a detached brick apartment building that was once a single-family home. She seemed dubious at first, and maybe a bit nervous, and, of course, I was a bundle of nerves myself, not only because I'd taken so few female histories to this point but because of her race and the surroundings, the close, vaguely yellowish walls, the neatly made single bed that might have been a pallet in the penitentiary, the harsh light of the naked bulb dangling from the ceiling on its switch cord. Fifteen minutes into the interview, when she saw what it was, she relaxed, and I do think I did a very professional job with her that night (though, to be honest, I did find myself uncomfortably aroused, as with Mrs. Foshay).

Her history was what you might expect from a girl in her position—relations at puberty with both her father and an older brother, marriage at fourteen, the move north from Mississippi, abandonment, the pimp, the succession of johns and venereal diseases—and I remember being moved by her simple, unnuanced recitation of the facts, the sad facts, as I hadn't been moved before. Unprofessionally, I wanted to get up from my chair and hug her and tell her that it was all right, that things would get better, though I knew they wouldn't. Unprofessionally, I wanted to strip the clothes from her and have her there on the bed and watch her squirm beneath me. I didn't act on either impulse. I just closed down my mind and recorded her history, one of the thousands that would be fed into the pot.

The second woman—she was older, thirty or thirty-five, and she had a white annealed scar tracing the line of her jawbone on the right side of her face—came to the door the minute the first girl had left. This second woman had a belligerent look about her—a striated pinching of the lips, the weather report of her brow, the prove-it-to-me stance of her legs as she stood there arms akimbo at the door—and before she stepped into the room she demanded the dollar we were paying out to each of our subjects that night. I dug around in my pockets and came up empty—Prok had the billfold of crisp green singles he'd withdrawn from the bank the previous afternoon and he'd neglected, in the confusion of sorting things out vis-à-vis appropriate interviewing venues, to give me more than the one I'd handed to the first girl. "I, well, I'm sorry," I said, "I guess I'll have to, well—"

"Yeah, sure, you're sorry," she said, her brow contorted, "and so am I." She let out a curse. "And after I've went and dragged my sweet ass all the way over here in the rain too—"

"No," I said, "no, you don't understand."

"You just some schemer," she said, "like all the rest. Somethin' for nothin', ain't that about right?"

It took all my powers of persuasion, which, believe me, weren't much more than marginally developed at that point, to convince her to have a seat on the bed while I made a mad dash down the stairs, out into the street and back along the two blocks to where Prok sat in the Nash, interviewing his own colored prostitute. He wouldn't be thrilled over the interruption. It was a rule, hard and fast, that all interviews must be conducted straight through in a controlled and private location, without any distractions whatever that might compromise the rapport established with the subject, no telephones ringing, no third parties hovering in the background, no emergencies of any sort. I knew this. And I knew what Prok's impatience—and his wrath—could be like. Still, I had no choice. I ran hard all the way, afraid that my subject would get fed up and leave, and I rounded the corner by Shorty's in full stride, the dark hump of the Nash rising up out of the black nullity of the pavement like something deposited there by the retreating glaciers. There was a light on inside—Prok's flashlight—and the silhouettes of a pair of heads caught behind the windshield. Out of breath, I skidded to a halt on the wet sidewalk, took half a second to compose myself, and rapped gently at the driver's-side window.

That was the precise moment when the police cruiser rounded the corner behind me and the lights began to flash.

I had never in my life been in trouble with the law and had no reason to expect anything but courtesy and neighborly assistance from the two peace officers who emerged from the cruiser, thinking absurdly that they'd come to help us contact as many prostitutes as possible so as to make it easier for us to line up our interviews. Events proved otherwise. Events, in fact, moved so swiftly from that moment on that I didn't really have a chance to make sense of them until much later. The two patrolmen, both short and stocky, with the barrel chests and bandy-legged gait of rugby players, converged on me where I stood arrested at the window of the Nash. The first of them—he looked to be Prok's age, with a pug nose and inflamed features—strode directly up to me, and without saying a thing took hold of both my arms, jerked them round behind me and clapped two conjoined discs of metal over my wrists. In a word, handcuffs.

"But, but what are you doing?" I demanded. Or rather, stuttered. The rain was in my face, soaking the sleeves and shoulders of my jacket and infiltrating the pomaded weave of my hair, which sprang loose now in a sad barbaric tangle (in my urgency, I'd left both hat and overcoat in the room). "No, no, no, this is all wrong. You see, you, well, you don't understand what—"

The second policeman—he was fair-haired, with pale eyebrows and a little mustache that vanished like Paul Sehorn's when the lights of the patrol car illuminated his face—had taken up my position at Prok's window. His rapping, with the business end of a nightstick, was more insistent than mine had been. The window rolled down and I saw Prok's astonished face framed there a moment, and then the policeman had his hand on the door and was jerking it open. "Okay," he said, "out of the car."

All the way to the station house, as we sat wedged in on either side of the prostitute (Verleen Loy, five foot five, one hundred twenty-seven pounds, D.O.B. 3/17/24), Prok remonstrated with the patrolmen in his precise, wrathful tones. Did they know who he was? Did they know that the NRC, the Rockefeller Foundation and Indiana University supported his research? Were they aware that they were holding up vital progress toward understanding one of the most significant behavioral patterns of the human animal?

They weren't aware of it, no. In fact, one of them—the red-faced policeman who had handcuffed me and subsequently shoved me up against the brick wall at my back for no earthly reason—swung round in his seat at this point and addressed the prostitute in a tone I could only think was both crude and offensive. "Hey, Verleen," he said, grinning wide, "are we holding up progress here?"

The passing aura of a streetlight caught her face then. She had battered-looking eyes, teeth that seemed to have been sharpened to points. Her voice was reduced, hardly audible over the swish of the tires on the wet pavement. "You ain't holdin' up nothin'," she said.

At the station house, things seemed to take a turn for the better. The night captain, though he was deeply skeptical, was impressed by Prok's manner and his dress (and I think he took pity on me too, with my disarranged hair and hangdog look). After determining that Prok was who he claimed to be, the night captain allowed him to put a call through to H.T. Briscoe, Dean of the Faculties at IU. I stood there looking on, the handcuffs digging at my wrists, as Prok recited the number from memory and the night captain conveyed it to the operator.

It was past two in the morning. Verleen had been taken off and locked up in a cell somewhere, and I could hear the occasional shout or whimper emanating from the men's cell block in the rear. I was frightened, and I'm not ashamed to admit it. I wasn't yet twenty-three, I'd seen little or nothing of the world, and here I was, on the wrong side of the law and facing some sort of convoluted morals charge that would blemish my record forever, and I was already frantic over what I would tell my mother—what I would tell Iris, for that matter. Solicitation. Wasn't that what they charged you with? What about Sodomy? Fornication? Corrupting the morals of a minor? I saw myself at the work farm, in prison stripes, shuffling out to rake the yard.

But then I heard Prok's cool, collected tones as he explained the situation to Dean Briscoe, rudely awakened from his bed in a cozy room in a comfortable house back in the very Eden of Bloomington, and then I watched the night captain's face as Prok handed him the phone and Dean Briscoe delivered his authoritative testimonial on the other end of the line, and it was only then that I knew the crisis had passed. Unfortunately, I never did recover my overcoat and hat, and we managed only six interviews on that trip, but on the positive side, it taught us a lesson—from then on, Prok never went anywhere without a letter from Dean Briscoe explaining his project and its validation by the highest authorities of Indiana University, said letter to be produced "in the event that the nature of his research takes him into localities where the purpose of what he is doing might not be clearly understood."

BACK SAFE IN Bloomington, I gave Iris a truncated version of our little contretemps, tried to make a joke of it, in fact, though my psychic wounds were still open and festering, but Iris didn't find the story amusing, not at all. We were taking dinner together at the Commons (the roast pork with brown gravy, fitfully mashed potatoes and wax beans cooked to the consistency of cud), and she'd innocently asked how the trip had gone. I told her, glossing over some of the seamier details, and winding up with an extended lament over the loss of my hat and overcoat (for which Prok would make allowance in my next paycheck, incidentally).

"Prostitutes, huh?" she said.

I nodded. The overhead lighting made a gargoyle's mask of my face (I know because I was staring into my own reflection in a long dirty strip of mirror on the wall behind Iris). Outside, it was raining, a local manifestation of the same pandemic storm that had dogged us in Gary.

Iris's face was very pale and her mouth drawn tight. She laid her knife and fork carefully across her plate, though she'd barely touched her food. When she spoke, her voice was thick with emotion. "Do you often go with prostitutes?"

"Well, no," I said. "Of course not. That goes without saying."

"Do you ever—do you sleep with them?"

I didn't like the implied accusation, didn't like the criticism—or belittling—of my professionalism and my work. And I was especially annoyed after what I'd been through the previous night. She couldn't begin to imagine. "No," I snapped. "Don't be ridiculous."

"Did you ever?"

"Iris. Please. What do you think I am?"

"Did you?"

"No. And if you want to know the truth I never laid eyes on a prostitute in my life till last night and I wouldn't treat them, prostitutes,
that is, any different from anybody else. As far as interviews are concerned. You know perfectly well that for the project to succeed we need
everybody's history, from as wide a range of people as we can manage to
contact, ministers' wives, Daughters of the American Revolution, Girl
Scout leaders"—and here the image of Mac, naked, flitted quickly through
my brain like one of the flecks and blotches on the screen when the projector first flicks on—"and, yes, prostitutes too."

She looked away, caught in profile, her hair a small conflagration of
shadow and light. "Did you ever sleep with anybody?" She spoke to the
wall, her voice a whisper. "Besides me?"

"No," I said, and I don't know why I lied when the whole ethos behind the project was to bring human sexuality out of the dungeon to
which the priests had confined it and to celebrate it, glory in it, experience it to the full, without prohibition or inhibition. But still, given the
moment and the situation, which was fraught to say the least, I lied.

"But why not?" she said, lifting her head to give me a sidelong glance,
the glance of the executioner and the hanging judge. "Isn't that—sleeping with people, I mean—exactly what Dr. Kinsey—*Prok*—says is the
right thing to do? Isn't it part of the program? Sexual experimentation,
I mean?"

"Well," I said, and a gobbet of meat, soft as a sponge, seemed to have
climbed back up my throat, "not exactly. He *is* happily married himself,
you know, and he, he wants us to be too—"

Her face was flushed. The crucified pork congealed in its gravy on the
table before her. I felt a draft come up, somebody opening a door somewhere, and I craned my neck to pinpoint the source of it. "Do you feel a
draft?" I said.

"You're lying to me," she said. "I know you've slept with people."

"Who?" I demanded.

She was working loose the ring I'd given her, twisting it back and
forth to get the band over the bone of the finger joint. It was a diamond

solitaire, and I'd borrowed twenty-five dollars from Prok, as an advance on my salary, to put a down payment on it. I had never in my life purchased anything so lavish—had never even dreamed of it. I watched her jerk it off her finger now and set it on the table between us. She was feeling around her for her jacket, all her emotions concentrated in her eyes and the unforgiving slash of the drawn-down wound of her mouth. "Mac," she said. "Mac, that's who."

8

TALK OF WOMEN'S intuition, of the subliminal signals the sex is somehow able to pick up on, in the way of the dog that knows its master is coming home when the car is still six blocks away or the cat that lifts its ears at the faintest rustle of tiny naked feet in the farthest corner of the attic. For a solid week I walked around with that ring in my pocket, and I made no attempt to contact Iris or convince her that she was wrong, other than what I told her that night at the Commons—that she was out of her mind, that Mac was a surrogate mother to me, and far too old, and married, and that I wasn't attracted to her in any case. Iris listened, wordlessly, as if to see how far I would go before I stumbled, and then she was on her feet and stalking across the cafeteria to the door at the far end of the room. Which she slammed behind her.

This was our first tiff, the first round in a long series of preliminary bouts and featured attractions, and I was miserable over it—miserable, but not about to give in. What had I done, after all? Interviewed a couple of prostitutes? That was my job, couldn't she see that? And if such an insignificant thing could set her off, I dreaded to think what the future would bring, when certainly we would be obliged to interview a hundred more prostitutes, not to mention whole busloads of sex offenders of all stripes. I wanted to call my mother and tell her the engagement was off, but, as I say, I'd always had difficulty confiding in her because she never seemed to see things my way—she would take Iris's side, I was sure of it, and lay me open like a whitefish she was filleting for the pan. In the end, I went to Mac.

I chose a time when I knew Prok would be in class and the children at school. I made my way down the familiar street, the sun in my face, leaves unfurling on the trees, the world gone green with the April rains.

The garden was coming along nicely, just as Prok had said it would, though we were devoting less time to it this spring because of the accelerating schedule of our travels, and I might have lingered over the flowerbeds for a moment or two before I screwed up the courage to ring the bell. All I could think of was Iris and what I could do to extricate myself from the sheath of lies I'd constructed around me—a marriage counselor, I needed a marriage counselor even before I was married— and I was more than a little tentative with regard to Mac too. She'd given us her blessing, just as Prok had, and she couldn't have been more excited if one of her own children were getting married. I wondered how I could turn around now and tell her that it was all off—off because of what we'd done between us, in the garden, on the bentwood sofa in the living room and on the marital bed in the room upstairs. So I stood there, vaguely aware of the life seething around me, the insects descending on the flowers and the sparrows squalling from their nests in the eaves, took a deep breath and put my finger to the bell.

Mac came to the door in her khaki shorts and the matching blouse with the GSA insignia over the breast pocket, but she was wearing a cardigan too. (The house was cold this time of year because Prok, always frugal, shut down the furnace on the first of April, no matter what the weather—a habit I've taken up myself, by the way. Why waste fuel when the body makes its own heat?) She'd been in the kitchen, fixing a pot of vegetable soup and bologna sandwiches for the children's lunch, and she was expecting the postman, one of the neighbors, a traveling salesman—anybody but me. I saw it in her eyes, a moment of recognition, and then calculation—how much time did she have before the children came tramping up the path? Enough to pull me in and wrestle off my clothes? Enough for a quick rush to climax with her shorts at her knees and the blouse shoved up to her throat?

"Hello," I said, and my face must have been heavy because the kittenish look went right out of her eyes. "Have you—may I come in for a minute?"

She said my name as if she were sleepwalking, then pulled back the door to admit me. "What's wrong?" she said. "What is it?"

I stood there, shaking my head. I don't think I'd ever felt so hopeless as I did in that moment.

Mac knew just what to do. She led me to the kitchen, sat me down at the table with a cup of tea and set about feeding me what she could spare of the children's lunch. I watched her glide round the kitchen, from stove to counter to icebox and back, a whole ballet of domestic tranquillity, and I began to let it all out of me. I remember there was a sound of hammering from the yard two houses over where they were putting up a garage and it seemed to underscore the urgency of the situation—and the hopelessness. "I don't know what I'm going to do," I said, and the hammer thumped dully, then beat a frantic tattoo.

To this point, Mac hadn't offered much, other than the odd phrase—"And then what?" or "Do you take mustard, John?"—and I had the sudden intimation that she was jealous somehow, jealous of Iris and what she meant to me. Mac was masterful at inhabiting her role—dutiful wife of the scientist, selfless helpmeet, hostess, cook and mother—but I wondered how she really felt about things. About me, that is, and our relationship and how this would affect it—how it already had.

"Should I—I mean, do you think I should be the one to, to—?" I wanted her to tell me to go to Iris and make it up, to say that honesty was the best policy, to let the truth come out and we'd all be the better for it, but, as usual, I fumbled round the issue.

Mac pulled out the chair across from me and sat at the table, her own cup of tea in hand. She leaned forward to blow the steam off the cup, then sat up and stirred the dark liquid with a spoon. "You do love her, John," she said. "You're sure of it?"

I did, I was sure I did, and it wouldn't be the first time I'd confessed it to Mac, but now, sitting in the gently percolating, sun-grazed kitchen where we'd copulated on the linoleum tiles in front of the stove—the two of us, Mac and I—it felt awkward to admit it.

"Yes," I said, and the hammer came down twice. "I'm sure."

She took a long while over it, blowing at her tea with pursed lips, then lifting the cup to her mouth and watching me over the edge of the ceramic rim. Her hands were beautiful, her eyes, the imbricate waves of her hair. I was in love with her too—with Mac—and I'd been fooling myself to think it was purely biological. And what had Prok said to his critics, to the Thurman B. Rices and all the rest who accused him of taking the spiritual essence out of sex, of regarding it in a purely mechanistic way? *They've had three thousand years to go on about love, now give science a chance.* I'd agreed with him, taken it as a credo and worn the credo as a badge. It was us against them, the forces of inquiry and science against the treacle you heard on the radio or saw on the screen. But now I didn't know. I didn't know anything. I set down my sandwich, too upset—too confused—to eat.

Mac was smiling suddenly, even as the first footsteps hit the porch out front and the squeal of the hinges and the slamming of the door came to us in quick succession. "You know what?" she said, and the hammer pounded with a slow, deliberate rhythm that was like the drumbeat of a funerary march. "I think I'll go have a talk with her."

AGAIN, THOUGH, I can't help thinking I'm straying off the path here, because this is about Prok—or it should be. Prok was the great man, not I. I was just fortunate to have been there with him from the beginning and to have been allowed to contribute in my small way to the greater good of the project and the culture at large. Prok was defined by his work, above all, and his detractors—those who find sex research a source of prurient jokes and adolescent sniggers, as if it weren't worthy of investigation, as if it were some pseudoscience like studies of spacemen or ectoplasm or some such thing—might like to know just how consumed by it he was. I'll give one example from around this period— I can't really recall whether it was before or after Mac and Iris had their little tête-à-tête—but it speaks volumes of Prok's single-mindedness and dedication. And it's of interest for another reason too—it was the one occasion when our roles were reversed, when I was the teacher and he the pupil.

But I'm already making too much of it. Anybody, any man on the street, could have given Prok what he required—I just happened to be available, that was all. In any case, we were in the office one evening—it must have been around six or so—and I don't think we'd exchanged a word in hours, when I heard Prok get up from his desk. I had my head down, busy with one of the preliminary graphs on sources of orgasm for single males at the college level, and so I didn't look up, but I did register the sound of the file drawer opening and closing again, of the turning of the key in the lock, signals that Prok was getting set to shut down the office for the day. A moment later, he was standing over me.

"You know, John," he said, "since Mac and the girls are away on this Girl Scout Jamboree, or whatever it is they call it, and my son seems to be absorbed in a school project he's doing over at his friend's house—the Casdens, decent people—I wonder if we shouldn't spend the evening together—"

I thought I knew what he meant, and I no doubt did have plans—brooding over Iris would have topped the list—but I nodded in compliance. "Yes," I said, "sure."

He was opening up that dazzling smile, pleased, delighted—and, oddly, he reached across the desk and shook my hand as if I'd just given him the keys to the kingdom. "A bite of dinner, maybe, and perhaps we can combine that with what I had in mind, a little practice in one of the areas where I find myself sadly deficient—with an eye to improving my technique, that is."

"Technique?"

"Interviewing, I mean."

I gave him an astonished look and said something along the lines that he was the consummate interviewer and that I couldn't imagine how he could expect to improve on what was already as close to flawless as anyone could hope.

"Kind of you to say," he murmured, giving my hand a final squeeze and releasing it. "But we're all capable of improvement, and, you know, I think, that I'm not as comfortable as I should be around revelers."

"Revelers?"

"Where do we spend most of our time—in the field, that is?"

I didn't have a clue as to what he was talking about.

"In taverns, Milk. In barrooms, roadhouses, beer halls, at parties and gatherings where smoking and drinking are de rigueur, and you know how I—how awkward I am, or perhaps *untrained* is a better word, with those particular sybaritic skills."

I still wasn't following him. "Yes? And?"

He laughed then, a short chopped-off laugh that began in his throat and terminated in his nose. "Well, isn't it obvious? You're the expert here, Milk. I'm the novice."

"You mean you want me, to, to—?"

"That's right. I want you to give me lessons."

We went back to the house on First Street that night with a brown paper bag of ham sandwiches, three packs of cigarettes, two cigars, a quart of beer and a fifth each of bourbon, scotch, gin, rum and vodka, as well as the standard mixers. It may have been raining. The house was cold. Prok built up a fire in the hearth and we spread our acquisitions out on the coffee table, set ourselves up with the proper glasses, ice and ashtrays, and started in.

First came the cigarettes. "You don't have to inhale, Prok," I said, knowing how much he loathed the habit. "Just let the thing dangle from your lips, like this"—I demonstrated—"bend forward to light it, squelch the match with a flick of the wrist, take the smoke in your mouth, like so, hold it a moment, exhale. No, no, no—just leave the cigarette there, right there at the corner of your mouth, and let the smoke rise. That's right. Squint your eyes a bit. But you see? Now your hands are free, and you can pick up your drink or, if you're interviewing, go right on with your recording. Yes, yes, now you can remove it—two fingers, index and middle—and tap the ash. That's it. Right. Very good."

Of course, he hated it. Hated the smell, the taste, the idea, hated the smoke in his eyes and the artificial feel of the dampening paper at his lip. And on the second or third puff he inadvertently inhaled and went into a coughing fit that drained all the color from his face and swelled his eyes till I thought they would burst. The cigars were even worse. At one point he went to the mirror to examine how he looked with the sodden stub of a White Owl clenched in the corner of his mouth, and then wordlessly came back across the room and flung the thing in the fireplace. "I just don't understand it," he said. "I just don't. How can people derive enjoyment from burning weeds under their noses—from burning weeds anywhere? From *inhaling* burning weeds? And what about men with facial hair, with beards—what do they do? It's a wonder every barroom in America hasn't burned to the ground by now." He was stalking back and forth across the floor. "It's maddening is what it is. Maddening."

We did better with alcohol. I started him off with bourbon, my drink of choice, and I tried to have him dilute it with water or soda, but he insisted on taking it straight, reasoning that if he had to choose a favorite, something he could order casually at some gin mill to help put potential subjects at ease, he ought to know what it tasted like in its unadulterated form. I watched him sniff the sepia liquid, tip back the drink, swish it around in his mouth, and then, after a moment's deliberation, spit it back into the glass. "No," he said, giving me a grimace, "bourbon, I'm afraid, is not—*viable.*"

And so on, through the other candidates (the beer, he said, had the smell of swamp gas and the taste of an old sponge that had been buried in the yard and then squeezed over a glass), until we got to the rum. He poured it, sniffed it, swirled it in his mouth and swallowed. The grimace never left his face and my impression was that the experiment had been a failure. But he leaned forward and poured a second drink, a very short one, and drank that off too. He gritted his teeth. Smacked his lips a time or two. His eyes were red behind the shining discs of his glasses. "Rum," he said finally. "That's the ticket. How does the song go?—'Fifteen men on a dead man's chest, Yo-ho-ho and a bottle of rum.'"

In fact, we didn't have Iris's history. I knew, though, almost exactly how it would tabulate—she'd been sex shy, inhibited by her upbringing and her religion; she'd masturbated guiltily while thinking of a boy in her class or some screen actor; she'd dated frequently, but not seriously, and had never, until now, allowed anything more than deep kissing and perhaps some awkward adolescent manipulation of her breasts; she'd had one sexual partner and had lost her virginity at the age of nineteen in the backseat of a Nash. And more: she loved that partner and intended to marry him. Or at least she had until a week ago.

Though he tried not to show it, Prok was irritated that we hadn't collected her history—how would it look vis-à-vis the project if the prospective wife of his sole colleague had decided against volunteering? Bad, to say the least. Unreasonable. Hypocritical. Even worse, it would tend to undermine everything we were trying to project with regard to openness about sex on the one hand and absolute confidentiality on the other. What was Iris thinking? Was she going to wind up being a detriment to the project? And if she was, would it cost me my job?

The pressure was subtle. There was that initial inquiry of Prok's on the afternoon he congratulated me on my engagement, and then, in the days and weeks that followed, the odd passing reference to Iris's sexual adjustment or to the history he'd recorded of some coed in his biology course, who just happened to remind him of Iris—"Same build, you know, same bright sparking eyes. A peach of a girl, a real peach." But once he'd found out—from Mac, I presume—that the engagement was off, he withdrew a bit, no doubt brooding over his options. He wanted me married, no question about it, and he wanted Iris's history as a matter of course, but since I hadn't yet chosen to confide in him, he couldn't very well give me unsolicited advice or exert the direct pressure with which he was so much more comfortable. All that week—the week I walked around with the weight of the ring like an anvil in my pocket—he said nothing, though I could see he was bursting with the impulse to interfere, to lecture, advise, hector and, ultimately, set things right.

As it turned out, it was Mac who held the key. The day after I spoke with her she asked Iris over to the house for tea, and I don't know how much she revealed (or I didn't then) or just how she put it, but Iris seemed mollified. Mac called me at the rooming house—shouts, the tramping of feet up and down the stairs, *Phone's for you, Milk!*—to tell me in her soft adhesive tones that I should go to Iris as soon as I could. It was past seven in the evening. I'd had an early supper alone at a diner (where I'd looked up from my hamburger to see Elster, my old antagonist from the biology library, giving me a look of contempt and naked, unalloyed jealousy), and I'd been stretched out on my bed ever since with a pint of bourbon, listening to the sad, worn, gut-clenching voice of Billie Holiday drifting over her sorrow. Was I drunk? I suppose so. I gave my effusive thanks to Mac, fought down my hair in the mirror, and then flung myself out the door.

The campus. The dorm. A sound of frogs trilling along the creek. The RA and her welcoming smile. "Hi, John," she said, and she gave me a wink. "Glad to see you're back." The big pale moon of her face rose and set again. "I've already rung her," she said.

As it happened, two other girls came through the door before Iris and I caught a glimpse of her on the stairs before the door wheezed shut, and in the interval between its closing and springing open again, I had a chance to compose myself. I smoothed down my hair, cupped a palm to my mouth and evaluated my breath (which smelled, essentially, no different from the neck of the bottle I'd left back in the room). What I needed was a stick of gum, but I'd given up the habit because Prok forbade it in the office and disapproved strenuously of it everywhere else. I fingered the ring in my pocket and stood rigid, awaiting my fate.

She was wearing her best outfit, one I'd repeatedly praised, and it was evident that she'd spent a great deal of time on her hair and makeup. And what was she doing? Making me aware of what I'd been missing, of what she had to offer, of what she was worth, and as I watched her cross the room to me I tried to read her face. How much had Mac told her? And the lie. Was the lie still intact? I was drunk. I wanted to spread my arms wide and hold her, but her smile stopped me—it was a pinched smile, brave and artificial, and her chin was trembling as if she might begin to cry. "Iris," I said, "listen, I'm sorry, I don't know what I've done or what I can do to, to make it up, but—"

The RA was glorying. A study date indented the sofa nearest us, but there was no studying going on in that moment—or at least not of books and notes.

"Not here," Iris said, and she took me by the hand and led me out the door.

The night was soft, a warm breath of air hovering over the dark unspooling stretches of lawn, streetlights masked in fog. The frogs trilled. Other couples, derealized in the drift of the night, loomed up on us and vanished. We wandered round the campus, hand in hand, not saying much, till at some point we found ourselves out front of Biology Hall, and we wound up sitting on the steps there till curfew. For the first hour we just held each other and kissed, murmuring the usual sorts of things—clichés; love thrives on them—until we got progressively more worked up and I asked her in a husky voice if I shouldn't run for Prok's car.

We were fully clothed, exposed to the eyes of anyone who happened by, but I suppose my hand might have been on her thigh, under her skirt. And her hand—her hand had been pressed against the crotch of my flannel trousers, and the pressure it exerted, the slow sweet calculated friction, told me everything I needed to know. "No," she said, and she didn't withdraw her hand, "not tonight. It's too late."

"Tomorrow, then?"

She kissed me harder, kept rubbing. "Tomorrow," she murmured.

It took me a moment, floating there on the breath of the night as if I'd gone out of my body altogether, and I wasn't thinking about Mac or versions of the truth or anything else. I was fumbling in my pocket for the ring. "In that case," I said, releasing her lips and lifting her hand from my lap for the instant it took to slip the ring back in place and not a second more, "I guess the engagement's back on, then?"

THE WEDDING WAS modest, as it had to be, considering my salary, the financial status of Iris's parents—her father delivered milk for Bornemann's Dairy in Michigan City and environs—and the instability of the times. Which is not to say that it wasn't a joyful, inspiriting ceremony and a celebration I'll remember all my life, the emotional core of the scene worth all the palatial weddings in the world. The bride wore white tulle, the lace veil setting off her hair and the uncontainable flash of her eyes, and the bridegroom found himself in a rented tuxedo, the first he'd ever pulled over his shoulders and forced down the slope of his chest. Tommy was best man, Iris's roommate the maid of honor (a trembling tall horse of a girl, with pinpricks for eyes and a mouth that swallowed up her lower face, and it's odd that I can't remember her name now, though it hardly matters: she was there, dressed in a strapless gown, doing her part). At first, Iris's parents had pushed for a church wedding, presided over by a priest, but Iris had begun to drift (or rather, swim, head-down, against the current) away from the Roman Catholic faith since she'd come to college, and I, a lapsed Methodist, had no real desire to join any church of any denomination, and certainly not one so compromised by mystery, superstition and repression. And, of course, to Prok, who was hosting the affair, all religions and religious persons were anathema.

But a word about Iris, because I see I haven't given her her due here—and she *is* central to all this, to Prok's story, that is, because on that day at the end of May in 1941 she was to become the fourth member of the inner circle, taking her place alongside Prok, Mac and me, and everything that's happened since concerns her as much as it does anyone else. She was—well, she had an independent streak. She thought for herself. Formed her own opinions. And while I didn't necessarily recognize it at the time, so caught up was I in the project and what we'd set out to accomplish, I would say that her independence grew over the years until it was almost antithetical—a rebellion, very nearly a rebellion—against what we believed in. But that's off subject. Iris. Let me put her down here in a few words. Beautiful, certainly. Stubborn. Witty (I've never encountered anybody so quick except maybe Corcoran). Smart as a whip. Organized. She played clarinet throughout high school and college, and until her senior year, when we were already married, she put on a starched uniform every Saturday morning and marched across the shimmering greensward with the band. She was a conscientious student, though her grades weren't nearly as high as mine (not that it matters, of course), and she had a stunning artistic sense, able to make a household, our eventual household, that is, look nothing short of elegant on just the barest of means. What else? Her smile. I wanted to sail away on that smile, and I did, for a long while. And her sexual response, of course—I can't leave that out, not in an account of this nature. What

I'd told Prok was true, more or less. She'd opened up to me—she loved me—and as we became more acclimated to one another, as we spent more and more time in the backseat of Prok's car and then, as the weather warmed, on a blanket in a hidden corner of the park, she let her passionate side emerge. We began to experiment, and she was increasingly enthusiastic, on several occasions even climbing atop me in the female-superior position without any prompting on my part. And while she wouldn't dream of using crude language in any situation, she used it then, used it when her eyes began to roll back in her head and her hands jerked at my shoulders as if she wanted to pull me right down inside her rib cage and beyond, into the ground beneath, and deeper, deeper yet: "Oh, fuck," she'd say. "Fuck, cunt, fuck."

Prok had arranged for the justice of the peace to perform a simple civil ceremony under the persimmon tree at the rear of the house, and he'd gone to considerable trouble to move the piano out of doors as well so that we could have the bridal march to put the official seal on the ceremony. (I haven't mentioned that Prok had dreamed of becoming a concert pianist when he was a boy and gave it up only when he'd discovered his true vocation in science. He was good, as accomplished as anyone you might find on the stage in the concert hall down the street, and he serenaded us not only with the wedding march that afternoon, but with a host of selections from *Peer Gynt*, which went eerily well with the fairy-tale setting.) Prok at the piano, Iris in my arms, Tommy at my side: it was as close to heaven as I'd yet come. And my mother, of course. She was there with Aunt Marjorie, a small distant smile on her face, and I think she drank too much that day (rum drinks—Prok had gone mad for them, not so much because he enjoyed drinking all that much himself, but because he was swept away with the idea of collecting recipes, and so we had Zombies that afternoon, and something called Charleston Cup in a crystal bowl set in a bed of ice). She didn't cry, though Mac did, briefly. For my mother, never one to sentimentalize (she'd described herself to me as a fatalist on more than one occasion), the ceremony must have brought her back to her own wedding day so many years ago and the wreckage that had been left in place of the dreams of a young bride. Still, she did approve of Iris because she felt that Iris had grit and grit was the only thing my mother understood in terms of getting by—you needed grit and toughness, especially if you were a woman, in order to survive in a world of war and depredation and boating accidents.

Somebody—Tommy, the maid of honor, Paul Sehorn—tied a potpourri of old pans and graters to the bumper of the Nash, and Prok, erect as a chauffeur up front with my mother and Mac erect beside him, grimaced at the noise all the way to the station while Iris and I clung to each other on the soft wide leather seat we knew so well.

9

OUR HONEYMOON TOOK its cue from the one Prok and Mac had pioneered twenty years earlier—that is, we went on an extended camping trip, not to the White Mountains of New Hampshire as the Kinseys had done, but to the Adirondacks, a region that had always fascinated me as a boy growing up among the scrub hills and dunes on the shores of Lake Michigan. Iris wasn't much of a camper, nor was I, if truth be told. But it seemed like an adventure, and it had the added virtue of being cheap (which was one of the motivating factors for Prok back in his day, though of course he was a naturalist who'd been camping all his life and could happily have subsisted on tubers, berries and mast if he had to, something, needless to say, I was neither able nor willing to do). To give her credit, Iris was game, though she'd lobbied for a more conventional honeymoon in Niagara Falls, and we did pay a visit there and spend a single night in a hotel room that cost as much as the rest of the trip combined. Looking back on it, I do have fond memories of that journey—Iris in a swimsuit and horripilated flesh perched over a lake barely clear of ice, the smell of the pine woods and the intoxicating smoke of our cookfires, the touch of her hand, our vagrant lovemaking in a sleeping bag designed for one in the core of a blackness absolute and a silence deeper than all of history—but overall it did have its limitations. I won't really bother to go into detail—it's not relevant here—but I will say that the insects were merciless, the tent barely adequate to its function, the weather horrible and the ground as hard as a rail rolled off the line in a Gary steel mill.

None of that seemed to matter (or it mattered, but we fell all over ourselves trying to assure each other it didn't), because we were together, just the two of us, for the first time in our lives. We made an erotic playground of the big white bed in the hotel room in Niagara Falls and engaged in activities—fellatio, cunnilingus, rear entry—I'd been too timid, and too hurried, to try with Mac. Ironically, though we didn't know it at the time, the two weeks of our honeymoon would be our last opportunity to experience that sort of freedom for almost a full year. That is, when we got back to Bloomington, Iris returned to her dorm—where she would stay on for summer session in the hope of accelerating her matriculation—and I to Mrs. Lorber's. Though we spent every available minute tramping through apartments, spare rooms, converted basements and various outbuildings posing as rental units, we found nothing we could both tolerate and afford, and so, though we were married now and though I was an adult with a full-time job, we went back to the blanket in the park and the backseat of Prok's antiquated Nash (not that Prok was unsympathetic, but you have to understand that the lion's share of the money for the project was at that time coming out of his own pocket—that is, from his earnings at IU and the royalties on his biology textbook—and it was all but impossible for me to expect him to raise my salary even by a few dollars a week).

In any case, Iris and I made do, as countless other separated couples had throughout the Depression, and we saved our money and painted vivid dreams of our first household as the summer imperceptibly coalesced with the fall and the news from abroad went from bad to worse. It was a strange, unsettling period, that interlude between our marriage and the war. On the one hand we were hopeful, and yet on the other, everything we did, even the simplest things, gave rise to doubt—why bother to put that extra dollar away, look after the condition of your teeth and your diet or dare to dream about your wife and an apartment and the future when the ax was poised to fall? A lot of men I knew despaired. Others just burned up all they had of energy and resources, day and night, carpe diem.

My own crisis came at the end of October, on a day when Prok and I had been in a jubilant mood over the correlations we were discovering between educational levels and number of sexual partners in adolescence (it was predictive, and that was the wonder of it, those who would not go on to college having a much wider and more complete range of sexual activity than those who would), and I remember feeling elated as I came through the door at Mrs. Lorber's. I was looking forward to dinner with Iris, a picture show and then some mutually productive time spent in the backseat of the Nash, and when I saw the official-looking envelope sitting there atop the pile of circulars on the little table in the vestibule, it didn't at first register on me. UNITED STATES GOVERNMENT, SELECTIVE SERVICE AGENCY, it read, OFFICIAL BUSINESS. I'm sure you're familiar with the form of the thing, with the language that sounds so clinical it might have been describing the latest method of relaxing the bowels or the proper way to install a new condenser in your Zenith, and yet manages to rivet your attention all the same:

Greetings:
Having submitted yourself to a local board composed of your neighbors for the purpose of determining your availability for training and service in the land or naval forces of the United States, you are hereby notified that you have been selected . . .

It wasn't that I didn't want to go—already the campus was beginning to teem with young men in uniform, already the girls were looking right through anybody in civvies and practically wrapping themselves in red, white and blue, and add to this the fervor that was building in all of us and my honest and true desire to go out and defend my country, to defend freedom and liberty and rescue all those besieged Britons from the terror of the Luftwaffe and the Albanians from the Italians and all the rest—but still, to come through the door on an otherwise tranquil afternoon and find the envelope there on top of the pile where Mrs. Lorber had no doubt left it after examining it from all angles and in every light available, was a shock. I was newly married, just getting started in a career, I had money in my pocket (not a lot, but money nonetheless) and an automobile at my disposal, and now I was going to have to start all over, with nothing. And in a strange place, among strangers. It wasn't that I was afraid. I was too young and blandly healthy to dream even in my worst imaginings that I could be maimed, injured or even killed;

that sort of thing didn't happen to the individual—to me—but to some faceless member of the generality in the newsreel footage before the main feature came on. The problem was the uncertainty of it—of putting oneself in the hands of such an arbitrary and manifold organization as the United States Army and having to trust for the best.

I must have stood there in the vestibule for a good five minutes before the tramp of feet on the outside steps, closely followed by the violent wrenching open and then slamming of the front door, brought me out of it. Ezra Voorhees had just come in from class. Ezra was a student of business, or business as it applied to agriculture, that is, and his ambition was to improve production on his father's poultry farm, with an eye to running it on his own someday. He was nineteen and more or less harmless, but he was loud and excitable, he'd chosen not to give up his sex history to the project (though I'd all but gone down on my knees and begged him) and he wasn't overfussy about washing his clothes—or his person, for that matter. "John!" he cried, giving me a look of surprise, as if I were the last person he'd expected to see there in the vestibule of the house in which we shared a room. And then, snatching the letter from my hand: "What's this? Oh, Jesus, Jesus. It's your induction notice."

I held my hand out stiffly, too numb to be irritated. He handed the letter back.

"You going to enlist?"

"Well, I—I don't know. I hadn't thought about it." I had a sudden vision of myself in uniform, erect and proud, my hair a perfect glaze cut crisply over the ears, the stiff-brimmed hat tucked under one arm, saluting. My mother would be proud. Iris would hate it. And Prok—Prok would be apoplectic.

"Enlistment's the route to take, believe me. I've been talking with Dick Martone and some of the other guys—Dave Frears, for one—and we were thinking about the Marine Corps, about enlisting, I mean. To get a jump on everybody." Ezra was tall—two or three inches taller than I—and thick-bodied, but with a disproportionately small and oddly shaped head, the crown of which he began to scratch now in a leisurely, thoughtful way. "Enlist," he said, "and you're right in the thick of things, overseas, in France or Belgium—or Italy, Italy, where the real fighting's going to be."

I went to Iris first. We met in the Commons for dinner (beef roasted white, with a puddle of butterscotch-colored gravy, disheartened potatoes and peas that had been harvested and canned before the New Deal went into effect), and I waited till we were seated, till we'd buttered our bread and peppered our meat, before pushing the envelope across the table to her. I watched as she bent her head and absorbed the contents of the letter even before she'd finished ironing it out on the placemat in front of her. Her chin was trembling, and when she raised her head again her eyes had taken on a harrowing look. "I don't believe it," she said. "You can't—isn't Tommy enough for them?"

"I don't know."

"You're not going to go, are you?"

I shrugged. "What choice do I have?"

"But you're married."

Another shrug. "Lots of people are married—and how many of them got married in the last six months just to evade the draft? They don't care about that in Washington. And the way it's looking—well, Wilkie didn't win the election, did he?"

She took hold of both my hands then, across the table, interlocked her fingers with mine and squeezed as if she wanted to crush them in her own. "I won't let you go," she said. "I won't. It's not our war. It has nothing to do with us."

But of course she was wrong, as the whole country—even the most diehard America Firster—would know in less than two months when the Japanese attacked Pearl Harbor. That night, though, with a cold wind scuttling leaves across campus and her hands locked in mine as students all around us sat gumming their overcooked beef and burying their heads in their textbooks or the funny papers or just laughing aloud in an excess of high spirits, it seemed as if the force of her words was enough: *I won't let you go. I won't.*

THE NEXT MORNING, I took the letter to Prok. He was in the office before me, as usual, head down, engaged with his work. I didn't want to interrupt him, but he looked up and greeted me with a smile as I came in, and I calculated that this was as good a chance as any to give him the bad news. "Good morning, Prok," I said, and already his eyes were dropping back to the page, but I forged on, if a bit awkwardly. "Prok," I repeated, and his gaze lifted again, even as the smile vanished, "there's something—well, I just wanted you to know, that, that, well, here," and I handed him the notice.

He gave it a cursory glance, then rose to his feet, folded it carefully and handed it back. "I've been afraid of this for some time," he said. For just a moment he looked defeated, the shadow of resignation flitting over his face, his jowls gone heavy, but then he squared his shoulders and let out a sharp burst of air, as if a teakettle had come on to boil. "Damn it," he said, and this was as close to cursing as I've ever heard him come, before or since, "we're going to fight this thing, even if we have to take it to the Secretary of War himself." And then he paused a moment and gave me a questioning look. "Who is the Secretary of War anyway?"

I told him I didn't know.

"That's all right. It doesn't matter. What matters is the research, and I wonder if any of these people"—and he let his hand rise and fall in a characteristic sweep, as if all the politicians, the forces of the Army and Navy, as well as Hitler and his Wehrmacht were no more than errant students who'd missed a key question on a biology exam—"if any of them have even the slightest idea of what it takes to train an interviewer? No," he snapped, answering his own question, "I doubt if they do. But you know, John, don't you?"

I nodded. We'd sat together through hundreds of hours of training, Prok quizzing me unceasingly, jumping up impatiently to snatch the position sheet out of my hand and make his own corrections, looking over my shoulder for hours at a time, putting me through mock interviews—I must have taken his history fifty times—and sitting perched behind me like a wooden Indian as I conducted my first live interviews. As I've said, he was a perfectionist, and he knew no other way to do anything but the Kinsey way, and whether that can be considered a flaw or not, I can't really say. His method worked, no question about it, and worked in an arena where so many before him—Krafft-Ebing, Hamilton, Moll, Freud, Havelock Ellis—had fallen short. But he had a point: the training was not to be undertaken lightly. And certainly you had to have a certain type of personality—the personality of a recruit, I suppose, or maybe even a disciple—to undergo it in the first place.

He'd come out from behind the desk now and he was striding back and forth across the confined space of the office, hands pinned behind his back. "No," he said finally, drawing himself up before me so that our faces were no more than inches apart, "no, I simply will not allow it."

And so, Prok began a vigorous campaign to keep me at his side throughout the war, though it may be interesting to note that he never really consulted me on the matter, but operated on the assumption that I was one hundred percent in accord with him, that sex research—the project and the advancement of human knowledge—was more vital to the welfare of the country than prosecuting a war on the European Front or in the Pacific. He never pressured me. Never knew, in fact, that I spent long hours propped on the edge of the bed in my room with Ezra and Dick Martone and some of the others, debating the merits of joining up, of doing my part, of sacrificing everything for the cause of freedom. In the end, I acquiesced. That is, I did nothing, and let events take their course.

IN THE MEANWHILE, even as Prok was filing an appeal and soliciting letters on my behalf from President Wells, Robert M. Yerkes of the National Research Council and other purveyors of influence and power, he was at the same time very seriously contemplating the hire of another researcher to increase our strength. That researcher, as most people will know, was Purvis Corcoran. Corcoran, as I've said, was a smoothly handsome and outgoing young psychologist and sexual wunderkind, who had taken his degree some ten years earlier at IU, completed his Master's in Chicago and was working incrementally toward his Ph.D. He was married—his wife's name was Violet—and the father of two small children, both girls. Prok first met him after lecturing to a group of social workers ("the most prudish and the most restricted in their understanding of sex you could find") in South Bend, while I was away on my honeymoon. Corcoran volunteered to give his history—which was extensive to say the least, both in heterosexual and H-experience—and Prok was impressed by him. So impressed, in fact, that he invited him to Bloomington, to visit the Institute (as we were now officially calling our cramped quarters) and interview for a position with us.

When I mentioned it to Iris—that Prok, in anticipation of new grants both from the NRC and the Rockefeller Foundation, was bringing Corcoran to town for a job interview—she was suspicious of the whole thing. "Can't you see he's trying to replace you," she said. "He's letting you go, leaving us high and dry, and I'll be here all alone and you'll be God knows where—in some desert in Africa fighting Rommel or whoever he is, some goose-stepping Prussian with a gun and bayonet."

We were in the Nash, parked in our favorite spot overlooking the black serene waters of a quarry and its ghostly monuments of rock, having a post-coital smoke. "You're wrong," I told her. "It has nothing to do with the draft or the war or anything else—we need more hands, that's all."

She was silent a moment. "You know," she said, "he's been making overtures—"

"Who?"

"Your boss."

"Prok?"

It was very dark in the car, but I could just make out the nod of her head. We were naked and the smell of her sex was all over me. I put an arm round her, drew her to me and began fondling her breasts, but she pushed away. "Yes, *Prok*," she hissed. "He's—when I was waiting for you the other day? He told me he was going to do everything he could to get you off, letters to the draft board back home, even a personal appeal if it comes to that—you know, because the research is vital to the national security and all the rest, and I said I was grateful. But it was more than that. I guess I just about got down and kissed his feet, because you know how strongly I feel about this—you are not going to war, not while I'm alive, John Milk—and he gave me a look, and I know you think he's God

156

Himself come down from on high with all the angels singing in rapture, but it was the coldest look anybody's ever given me in my life. And you know what he said then, as if it were some kind of bargain we were entering into? He said, 'We don't have your history yet, Iris, do we?'"

"Yes," I said, "and so what?"

"So what? Aren't you listening to me?"

"Look, Iris," I said, and all the wind went out of me, "I've told you myself, a thousand times, you have to give up your history because of how bad it'll look if you don't—how bad it already looks."

"He's a blackmailer."

"A blackmailer? Have you gone completely nuts?"

"Don't give me that, don't pretend you're blind." I reached out a hand to her again, but she shifted away until her shoulders were pressed up against the window and the light of her cigarette revealed her face there, in shadow. "I give him my secrets, I tell him what I've never told anybody, not even you, and he'll get you off." A beat, time enough for the bitterness to saturate her voice. "And if I don't—well, goodbye, Johnny, huh?"

A WEEK LATER, Corcoran arrived. He'd come alone, without his wife, arriving early one Saturday when I was off someplace with Iris—at Prok's behest. Prok was interested in my impression of Corcoran, of course, but on that first day he wanted him to himself, and I didn't know what, if anything, happened between them, but Prok, I'm sure, was his usual courtly self and wound up giving Corcoran the VIP tour of the facilities, ending up with an intimate, Mac-prepared dinner at the faerie cottage on First Street. The following evening, on Sunday, Iris and I were invited to Prok's for one of his weekly "musicales" as he called them, in order to socialize with a select group of his friends and colleagues, listen to a recorded program Prok had selected for the occasion, and, expressly, to meet Corcoran.

We were a few minutes late, nothing to worry over, though Prok had asked me to come early so as to have some time with Corcoran before the others arrived. Iris was the one at fault here. She seemed to take forever with her dress and makeup—maddeningly so—and I must have had the RA ring for her five times before she finally came down the stairs and through the door at which I'd been staring so hard and for so long I actually began to believe I could force it open by will alone. I was impatient, maybe even a bit angry, though I have to admit it was worth the wait: Iris was stunning that night, all in black, with a single strand of heirloom pearls her mother had given her and an especially vivid shade of lipstick that lent her all the color she needed. I don't know what it was—the pearls, maybe—but she looked transformed, as if she'd suddenly gained five years and the sophistication of a socialite, and forgive me if I couldn't help thinking of Mrs. Foshay and her savoir faire.

Most of the guests had already arrived by the time we got there. I suppose there must have been fifteen or twenty people present, professors and their wives, Prok's next-door neighbor, two awed-looking undergraduates who seemed afraid even to glance at the crackers, nuts and chocolates Prok had set out around the room in cut-glass dishes. Mac greeted us at the door. "John," she puffed in her airless voice, drawing me to her for a kiss on the cheek, "and, Iris, so nice of you to come," and she took both of Iris's hands in her own and embraced her as if they'd been separated for years.

They held on to each other just a moment longer than I thought appropriate, and I was beginning to feel uncomfortable, as if I'd been deserted there in the entrance hall, the eyes of the guests beyond already roving toward us. "But, Mac," Iris said, fixating on her face as if they were exchanging telepathic secrets, "you know I wouldn't miss it for the world." She was smiling, beaming, as happy as I'd seen her since the draft notice arrived, all her irritation over Prok dissolved in that instant. She was genuine, I'll give her that. "You're simply the best, you are, and I—we, John and I—we're always thrilled to come visit. You know that. I just wish we could return the favor . . ."

"Don't you worry," Mac said, taking our coats and leading us into the living room, "something'll turn up. Prok and I went through the same sort of thing after our honeymoon, and the place we did find—well, you kids probably wouldn't look twice at it today."

Iris cooed something in response—I still hadn't got round to broaching the subject of Mac with her, and I know it was ridiculous and maybe even cowardly, but I think too that anyone in a similar situation will understand the temptation to let sleeping dogs lie—and then we were among the company and Mac had excused herself to dart off to the kitchen. I didn't know everyone there, though I'd attended several of Prok's musicales in the past—the cast of invitees was forever shifting—and so I wasn't able to pick out Corcoran right away. We were distracted by Professor Bouchon of the Chemistry Department, and his wife, who appeared to suffer from logorrhea, and then we were separated, and I found myself wedged into a corner and nodding at what seemed appropriate junctures as Mrs. Professor Bouchon told me in exhaustive detail of the defects of the German character and the privations she'd suffered as a girl in Nantes during the first war. Iris was across the room, clutching a long-stemmed glass of greenish liquid (one of Prok's herbal liqueurs) and talking guardedly with Professor Bouchon and a gaunt, hunched man in a flannel suit who was too old to have been Corcoran. It was only then that I realized that Prok wasn't among us.

But a word here on the musicales: Prok, always the inveterate collector, had amassed a personal library of over a thousand records, and for the past decade or more he'd been hosting these weekly gatherings in order to share the musical wealth. There was a high tone to these evenings, and the shape of the program was uniform and even fairly rigid—Prok was in charge, and Prok would do as Prok would. The guests gathered, as we were doing now, for a brief period of socializing, Prok delivered a lecture on the pieces and composers he'd selected, and then there was the listening. Seated in a semicircle facing the gramophone, the audience watched in silence as Prok wiped the record free of dust, sharpened the cactus needle and gently laid it on the revolving disc; this was succeeded by a moment of tense anticipation, during which the guests sat rigid and expressionless through the initial poppings and crackles until the music began with a characteristic roar and they settled into their listening postures. The records were always played at full volume, because that was the only way, Prok believed, to pick up on the nuances of the pianissimo movements and the full complexity of the interweaving of the various instruments, and for the duration of the symphony or quartet or whatever it was he'd chosen for the evening, absolute silence was required on the part of the audience. I remember one evening on which the wife of a first-time guest seemed especially restive and kept shifting in her seat, though Prok threw her one admonitory glance after another—her chair was squeaking and she couldn't help herself. Afterward, during the break for refreshments, Prok ignored her. She was never asked back, as far as I knew.

But this evening was different, in deference to Corcoran. The pre-concert gathering was more elaborate and animated than usual, as if this were a dinner party rather than a musical evening, and I was just about to excuse myself and go looking for Prok, when the door from the kitchen swung open and he strode into the room with the crystal bowl from our wedding party held out before him in both arms. Right behind him, holding the door, was Corcoran.

The first thing I noticed about Corcoran was the look on his face—not smug, exactly, but utterly relaxed and self-assured—and then the physiognomy itself. It's been discovered (not by us, but by other researchers in the field) that the most appealing face in either sex is the one that most closely approaches perfect symmetry, and Corcoran's certainly fit the bill. He was handsome, no two ways about it. Eyes the color of a calfskin wallet, sandy hair, the perfect expanse of brow, everything about him sleek and neat to a degree that was just pleasing, simply that. You saw him and you liked him, and when he smiled, and then when he spoke, you liked him even more. That was Corcoran: handsome, charming, gregarious. He was just slightly taller than average, five eight or nine, I guess, and he didn't look particularly athletic—too slack, somehow, too insouciant, as if there were an invisible bellpull hanging in front of him and he had only to give it a tug to summon a whole team of servants at a trot.

In the bowl, trembling at the cut-glass rim, was a deep ochre liquid in which floated the carapaces of three or four bright emerald limes, and I recognized this immediately as Prok's special version of Planter's Punch (two parts dark rum to one part triple sec, orange and pineapple juice in equal proportions, squeeze of lime, dash of grenadine, to be shaken and poured over ice and garnished with an orange slice and maraschino cherry). Prok looked bemused as he set the bowl down on the coffee table, obviously still turning over in his mind some little witticism of Corcoran's, and then his face was neutral again as he focused on the task of preparing the individual glasses of punch and handing them out to his guests. Corcoran, meanwhile, had turned to Dean Briscoe and his wife, and was already talking animatedly with them, gesturing, smiling, as slick and frictionless as a tail-walking trout, and then, even as Mrs. Professor Bouchon reminded me for the third time of how she'd subsisted entirely on turnips for a period of nine weeks in the autumn of 1917, I saw him register Iris's presence. She was in the far corner, still engaged in conversation with Professor Bouchon and the stooped, skeletal man who was too old to be Corcoran, and I watched Corcoran's head swivel on its axis and then fix on her.

"A toast!" Prok proclaimed, though he was holding up a nearly empty glass himself and had never before offered any alcoholic beverages of any kind—even his liqueurs—prior to a musicale. The room fell silent. "To Purvis Corcoran," he said, raising his glass high, "a fine and a talented young man—one who is certainly not sex shy, not in the least, and who I understand just might be willing to join us in our endeavors here . . . that is, if we can ever manage to lure him away from the cultural and physical charms of South Bend."

There was an unfocused laugh or two in appreciation of Prok's attempt at humor, and then we drained our glasses, Prok setting his down untouched and immediately looking about him as if he'd misplaced something. I patted at my lips with a napkin, smiled absently at Mrs. Professor Bouchon. She was a bore, of course, but I was nothing if not polite and attentive—that was my nature, and that was my job. But now Prok was motioning me to him even as Corcoran disengaged himself from the Briscoes and began a peculiar shuffle in the direction of my wife (it was almost a dance, and the verb "to sidle" doesn't begin to do it justice—he was skating, that was what he was doing, skating across the polished floor as if it were the municipal rink).

"Milk," Prok was saying, "Milk," as I mumbled something excusatory to the professor's wife and strode across the room. "And, Corcoran," he called, causing my future colleague to whirl round on his heels as if he were a human gyroscope Prok had just set spinning, "I'd like to introduce you to John Milk."

The chatter had started up again, fueled now by the bite of Prok's rum. I felt it myself—the rum—as a sudden stimulant, as if there were a flap at the back of my head and I'd poured it directly into my brain. At the same moment I caught a glimpse out the window of the denuded persimmon tree, framed over Corcoran's big smooth head like the standing remnant of some ancient conflagration. Corcoran was smiling. He held out his hand, the happiest man alive, the best-adjusted and most relaxed, an emperor in his own bedroom, and I took it in my own.

"It's a real pleasure," Corcoran said, pumping my hand. "Dr. Kinsey's been singing your praises for two days now. I feel I know you already."

And there was Prok's face, creased, jowly, the keen-edged eyes and accipiter's crest, hanging there between us. Prok was nodding, nodding and approving.

"Yes," I said, registering the touch of the man's skin on my own, "me too. I mean, yes, it's a, well, pleasure."

"He's turning into a first-class interviewer," Prok interjected, turning to Corcoran. "And that is no mean feat, as I expect you'll come to learn as soon as we can put things on a firm footing."

I bowed my head at the compliment to show how little I deserved it. Both men were studying me now, as if I were some rare object in a museum. "You're too kind, Prok, really you are." I focused on Corcoran. "It's all in the teaching. And Prok, he's, well—"

"I'm sure he is," Corcoran said, giving Prok his soberest look.

"A firm footing," Prok repeated, all business now. "And I certainly hope you won't keep us in suspense, Corcoran, because the project requires data, and we do have several other candidates lined up at this juncture, quite capable men, like yourself." If there had been an air of festivity to this point, Prok had erased it. I could see that he was impatient with the whole process, eager to get on with the musicale—to get it over with, though he treasured these evenings as a way of giving himself over to the emotional side he so rigidly suppressed in his workaday life—and beyond that to get Corcoran hired, trained and out in the field. He looked at us shaking hands and sizing each other up, and he saw nothing more than data, data accumulating at the rate of fifty percent more rapidly.

Mac went round with a tray to collect our glasses, and we took our seats. Prok insisted on ushering Iris and me into the front row beside Mac, and I had a brief moment of panic over the seating arrangements before opting to interpose myself between the two women, who immediately leaned across me and exchanged a birdlike flurry of conversation, not a word of which I caught. Corcoran, as guest of honor, was seated in the front row along with us, taking his place beside Iris. The room quieted. Professor Bouchon's wife returned from the lavatory and ducked into her seat at the end of the second row, while another woman (middle-aged and doughy, someone I didn't recognize, or at least didn't remember) pulled out her knitting and began counting stitches with a mute movement of her lips. There was the fragment of a moment during which Prok turned away to check the gramophone and I was able to lean across my wife and make a hurried introduction—"Iris," I whispered, "this is Purvis Corcoran; Corcoran, my wife, Iris"—and then Prok started his lecture.

"This evening we have a real treat for you—two versions of Gustav Mahler's exquisite and powerful Symphony Number Four in G Major, the one conducted by the immortal Leopold Stokowski of the Philadelphia Orchestra (though some of you will no doubt remember him from his early days with the Cincinnati Symphony Orchestra), and the other by his protégé and successor, Eugene Ormandy, the new kid on the block, as it were." Prok went on, in full lecture mode, to give a brief biography of Mahler, a discography of known recordings, both in the United States and Europe, and then a summary of the contrasting styles of Stokowski and Ormandy. "Now," he said, his fleshy face and oversized head hanging there before us like a great ripening fruit, legs slightly spread for balance, right hand gesturing, "I intend to play alternate movements, beginning with the Stokowski for the first and third and Ormandy for the second and then the fourth and final movement, but I will then conclude by playing that final movement as well in the Stokowski version. Now, of course, that movement contains the stirring soprano solo, 'Wir geniessen die himmlischen Freuden' as sung by"—and here he named two singers I'd never heard of—"but I don't want you to be distracted by the distinctions in vocal coloration, but rather attune yourselves to the tempo work of the respective conductors, all right?"

There was a vague murmur of assent, which seemed to satisfy him. Prok clasped his hands in front of him briefly, in what might have been prayer, or, more likely, conciliation, then turned away from us to start the record. We heard the needle hit the vinyl surface with a jolt, a blast of static, three distinct pops, and suddenly Mahler was there with us, at full volume.

We lingered for half an hour or so once the concert was concluded (again, the evening was unusual in that Prok generally scheduled an intermission and finished up his program with a few light pieces, but not tonight), and stood around in little groups, sipping coffee and remarking on the music and the clear differences between the two conductors, at least when those differences were made apparent in a demonstration such as this. I had entertained fond hopes of spiriting Iris off somewhere in the Nash, but it was late and there was work in the morning for me and classes for her, so I just stood there stupidly with a coffee cup in one hand and a ladyfinger in the other while Professor and Mrs. Bouchon boxed me into a corner and made appreciative noises about the music we'd just heard. Since I knew nothing about classical music, other than what I'd just picked up from Prok's remarks, I essentially just stood there listening while Professor Bouchon reminisced about having seen Stokowski in action once—it was in either Philadelphia or New York, he couldn't be sure which—and his wife pointed out that thanks to the Germans her family's piano had been destroyed, and all her joy in music along with it.

Across the room, Iris and Corcoran were getting acquainted. Corcoran had somehow managed to talk Prok into bringing out his tray of liqueurs again, now that the time was appropriate, and I watched as he leaned over to pour something the color of urine into her coffee. She hadn't enjoyed the concert. That much I was sure of. She always claimed that Prok's clinical dissection of the pieces took all the spirit out of them, and as the years went on she would come to view these musical evenings more and more as a duty than a pleasure. But on this night, as she stood there with Corcoran in the shadow of the far corner, framed by the slick black architecture of Prok's furniture and the dark stain of the walls, she seemed to be having a high time of it.

How did I know? I could tell from the way she held herself—and from her face. I knew that face better than I knew my own, and I could see by the way she widened her eyes and pursed her lips as he spoke (and what was he telling her, what was so fascinating?) that she was fully engaged. And, too, there was a way she had of ducking her head to one side as she laughed, tugging unconsciously at her right earring and shifting her weight from foot to foot as if the floor had caught fire beneath her. Body language. I'd become a student of it, of necessity. Was I jealous? Not in the least, not yet, anyway. Why should I have been? I loved her and she loved me, there was no doubt about that—and there never has been, not to this day—and all the rest, as Prok had taught me, was nothing more than a function of the body, physiology at its root, stimulus and response. I listened politely to Professor and Mrs. Bouchon, nodding and smiling when it seemed appropriate, and then I excused myself and crossed the room to collect my wife, thank our hosts and head out into the night.

THE WALK HOME was—well, I suppose you'd call it stimulating. Not in a sexual sense (as I said, we didn't have the luxury of being sexually stimulated that night), but in an emotional one. For the first minute or so we fussed with the buttons of our coats, pulled our collars up against the breeze and leaned into each other as we hurried down the street, not a word exchanged between us. There was a premonitory scent of winter on the air, of the cold rock-strewn Canadian wastes and the stiffened fur of all the hundreds of thousands of beasts creeping across the tundra up there, and the sky was open overhead, the stars splashed from horizon to horizon like the white blood of the night. I felt like going out somewhere for a nightcap, but I knew Iris would refuse—absurdly, though she was a married woman, she was still under jurisdiction of the dorm, the RA and curfew—so I found myself instead saying the first thing that came into my head. "So what about Corcoran," I said. "What did you think of him?"

Her head was down, her shoulders slumped, one hand at the collar of her coat. She was moving along at a brisk pace—we both were. "Oh, I don't know," she said. "He seems all right."

"All right? Is that all?"

My hands were cold—I hadn't thought of gloves; it was too early in the season—and I'd looped my arm through hers and forced my right hand into the pocket of my coat. The left I stuffed down into my trousers pocket and kept it there, though I found it awkward to walk off-balance like that. Leaves scuttered before us. There was the sound of a car backfiring up the street behind us, where the other guests were leaving Prok's party. "I don't know," she said again. "Persuasive, I guess."

"Persuasive? What do you mean?"

"He's a good talker. Smooth. He'll make a sterling interviewer, I'm sure."

"Do I detect a note of sarcasm?"

She turned her face to me, a cold pale oval of reflected light, then looked down at her feet again. "No, not at all," she said. "I'm just being practical. He's a perfect fit. He'll take your place without so much as a ripple—"

"He's not going to take my place."

"Did you see the way Kinsey looked at him?"

I was shivering, I suppose, my coat too light, the wind knifing at my trousers. A chill went through me. I saw Corcoran's face then, saw Prok hovering over him throughout the evening, as proud as if he'd given birth to him himself, and I knew in that moment what there was between them—the same thing Prok and I had together. I couldn't help myself. I was angry suddenly. Jealous. "So what?" I said. "What's it to me? I keep telling you, we need more hands."

Iris said nothing. The leaves crunched underfoot. After a moment, she said: "But he *is* persuasive."

"Really," I said, and I wasn't thinking, not at all. "What did he persuade you of? I'd like to know. I really would."

We were at the end of the block now, turning right, toward campus. The wind came naked round the corner. A pair of automobiles, one following so closely on the other they might have been tethered, slammed over a branch the wind had thrust in the street and the sound was like a burst of sudden explosions. "To give my history," Iris said, but I thought I hadn't heard her right, and so I said, "What?"

"To give my history. To Kinsey."

I was dumbfounded. I'd been nagging her for months, and here this new man—this persuader, this *Corcoran*—had won her over in what, ten minutes' time? "Good," I said, numb all over. "That's good. But how—I mean, why listen to him if your own, well, your own husband can't convince you, and after all this time?"

The taillights of the two cars receded up ahead of us. They both turned right on Atwater, in front of the campus, and were gone. "He just seemed to make sense," she said, "that was all. For the good of the project, like you've been saying. His wife's already arranged to give her history on your next trip to South Bend—maybe you'll get to take it, John, and wouldn't that be just swell, keep it in the family, huh?"

"And so, what's your point? I see nothing wrong with—"

"Kinsey said he'd get him a deferment."

We walked on in silence. Of course Prok would get him a deferment—he was going to get me a deferment too, for the sake of the project, and it had absolutely nothing to do with whether our wives gave their histories or not. I should have been gratified, Corcoran's first day on the scene and he'd convinced Iris to join in for the sake of team spirit, and that was wonderful, terrific news, hallelujah to the heavens, but I wasn't gratified, I was rankled. "That has nothing to do with it," I said.

The campus loomed up before us, the odd office lit in a random grid against the backdrop of the night, the frost-killed lawn underfoot, more leaves and the advancing crunch of our footsteps. "What about Mac?" she said then.

"Mac?" I echoed. I wasn't following her. "What do you mean, *Mac*? Was Mac in on it? Did she persuade you too—or help persuade you? Is that what you mean?"

"No. Mac as a wife. As part of the inner circle. Now it'll be three husbands and three wives—*if* I give my history to Prok, that is, and *if* he goes to the draft board."

"He will," I said, simply to say something, to keep it going. "He has, I mean. He's trying his best."

"But what about Mac?" she repeated. We were crossing the quad to the women's dorm, figures gathered there by the vault of the door, couples in the shadows, the rooms overhead radiating light as if all the life of the campus were concentrated there. And it was. At least at this hour.

"What about her?"

Iris suddenly jerked her arm away from my mine and quickened her pace. "You slept with her," she said. "She told me all about it." The light from the high bank of windows was on her face now, on her hair, silvering the shoulders of her coat and the dark crenellations of her hat. "She told me," she said, and there was a catch in her voice, an amalgam of rage and despair strangling the words in her throat, "and you lied to me." She swung round suddenly and planted herself right there in front of the building. "You," she said. "You, John Milk. My husband."

I didn't know what to say. It would have required a speech, would have required hours, days, would have required a whole heterogeneous philosophy delivered and debated point by excruciating point, and we had ten diminishing minutes till curfew. "I didn't want to, to *surprise* you," I said, and that was the best I could come up with. "Or, or hurt you, if, I mean, if—"

"Liar." She spat it at me. Heads turned. The lovers in the shadows came out of their clinches for one hard instant. "You're a liar," she said, then swung round, went up the steps and into the arena of light even as I stood there and watched her jerk open the door and slam it behind her.

A week later, Iris made an appointment with Prok and gave up her history. As I remember it, there was an unusual amount of rain that fall, and then an early snow. Everything was locked in, the weeks seemed to conflate, and then Corcoran sent word that he was accepting Prok's offer and the Japanese climbed into their planes in the hour before dawn and descended on Pearl Harbor. And nothing was ever the same again.

10

GIVEN WHAT I'VE already revealed about myself, I suppose it will come as no surprise if I tell you that the first chance I got (when Prok was away on his own, lecturing to a civic group in Elkhart, and, incidentally, taking Violet Corcoran's sex history in neighboring South Bend), I went straight to the files to look up two histories of special interest—Corcoran's and my wife's. Can I tell you too that I didn't feel the slightest guilt or compunction? Not this time. Not anymore. Prok was away, and it was only his intervention that would have stopped me, and nothing short of it. I broke Prok's new ironclad code within the hour, pulled the files and spread them out side by side on the desk before me.

It was just before the holidays, the whole country whipped into a froth of martial hysteria and Prok already fretting over the rumored rationing of gasoline, tires and the rest, insisting we'd have to take the train more now, the train and the bus. Everyone was distracted, shocked, outraged, so caught up in the events of December seventh that even Christmas itself seemed inconsequential—who could think of Santa Claus when Tojo and Hitler were loose in the world? As I remember, we were having a cold snap, the sky the color of shell casings, snow flurries predicted for later in the day, and I was in the office early, with a number of tasks ahead of me. There was the endless tabulation of data, the drawing up of tables and graphs, and correspondence too, though of course the volume was nothing like what we—Prok mostly—had to contend with after publication of our findings in '48. By that time, Prok was receiving thousands of letters a year from absolute strangers seeking advice or adjustments of their sexual problems, offering up their services as friends of the research, sending on explicit photos and sex diaries, erotic art, dildos, chains, whips and the like. I remember one letter in particular, from an attorney representing a client who had been charged with "knowing a pig carnally by the anus," and requesting Prok's expert testimony as to the overall frequency of such acts with animals (six percent of the general population; seventeen percent of the single rural population). Prok declined. Politely.

At any rate, there I was, bent over the desk, a Christmas carol infesting some part of my brain (Iris and I had attended a choral concert the night before), one of Prok's colleagues clearing his throat or blowing his nose down the hall somewhere while secretaries in heels clacked on by as if so many miniature locomotives were running over the rails of a miniature train set. I turned to Iris's history first, and there were no surprises there, just as I'd assumed. She hadn't even known what the term "masturbation" meant until she was seventeen and already in college, and then she was too consumed with her own inhibitions to try it more than two or three times, and never to the point of orgasm; she'd experienced both manual and oral stimulation of her breasts on the part of men—boys—other than me, but no petting and no coitus until the time of her engagement and marriage. She'd had limited experience with her own sex, and that at a very young age, no animal contacts, few fantasies. She'd never employed foreign objects, never (till now) taken the male genitalia into her mouth.

There was nothing there I hadn't seen a hundred times already, and I wondered why she'd been so reluctant to give up her history—truly, it was as pedestrian as could be—and then I wondered if that wasn't it, that she was ashamed of having so little to offer us, as if all we cared about were the extreme cases, the sexual athletes, the promiscuous and jaded, the individuals who dropped off the end of the bell curve. Could that have been it? Or was it something deeper, some resistance to the tenor of the study itself? To Prok? To me? For a minute I felt my heart would break—it hadn't been easy for her, and she'd done it for me, for me alone, and if it weren't for that she'd never have offered herself up to the project. It just wasn't in her nature. I might have taken a moment then to stare out the window into the sealed gray crypt of the sky, might have spoken her name aloud: *Iris.* Just that: *Iris.*

She was so nervous the day she came in, so tightly wound, so shy and soft and beautiful. "Dr. Kinsey," she said in a voice that was barely audible, "hello. And hello, John." I'd known she was coming, and I'd been in a state myself—all day, in fact. Every time I heard a footfall in the corridor, and never mind that it was hours still until her appointment, I couldn't help shifting in my seat and stealing a glance at the door. I thought I was ready for her, ready to put this thing behind us as if it were the last in a series of marital rites, like an inoculation or the VD test required for the license, and yet still, though I'd been watching the clock and there was an ache in the pit of my stomach as if I hadn't eaten in a week, when it came to it I was almost surprised to see her there. I'd been working on a calculation that was a bit over my head (standard deviation from the mean in a sample of men reporting nocturnal emissions) and she'd come in noiselessly, as soft-footed as a cat. I looked up and there she was, stoop-shouldered, waiflike, sunk into her coat like a child, her gloved hands, the hat; the quickest, fleeting, agitated smile on her lips. Prok and I rose simultaneously to greet her.

"Iris, come in, come in," Prok was saying, all the mellifluous inflection of his smoothest interviewer's tones pouring out of him like syrup, "here, let me help you off with your coat—bitter out there, isn't it?"

Iris said that it was. She gave me a smile as she shrugged out of her coat and Prok bustled round her, hot on the scent of yet another history. Did she look tentative, even a bit dazed? I suppose so. But I didn't really have much time to think about it one way or the other because Prok immediately turned to me and said, "I expect you'll want to go home a bit early this afternoon, Milk? Or better yet, perhaps you'd like to take your work down to the library—?"

And then there was Corcoran's history.

But Corcoran's history—and it was, as I've said, extensive, the most active single file we'd yet come across—isn't perhaps as important at this juncture as sketching in the denouement of that scene with Iris on the steps of the dorm, because that has more than a little bearing on all of this, and all that was to come. She called me a liar. Slammed the door. Left me in the cold. As I stood there in the unrelenting wind, undergraduates and their dates slipping round me like phantoms, I was faced with two incontrovertible facts: Mac had told her everything, and she'd known about it all this time, through our reconciliation, our wedding and honeymoon and the dawdling intimate Sunday afternoons of summer and on into the fall, and she'd never said a word. She'd just watched me, like a spy, awaiting her opening. Well, now she had it. The door slammed behind her, the dorm swallowed her up and I staggered across campus like an invalid till I found a pay phone and rang her number.

The RA answered. "Bridget?" I said. "It's John Milk. Can you get Iris for me?"

"Yes, sure," she said, but her voice was distant and cold, and I wondered how much she knew. The phone hit the table with a hard slap, as of flesh on flesh, and then I was listening to the buzz of static. After a moment, the usual sounds came through: the scuffing of feet in the background, a giggle, a man's voice. "Good night," somebody said, another man, and then a girl's voice: "One more kiss."

When Iris finally came on the line—it might have been two minutes later or ten, I couldn't say—she sounded as if she were speaking to a stranger, an unsolicited caller, somebody selling something. "What do you want?" she demanded.

"I just, well, I just wanted to, well, *talk*—that is, if, if—"

"What did you think you were doing?" she said then, and she sounded better now, sounded like herself—furious, but in some way resigned. "Did you think I was stupid or something? Or blind? Was that it?"

"No, it wasn't that. It was just that, well, I didn't think I'd done anything wrong, but I didn't want to upset you in any way, that was all. It's the project. It's the human animal. There's nothing to be ashamed of, nothing at all."

She was silent. I listened to the blitzkrieg of static over the line and she might have been a thousand miles away instead of just across the quad.

"Listen, Iris," I said, "you're going to have to try to overcome these antiquated notions about, well, *relations* between consenting adults—this is the modern age and we're scientists, or we mean to be, and all this superstition and fear and blame and finger-pointing is holding us back, as a society, I mean. Can't you see that?"

Her voice came back at me as if she hadn't heard what I was saying at all, a small voice, quavering around the edges: "And Prok?"

"What about him?" I said.

"You and Prok?"

I was in a phone booth, bathed in yellow light. It was cold. The wind rattled the door, seeped through the cracks where the hinges folded inward. I was shivering, I'm sure, but this was my wife, this was Iris, and I had to get everything out in the open, had to be straightforward and honest from here on out or we were doomed, I could see that now. "Yes," I said.

What came next was a surprise. She didn't throw it back at me, didn't shout "How could you?" or demand to know the occasions and the number of times or ask me if I loved him or he me or where she and Mac fit into all of this, and she didn't use any of those hateful epithets people are so quick to make use of, invert, tribad, fag. She just said, "I see."

What did I feel? Shame? A little. Relief? Yes, certainly, but it was as tenuous as the connection that fed our voices through the superstructure of the night. "I love you," I said. "You, and nobody else. The rest is all—"

"A bodily function?"

"Iris, listen. I love you. I want to see you face-to-face, because this isn't—we shouldn't, not over the phone—"

"Mac," she said, and I couldn't be sure—the connection was bad—but there was a knife edge of sorrow to her voice, a slicing away from the moment that made me feel she was about to break down in tears. "Mac and I talked. She's like a mother, but you know that, don't you? She, she told me the same thing you did. It doesn't mean anything, not a thing, it's just—just what? Animals rubbing their parts together."

"Iris," I said. "I love you."

There was a long silence. When she finally spoke, her voice was re-

174

duced to nothing. "What about me and Prok then?" she whispered. "Is that what you want?"

I might have been carved of cellulose, absolutely wooden, the effigy of John Milk propped up inside a phone booth on the far side of the quad on the IU campus on a blustery autumn night. Hammer nails into me, temper me, whittle away with every tool at your disposal: I was insensate. "No," I said. "No, I don't want—that's not . . . You don't have to do anything you don't want to do."

"But I'm giving up my history, aren't I? Why not give up the rest of me too?" A pause. The wind rattled the booth. "It doesn't mean anything, does it?"

I was made of wood. I couldn't speak.

"John? John, are you still there?"

"I'm here."

"Your—what should I call him? Your colleague—Corcoran," and now a new tone came into her voice, a tone I didn't like at all. "He certainly seemed interested. Did you see him tonight? Did you? He was on me like a bird dog."

And so I went for Corcoran's history. After things had settled down, that is—after Iris and I had talked it out a hundred times, after we'd reaffirmed the vows we'd taken before the justice of the peace and loved each other in the backseat of the Nash and scraped our money together to put down a deposit on our first apartment because this was intolerable, this separation, this yearning, these *misunderstandings,* and it was all right, it was going to be all right as far as I could tell on that hollowed-out December morning when Prok was away and I went to the files and saw what Corcoran was. What can I say? I sat there under the lamp and ran my finger down the interview sheet, noting acts, ages, frequencies, reconstructing an ever-expanding scenario of experimentation and sexual derring-do. Corcoran, in fact, was very nearly my diametrical opposite so far as experience was concerned. He'd matured early and taken advantage of it, precisely the type of individual we would later label as "high raters," who consistently, throughout their lives, experienced more sex with more partners than the average, and far more than the "low raters" on the other end of the scale.

Corcoran was raised in Lake Forest, the son of a professor who later (when Corcoran was fourteen) moved the family to South Bend in order to accept a position at Notre Dame University. His father was Catholic, but only minimally involved in the church, and his mother was Unitarian, and something of a free spirit. There was nudity in the household, both parents having been involved at one time with the Nudist Movement, a fact his father took pains to conceal from his superiors at the university, just as Prok had to keep his own private affairs sub rosa in the IU community. Corcoran could remember having experienced erections in childhood, and his mother assured him that he'd had them in infancy even—she used to joke about it, in fact, saying he was like a little tin soldier, poking right up at her every time she went to change his diaper—and while this is unusual, our research into childhood sexuality has shown that it is not at all anomalous, especially among high-rating individuals. When he was eleven, he had his first orgasm, after which he participated enthusiastically in what in the vernacular would be called "circle jerks" with other neighborhood boys, first in Lake Forest and then in South Bend, where it seems he was the initiator of a whole range of sexual activities involving both boys and girls.

First coitus came at the age of fourteen, at a summer cottage on one of the lakes in the upper Michigan peninsula. There were, apparently, a number of like-minded individuals taking summer cabins in the region—nudists, that is—and he and his two sisters went without clothing throughout the summer, "tanned," as he later put it, "in every crevice." It was his aunt—his mother's sister—who first initiated him, and from there he went on to the sixteen-year-old daughter of one of the other campers, with whom he pursued every means of gratification he could think of. He found, as he liked to say, that he had a talent for sex, that he enjoyed it more than any other activity he'd ever discovered, and before long he'd lost all interest in the boyish pastimes of baseball, trout fishing, picture shows and adventure novels, devoting himself almost wholly to satisfying his urges in as many ways and with as many partners as he could. He met his wife, Violet, in college, and she was, from the beginning, a sexual enthusiast as well (at this juncture I could only configure her in my imagination, and I have to confess that I found myself becoming stimulated at the thought of transcribing her interview for our records). They had two children, both girls, of seven and nine years of age respectively. On occasion, they entertained other couples, Corcoran himself indiscriminate as to whether he had sex with the men or the women or both (he rated himself no higher than a 3 on Prok's 0–6 scale and thought of himself as fully bi-sexual). Finally, and this was to endear him to Prok and provide an ever-accumulating source of data for our files, he kept a little black book of his conquests, which ran, at this point, into the hundreds.

Of course, much of what I've related here is what I've gleaned from my personal knowledge of the man—we've been colleagues for fourteen years now and certainly we've kept no secrets from each other— and yet the basic information was there in the files when on that December morning a week before the uncertain Christmas of 1941 I violated Prok's proscription for the second (but not the last) time. I can remember sitting there among the dried-out galls, my heart racing as I scanned the file of my prospective colleague, "Hark the Herald Angels Sing" banging around in my head, the fading tramp of students' feet trailing down the corridor. How could I ever hope to match him?—that was what I was thinking. I was sure suddenly that I'd been fooling myself all along, that Iris had been right—Corcoran was here to displace me, here to take my desk and my salary and my interviews, to unseat me in the hierarchy of the project I'd been the first to sign on for. A kind of panic took hold of me and I had to get up and pace round the room to calm myself. I made a mental list of my own virtues—loyalty, affability, a knowledge of the research second only to Prok's, my seniority on the job—and yet, no matter how I turned it over in my mind, I had to admit that Corcoran was my superior in every way, at least on paper: eight years older, the father of two, holder of an advanced degree and so high a rater he'd wind up at the top of any number of our graphs and charts. Guilty now—self-accused and suddenly ashamed—I slipped the file back in the cabinet and turned the key in the lock.

WE TOOK POSSESSION of the apartment on New Year's Day. It was far from ideal—ten footsore blocks from campus in what must have been the shabbiest neighborhood in Bloomington and damp as a tomb because it was situated at the bottom of a hill on land reclaimed from a marsh, three rooms with a bath and a perdurable smell of the old lady who'd died there (Mrs. Lorber's elder sister, if that tells you anything of its provenance)—but it was ours, and Iris, with her genius for interior design, soon transformed the place. She strung a bead curtain to separate the kitchen from the sitting room, stripped the faded Victorian wallpaper and replaced it with an almost austere modern design in beige with an overlay of gray-and-white interlocking rectangles, then, after deliberating all of one afternoon and into the evening when I got home from work, directed me in hanging the four framed woodcuts depicting scenes from *Wuthering Heights* she'd found in the back corner of a secondhand shop. Our sofa and armchair came courtesy of the want ads in the back of the paper, and Prok was kind enough to lend us the Nash to serve as moving van and Ezra helped me maneuver the things through the narrow front door. There was the bed—a double, made of painted iron and dug out of an antiques shop at a basement-bargain price—and the mattress, marked "just like new," to fit it, a bookcase to lend stateliness to the barren wall across from the sofa, my radio, an assortment of blue glass vases featuring various arrangements of dried flowers and an aspidistra Mac gave us, along with a set of pots and saucepans, as a wedding present. And Prok had been more than generous too, with a Christmas bonus that came at just the right time and the promise of a five-dollar raise to fifty dollars a week beginning the first of the year.

We had sandwiches out of a brown paper sack that first night, sitting cross-legged on the mattress we laid out on the floor because we were too exhausted to set up the bed, and we passed a quart of beer back and forth till it was gone, and then we opened another. I had the radio on—Benny Goodman playing "Don't Be That Way," or maybe it was something softer, sweeter—and I lay back against the soon-to-be-stripped wall with Iris in my arms and just held her. The smell of her hair, newly washed in our very own bathroom sink, was the smell of a new beginning, the beginning of life on our own, adult life, together and inseparable. I can't describe the peace I felt that night. We must have lain there on our new mattress, admiring our new walls, our new front door and the new bead curtains till past midnight, the beer setting us gently adrift, the music swaying softly beneath it, borne up on its own currents. Mrs. Lorber and the various RAs were no longer a part of our universe. Ezra could bathe or not as he pleased and it was nothing to me. The backseat of the Nash was a thing of the past. We had our own place now—our own home—and we could do anything we wanted, anytime, day or night, and never have to worry about the headlights of another car pulling up behind us or the fumes from the exhaust or the night that lay round us like hostile territory.

When I came in from work the next day, Iris had her hair up in a kerchief and she was wearing an apron. The apartment smelled powerfully of something other than Mrs. Lorber's deceased sister and the ineradicable ribbons of black mold that traced the lines of the fixtures she'd left behind. "What is that, Iris?" I asked, swishing through the bead curtains. "It smells, well, good—or different."

The kitchen table, layered with coats of ancient kelly-green paint and unstable on its legs, was a scene of devastation. Every plate we owned— used plates, chipped variously round the edges, a legacy of my mother and the trove of our basement in Michigan City—was either crusted with or dripping something. There was a scattering of flour, eggshells, sugar, mounds of potato and apple peelings, what looked to be ketchup and Worcestershire, and spices—marjoram figured prominently in the display, as I recall.

She gave me her smile, two arms conjoined round my neck, and a kiss. "Meat loaf," she said, "with scalloped potatoes, string beans and apple pan dowdy. The meat loaf and potatoes come courtesy of my mother, and yes, I was standing right beside her in the kitchen all those years in high school, learning how to be a good little housekeeper, thank you very much." She was grinning, pleased with herself, and so what if the place was a mess—we'd just moved in and she was cooking for me. "As for the apple pan dowdy, I found a recipe in a magazine at the library, and I didn't have a pencil so I tore it out." And there it was, a square of glossy paper, Scotch-taped to the cabinet over the stove.

I must have given her a look (she knew full well that as a former librarian I would disapprove of her defacing library materials of any kind, even ephemera like magazines), because she added, "Don't pout, John. The IU library isn't going to miss one little recipe—or do you think all the coeds are lined up at the checkout desk right now, sobbing over the apple pan dowdy that might have been?"

Inside the pocket of my overcoat, which I hadn't yet removed, was a bottle of bourbon. I thought this might be an auspicious time to draw it out and set it amid the clutter on the table. "A little celebration," I said, lifting two glasses down from the shelf and pouring us each a drink. "To you," I said, and we clinked glasses even as she corrected me: "To us!"

Can I say that that meal was the best I've ever had? Because it isn't just the quality of the ingredients or the expertise of the preparation or the elegance of the surroundings that make for a great meal, but the mood of the diner—in this case a mood elevated by the situation, by the bourbon, by *love*—that can make every bite seem as sensual as a kiss. Apple pan dowdy. Meat loaf. I ate like a man who'd been shipwrecked for a month, ate till I could eat no more, then killed the bottle of bourbon—it was a fifth and it got both of us pretty giddy, I'm afraid—and fell on my wife like that same shipwrecked sailor, or maybe his admiral.

That was in the beginning, and that was what our life was like through every day and every night. It's called happiness, and we had it in spades, as they say. The war loomed over us, of course, as it loomed over everyone in those days and months after Pearl Harbor, but Prok was good to his word and did finally manage to get me an occupational deferment, using the full arsenal of his rhetoric and all the weight of his position to bring the draft board around to the view that our research was crucial to the war effort. For her part, Iris was determined to finish out her final semester and get her degree in elementary education, but she did take a part-time job at the five-and-dime, and the money she earned there, along with the raise Prok gave me, helped lend us as much a sense of security as anyone could expect under the circumstances. Which is not to say that we didn't have to budget pretty strictly, and I cut back on smoking, we did our drinking at home and rationed ourselves to one picture a week.

Was it all idyllic? No, of course not. There was still the unresolved business of our relationship with Prok and Mac—they invited us for dinner and musicales on a regular basis, and, of course, I traveled with Prok much more than Iris would have liked, a sore point that seemed to get sorer and sorer as the years went on—and beyond that there was Iris's growing disenchantment with the project itself. "We're at war," she would say. "The whole world hangs in the balance, and you're out there somewhere in the hinterlands measuring orgasms—I mean, doesn't that strike you as trivial?"

"But you never wanted me to go, don't you remember?" I countered. "You were the one. You were adamant—you could have been Lindbergh's speechwriter, for Christ's sake. 'I will not let you go,' you said. 'It's not our war.' Remember?"

She had a way of curling her underlip, as if she'd just been poisoned, had just set down the vial and was about to turn on her perpetrator—me—with all the moribund strength left in her. "Don't give me that crap, John. I might have been against it, but that was before the Japs came into it. Now it's almost as if, as if—I don't want to say it, John. But *orgasms*. I mean, what could be more ridiculous?"

I remember a night from that period, sometime in the winter or early spring, when we had our first dinner party, and Ezra and Dick Martone, who were quitting school to enlist, came to the apartment with two girls and three tall bulging sacks of beer—and gin, which was Dick's drink of choice. Gin, in a silver bottle, with a seltzer squirter full of tonic. The girls were plain, with dead-looking hair and acne scars—they were sisters, I think, maybe even twins—and their chief attraction, aside from the lushness of their figures, was their unabashed carnality. They talked dirty, drank like sponges and had "given out" to half the men on campus. What they especially liked, being patriotic girls, was uniforms.

At any rate, we had a going-away party and Iris made a leg of lamb with pan-roasted potatoes, carrots and creamed corn, hot-from-the-oven biscuits, and a homemade peach cobbler for dessert. I spent the afternoon—it was a Saturday—running a carpet sweeper over the rug, peeling vegetables and dashing out to the store for mint jelly, cloves of garlic, a pound of margarine and whatever else she discovered she needed at the last minute. I told her it was no big deal, that it was only Dick and Ezra and their dates, a couple of girls we'd never see again and who were there for one purpose only, but Iris had worked herself into a state. "It's our first dinner party, John," she said, busy at the sink, her back to me. "The first time we've ever entertained people in our own home."

The water was running, steam rising, the heady fragrance of the roasting lamb infusing every corner of our three rooms and bath with a richness and prodigality that made me feel like a robber baron, like a sultan lounging on his multicolored carpets while the exotic smells of dinner wafted up from the royal kitchens below. I put my hands on her hips, kissed the back of her ear. "I know you," I said, leaning into her, pressing my groin into the swell of her buttocks, "you just want to show off."

She stiffened, her shoulders gone rigid, the dishes in the sink flying from the suds to the rinse pan and off to the dish rack as if an automaton were at work. "You could help," she said, without turning around. "You could dry. Because we're going to need these dishes for the table and our guests are going to be here in less than an hour."

"Sure," I said, "sure," and I picked up the dish towel and moved in beside her. "But really, you don't have to make such a production of it, not for Dick and Ezra—"

She turned to me in half-profile, showing me the underlip and a quick darting leap of her eyes. "And so what if I want to show the place off—and my husband too. I'm proud of it. Aren't you?"

I told her that I was and I tried to embrace her with a wet platter in my hand, and I suppose I was a bit awkward—not drunk yet, not by any means, but I will admit to having had a nip or two in anticipation of the party—and somehow the platter wound up on the floor. In pieces. We both stood stock-still a moment, staring down at the wreckage. This was the only platter we had, the platter on which the lamb was to have been served, and the crisis of the moment proved too much for Iris. She gave me a savage look, plunged through the bead curtains and stalked down the hallway to the bedroom, where she slammed the door behind her with an excess of force. I wanted to go to her and apologize—or no, I was angry suddenly and I wanted to kick the door, rattle the knob and shout at her, because it wasn't the end of the world, it was only an accident, and why take it out on me? *Why don't you just tear the goddamned thing off its hinges, huh?* That was what I wanted to say, what I wanted to scream. But I didn't. I got as far as the door, but the door was locked. "Iris," I said. "Iris, come on." I listened for a moment—was she crying?—then went back to the kitchen, poured another drink and got down on my knees to pick up the pieces.

For all that, the party went off as well as could be expected. Or better, even. Dick and Ezra and the two girls—let's call them Mary Jane and Mary Ellen—were pretty well lit when they arrived and I don't think they would have noticed or cared if we'd served the lamb on a skewer. As it was, I carved the meat at the stove and arranged the slices on an ordinary dinner plate, after Iris had made sure that everyone had a chance to admire it in the pan, that is, and by the time the pie and coffee were served we were laughing over the lost platter and the inept husband who couldn't be trusted in the kitchen. Mary Ellen, seated on my right, gave me a playful cuff on the shoulder and called me "butterfingers." "You butterfingers, you," she said, and both sisters let out a scream of laughter.

I brought out the bourbon to spike our coffee and Ezra poured his cup full to the brim and bolted the whole business while it was still too hot for anyone else even to sip, and then asked for more. A vacant look came into his eyes after that, but he sat there happily, one redolent arm thrust over Mary Jane's shoulder while his free hand maneuvered his fork round a second piece of cobbler. He and Dick, who'd stayed on through the fall for graduate school and a teaching assistantship in the Engineering Department, were leaving in the morning for basic training. This was their last night of freedom, their last fling, and I wanted—Iris and I wanted—to make it memorable for them. There was beer left still, and when we moved away from the table and into the sitting room, Dick poured a fresh round of gin and tonics for himself and the girls.

At some point, and I didn't really recall too much of it the following morning, let alone what I can summon up at this juncture, the conversation turned away from the war and how Dick and Ezra were sure to turn the tide, whip Hitler with one hand tied behind their backs and come steaming home triumphant by fall, to me and my situation. Dick was sunk into the couch, his arm fastened round Mary Ellen and his hand resting lightly on her left breast. The radio was on, the volume turned down low out of respect for the neighbors, something moody and blue seeping in out of the airwaves. "Kinsey really did get you that deferment, huh?" he said.

"Kinsey?" Mary Ellen said. "You mean *Professor* Kinsey? Dr. *Sex*?"

Mary Jane, who'd been locked in an embrace with Ezra in the easy chair, lifted her head a moment to let out a giggle.

"That's right," I said. "Yes. Dr. Kinsey. I work for him."

"Doing research," Iris put in. "He's terrific with statistics, he does all the figures—"

Ezra let out a snort. "I'll bet he does—but what do you do with all those *figures*, huh, John?" And he and Dick shared a lascivious laugh.

Mary Ellen was slow to form the next thought, but I watched her compose her features and struggle with the notion till she got it out. "You mean . . . you, you're a sex researcher?"

I was seated on one of the hard-backed kitchen chairs I'd dragged into the sitting room to make space for everyone. As I've said, I had no qualms whatever about the work—I was Prok's right-hand man, his disciple in everything—but I didn't like having to defend it, not in mixed company, not in my own living room. I looked into Mary Ellen's eyes—she had nice eyes, her best feature, along with her consequential figure—and just nodded.

She made a cooing noise, turned to Dick and kissed him full on the mouth. When she came up for air she treated us to a coy smile and said that sex was the most fascinating subject she could think of. "I love sex," she said, cooing still. "I love men, I'm sorry, but that's just who I am." A pause. "Do you get to watch? I mean, when people are . . . when they're"—she looked to Iris to see how far she could go—"you know, *doing* it?"

I was long past the stage of coloring, but I felt the heat in that room and my wife's eyes on me, and Dick's and Ezra's too. "No," I said, raising a hand to smooth back my hair, "no, we just—"

"They just ask questions," Iris answered for me. She gave me a look I couldn't fathom. "Isn't that right, John?"

Mary Jane had come back to consciousness, sprawled in Ezra's lap and with her lipstick smeared in broad ovals at the corners of her mouth. Her eyes were dull with drink and the lateness of the hour. The faint wail of a saxophone rose from the radio like the cry of a strangled soul, then faded out again. "Questions?" she said. "What kind of questions?"

"How much do you masturbate?" Iris said, and she was still looking at me. "How many men you've been with, how many orgasms you have, how often you fellate your boyfriends. That sort of thing."

There was a silence. Dick lifted his head as if he hadn't heard a thing we'd said for the past five minutes. "I don't know," he said, "but I guess you've got a wife and all that, so I can't blame you for taking the deferment, I really can't."

Another silence. The comment just sat there crouching over the evening, and no one wanted to touch it, least of all me. The announcer came on then to inform us that the station was signing off for the night, and we all stared at the radio till the fuzz of static replaced the broadcast and I began to think it was time to turn in. Finally Mary Jane roused herself again long enough to ask, "What's fellate?"

Iris and I had agreed beforehand that we would retire early and let the two couples have the benefit of the couch and easy chair and the equable temperature produced by the furnace rather than having to make do in a frigid hallway somewhere or the backseat of a borrowed car, and so we went to bed not long after that and left our guests in the front room. I was fairly well gone at that point, and so was Iris, and I don't think I even got around to brushing my teeth before I fell into the bed as if I were plummeting from a high dive. Instantly, I was asleep.

I woke sometime in the night with a dry throat, a condition that often afflicts me when I've been drinking. I was having a dream about walking into the drugstore and ordering a chocolate phosphate that magically turned into a Coca-Cola on ice with beads of condensation standing out on the glass that was like a cold compress in my hand, and then I was up and out of bed and heading toward the bathroom in my bare feet. But it wasn't just my feet that were bare. I've always slept in the nude, at least ever since puberty when my mother stopped looking in on me at night, and in the disorientation of waking I'd forgotten entirely that there were guests in the house. The truth of it was, I was still drunk. Even so, something alerted me to the situation—a scent, the sound of a furtive movement, the faint trembling light of the candle Iris had left burning in the main room.

It took me a moment, fumbling my way down the hall step by faltering step, to realize that I was not alone. There was someone else there, a deepening shadow that seemed to concentrate the darkness against the wall just in front of me. I reached out a hand and felt flesh, a woman's flesh, two complicit breasts to linger over, the heat of her skin, of her tongue, and a whisper: "I was looking for the bathroom . . ."

What would the proper host have done? Escorted her to the lavatory, I suppose. Provided her with fresh towels, a bar of soap, eau de cologne. I didn't do any of that. I didn't even have time to think, really—one minute I was asleep, and the next I was making tactile contact with the smooth hot inflammatory skin of a strange naked woman in my own hallway even while the sounds of distant snoring and the ticking, somewhere, of a clock, came to me. Her nipples were hard, her vagina was wet. Instantly, we were inseparable, and I don't blame myself, not in the least, because it was the natural impulse of the moment, uncomplicated, salubrious, research on the fly, as it were.

I never did discover whether the friend of the research that night was Mary Ellen or Mary Jane, not that it mattered.

11

Automobiles were on my mind that winter, even as rationing went into effect and the auto assembly lines switched over to war production. In December, just before the Japanese struck, Prok had turned his considerable investigative energies to seeking out a second car, reasoning that it was unfair to deprive Mac and the children of transportation for such long stretches when we were out on the road lecturing and collecting histories. After having examined a dozen or more vehicles for sale around town, he finally settled on a late-model Buick that featured almost-new tires and an unblemished finish in a shade of blue so deep it was almost black. The car had belonged to one of his colleagues at IU, an elderly music professor who had passed on the year before and left the car garaged with his widow, who'd never learned to drive it. Prok sat down with the widow over tea one afternoon and collected not only the car (at a rock-bottom price), but her sex history as well. I was there, at the house on First Street, with Iris and Mac and the children, all of us waiting on pins and needles to see if Prok could pull it off, and I remember the celebratory flash of the sun catching the windshield as he swung into the driveway and the look of naked triumph on his face. Ostensibly, by the way, this was to be Mac's car, while we continued to rely on the wheezing, unsteady Nash for our peregrinations, but in fact, from the day Prok motored into the driveway with it, the Buick was ours.

Of course, since Iris and I were to set up our household a few weeks later, our need for a car wasn't quite as urgent as it once was, but still I think I wanted an automobile of my own at that time as much as I'd ever wanted anything. On Sunday afternoons Iris and I would bundle up and walk across town—and sometimes even out into the nether areas where the houses gave way to farms and open land—just to have a look at this or the other ancient collapsing Tin Lizzie we couldn't have afforded in any case. But we looked, because you never knew. Every time I saw an ad—"1929 Model A, good tires, needs work, best offer; 1934 Chevy, clean"—I built something in my mind, and every time, without fail, I was disappointed. I wasn't a mechanic. Didn't, in fact, know the first thing about spark plugs or flywheels or transmission oil. I had hope, though. I was looking for something reliable, something cheap and efficient, with a sound engine and rust-free chassis, and I didn't care about make, model or year. Because, as I've said, the road out of town always beckoned to me and I sometimes felt—as both student and married man—that I was stranded in Bloomington, surrounded and given up for dead. There were buses, the train and my trips with Prok, sure, but if I had four wheels under me I could be my own master and go where I liked, when I liked.

It must have been toward the end of February, and I can't really recall whether it was before or after our little farewell party for Dick and Ezra, when Corcoran came to Bloomington to stay. There had been a break in the weather—clear skies and daytime temperatures that climbed up into the forties—and I remember I was just leaving Biology Hall to run an errand for Prok when a horn tooted and a car pulled up to the curb in front of me. It was a yellow Cadillac La Salle convertible with crisp whitewall tires and chrome hubcaps, and the top was down. At the wheel, in a tweed jacket and with a pipe clenched in the corner of his mouth, was Corcoran. He thrust both arms up over his head and waved them in transect as if he were lost at sea. "John," he called, "hey, John! I've arrived!"

I don't know what I said to him in response, something about the car, I suppose. It was the sort of thing you came across in magazines, hands down the sportiest vehicle Bloomington had yet to see.

"You like it?" he crowed, sliding out the door and pumping my hand. "Just got it a week ago. And you should have seen the thing cruise on the way down here, my hand on the horn the whole way because all you cows and you farmers in your hay wagons, just look out, here I come."

I made admiring noises, traffic passing by on the pavement, students pausing to gawk, the barren trees jammed into the ground up and down the street like so many gibbets. There was a suitcase on the passenger's seat and a new tan fedora atop it. I was wondering how Corcoran could have afforded such a car on a social worker's salary (his wife's people had money, as I was later to learn), and wondering too how much Prok had offered him to come work with us—more than I was getting, that was for sure—when he looked from me to the suitcase and back again and said, "You think this'll be okay here? The suitcase, I mean. Just for a minute?"

"Well," I said, "I guess, well, sure—"

"You wouldn't want to keep an eye on it, just for a minute, would you? See, I wanted to dash up and let Prok know I'm here—the apartment I can find afterward, that's no problem . . . and by the way, I wanted to thank you, and Prok, I guess, for finding me the place."

This was the first I'd heard of it, and my face must have showed my confusion, because he added, "Or whoever was responsible. It was kind. It really was. See, I'll need the next couple of months, while I'm batching it, to find something suitable for Violet and the kids, and this is really—well, I know how hard it is to find something in the middle of the semester . . ."

As it turned out, I must have stood there at the curb for half an hour while flocks of students, townspeople and the odd professor ambled by, watching over the car and maybe even pretending it was mine. I did inspect the thing pretty thoroughly, even looked into the engine compartment and the trunk (tennis racket, a set of golf clubs, a pair of two-tone shoes and another suitcase), and toward the end of my little wait I sat at the wheel, just to get the feel of it. I was beginning to feel a bit uneasy—Prok would be wondering where I was—when I saw Corcoran and Prok emerge from Biology Hall and start up the walk toward me. Prok was moving along at his usual stiff pace, and Corcoran was keeping right up with him, stride for stride. They were both smiling, gesturing, deep in running conversation. Guiltily (though I don't know why I should have felt guilty—I *had* been asked the favor of minding the car and suitcase, after all), I slid out from behind the wheel and eased the door shut. When they got to the car—to me, that is—both men looked up as if surprised to see me there, and Prok went immediately to the passenger's side, lifted out the suitcase and handed it to me. He climbed in and shut the door without a word, then looked up at me and said, "See if you can fit that in down behind the seat, Milk, will you?" And then to Corcoran: "Very impressive, Corcoran, I must say. But a bit flashy, isn't it?"

I could see that Prok was getting a very high reading on his frugality monitor, not to mention his concern over any of his employees drawing undue attention to himself. The look on his face told me everything: *A yellow convertible,* he was thinking. *And what next?* No doubt too he was calculating how Corcoran's layout for expenditure could have been more propitiously budgeted to the project, though that wouldn't have been fair, *but still—*

Corcoran was oblivious, as he so often was—this was one of his talents, as I was soon to learn. He coasted through life on greased wings, and he took what he wanted and gave what he liked in return. If the situation was oppressive or difficult in any way—and as the project took off and the public descended on us there were any number of occasions that caused me to squirm, to say the least—he simply ignored it. I don't think it was because he was insensitive, quite the contrary, but just that he didn't care. He was blithe. He was insouciant. He was Corcoran— and the world had better look out. All he said to Prok now was: "V-8 engine, Prok, runs like a dream. And does it have *power.*"

I managed to fit the suitcase in the space behind Prok's seat, and then Prok gave my hand a pat and said, "Go on back up to the office, Milk— I'm just going to take a few minutes here to settle Corcoran in at his apartment, just to get it over with. We'll be back inside of an hour, and then"—with a glance for Corcoran—"then we'll get some real work done."

Corcoran put the car in gear, revved the engine and took off with a squeal, Prok already beginning to gesticulate, no doubt giving him the first in an unending series of driving instructions. I stood there and watched the car recede down the block, then I turned round and went back up to the office in Biology Hall, the errand—whatever it was—all but forgotten.

THERE WAS A dinner party that Saturday evening, then a musicale the following Sunday for a select group of Prok's colleagues, including the Briscoes and President Wells (Prok was showing off his newest acquisition, this handsome, shining, confident young man with the yellow convertible, and that was only to be expected), and then the three of us were off on our first collective trip in the streamlined shell of the Buick. Prok drove, Corcoran in the passenger's seat beside him, while I sat in back and gazed out on the countryside. As usual, Prok never stopped chattering from the moment he and Corcoran swung by the apartment to pick me up till we arrived at our destination, Corcoran, as new man, doing his best to punctuate some of Prok's fluent observations with thoughts of his own, and I just leaning back with half-closed eyes and letting it all drift over me. Was I disillusioned over having my place so immediately and completely usurped? Yes, of course I was, at least at first. But I quickly began to see the advantage in it—I now had someone to divide Prok's attention, absorb some of his excess energy as well as his criticism, his rigidity and, not least, his sexual needs. And so, as I sat back against the seat in the relative luxury of the Buick, half-listening to the conversation up front and replying with a nod or grunt when I was directly drawn into it, I began to feel that things were definitely looking up and that some of the pressure I'd been under was bound to lift.

Because I *had* been tense. In the weeks before Corcoran's arrival Prok and I had been working on our grant proposals as well as pushing ourselves to travel and collect as many histories as we could before rationing went into effect, and Prok had become increasingly demanding under the sway of his own pressures. Perhaps it was the uncertainty of the times (he never said a word about the war, never followed developments or mentioned world events except as they related to the research, and yet it was clear that he was increasingly concerned over the potential damage to the project), and perhaps too it was that he felt me drawing away from him emotionally since I'd moved in with Iris. He wanted sexual relations and I acquiesced, but there was no joy in it, and he must have felt that. I remember one night in a motor court outside Carbondale when he came to me naked and erect after a long day's driving and interviewing and all I wanted was to turn over and go to sleep, and I told him as much. "What's the matter," he said, easing down on the bed beside me, "you're not getting sex shy on me, are you?"

"No," I told him, "no, I'm just tired," but I did what he wanted, and all the time I was thinking of Iris, back at home, waiting for me.

On this particular trip—the first of a hundred or more the three of us would make together over the years—we were on our way to Indianapolis, where we were planning to interview prostitutes and, if possible, their johns, Corcoran looking on in the role of apprentice till he could acquire the necessary skills to join in. Prok was in high spirits, more talkative even than usual, and though he drove erratically, also as usual, and tried to maintain an even speed so as to conserve on fuel, we made good time and got to our hotel early enough to have a collegial dinner before going out on the streets. I'd wanted a highball before the meal, and so had Corcoran, but Prok wouldn't hear of it—we'd be in and out of bars till all hours, and as that would almost certainly involve the consumption of a certain unavoidable quantity of alcohol there was no reason to start now; the last thing he wanted was an inebriated interviewer. Didn't we agree? Yes, of course we did, albeit reluctantly, and after the waiter took our menus, Corcoran and I exchanged a glance over our glasses of virgin soda water and I thought I'd found an ally. We were under Prok's thumb—always, and willingly—but we could rebel too, in our own quiet, complicit way, and that made me feel ever so slightly wicked, as if I'd found an elder brother to kick under the table when our father's back was turned.

So we sipped soda water while Prok had a Coca-Cola ("I don't really like the taste of the stuff," he claimed, though his sweet tooth was legendary, "but it's good for the caffeine, keeps me alert, you know") and outlined our plan of attack for the evening. "Actually," he said, pausing to look round him at the nearly deserted hotel dining room, "I have no doubt but that we'll pick up some excellent data tonight, the sort of high-rating, lower-level histories we're always seeking for balance—and you remember Gary, Milk, and how rich an arena that was—but I've been thinking that it's not enough."

The hotel was in the low- to mid-price range, and its restaurant was nothing to write home about (again, Prok's thinking was, Why waste project funds on some fleeting luxury?), and he set his knife and fork down carefully beside the salad plate, on which three slices of pickled beet remained in a gory pool beside a brownish fragment of lettuce.

"What do you mean?" Corcoran asked. "No one's ever accumulated data as accurate and complete as what you've showed me, you and John, I mean."

Prok shot another glance round the room to make sure no one was listening, then leaned in over his plate. "What I'm thinking is this: while it's all well and good to record direct accounts of sexual activity—while it's essential, the backbone of everything we're trying to accomplish— nevertheless we could be doing more, much more."

Corcoran's eyes jumped to mine and I gave him the faintest shrug of my shoulders. I couldn't imagine what Prok was getting after.

"I've arranged something a little different for tonight," Prok said, picking up his fork as if he'd never before seen a utensil, then setting it down again as if he couldn't guess at its function. "Let me put it this way," he went on, "while we have been able, as a species, to domesticate animals and breed them into their many varieties—to observe and ma- nipulate, as it were, their sexual activity—we've never had the opportu- nity to do the same with human beings. To observe, that is."

"Yes, of course," Corcoran said, jumping on the notion, "because while we all participate, we're never exactly watching, are we? Or even wearing our scientist's hat—isn't that right, John?"

"Well," I said, "yes, sure," and I gave him a grin. "In the heat of the moment, you're not thinking in scientific terms; no one is—"

"Right. And where's your objectivity?" Corcoran's face was lit with pleasure. He was on the trail of something. The moment was his. "When you're with a woman, in the throes of passion, everything else, every other consideration, goes right out the window, and at a certain point you don't even care what she looks like, just as long as—"

"Exactly." Prok gave us a satisfied look, the blue claws of his eyes pulling us to him even as he paused at the approach of the waiter and the three of us sat in silence as the steaming plates appeared before us. The waiter hovered expectantly—Could he bring us anything else?—and Prok waved him off. When the man had retreated to the far side of the room, Prok took a moment to poke at his entrée—corned beef and cabbage, sans potatoes, one of his alimentary prohibitions. "Tonight we're going to do what no one in the field has even so much as dared before, at least as far as I know—that is, we're going to observe the act itself, in commission. It's all been arranged."

We waited in a kind of palpitating silence, till he added: "With one of the young women, that is. We'll be secreted in the room—in the closet, actually—when she entertains her tricks."

"You mean"—I couldn't help myself—"we'll be peeping then, as if we were, well . . . you mean, like Peeping Toms?"

"Voyeurs," Corcoran pronounced with a faint smile.

Prok gave each of us a look. "Yes," he said. "That's it exactly."

JEAN SIBELIUS—one of Prok's particular favorites—had been the focus of the previous week's musicale, and I remember having gone to Prok's without much enthusiasm only to find myself pleasantly surprised. As I've said, swing was more to my taste than classical, but the music Prok chose that night was melodic and warm—almost dreamlike—and before I knew it I'd lost all consciousness of my surroundings and let it sweep over me like some natural force. I suppose something similar happened to jitterbuggers out on the dance floor—to Iris and me when we danced before a bandstand—but all that was driven by the intoxication of the moment and the coronary thump of the bass drum. This was different. Once the record began I found myself slipping into a reverie, utterly calm and at ease, my thoughts bumping along from one repository to another without logic or connection. For the first time I began to understand what Prok saw in his music and why he was so devoted to it.

Iris and I had been on time, for a change, and I'd taken a seat in the front row, as Prok expected me to, with Iris on my right and Corcoran seated beside her, the preliminaries this time reduced to a few minutes of strained chitchat with President Wells over a plate of stale crackers and rumless fruit punch, and I remember speculating about Wells even as he eased into the seat beside me. He was a short, energetic, rotund little man, and a great supporter of Prok against the storm of criticism, invective and innuendo that continually came our way, and yet he was unmarried in his forties, and that seemed odd—very odd—given the time and place. I made a note to myself to pull his history the first chance I got.

The room was cold that night, Prok having turned down the thermostat in the expectation that the aggregate body heat of his guests would be sufficient to warm the place up—that and the coloration of the music. There was a small fire going in the hearth, but it was dying because Prok didn't like to fuss with tending a fire when a record was on the turntable, and who could blame him? So we were cold, and I suppose I must have felt a bit sorry for the first-time guests who hadn't dressed for what might as well have been an outdoor concert, as Iris, Corcoran and I had. For all that, Prok was his usual warm and outgoing self, entertaining us with a brief lecture on the composer's career and the piece we were about to hear. He talked of Sibelius's love of his native Finland and the charm of his sylvan settings and how the majority of his symphonic poems were based on Finland's great epic, the *Kalevala*.

Then the room hushed as he retreated to the gramophone, sharpened the needle and let it fall. We heard "The Swan of Tuonela" that night and selections from "Pohjola's Daughter," and, as I say, I simply closed my eyes and let the music carry me away. There was an intermission, during which Mac served refreshments—non-alcoholic—and the guests got up and mingled, and then there were a few songs ("Was It a Dream?" and "The Maid Came from Her Lovers' Tryst," both of which I remember distinctly because as soon as I was able I went out and purchased a recording of them, which I treasure to this day), and then the party broke up. The reason I mention all of this, is because of what happened during the intermission—or what might have happened, because I can't say for sure that that was the beginning of it, though I have my suspicions.

In any case, I was doing my best with a fistful of stale crackers and a cup of tepid punch while Prok pinned me in the corner along with President Wells, expatiating on the music we'd just heard (and on the research, of course), when I looked across the room and saw that Iris was alone with Corcoran, just as she had been on the last occasion—back in the fall—when we'd all three gathered for a musical evening. I wouldn't have paid it any attention really if it weren't for what she'd said that night over the wire while I sank miserably into the glass crevice of the phone booth: *He was on me like a bird dog.* Prok was informing President Wells and me (though I'd heard it before) that he liked to study the faces of the audience during musical performances for signs of sensual transport—one professor emeritus in his seventies had actually become physically aroused one night over Mahler's *Das Lied von der Erde*—but I was watching Iris, watching her face, watching Corcoran and how he seemed to anticipate her every movement, as if they were dancing to an imaginary orchestra. "Prok," I said, cutting him off, "President Wells, I, just, well, if you'll excuse me, please, and I'll be right back—"

Prok gave me a wondering look, but he didn't miss a beat. As I wandered off, making sure to head in the direction of the lavatory, I heard him say, "Of course, I would never name that gentleman, for fear of embarrassing him, but really, there's absolutely nothing to be embarrassed about—"

I came up on Corcoran and my wife from behind, having made a detour past the lavatory in the event that Prok and Wells were watching, and I seemed to have startled them. Whatever they'd been talking about so intently just a moment before fell off a conversational cliff and the two of them looked up at me in confusion. I wanted to say something blithe like, "Am I interrupting anything here?" but when I saw the looks on their faces the words died in my throat. "Hello," was the best I could manage.

Corcoran treated me to a smile. "Oh, hi, John. We were just discussing the way Prok seems to have taken charge of our president." He gave a sidelong glance to where the two of them stood in the corner still, Prok lecturing, Wells stifling a yawn.

Iris said, "He never misses an opportunity, does he?"

I was angry suddenly, or testy, I suppose—testy would be a better word. "He has every right," I said, staring her in the face, and I wasn't smiling, wasn't keeping it blithe and light. "Because you'd be amazed how much each department has to fight for funding. And we've got the prospect of expanding our grant base, which in turn should help convince Wells—or the university, I mean—to give us more for salary, materials, travel expenses and the like."

Iris was wearing a little smile of amusement. "So?" she said.

"So don't go accusing Prok, of, of—*pandering*—or whatever you want to call it, because if it weren't for him we'd be—"

"Up shit's creek without a paddle," Corcoran said, expanding his smile. He had a glass of mauve-colored punch in his hand and he was rotating it against his palm as if he were about to snatch up three or four others and start juggling them to break the ice and get the party rolling, irrespective of Prok and Wells and the high tone of the evening. But then he laid a hand on my arm. "It's okay, John," he said, and Iris warmed up her smile too, "we're on your side. We're all in this together, aren't we?"

I SUPPOSE THAT was when I first began to have my suspicions—Corcoran, the sexual Olympian on the loose, and Iris, the love of my life, stinging still over what I'd done in bed with Mac and with Prok—but I was paralyzed. I wanted to believe that there was nothing between them beyond the usual goodwill that existed between one colleague and the spouse of another, and I was afraid of any sort of confrontation with Iris, because I knew she'd throw it back at me, every phrase, every excuse and rationale, every occasion on which I'd ever spoken of our animal nature and sex as a function divorced from emotion of any kind, no different from hunger or thirst. Of course, I dropped hints. Put out probes, as it were. I came home from work, complimented the aroma of whatever was cooking, poured a drink, sat with her and reviewed my day, and of course my day included Corcoran—I dropped his name whenever I could, scanning her face for a reaction. There was nothing there.

But what did she think of him? I pressed. Oh, he was nice enough, she said. Better than she'd thought. She really did think he was going to work out, and she was sorry if at first she'd seemed negative about him. "Yes," I said, "I told you, didn't I?" And then a smile, as if it were all a joke, "And what about his bird dog propensities?"

She was busy suddenly—a pot was boiling over on the stove, there was an onion to be peeled. It was a joke, sure it was, and she just laughed. "He's like that with all women," she said. "And men too. But you would know better than I, John."

If I were a turtle—one of Darwin's Galápagos tortoises Prok was always talking about—I could have pulled all my exposed parts back into my shell, and I suppose, in a metaphorical way, that was what I did do. We went to Indianapolis, the three of us, colleagues on a mission, and Corcoran and I sat across the table from each other exchanging our own private signals while Prok informed us that we were going to do something illegal, if not immoral, despite the testimonial letters from Dean Briscoe, President Henry B. Wells and Robert M. Yerkes: for this night, anyway, we were going to be Peeping Toms.

The idea of it, I have to admit, made my blood race. I think we all have the capacity for voyeurism, we all burn to see how other people live through their private moments so that we can hold them up against our own and thrill with a feeling of superiority, or perhaps, on the other end of the spectrum, feel the sharp awakening slap of inadequacy. *So that's how it's done,* we think. *I could do it that way. Or could I? Yes, sure I could, and I could do it better too. I'd like to be doing it right now—but look at her, look how she clings to him, how she rises to meet him, how—*

Beyond that, of course, we were scientists, and we convinced ourselves that we had a duty to the research that rated above all other considerations. We needed to do fieldwork, like any other investigators, needed to engage in direct observation of sexual experience in all its varieties, else how could we presume to call ourselves experts? How could our data have the kind of validity we sought if it were paper data only? If you think of it, everything we were attempting to accomplish, every close observation, every measurement, should have been rendered redundant by a hundred studies that had come before us. But there weren't a hundred studies, there weren't fifty—there wasn't even one. We'd built our civilization, gone to war, delved into the smallest things, the microbe and the atom, and still the hypocrites and the lily-whites were there to shout us down: sex is dirty, they said. Sex is shameful, private, obscene, unfit for examination. Well. We got up from the table, paid the check and walked out into the night to prove them wrong.

This time it wasn't raining, wasn't even all that cold, considering the season. Prok wasn't wearing an overcoat, though the streets were damp from a series of rainstorms the previous week and he'd pulled a pair of rubbers on over his shoes. Corcoran was wearing his tan fedora and a pale camel trench coat, as if he'd just stepped off the set of a picture about foreign agents and the assignations of war. For my part, I was dressed as usual, coat and tie, no hat, and my feet—in a pair of fresh-polished cordovans—would just have to get wet if I wasn't absolutely vigilant about the puddles in the street. "All right," Prok said, gathering us to him on a street corner, "I think it's this way, down this street and one block over to the left—and the contact, incidentally, is a young woman, a redhead by the name of Ginger."

We found Ginger without any trouble, dressed in a cheap imitation fur and sipping a soft drink through a straw on a bench in the back of the local pool hall. There was a man slouched beside her, a sharp dresser with a flashy tie and elephantine pants that concealed the boniness of his legs, till he leaned back to light a cigarette and crossed his ankles, that is. He regarded the three of us with suspicion—he was the pimp, and his name was Gerald—till Prok won him over with a brief speech in the vernacular and a contribution of three dollars to the support of his staff and a dollar more for each history he brought us, including his own. Ginger was a big girl, five eight or five nine, twenty-two years old, with a solid, thick-fleshed physique that would sink her in fat by the time she was thirty and the milky coloring of a natural redhead. She didn't make a move. Just sucked at the straw within the red bow of her mouth and watched her pimp fold Prok's bills and tuck them away in the voluminous pockets of his trousers. "Okay," Gerald said then, "okay," and he smiled to reveal a set of hopeless teeth, variously colored. He looked to Ginger and the smile vanished. "So what you waitin' for? Go peddle your goods—and take these gennemen with you."

Then we were outside, dodging puddles, Prok at Ginger's side as if he were escorting her to a cotillion that would miraculously appear round the next corner in a pure white outflowing of light, Corcoran and I bringing up the rear. It was an awkward scenario, none of us—even Prok—inclined to say much, Ginger leading us on with a hypnotic shake and roll of her hips, faces appearing out of the dark to dodge away again, slatted eyes assessing us as potential johns or mugging victims. Ginger had a ground-floor room, convenient to the street, in a house from the Victorian era that was in serious need of repair and paint too, and she separated herself from Prok and strolled right in through the unlocked door without turning around to invite us in or even to see if we were still there.

The room itself was a shambles, but that's about all I remember of it. Except that it had a high ceiling and a big, walk-in closet that had once been an anteroom of some sort and was now separated from the bedsit by a finger-greased quilt stretched across the doorway on a wire. Ginger's dresses—a dozen or more, smelling of her underarms and the cologne she used to mask the smell of her tricks, one from the other—hung on wire hangers in the forefront of the closet, while her shoes and undergarments were scattered underfoot. "Here it is," she said in a high, fluting voice that could have belonged to a woman half her size, to a child, and she held out her hand, palm up, to receive the dollar Prok had promised.

"Swell," Prok said, reverting to the vernacular. "Just grand." He'd swept back the quilt to inspect the arrangements and the grin he gave her was almost ghoulish—the light was bad, yellowed and corrupt, issuing from a lamp at the bedside over which Ginger had laid a saffron scarf for effect, and it made his whole face seem to sag under the weight of his satisfaction. I glanced at Corcoran. He looked like a ghoul too. I wondered what my own face looked like. "This is just the ticket," Prok said, laying the dollar bill across Ginger's palm while we looked on as if we'd never seen money exchanged before, "but I wonder if you could do me a favor, Ginger? Just a tiny little one?"

She'd turned her back to secrete the money somewhere on her person, and now she swung back round suspiciously. "Depends what it is."

"Would you mind if I"—Prok crossed the room and lifted the scarf from the lamp—"just removed this for the evening? Unless you're really stuck on it—"

A slow smile crept over her face. "Yeah," she said, "yeah, sure. You're the doctor."

When she'd gone off in search of her first trick (and I don't know if I've explained this previously, but "trick" was the term prostitutes used then to describe their johns, and, of course, it's still in current usage, though in those days only our lower-level subjects would have been conversant with it), we did what we could to make the closet comfortable, shifting some of Ginger's underthings from the floor and moving the room's only chair into the closet with us. We agreed to take shifts in the chair, so as to relieve the tedium of standing—this was going to be a long night, and we couldn't afford to give ourselves away by any stretching or cracking of joints, let alone the fatal cough or sneeze. We talked in whispers now, all three of us keyed up with anticipation. What was it like? Like the juvenile thrill of hide-and-seek, I suppose, only with the delicious adult taint of the verboten layered over it. Living sex. We were about to witness living sex.

It didn't take long. There was the sound of footsteps on the porch, a low murmur of voices, then the click of the doorknob, and the three of us froze in place. The way Prok had arranged the quilt—and we'd all examined it from the outside to make sure we were completely hidden—gave us two points of access. Corcoran was at one end of the closet, peeping through the slit there, and Prok and I at the other. Prok was in the chair, perched at the very edge of it, as motionless as a fakir on a bed of nails, and I was hovering over him, so close we were practically conjoined. Movement, voices. I felt him tense. I didn't dare breathe. From where we were stationed, we had a view of the now brightly lit bed, but we couldn't see the door or what was happening there as Ginger and her john apparently embraced, clothes rustling, the allision of their shoes on the floorboards, and then the sudden startling basso of the man's voice. "Shit, is this it?" he said, and the voice thrilled me, resonating from the cerebral cortex that registered it all the way down to the soles of my feet. "Well, shit," he said again, movement now, and there they were—there *he* was—not five feet from us. I'd like to report that the man was some sort of bruiser, a tattooed sailor stranded ashore, a *specimen*, but that wasn't the case. He was slight of build, average height, average in every way, with skin that seemed granulated under the harsh accounting of the light. Ginger was there, looming, the meat of her rump, her breasts. "You going to blow me," he said, "or what?"

"Anything you want, honey," she said, bending to run her hand up the crotch of his pants. "You're the doctor."

She wasn't wearing underpants—stockings, yes, supported by black garters at the swollen midpoint of her thighs—and she was reluctant to fully undress, though that was what we wanted, as Prok had made clear beforehand. (From her point of view, removing her dress and brassiere was both a bother and a waste of time, an impediment to moving her johns in an efficient conga line in and out of the room, but from ours it was essential, if we were to observe the way the female corpus responds to sexual stimulation.) The man—the trick, the john—let her undo his fly while she was still fully dressed, and he massaged her scalp, squeezed her head as if it were a bowling ball he was about to pluck up and fling down the alley, as she fellated him. Her lips shone with the viscous fluid released by the Cowper's glands by way of lubrication, and she took the whole thing into her mouth—and this was amazing—his entire phallus, right down to the root, as if she were a sword-swallower performing at the carnival. We were later to discover, incidentally, that among the many physiological modifications occurring during sexual activity, suspension of the gag reflex occurs in a high percentage of both women and men, thus demonstrating the adaptive role of the oral component in sexual response. But all that aside, can I tell you how amazed I was? How—unprofessionally—titillated?

He pulled away from her before he reached orgasm, and only then did he begin to tug down his trousers. "On the bed, sister," he told her, "because if you think you're getting off that easy, you're nuts. I paid for a fuck, didn't I?"

Ginger stretched out on the bed in compliance, hiking her skirts to display her nakedness, but then she seemed to remember her mission— we were in the closet, her auxiliary johns, and we'd paid for our fuck too—and she sat up again, took his penis in her hand and caressed it a moment, then pulled the dress up over her head and reached behind her to release the snaps of the brassiere and let her breasts fall free. Immediately he was on her, stimulating her nipples both with his fingers and tongue even as she guided him into her, but then, suddenly, he stopped in mid-thrust. "The light," he said. "What gives with the fucking light? Don't you know nothing about romance, sweetheart?"

She did. Or at least apparently she did. Because until the moment he pulled out of her and snatched for the light, she'd been moaning and singing out to him as if there were no man better in the world and no moment richer than this. "Leave it on, honey," she said. A theatrical pause, one finger stuck in the corner of her mouth. "I want to see every inch of you."

12

The first thing I did when we got back to Bloomington three days later was go straight to Iris. It was past two in the morning, I was dirty, exhausted, hungry—famished, actually, since we hadn't stopped to eat—and I could still feel the throb of the Buick's engine like a permanent dislocation in the back of my skull. I'd personally recorded eight histories, including Gerald's and Ginger's, and I'd watched from the closet with Prok and Corcoran as Ginger entertained sixteen different men over the course of the three nights we spent in her company. Surprisingly, there really wasn't all that much variety, and while I admit to being in a state of permanent sexual excitation throughout the entire time we were there, the novelty did tend to wear off after a while. The men were hirsute, glabrous, tall, short, fat, thin, they wore long johns, boxer shorts, sports coats and flannel shirts, galoshes, boots, tennis shoes. They had moles, birthmarks, tattoos, they were circumcised and uncircumcised, their penises angled to the left or the right or straight up, and they folded their clothes neatly atop the bureau or threw them on the floor in a twisted heap. As for the sex, it was entirely conventional, beginning with a brief period of fellatio in about half the cases and a certain degree of fumbling, licking and squeezing in the others, followed by penetration, the pumping of the naked white buttocks that were variously flaccid or tight with the strain of the gluteal muscles, Ginger's increasingly theatrical simulation of orgasmic ecstasy, and then the decline and fall and the absolute lack of interest in the female's nudity, her exposed genitalia or even her face and eyes as the clothes were silently gathered up and hurriedly pulled back on and the door swung open and shut again.

But I went to Iris. Went directly up the walk from the backseat of

Prok's car and into the apartment, which was utterly still and dark now but for the light leaching in from the streetlamp and the moon that hung over the town with all its symbolic heft. I went straight into the bedroom. She was asleep. Bundled in the blankets against the cold, her hair splayed out on the pillow, one eye winking open as I switched on the light beside the bed and the clock glowing and no sound anywhere in the bottomless cavern of the night. I was stripping off my clothes, jacket, shirt, trousers, and the light was on. I wanted her to see me, wanted her to admire me and the souvenir I'd held on to for her through three grueling days in a whore's closet in Indianapolis. "John?" she murmured. "John? What time is it?"

There was the smell of her, a smell I can't describe, her own personal fragrance that was like no other, a compound of body heat, the emollients she used on her face and hands, the traces of her shampoo and her perfume and the natural oils of her scalp. "Shhhh," I said, and I waited for her to acknowledge me, to see what I'd brought her, and yes, I know that our published research has shown that the majority of females are unaffected by a display of the erect phallus and that a portion are even offended by it, but it didn't matter a whit that night. I was stimulated to the point of bursting and I wanted her to see that, to know it and feel it. "Shhhh," I repeated, and I threw back the covers, all that warmth, the sight of her naked feet and ankles, her face turned to me now and her arms spreading wide in invitation. I slipped between the covers and lifted her nightgown and we never did shut the light off, not till morning.

One night in a thousand nights, in five thousand nights, a man and his wife—a sex researcher and his wife—gratifying each other's needs. It was the most ordinary thing in the world—or no, it was celebratory, celebratory still because we had the license of our own apartment and no John Jr. to worry over or anything else. We had intercourse six or seven times a week. We experimented with extended foreplay, with teasing, strip poker, with all the coital positions we could imagine. And all the while the project went forward, gained momentum, and Corcoran and I became ever more deeply involved—as friends, as colleagues—even as we jockeyed for position with Prok.

Corcoran offered me a ride home after work one evening, and we wound up stopping off at a tavern for a drink. I thought of calling Iris, to tell her I'd be late, but there was no need really—the hours were never regular when you worked for Prok, and there was no telling when I'd be home on a given evening, but it was rarely earlier than seven. The tavern was the same student hangout I frequented senior year, the place where I'd sat breathless and palpitating with Laura Feeney and her friends in the wake of Prok's arresting slide show. I remember smiling at the memory. It had seemed like a hundred years ago—and it was, in terms of what I'd learned and experienced since. Corcoran laid a bill on the bar and asked me what was so amusing.

"I don't know," I said. "It's this place, I guess. I used to come here as a student."

At that moment, both of us, as if we were being manipulated by a force beyond our control, turned to watch a coed in a pair of slacks saunter by on the arm of a boy who couldn't have been more than eighteen. "What a waste," Corcoran said.

I was grinning. "Oh, yeah," I said, "yeah. A real waste."

He was staring off into the distance now, idly tapping a knuckle on the bartop. "I could relate to her," he said. "Couldn't you?"

I said that I could, and then the bartender appeared and we both ordered martinis, up, with a twist, though I didn't really care all that much for gin—Corcoran ordered first, that was all, and he made it sound good, so I said, "Second that."

What did we talk about that night through three martinis and a kind of delirium that made my head feel as if it were a pan full of sloshing water? Sex, certainly. The project. Prok. The immediate future, as in our next trip, scheduled for two days later. At some point, there was a pause, and he leaned forward to light a cigarette. "How do you feel about that, the trips, I mean?" he said, shaking out the match. "Is it—I don't know—difficult at all? With Iris?"

I looked out over the room a moment, caught the gaze of the coed we'd tracked earlier, and immediately dropped my eyes. "Well, yes, sure." The third martini had lost its chill. The roof of my mouth felt as numb as if I'd been given an anesthetic at the dentist's—gin, I didn't like gin, and I didn't know why I was drinking it. "But it's part of the job. She understands that. We both do." I lifted the thin-stemmed glass to my lips, conscious all at once of its fragility. "But what about you? You don't, well—what about your wife?"

Corcoran turned a bland face to me. There were golden highlights in his hair. He gave an elaborate shrug that began in his upper arms, migrated to his shoulders and finally to his neck and the rotating ball of his head. "It's hard, but Violet's got to keep the kids in school till June—we couldn't very well uproot them. And when I do manage to see her—you remember I drove up there weekend before last?—when we do get together, believe me, the sex is terrific, red-hot, like you wouldn't believe."

I didn't know what to say. To this point I'd laid eyes on Violet Corcoran just once, when she'd come to town on the bus one weekend to get her bearings and help motivate her husband to find a suitable place for the long term. She was attractive, certainly—of Italian descent, with skin the color of olive oil, very dark eyes and a mouth that turned up in a natural pout, even at rest—but she was nothing compared to Iris. Maybe I was prejudiced—of course I was—but to my mind Iris was a true natural beauty and Violet Corcoran wasn't in that category at all. I tried to picture her with her clothes off, picture her in bed with Corcoran, but the image flickered and vanished before I could get hold of it. Finally I said something like, "I guess there are some advantages, then, hmm?" And tried for a complicitous smile.

There was traffic in and out of the bar, the high whinny of a laugh, the squeak and shuffle of men's shoes. The jukebox was playing something I didn't recognize. Corcoran squinted against the smoke rising from his cigarette, and I couldn't help thinking he should be the one to give Prok his lessons in savoir faire. "Yeah," he said finally, "but there are other advantages too, if you know what I mean."

"No," I said, "what?"

He drew at the cigarette, exhaled, set it down carefully in the corner of the ashtray and picked up a hard-boiled egg, which he began delicately tapping against the surface of the bar. I watched him for a moment as he peeled back the shell and the membrane beneath it, salted the slick white surface and took the entire thing into his mouth. "You know, batching it," he said, chewing around his words. "Opportunities arise. Not that they wouldn't if I were back home in South Bend—and you know I never let convention stand in my way—but it's just that it's, well, easier if you're off on your own. Less complicated, you know?"

I thought about that a moment, thought about him and Iris at the musicale, thick as thieves. I had nothing to add.

"But you," he said, turning to me, his face as bland and ineluctably handsome as any movie star's, "don't you . . . get out a bit yourself?"

As I've said, I was past the stage of reddening—that sort of emotional report card was strictly for adolescents—but I did feel my heart pound out of synchronization for just a moment even as the lie flew to my lips. "No," I said, thinking of that dark groping encounter in the hallway of my own apartment, "no, not really."

THEN THERE CAME a night when I did get home early—just past six—and Iris wasn't there. I'd been in the biology library all afternoon, sequestered in a back corner working on a series of tables *(Accumulative Incidence: Pre-Adolescent Orgasm From Any Source, By Educational Level; Active Incidence and Percentage of Outlet: Petting to Orgasm, By Decade of Birth)* in support of our grant proposal to the Rockefeller Foundation, my head down, minding my own business, while Elster stalked back and forth and glared at me from his desk as if the scratch of my pencil or the setting down of my ruler and T square were exploding the bibliographical calm of the place. I tried my best to ignore him, but whenever he came into my range of vision with an armload of papers or a cart of books, I couldn't help wondering why he hadn't been called up to fight our enemies in Europe, Africa or the Pacific. But then I studied him for a moment when he was busy at his desk—the slack posture, fleshless limbs, the glowing bald spot on the crown of his head that was like the stamp of early senescence—and came up with the answer to my own question: he was IV-F, IV-F without a doubt.

And what was I doing in the library in the first place? Simple. Prok had evicted me for the afternoon so that he and Corcoran could conduct simultaneous interviews of a cohort of southern Indiana psychologists who were attending a conference on campus. I'd interviewed two of them already that morning and early afternoon, and now Prok was putting Corcoran to the test, checking Corcoran's position sheet against his own the minute the subject had left. And so I got home early, and Iris wasn't there.

I saw that she'd made a casserole—tuna and macaroni, with layers of American cheese spread atop it—and left the morning's dishes to dry in the rack, and that was fine, nothing out of the ordinary there, but where could she be? Had she forgotten something at the store, some essential ingredient—coffee, margarine, a cake mix for dessert? Perhaps she'd just stepped out for a minute to go round the corner to the grocer's. Or maybe it was some sort of emergency. Maybe she'd cut herself or fallen—or it might have been one of the neighbors. I thought of the old lady upstairs who'd been the special friend of Mrs. Lorber's sister. Mrs. Valentine. She was so frail—so winnowed and reduced—that she could have gone at any moment and no one would have been surprised. But it wasn't anything to concern myself over. If something had happened, there was nothing I could do about it. I would hear in due time, so why worry? The casserole was in the oven, the bourbon on the shelf. I poured myself a drink and went to the radio to see what was on.

I was on my third drink and the top layer of the casserole had developed a color and texture I'd never before seen in a baked dish, not that I'm much of a cook, when I began to feel concerned (about Iris, that is; for all I cared the casserole could find its way into the trashcan and we'd make do with sandwiches and three fingers of bourbon). I'd listened to *Vic and Sade,* then a program of war news and Kate Smith singing "God Bless America," and now I began to pace round the room and peek out through the curtains every time I thought I heard someone coming. Could she have gone to the office to surprise me? Was I supposed to have met her somewhere? Did we have concert tickets for the student-faculty orchestra? Were we dining out? But no, there was the casserole, irrefutable evidence to the contrary. I decided to go back to campus, to the office, just to check if she was there, to see if I'd somehow managed to get my signals crossed, and so I shrugged into my coat and hat and started out the door.

The light had faded from the sky and the streets were pretty well deserted. I had the bourbon to fuel me, and, as I say, I kept myself in tip-top shape, so I was able to make the ten blocks to campus in what must have been record time, though I wasn't running or even jogging, but moving along expeditiously for all that. I climbed the familiar steps of Biology Hall, went in through the unlocked door and mounted the stairs. I found the office dark, the building silent. Perhaps I rattled the knob of the office door a time or two—I could have used my key, but what was the sense?—and then turned and went back down the stairs. I thought about another drink, about stopping somewhere, but I didn't.

All the way back, I kept thinking how odd this was, how unlike Iris. She was taking classes still, of course—this was her last semester—and that involved research papers, library work and such, but she'd always taken care of that sort of thing during the day so we could be together at night. I set a brisk pace on the way back, because I was concerned now, frustrated in the way I got on the rare occasions when I misplaced something and wound up endlessly retracing my steps, running round in circles till I either found it or gave up on it altogether. My pen, for instance. I had a sleek silver Parker pen Iris had given me for my birthday, and one afternoon after lunch I couldn't seem to find it. Up and down from my desk I went, back and forth to the filing cabinets, the bookshelves, the anteroom, till Prok lifted his head from his work and asked in an irritated voice what exactly I thought I was doing. I told him, and he gave me a long wondering frown before going back to his papers, but I was up and down all afternoon until finally, on my sixth or seventh trip, I found the pen in the men's washroom, on the metal tray above the sink, where I'd scrawled a note to myself after washing up. It was a bit neurotic, I suppose, but when I felt that things were out of my control, that something was wrong, that I'd fouled up somehow, I had difficulty breathing and I'm sure my blood pressure shot up. Jittery. I felt jittery, as if I'd consumed one too many cups of coffee. That was how I felt now, coming up the final block in the dark, when I should have been home with my wife and a casserole.

A car door slammed up ahead, I saw the red flash of the taillights like cigarette burns in the dark garment of the night, and the car—it was light-colored—passed under the streetlight and disappeared at the far end of the block. Was there a figure there, a shade against the shade, moving up the walk of one of the houses on our side of the street? It was dark. I couldn't be sure. Two minutes later, I came through the door and Iris was there, bent over the oven.

"Jesus, Iris," I said, "where've you been? I was, well, I was here and I turned off the casserole—"

She looked flushed, as if she'd been running laps or springing up off the trampoline at the gymnasium, an exercise she loved, incidentally, and I'd watched her at it, the tight focus of her concentration, her arms flapping as if she were about to take wing and her hair rising straight up off her head in defiance of gravity. The casserole was in her two hands, the red pot holders climbing up over the handles. She set it down on the counter and gave me a smile that faded as soon as it bloomed. "That was the right thing to do," she said. "Because it would have burned."

I was in the kitchen now, the bead curtains rattling behind me like a swarm of angry insects. "But where were you? I was worried. I, well, I went all the way back to the office, just to see if, you, well, if you were there."

"I'm sorry, John. I didn't expect you so early." She was opening a can of peas, her back to me so I couldn't read her face, brisk movements, the pot, the flame, and then to the table to set out the plates and cutlery. "Do you want milk with this tonight—or will water do? Or juice?"

"What was it?" I said. "Studying? Didn't you just have an exam last week?"

She was in motion, brushing by me, the beads rattling, to the table and back. She wasn't looking at me, her eyes fixed on anything but me— the table, the icebox, the floor. "Studying," she said, "that's right. I was studying."

"Where? At the library? Because I was in the bio library all afternoon, and you should've—but you needed the main, right? For what, for Huntley's class?"

The casserole had gone to the trivet in the center of the table and she'd poured me a glass of milk, staunch and white, the glass standing beside the plate in a still-life representation of the ordinary. She looked harried. Looked unhappy.

"What is it?" I asked. "What's the matter?"

She held herself right there, the peas in a slotted spoon, the hot pan balanced at the edge of the table. "Oh, John, I'm not good at this. I'm just not."

This was the fever, this was it, the moment that had my heart pounding. I didn't say a word.

Two scoops of peas, one on each plate. "You might as well know—I was with Purvis. I—I went to the office, looking for you, to surprise you, and he was just locking up . . ."

"That was his car? Just now, when I came up the street?"

She nodded.

"Well," I said. "And so? Did he give you a lift home, did you go out with him for a drink or what?"

"No," she said, her eyes dodging mine. "Or, yes, he gave me a lift home."

I shrugged. He'd given her a lift. Case closed.

She was still holding the pot of peas, still hovering over the table. "But I'm not going to lie to you, John, neither one of us is. I'm not that sort of person, and I think you know that." There was a pause then, and I suppose somewhere in the world ships were passing in the night, freighters foundering, the ice narrowing in the narrow passages. "We—we had a relationship."

I just stared at her.

"In the office. On the desk."

"In the office," I repeated.

"Purvis and I." Her eyes went cold a moment. "It's nothing to worry over," she said, and the pot found its way to the table even as she wiped her trembling hands on the apron at her hips. "You know, John," she said. "The human animal."

IT WAS AROUND this time that we began to conduct our first interviews with children, which, as most people will know, served not only to break a long-standing taboo but to lay the foundation for the many studies into childhood sexuality that were to follow. In fact, in trying to reconstruct events, I'm almost certain that our initial foray into the field must have come just after that unnerving scene with Iris—the very next morning—because I remember distinctly how unsettled I was, turning the situation over and over again in my mind as if it were a sharp-edged object I could worry until it was as smooth as fired clay. It was odd. As I sat beside Prok in the front seat of the Buick on our way to the Fillmore School in Indianapolis, listening to him chatter on about infantile sexuality and the preadolescent awakening of desire, I couldn't help feel that my emotions were on a collision course with my objectivity. I kept telling myself that I was a researcher and that sentiment had no place in the scientific ledger, no quantifiable value at all. It was a negative, a disqualifier, a weakness that had to be conquered. Prok had indoctrinated me well, and I was getting there, almost over the hump, but I kept slipping back. I couldn't help myself.

"Are you all right?" Prok asked, giving me one of his hooded, searching looks.

I must have been twisting in my seat, jittering a knee, lifting my chin to the flicker of roadside light as if I were on my way to martyrdom, but at least I didn't have to face Corcoran, not yet anyway—Prok had given him three days off to see to his affairs and attend his daughters' Easter pageant back in South Bend.

"Milk?" Prok said. "Milk, did you hear me? I said are you all right?"

"Yes," I said. "I'm fine."

The motor hummed beneath the floorboards. Scenery flitted by. Prok cocked his head and shot me another glance. "Getting enough sleep? Because really, Milk, you look like one of the living dead—"

"No, I—well, not last night, I guess."

He went off on a mini-lecture about the vital importance to health of the three telling factors—diet, exercise and sleep—and was in the middle of one of his long, artfully congested sentences when he suddenly caught himself. "But, John," he said. "Are you—do you have something caught in your eye?"

I told him that I was allergic, that was all. "Hay fever," I said.

He was silent a moment. Then he turned his face to me, his eyes shifting focus briefly and then darting ahead to the road. "A bit early in the season, isn't it?"

In the end, I hadn't confronted Iris—how could I? How could I have said anything without looking like a hypocrite? We'd eaten our dinner in silence, listening to the radio. She had a text—*Modern British Poetry,* my old marked-up copy—spread out on the table beside her plate, and she never lifted her eyes from it, though I didn't see her turn the page, not once. When we were finished, I tried to get up and clear off the dishes, but she wouldn't let me. "No, no," she said, taking the dirty plate from my hand—I'd eaten nothing, the macaroni like sodden cardboard, though I'd chewed as if my jaw would break—"let me do it. You must be tired."

Her face was bloodless, her hair hanging limp, and I didn't want to think of what had happened to the curl she spent so much effort on every night and worked so hard to bring to perfection each morning. I *was* tired. So tired I could barely lift my arms from the table. "Sure," I said. "Okay."

I made it as far as the couch and just lay there with one hand laid flat across my forehead while the radio spat and crackled and the water ran in the sink. For a long while I listened to her move about the kitchen, the cabinets opening and closing, the hiss of the water, the clink of glass and crockery, and then I lit a cigarette and studied the ceiling. There was band music from somewhere, a variety show, the Chiquita banana jingle—I must have heard that ten times over. Finally, she came to me. I felt her there, standing over the couch, but I never turned my head. "John," she said, "John, please," and I could hear the emotion saturating her voice, the plea for absolution that made me stiffen and harden all the more—mineralizing, I was mineralizing like a stick of wood buried over the eons in the deepest layer of sediment. I said nothing. She made a speech then, tearful, punctuated by sobs—she didn't mean to, it wasn't anything, the madness of the moment and somehow she couldn't resist him, Purvis, because he was so *persuasive*—but I never moved. After a while she went into the bedroom and shut the door.

Can I tell you now that I felt as if a stake had been driven through my heart? I knew why she'd done what she had—it didn't take a psychiatrist to figure that out. She'd had one man in her life, just one, and I'd had Mac and Prok and she could only guess whom else. The whole project, the whole regime, demanded that she acquire experience—we looked up to the high raters, didn't we, no matter how unbiased we tried to appear? I knew where the guilt lay. I knew who was at fault. But if I believed in what I preached, if I believed in my work—and I did, and still do, fervently—then I had no right to say *J'accuse*.

I went to bed late that night, so late there was the sound of birds stirring in the bushes outside the windows and a slow gray seep of light infiltrating the curtains. She was awake still. I saw her there in the bed and all the sadness of the world came to lodge in my throat, acidic and unforgiving, until I steeled myself and swallowed it down. What I wanted more than anything in that moment was to have her, to throw back the blankets, strip off her nightgown and bury myself in her.

She might have said my name, I don't know, I don't remember. But I remember this: we came together without preliminaries, without words, and I drove at her in an ecstasy of release and she responded in kind, fighting me, thrashing at me, furious with the sting of her guilt and the pleasure too, and all the while I was thinking she hadn't run the tub, hadn't washed Corcoran out of her, and he was right there with us, grinning like an actor.

Yes, and it felt odd too to be returning to Indianapolis, this time to sit with children from the local elementary school instead of some jaded prostitute and her string of faceless johns, and in the pure efflorescent light of day instead of in the shadows of the night. Prok had arranged the session with the principal and one of the kindergarten teachers, both of whom were friends of the research, and we'd modified the standard procedure to accommodate the children's level of apprehension. Also, we were careful to get the parents' consent beforehand—and the parents' histories, as well—and we conducted the interviews in tandem and with at least one parent present so that there could be no hint of impropriety.

We arrived early, the children still in their classes, the stiff, hacked grass of the athletic field greening round the edges and the sun hanging bright over the playground and its idle swings and seesaws and the rigid superstructure of the monkey bars. The school's principal—a Mr. McGuiniss, whose comfortingly unremarkable history we'd taken on our last trip during the diurnal hours when Ginger was unavailable— met us at the door and led us into his office. There was a flag, a stuffed owl, the crude, curiously mobile abstract paintings of very small children decorating the walls, and a window that gave onto the playground. "Dr. Kinsey," McGuiniss said—he was small, bald, his fingertips stained with nicotine—"and Mr. Milk, welcome, and thank you for coming. We have, as you know, several students who've volunteered, and their mothers are here as well. Everyone is very excited."

We began with two sisters, aged seven and five. The principal made his office available to us—he'd already furnished it with a few playthings and picture books to put the children at ease—and the girls' mother ushered them into the room. She was a tall brunette, not unattractive, with prominent cheekbones and a mass of healthy-looking hair swept up atop her head and held in place with a pair of mother-of-pearl barrettes. I knew her age—twenty-nine—because I'd taken her history myself on our previous visit. (She was monogamous, married eight years, eager to experiment with coital positions and oral-genital contacts, but as yet very much a novice and fighting her husband's resistance—he was a devout Catholic and typically repressed, and he was the only one of this particular cohort who'd declined to be interviewed himself.)

Prok and I rose to greet her, even as McGuiniss bowed out of the room with a sheaf of papers under one arm. "Mrs. Perrault," Prok cried, taking her hand and flashing his smile, "so nice of you to come. You know my associate, Mr. Milk, of course. And now"—turning to the girls and giving a formal bow that was calculated to charm them—"who are these beautiful young ladies?"

The girls—Suzy was the younger, Katie the elder—both had their mother's coloring and her outsized liquid eyes. They gave us prim little smiles, pleased to be the centers of attention, and yet they seemed a bit flustered too, uncertain as to what was expected of them. "I'm Katie," the seven-year-old said. "And this is my sister."

"Suzy," the sister put in, swaying back and forth over the pivot of one foot. "My name's Suzy."

"Ah," Prok said, and he was still bent at the waist, his face at a level with theirs, "so you're not princesses, then? I thought you were princesses for sure."

A giggle. More swaying. "No," the little one said, and they both burst out in laughter.

"And what do you think of having the principal's office all to ourselves? Pretty special, isn't it? Well, this is a special afternoon for some very special little girls. I'm Uncle Kinsey, and this"—indicating me, and I smiled as genuinely as I could to show everyone concerned how harmless I was—"is Uncle Milk."

Both girls gave me a brief examination, their smiles flickering uncertainly and then coming back to life again as Prok went on in his most facetious and whimsical tones: "And what of Mr. Owl—you see Mr. Owl up there? He's going to play a part too, because the game I've thought up for us is a camping game—do your mommy and daddy ever take you girls camping?"

Oh, yes, yes, they did. And where had they gone camping? A look to their mother and back again. "In the woods," Katie said.

"Good, very good." Prok had got down on the floor now, and he eased himself into a cross-legged posture, as if he were an Indian chief presiding over a sheaf of tobacco leaves. "All right, girls," he said, "sit right here with me, that's right, cross your legs just like this, because we're going to pretend that we are out in the deep woods sitting round a campfire roasting marshmallows—do you like marshmallows? Yes, good. Very good. Of course you do." And, magically, from his coat pocket, appeared two white puffs of the very substance.

I should say here that despite what you may have heard to the contrary—and I am aware of some of the more malicious and odious rumors spread by enemies of the project, people who choose to see dirt in everything—that Prok was as delicate, respectful and proper with our juvenile subjects as anyone I could imagine. And we all learned from him and attempted to adopt his methods, though none of us could ever manage to establish the instant rapport with children that Prok was capable of. This was one of his great gifts as an interviewer, and as a personality too. Just as he could sidle up to a urinal at Penn Station and immediately cultivate the trust of a homosexual hustler in search of action or wander the Negro neighborhoods of Gary and Chicago with the authentic argot dropping from his lips, so too could he relate in the most open and innocent way to children. And children's histories were vital to the research, because while we routinely asked our subjects about their initial sexual awakening, nearly all of them were at least somewhat hazy on the details, and we felt we could correct for the inadequacy of memory in our adult subjects by collecting data directly from children, whose experiences were still vivid and ongoing. That seemed to make sense. And yet, inevitably, there was criticism—we were sullying the children's minds, leading them astray, that sort of thing. But I can assure you that nothing could have been further from the truth.

On this particular day, as Prok led these two beautiful wide-eyed girls through an imaginary forest and sat with them round a fanciful campfire, ever so subtly and gracefully posing his questions, first to Suzy as her sister played in the corner, and then to Katie, I have to admit it was an education for me. The questions were entirely innocent, yet telling: *Do you play more often with girls or boys? Do you like boys? But boys are different from girls, aren't they? Yes? And how is that? How do you know?* I sat there in the principal's chair, clinging to a grin and exchanging the occasional glance with the mother while recording her daughters' responses, and I felt myself expanding into the possibilities. Children. I'd never really thought much about them one way or another. In fact, they'd always made me nervous and uncertain—I didn't know how to act around them, didn't have a clue—and now here was Prok, one of the most eminent men of his generation, a starred scientist, showing me the way. "Just talk to them," he said. "Just talk and listen."

All this sex, and what was it for? For this. For children. It came to me as a revelation that afternoon, my brain struggling with the insupportable image of Iris spread out naked on my desk and Corcoran rising above her even as the piping immature voices gave rise to opinions and qualified expectations. They trooped through the office, one child after another, shy, brassy, eager, reticent, and I found myself groping toward the beginnings of perspective. Those organs we'd so diligently focused on with Ginger and her clients, the acts, the consummation, the *reproductive tract*—it came to this, to children. And John Jr. wouldn't be born for another five years yet.

WE GOT BACK to Bloomington late on the third night, after having overstayed ourselves in order to record a number of serendipitous interviews that came our way at the last minute—the school janitor and his brother, who ran the filling station, and a local minister, his wife and their seventeen-year-old daughter. I came in the door and there was Iris, in her kimono, waiting up for me over her poetry text. "But you didn't have to wait up," I said, and she came to me, her eyes full, and held me, rocking gently with me there in the middle of the living room. "Don't you have class tomorrow?"

"Hush," she said, "hush," and then we went to bed, and I was made of wood. We had intercourse though, almost as soon as I could get my clothes off, and she might have broken down during the process—might have cried, might have buried her face in my chest and sobbed for all I know—but I was made of wood and I can't really say for certain. She was gone before I woke in the morning, and then I was at the office in Biology Hall, surrounded by galls and running a slow, lingering hand over the surface of my desk as if I'd never seen anything like it before.

13

THERE WAS THE sound of footsteps clattering in the stairwell, the faint reverberant echo of voices, growing louder now, coming closer, and my first thought was of Prok, returning from his early class with students in tow. By this time I'd recovered myself and I was settled in at my desk, organizing the material we'd collected at the Fillmore School and sinking numbly into the familiar grip of routine. I'd sharpened all the pencils, squared away the papers on the desk. A mug of black coffee stood at my elbow, giving off steam. Outside, beyond the windows, a mild drizzle softened the lines of Maxwell Hall, across the way.

But that was Prok's voice, no doubt about it, a sort of lucid mumble rising above the ambient sounds, and there was another voice attached to it, hearty and unflappable, a voice I couldn't help but recognize, and a moment later, there they were, Prok and Corcoran, ducking through the door. "Milk, good morning," Prok sang out, "sleep well?"

"Morning, John," Corcoran put in. He stood there hovering over Prok's desk, no more than ten feet from me, arms akimbo, exuding nonchalance—nothing wrong here, not a thing in the world. "I tell you, it's good to be back—the drive was killing, absolutely killing. And how was your trip?"

For the moment, I was at a loss for words. I suppose I'd thought of nothing really over the course of the past four days but Corcoran and what I would say to him, what he would say to me, how I'd face up to him and what it would mean for all of us—for the present and the future too. "We, well," I faltered. "I'm sure Prok—" I gestured vaguely, and then let my hand drop, too full of anguish to go on.

Prok was already seated at his desk. His head was down, and he was shuffling through his papers. "Splendid," he said. "Couldn't have been better. We got some fourteen juvenile histories, very interesting, very significant, and it just confirms in me the resolve to get more. Isn't that right, Milk?"

"Yes," I said. "It was, uh, a real experience."

Corcoran was watching me closely. "Oh?" he said. "How so?"

Prok's head rose as he glanced up to monitor my answer.

"I don't know," I said, reaching for the coffee cup to cover myself. "It was—I guess you'd have to call it an awakening. Of sorts."

Corcoran was smiling, always smiling. He was so at ease I could have killed him, could have leapt up from the desk and strangled him right there in the middle of the linoleum floor and never thought twice about it. I think he was about to press it further, ask for some clarification— because this was interesting, it was. He might have been about to say, *What do you mean?* Or turn it into a joke: *But how long were you asleep, then?*

Prok got there first. "Good," he said. "Well put. I felt it myself, and this is a new avenue—one we have to tread a whole lot more in future, but cautiously of course." There was a silence as we all three contemplated just what that caution entailed, and then Prok, in his briskest voice, said, "I'm going to need you to take some dictation, Milk—follow-up letters, and not just to the parents, but to the children as well." He glanced up sharply, as if I were about to demur. "Because, you understand, we have to be absolutely aboveboard here, and the parents will see the letters— follow-up, that is, and I can't stress how vital this is. And should be. My feeling is that if a volunteer goes out of his way to be a friend of the re-search, no matter how young or old, we are in that person's debt and should acknowledge it at the very first opportunity."

I should point out that these were still the early days of the Institute for Sex Research and we didn't yet have a full-time secretary or even ad-equate office space, though with the arrival of Corcoran, Prok had con-vinced the administration to incorporate the classroom next door into what was now a little suite of offices. A door had been carved out of a wall of the original office, giving onto this new space, and Corcoran's desk was located in there, as well as the overflow from our files and the ever-increasing library of material in the field that Prok had begun to amass (including the erotica collection so much has been made of recently). But truly, from humble beginnings . . .

In any case, I mention it only because of what came next—just to locate you in situ—so you can appreciate where all three of us were in relation to one another. The pleasantries were over, and Prok was the last to tolerate any procrastination—work was what he wanted and work was what we were there for—and yet still Corcoran hadn't moved. "John," he said, dropping his voice, "listen, I wonder if you and I could have a few words, later, after work, I mean. We must talk."

Prok lifted an eyebrow, shot us both a look. "That would be splendid, Corcoran," he said, "but I assure you I'll be more than happy to fill you in on the details of what we've learned, and what we hope to learn. Fascinating, really."

Corcoran's smile was fading. "No, it was another matter, Prok."

"Oh?"

For all my will power, I felt the color rising to my face. I stared into the coffee mug.

"A private matter," Corcoran said.

Prok's eyebrow lifted a degree higher. "Oh?"

"It's nothing, really. Just—well, just something between colleagues, isn't that right, John?"

What could I say? I'd been shot through the shoulder blades, brought down at a gallop on the high plains, hooves kicking futilely in the air. I felt the shaft of the arrow emerging under my breastbone, the hot sharp little tip of the skewer. "Yeah," I said. "Or, yes, I mean. Yes, that's right."

I don't suppose it will come as a surprise if I told you I had trouble concentrating on my work that day. As much as I tried to fight them down, I was prey to my emotions—stupidly, I know. Falsely. Anachronistically. I kept telling myself I was a sexologist, that I had a career and a future and a new outlook altogether, that I was liberated from all those petty, Judeo-Christian constraints that had done such damage over the centuries, but it was no good. I was hurt. I was jealous. I presented my ordinary face to Prok and, through the doorway and across the expanse of the inner room, to Corcoran, but I was seething inside, burning, violent and deranged with the gall of my own inadequacy and failure—my own *sins*—and I kept seeing the stooped demeaning figure of the cuckold in the commedia dell'arte no matter how hard I tried to dismiss it. I stared at Corcoran when he wasn't looking. I studied the way he scratched at his chin or tapped the pencil idly on the surface of the blotting pad as if he were knocking out the drumbeat to some private rhapsody. *Kill him!* a voice screamed in my head. *Get up now and kill him!*

Then we were locking up, the three of us gathered there at the front door of the office while Prok turned the key and we chatted, in a valedictory way, about the business of sex. Prok had his umbrella with him, and his galoshes, but no overcoat—it was too mild and he was the sort who could endure anything, in any case—and he made some comment about the two of us, Corcoran and I, needing to better attune ourselves to the weather as neither of us had any protection at all, save for sports coat and tie, and then he bade us good night and headed off down the hall. "Well," Corcoran breathed, hesitating, "shall we—do you want to take the car?"

I just nodded and we walked to his car in silence. As soon as we'd slammed the doors, Corcoran turned over the engine and the radio came to life, blaring out a popular dance tune, and it was that, as much as anything, that made my anger rush to the surface—I had to hold tight to the doorframe to keep from doing something I might have regretted for the rest of my professional career.

Corcoran had put the car in gear and we were moving slowly down the street, but I was so wrought up I barely registered the movement. After a moment, he said, "What about the tavern? How's a drink sound? It's on me."

There was a clarinet solo in that tune—the band was famous for its clarinetist—and we both listened as the instrument went slipping and eliding through its paces. "I never realized how much I hate the clarinet," I said, "not till now, anyway."

Corcoran reached out a cuff-linked wrist to flick off the radio. He seemed to decide something then, swinging the wheel hard to the right to nose the car in at the curb. "Listen," he said, "John, I hope you're not going to take this the wrong way, because it can get awkward for all of us, and there's no reason—"

Was I glaring at him? I don't know. All of a sudden, and this was the foremost thing in my mind, grown there full-blown like an instantaneous cancer, I was overcome with a fear of embarrassing myself, of showing my hand—of being petty, hidebound, of being the cuckold. "No," I said, turning away from him, and I didn't know what proposition or argument I was dismissing.

"It doesn't mean anything. Not a thing. Not between us." He was turned to me, studying me in profile, and I could feel him there, feel the heat of his breath against the carved wooden mask of my face. "Look, before I did anything I consulted Prok—"

At first I thought I hadn't heard him right—Prok? What did Prok have to do with this?—and then the single curt syllable began to reverberate in my head like a pinball ringing up the score. Maybe my ears reddened. Still I didn't turn to him, but just sat there staring out the window, fighting for control.

"Well, of course I did. You don't think I would just—hey, I might have an overactive libido, I admit to it, but I wouldn't do a thing without Prok's go-ahead, not anymore, not now, not with the situation out there in the world like it is. That'd be nuts, that'd be suicide."

Prok. He'd consulted Prok—Prok, but not me. As if—but I couldn't finish the thought, because Prok had known all along, Prok had approved, given him the green light and his blessing too, all for one and one for all. And I'd sat there stolidly through the morning while Prok loomed over me dictating letters, my fingers hammering away at the keys of the typewriter as if I were some obsequious little clerk in a Dickens novel. Letter after letter, and never a word about Iris or me. First there were the letters to the parents, then to the principal, the superintendent, the minister and the gas station attendant, and finally, the children.

Dear Suzy: Uncle Milk and I wanted you to have a very special letter all your own that the mailman will bring to the box just for you. We will

*write a special letter to your sister, Katie, too, and the mailman will
bring it just for her so that she can have one as well. What we want to
say, most of all, is how much we enjoyed meeting such a sweet and intelligent girl as yourself and how proud you should be for helping us with
our science. Yours Truly, Uncle Kinsey*

"And I think you know how he feels when it comes to the inner
circle—we have no secrets, we're bonded, each of us, together. John, listen, he encouraged me—for your good and mine. And Iris's, don't forget Iris."

I hadn't forgotten her, not for an instant.

Corcoran's face hung there in the car as if dissociated from his body,
the last light of the day laminating his features at the far blurring edge
of my peripheral vision, and still I was staring straight ahead. I wouldn't
look at him. I couldn't. There was a picket fence two doors up, fresh
white paint peerless against the unfolding copper-green leaves of the
climbing roses that were just then starting to take hold of it. "And there's
Violet, don't forget Violet. She's a very passionate woman, John, believe
me. And she'll be here sooner than you know."

IN MY HURT—in my hurt and my refusal to acknowledge it to Corcoran, Prok or Iris or anyone else—I went to Mac. I telephoned beforehand to let her know I was coming—it was Saturday morning, Iris
behind the cash register at the five-and-dime, Prok lecturing his biology
students on gametes and zygotes or the sex life of the fruit fly or I don't
know what, nest robbers, parasitic wasps, the cowbird and the cuckoo—
and she was waiting for me at the door in a light sweater and her walking shorts. "I thought you might want to go for a walk," she said, her
eyes searching mine.

I gave her nothing back, just nodded, and we went off empty-handed
down the street and through the familiar fields and into the woods beyond. It was coming on to high spring in southern Indiana, the wet
black furrows spread open under the sun, wildflowers in the clearings, a
smell of mud and ferment under the trees, birds everywhere. And gnats.

We swatted them as we moved along, ducking away from one swarm only to walk headlong into another. It was warm where the sun hit us, cool, even a little chilly, in the shade. Mac went out of her way to make small talk—if Prok knew, then she knew—and I give her credit for that, trying to defuse the situation in the way Corcoran had, nothing amiss here, life as usual, the study of sex and the free and unencumbered practice of it inextricably linked, and where were the grounds for complaint? We found a spot in one of the clearings where the sun invested a spike of weather-worn rock with its heat, and made ourselves comfortable.

For a long while I just sat there, my back against the rock, and let Mac do the talking. She wasn't saying much, nothing of substance, that is, and I knew what she was doing ("Isn't that a bluebird over there, on that branch just above the stump, right there, see? They're getting rare, aren't they, ever since the starlings invaded, anyway, but don't you love the smell of the outdoors, especially this time of year? I do. I can't get enough of it. When I was a girl, oh, no older than eight or nine—have I ever told you this?") but I didn't care, it was conversation as anodyne, and I let it wash over me. Gratefully. I don't know how long this went on—ten minutes, twenty—but eventually she fell silent. I leaned back, closed my eyes and let the sun probe my face. I wanted her, and we'd come here to engage in sex, but I was in no hurry—or maybe I was fooling myself, maybe I didn't want her at all.

Her voice seemed to come to me out of nowhere, out of some place in my head, and my eyelids, blue-veined, pulsing with the sleepy drift of floating bodies, snapped open. "John," she was saying, "John, listen, I know how you feel. I do. But you can't let it get to you, because that way of thinking—jealousy, recrimination, whatever you want to call it—is wrong. And it's destructive, John. It is."

She closed her hand over mine. The light was stark, flaming all around her as if she were on the apron of a stage, her pupils shrunk to pinpoints, a splay of lines radiating out from the corners of her eyes as if the skin there had been fractured or worked with a sharp tool—she was old, getting old, and the visible signs of it, the apprehension of it, made something shift inside me. "I'll tell you," she said, dropping her voice, "it wasn't easy for me in the beginning. You're not the first, you know. There was Ralph Voris—has Prok ever mentioned him?"

"Yes."

"And there were graduate students too, casual affairs—things with women."

I said nothing, but I may have flushed, thinking of the day I'd broken the code and pulled his file. And hers.

"He's highly sexed, Prok, and to be away so often, for so long—you don't know. It was before your time, ten years ago and more. He went to Mexico for three months, collecting galls with three healthy young men—and he was a healthy young man himself. Was I hurt? Did I complain? Did I resent being all but abandoned? Do I resent it now?"

"I don't know," I said. "Do you?"

She removed her hand, lifted both arms to pat her hair in place, and then she smoothed down her blouse and shifted position in the dry leaves at the base of the rock. "No," she said, "I don't think so. Not anymore. You see," and she moved in closer to me, so that I could feel the warmth of her hip sliding in against mine, "I love him, love him more than anybody else in the world, and that's all that matters."

The moment hung there between us, and Prok was proportional to it, each of us trying to fit him in and work around him at the same time. Then I leaned forward and kissed her and she brought both her hands to my chest and slipped them inside my shirt and ran them down the long muscles at my sides. We breathed in unison, and then she released me. "And I believe in him," she said, "believe in his work and everything he does—and so do you. I know you do."

THAT EVENING, when I went to pick up Iris at work, she wasn't there. I was right on time—six o'clock on the dot—and I'd got good at that, adopting the model of Prok's punctuality along with so many other things. The girl behind the counter said that Iris had left early, half an hour before, to make some urgent appointment—"Maybe with the doctor," the girl offered after studying the look on my face. "Yeah, I think she said the doctor," she added, and what did it matter if no doctor in the whole state of Indiana was keeping hours at six o'clock on a Saturday evening?

I went home then, to see if I'd somehow missed her, and I sat there brooding till seven. When the bell in the church tower two blocks over struck the hour I pushed myself up and walked the ten blocks to the office, and this time I used my key in the door. I hit the light switch and the shadows fled into the corners. It was very still. I stood there a moment in the doorway, and then I couldn't help but go to my desk and examine it—I bent down and sniffed it, actually sniffed the surface of my own desk as if I could somehow detect the residue of vaginal lubricants there, as if I were a bloodhound, as if I were some petty and heartbroken cuckolded fool stooping so low as to drop off the chart of humiliation, even—and I examined Corcoran's desk too, shuffling through his things, probing into his drawers, looking for something, anything, that would give me a clue as to who he really was and what he might want. And how did I feel then, standing there in the lamp-lit office rifling my colleague's desk while the sky closed down over the campus and couples were strolling out hand-in-hand to the dance, the pictures, dinner? Devastated. Devastated, certainly, but it was worse than that: I felt as if I'd somehow failed Iris, as if I were the one at fault. More than anything, and I hate even to remember it, I felt inadequate.

Our research would show that some twenty-six percent of women and fifty percent of men would engage in extramarital intercourse—I myself drew up the accumulative incidence curve on page 417 of the female volume—and we would conclude, in Prok's words, that "Extramarital coitus had attracted some of the participants because of the variety of experience it afforded them with new and sometimes superior sexual partners." Exactly. And yet the female volume was still a decade in the future—we'd only begun to accumulate the data at this point—and so my attitude was purely intuitive. I'd been with Mac. I could still smell her on my fingertips. But that didn't matter a whit, not now—all that mattered now was Iris, Iris and Corcoran.

I went back home—eight o'clock and no sign of her—and I poured a drink and brooded some more. When eight-thirty came and she still

hadn't appeared or even called, I copied out a poem, or a fragment of a poem, from her anthology, and left it on her pillow in the bedroom, then took the long walk to Corcoran's to see if his car was parked out front, if his windows were lit, if there was movement there, a silhouette on the shade, anything. The night had grown cold and I watched it stream from my mouth as I walked, my shoulders tense, all my emotions—rage, despair, scorn, vengefulness—wadded up like a bolus in the pit of my stomach. There was no yellow convertible drawn up to the curb outside Corcoran's apartment, and there was no sign of life inside. I stood there for two hours and more, then I turned away and went home, defeated.

Need I say that Iris wasn't there? The poem was where I'd left it, though, untouched, and it might have remained there all night and into the next day, for all I knew. I had no idea when she came home that night or if she came home at all because I bundled up some things in a suitcase—a change of clothes, toiletry articles, bedding—and dragged myself back to the office to sleep on the floor while the abandoned building, one of the oldest on campus, ticked and settled round me in a state of decline that couldn't help recalling my own. I wasn't yet twenty-four and already my life was over. I should have enlisted, I told myself. Should have gone to fight and kill and be killed, because anything was better than this.

The poem, incidentally, was from Hardy, bile-bitter and as grim as it gets. I suppose now it looks a bit sophomoric—the sentiments expressed, the whole gesture—but then it seemed to strike right to the heart of what I was feeling. It's called "Neutral Tones," and the speaker is looking back on the bleak day by a frozen pond when the smile on his lover's lips went dead. I left her with the last four lines:

> Since then, keen lessons that love deceives,
> And wrings with wrong, have shaped to me
> Your face, and the God-curst sun, and a tree,
>   And a pond edged with grayish leaves.

I slept in the office for two nights, never venturing within ten blocks of the apartment, because if she could make me suffer I could make her

suffer too. Let her stew, that was what I thought, let her stew until she's as sick at stomach as I am. But where was Corcoran? I waited for him that first morning with a dry throat and a pounding in my temples that was calibrated to a recurrent hormonal rush, and then eight o'clock slipped by, and eight-ten, and I put it to Prok as casually as I could, *Where is he?* Prok barely glanced up. It had slipped his mind, but he'd neglected to tell me that he'd given our colleague two days off to see to a personal matter, and that was where it ended—Prok barely lifted his head from his work all the rest of the day. There was no chatter, no humor, and the only relief from routine came when we interviewed two young women for the position of full-time secretary, and subsequently, one-on-one, took their histories.

At the end of the second day, having heard nothing from Iris, I went back to the apartment, but warily, looking for signs, coming up the walk and approaching the front steps with the slow deliberation of a sapper, as if the place had been mined and booby-trapped by the retreating forces. The first thing I noticed was the milk—there they were, two bottles, nestled side by side in the insulated box on the porch, undisturbed. There was no sound of the radio, no lights left burning. Everything sank in me. I turned my key in the lock and came in to a smell of nothing, of a tomb, of a place that was empty and had been empty and might never be inhabited again. It was as if the people who'd lived here had disappeared, that nice young couple, as if they'd been kidnapped and held for ransom and no one could tell if the sum would ever be raised.

Her clothes were there still, hanging in the wardrobe, her brushes and toilet things, her shampoo—it was all there. It probably took me fifteen minutes, a good quarter hour of poking through things in a kind of mind-numbing despair, until I noticed that the poem was gone, replaced by a few lines in her own hand, and I still don't know where she got them from:

I never again shall tell you what I think.
I shall be sweet and crafty, soft and sly. . . .
And some day when you knock and push the door,

230

Some sane day, not too bright and not too stormy,
I shall be gone, and you may whistle for me.

I couldn't breathe. I had to pour a drink and ease myself down in the armchair, so weak suddenly my legs wouldn't support me. *Gone? I shall be gone?* And what was that supposed to mean? I couldn't fathom it—was she saying she would leave me, that she didn't want me anymore, that Corcoran had taken my place and negated everything between us in the course of what, a week? Sane? No, it was insane. I loved her, she loved me. How could anything ever change that?

If I thought that was the low point, exchanging bitter poems, warfare by proxy, the drink and the chair and the empty apartment, I was wrong. Because even as I sat there in the armchair, the glass in one hand and the sheet of paper she'd inscribed in the other (and I'd sniffed that too, holding it to my nose and breathing deep in the hope of catching the remotest fleeting scent of her), there was the sound of her heels on the steps and her key turning in the lock, and in the next instant I had to look her in the face and listen to her tell me that she was in love.

There she was, flush with it, her hair disheveled and her clothes looking as if they'd been slept in (and they had, or no, they hadn't, and I didn't want to think about that either). She came straight into the room, threw down her purse and her coat, and told me she was sorry, but that was how it was, she was in love.

I don't get angry. I suppress my anger, drink it down like Angostura bitters, digest it, let it run through the bowels, shit it out—my mother taught me that. *Do what I say. Mind your manners. Live for me.* "We haven't even been married a year yet," I said.

She was frantic, she couldn't sit down, pacing back and forth while I clung to the chair as if the ship had gone down and this was all that was left to me. "I don't care," she said. "I'm sorry, and I don't want to hurt you—I'll always love you, and you're my first love, you know that—but this is something bigger than that, and I just can't help it. I can't."

"He's married," I said, and my voice was flat and toneless. The faucet was dripping in the sink, one thunderous drop after another hitting the greased porcelain of the unwashed plates and cups and saucers. "He doesn't love you. It's just sex—he told me that. Just sex, Iris. He's a *sex* researcher."

All the intensity of her face drew down to the frozen eyelet of her mouth and for a second I thought she was going to spit at me. "Is that what you call it—research?" She was trembling, lit up with the ecstasy of the moment, her eyes gone clear and hard. "Well, I don't care, I love him and it doesn't matter what happens. I can do research too. You'll see. You just wait and see."

THE NEXT MORNING, early, while Prok was still upstairs brushing his teeth and Mac presiding over the kitchen with her whisk and bowl and a mug of coffee, I went to the house on First Street and rapped on the door till one of the children let me in. I don't recall which one it was— it might have been Bruce, the youngest, who would have been thirteen or fourteen at the time—but the door swung open, the adolescent face registered my presence and then vanished and I was left standing there in the anteroom, unannounced, the door open wide to the street behind me. Two years earlier I would have been mortified to be put in this position, but now, as the sounds of the house percolated round me—three children preparing for school and the slap of Prok's razor strop echoing down from above—I felt nothing but relief, blanketed by normalcy, by the regular thump of footsteps overhead and the murmurous dialogue of the girls drifting down the hall. I stood there a moment, then shut the door softly behind me. There was a smell of coffee, butter, hot grease, and I let it lead me to the kitchen, even while I tried to calm the pounding in my chest. Mac was at the stove, beating eggs for the pan, her back to me. She was wearing a housedress and an apron, her feet were bare and her hair was uncombed, and when I spoke her name she started visibly.

She turned to me, puzzled. "John?" she said, as if she couldn't quite place me. "What are you doing here at this hour—are you and Prok off somewhere? I thought it was next week you were going back to Indianapolis?"

"No," I said, fumbling for the words I wanted, "I just, well—I came to see Prok, is Prok in? It's, well, it can't wait—"

She gave me a stricken look. There was danger here, and heartbreak too, and I was out of bounds—she could see that at a glance. "Have you eaten?" she said suddenly. "Because I can just add a couple eggs—and toast, do you want toast?"

"Is he upstairs?"

She might have nodded, or maybe she said, "Go ahead," but the permission was implicit—I belonged here, I was part of this, part of this household, this family—and in the next moment I was bounding up the stairs even as the two girls, Joan and Anne, were coming down, dressed for school. I suppose they might have given me a quizzical look and perhaps even a giggle or two (they were eighteen and sixteen respectively), but it was nothing out of the ordinary—I was there, on the staircase, and I'd been there before, John Milk, the handsome young man with the recalcitrant hair, Daddy's friend, Daddy's assistant, his colleague and traveling companion. I found Prok in the bathroom, standing before the mirror, shaving. The door was open, he was in his underclothes, and he'd just scraped the last of the shaving cream from his chin when he became aware of me standing there in the doorway. "Prok," I said, "I hope you won't—well, I didn't know where else to turn."

I couldn't eat—I was too wrought up for that—but the two of them, Mac and Prok both, insisted on sitting me down at the table with a plate of toast and scrambled eggs. Throughout breakfast, Prok kept fastening on me with that intent gaze of his, as if he were trying to reduce me to my constituent parts for a physiologic study of variations in the human organism under stress, but he talked exclusively of the project. "The children were really something, weren't they, Milk? And, Mac, you should have seen them, fully cognizant of sexual roles even at four and five years old, and by seven or eight a number of them had already seen the genitalia of the opposite sex, and there was that one girl, Milk, you remember her? The one in pigtails? She'd seen both her parents naked—*saw* them on a regular basis." When we were done—I barely touched my food—he got up in his usual brisk way, squared his bow tie in the hall mirror and informed me that we'd better hurry if we were going to be at work on time.

The minute we were out of the house he asked me what the matter was.

"It's Iris," I told him, struggling to keep pace with him as we swung through the gate and out onto the street. I was having trouble getting it out, the words colliding in my head, and the emotions too, choking at me in some deep glandular way. Prok shot me an impatient look. "She says she's in love with Corcoran, and that"—and here I felt myself breaking down—"that she wants to move in with him, to live with him. To, to—"

His head was down, his shoulders hunched, and he was already elongating into his no-nonsense stride, no time to waste, no time to stand still in the street and shoot the breeze when there was work to be done. What he said was, "We can't have that."

No, I thought, *no, of course we can't.*

"But you approved," I said, "or that's what Corcoran told me, that you said, well, that you gave your blessing. To the whole thing, I mean."

The look he gave me—sidelong, over his jolting shoulder—wasn't in the least sympathetic. It was fierce, irascible, the sort of look that came over his face when he was challenged, when the Thurman B. Rices and Dean Hoenigs of the world rose up to castigate him on whatever grounds, whether statistical or moral. "We're adults, Milk," he snapped. "Consenting adults. No one needs my permission to do anything."

I was right there now, right at his shoulder, drawn up even with him, and I came as close to losing control then as I ever have—there were accusations on my lips, I know it, and I wanted to throw his words right back at him, but the best I could manage was just another reflection of my own inadequacy, a kind of bleat of agony that might have come from the lips of a child. "It's eating me up inside," I said, and for all my conditioning I seemed to be out of breath, my legs pumping automatically, air in, air out. "I love her. I want her back."

We walked on in silence a moment, and I can't tell you whether the sun was shining and the squirrels clambering up the trees or the wind blowing a gale, because I was at the breaking point and nothing of the world of appearances held any interest for me, all of it just a backdrop now to the scene I was playing out, the heartsick lover, the cuckold, the fool in motley. "You say she wants to *move in* with him?" he said. He gave me the snatching look.

I nodded. We were hurrying along so fast I was on the verge of breaking into a jog. "She's been with him the past three nights and she, she came home only to get her things last night and she told me she was"— I felt ridiculous saying it, but I couldn't stop myself—"doing *research.*"

Suddenly we were stopped dead in our tracks, right there in the middle of the sidewalk, a pair of student lovers splitting up to edge around us on either side, the trees wheeling overhead and everything aside from Prok's face, his glasses, his eyes, rushing past in a blur of motion. "Research?" he said. "But that's absurd. It's wrong. And you know, John, you of all people, because I've emphasized it over and over again, how much our work depends on the public perception of it?"

"Of course. That's what I'm saying."

His jaw was set. The wind, if there was a wind, might have ruffled the stiff crest of his hair. "We can't afford to give them any ammunition."

"No, of course not." I wanted to look away. There was fluid in my eyes—tears, that is—and I didn't want to expose myself.

"You and Mac, for example. Mutually beneficial, just as I've said all along, pleasure given, pleasure taken. That's the way it should be. We need to break down our inhibitions and express ourselves to the fullest, I do believe that with all my heart. But it has to be kept strictly confidential, and every one of us—not just the husbands but the wives too—must understand that we're part of something larger here, much larger. And under scrutiny, under the microscope, John. You know that, don't you?" He caught himself. We were still rooted there, and he made as if to move off, but caught himself again. "Has anyone seen her with him, seen her go to his apartment?"

"I don't know," I said miserably. I was studying the pattern of the sidewalk. I couldn't look him in the eye. "But I don't see how, well, in a small town like this—or not for long, anyway."

Prok didn't curse. He never used expletives or indulged dirty jokes, though of course in later years he was deluged with them, but now, standing there in the street, he came as close to it as I can recall. He spat something out, some Latin term, and then we were walking again and he was muttering about Corcoran, about how he blamed himself for not making the situation "absolutely clear, so clear any idiot could see through to the truth and necessity of it." We crossed Atwater, then Third, moved up the walk and into the aegis of the big looming lime-stone buildings of the campus. "I'm sorry, John," he said, pinning me with his gaze as if I were the one threatening to bring the research down, "but we just can't have it."

Two weeks later, though her daughters' school was still in session and they would have to miss the last six weeks of the term, Violet Corcoran left South Bend and moved into her husband's cramped apartment on College Avenue in downtown Bloomington. She took charge of things right away, opening up an account at the grocery, arranging for a tutor and putting Lloyd Wheeler, the best real-estate agent in town, on the trail of a suitable property, with a yard for the girls, a garage for the Cadillac and shade trees to mitigate the summer heat. Prok had had a talk with Corcoran—he came right up the stairs of Biology Hall the morning I'd voiced my complaint, slammed into the back office and chewed him out, in no uncertain terms—and Corcoran had a talk with Iris five minutes later, on the telephone to his apartment. All the while I sat at my desk, drinking coffee as if my veins flowed with nothing else.

If I think about it now, I have to chalk the whole thing up to Iris's immaturity—she was just twenty when we married and, as I say, hadn't had any previous experience with men, and perhaps that was unfair to her, or certainly it was, especially in the context of the project we were all engaged in and the relations I'd had outside of the marriage. She had no way of gauging what she was doing, of putting a cap on her emotions and keeping things in perspective—she was infatuated, that was all, like so many of the teenage girls we interviewed over their first crushes and so on. Above all, she was stubborn. Once she set her sights on something, it was hard to turn her, and when she came through the office door an hour later, her face drained of color and her eyes red-veined and swollen, I can't say I was surprised, though I shrank inside. Prok happened to be standing over me, comparing a chart with one of mine, and Corcoran, the self-satisfied smile for once kneaded out of his features, sat hunched at his desk in the back room. "You can't do this," she said.

I was on my feet before I knew what I was doing, before I realized she wasn't talking to me at all. Corcoran swung round in his chair, his eyes shrunk back in his head. He was wearing his two-tone shoes, I remember, and he began to grind one foot into the floor as if he were putting out a cigarette. Prok laid a hand on my shoulder, and I felt a wave of shame wash over me.

Iris never moved. "You don't own me—or John or Purvis either."

"Take your wife out of here, Milk, will you," Prok said. "Take her home."

"No," she said, her voice rising, "no—not until you tell me who elected you God."

"Corcoran," Prok called over his shoulder, "will you come in here please," and we all watched as Corcoran pushed himself up from the desk and crossed the room on stiffened legs. He edged in beside us, looking unsure of himself, and still Iris hadn't moved from the doorway.

"All right, Corcoran," Prok said then, and I hadn't gone to my wife, hadn't touched her, the three of us ranged there against her like a scrum awaiting the drop of the ball. "Just tell me please if you've explained the situation to Mrs. Milk?"

Corcoran bowed his head. "Yes," he said.

"I'm sorry, I didn't hear you—"

Corcoran looked first to Iris, then to me. "Yes," he repeated.

"Good," Prok said, "very good. And, Iris, if you would"—and he was already moving forward, already taking her by the arm and guiding her toward the door of the inner room—"I'd just like to have a few words with you in private, if I may."

Then the door closed and I went back to work.

PART II

WYLIE HALL

1

I DON'T THINK ANY of us—not Prok, my fellow members of the inner circle, President Wells, the NRC or even the W.B. Saunders Company, Philadelphia, the book's publisher—was quite prepared for the furor that greeted publication of the male volume in January of 1948. Prok had chosen Saunders, a staid and colorless publisher of medical texts, over the big commercial houses in New York (and believe me, once word was out, they all came knocking), in a conscious effort to avoid any sort of misguided marketing effort or sanguine publicity that might cheapen or sensationalize our findings. Above all, what we wanted was to be regarded as scientists, to legitimize the field of sex research and elevate it to its proper place among the behavioral sciences, and yet at the same time there was a real reformer's zeal in Prok that made him want to deliver up our results to the widest possible audience. And so, yes, he did arrange for press interviews—press conferences, actually—so that the word would get out, but in a sober, rational and controlled way. And he chose Saunders to produce the book in a plain, no-nonsense hardcover volume that was indistinguishable from any other scientific or medical compendium sitting forgotten on the back shelves of bookstores, libraries and physicians' offices. It sold for $6.50, or more than twice what the average book retailed for at the time. There were 804 pages, including appendices, tables, bibliography and index. And it was dedicated, soberly enough, "To the twelve thousand persons who have contributed to these data and to the eighty-eight thousand more who, someday, will help complete this study."

"Sober," "staid," "clinical"—no matter what adjective you want to use, the press wasn't having it. Every magazine and newspaper in the country exploded with sensational headlines—"50% OF MARRIED

MEN UNFAITHFUL!" "PREMARITAL INTERCOURSE RAMPANT!" "KINSEY SAYS MEN REACH PEAK TEN YEARS AHEAD OF WOMEN!"—and that sort of thing, always in caps and tailed by the flogging exclamation point. The book began to fly out of the shops, 40,000 copies in the first two weeks, and it was soon topping bestseller lists across the country. By March, there were 100,000 copies in print, and by June 150,000. *Time* magazine called it the biggest thing since *Gone With the Wind*. And Prok, who'd authored every last word of it, was suddenly ubiquitous, his face staring out from the pages of every publication you could imagine, and his words—his statistics, *our* statistics—on everybody's lips. In fact, things grew so out of control that we could barely get in and out of the offices without a press of reporters, admirers and sensation seekers trying to run us down, and work on the project came to a decided halt for those first few months. (And can anyone forget those jukebox ditties, Martha Raye with her "Ooh, Dr. Kinsey," and Julie Wilson with "The Kinsey Report," and worst of all, "The Kinsey Boogie"?)

For me, it was nothing short of hellish. I've never been comfortable in front of a camera and while I do think I can hold my own as an interviewer on the job, as an interviewee I'm afraid I'm a bust. ("You're just shy, John," Iris would tell me, "not sex shy, just plain shy.") It was hard on Mac too. While the reporters tried to corner me and Corcoran—and Rutledge, because he'd joined us by this time—we were able to present a united front, and in the eyes of the press we were subsidiary in any case, mere sidemen to Prok's bandleader, but Mac was left exposed. If *Sexual Behavior in the Human Male* revealed men for what they were—human animals engaging in a whole range of activities, from anal intercourse to extramarital affairs and relations with nonhuman animals—then what was it like to live with the man who routinely quantified and correlated all this behavior? What was the *woman's* perspective on it?

In interview after interview, Mac bore up under the pressure and scrutiny as if she'd been born to it, but I knew different. It wasn't that she was reticent, like me, but simply that she'd always seen her role as an accommodator, as Prok's helpmeet, and she felt that the reward for all his tireless work and the genius of his conception should be entirely his, all the glory and the limelight, and that she should stand in the background and let him have his due. But they wouldn't let her. The women's magazines especially—*McCall's, Redbook, Cosmopolitan.* They were mad to feast on the details, to get in under her skin, poking and probing and hoping against hope to turn up something odd and out of the ordinary, something outré their readers could latch on to in order to put all this *male* business in perspective. He counted orgasms and he had a wife. Who was she? Who was she really?

Mac invited them into the house, one and all, to let them answer the question for themselves—she was just an ordinary housewife, that was all, no different from any of their readers, except that her husband went off to the Sex Institute every morning while theirs packed lunches for the factory or the downtown office—and she baked the journalists cookies and persimmon tarts and sat knitting in her rocker by way of demonstration. When they asked if her lifestyle wasn't about to change, if she wouldn't soon become wealthy off the royalties from the book and start swathing herself in furs and hiring maids to do the cooking and cleaning and child-rearing, she pointed out, dourly, that all proceeds from *Sexual Behavior in the Human Male* were pumped back into the Institute and that they never saw a penny of it, that, in fact, the book had *cost* them money because the writing of it had prevented Prok from revising his biology textbook, which at least would have brought them a small yearly something. Just take a look at Prok's wardrobe, she told them—he's only got one decent suit to his name. Rich? They were anything but. In fact, Mac projected exactly what Prok expected her to: a kind of safe and sterile warmth that would keep the critics at bay and the housewives of America satisfied to the point at which some of them might even begin to feel a little superior. It was a bravura performance.

But I'm getting ahead of myself. Why I bring it up at this juncture is to impress on you how vital it was for us to keep our activities secret— for all of us—and never to let slip even the faintest hint of impropriety or behavior that anyone could fasten on as deviating from the norm in any way. Thus, we were all married, and to all appearances happily married, and we all had children. We had to present an unimpeachable front to the public—we were the sex researchers and we were absolutely and rigorously normal, no prurience here, no wife-swapping or sadomasochism or sodomy on our platters—but as the years went by, and the public scrutiny intensified, it became ever more problematic. And Prok. Prok seemed to enlarge into his role, to try ever increasingly and recklessly to push the boundaries both personally and professionally, and in the later years we were all waiting for the roof to fall in, for Prok to be arrested and shackled and hauled off to the flash of photographers' cameras for soliciting sex in a public restroom or engaging in immoral acts at one of the bath houses he increasingly frequented on our field trips. It never happened. I suppose a part of it can be attributed to luck, but he *was* cautious for the most part, never admitting anyone into the inner circle unless he was absolutely sure of him, and on top of that there was the impregnability of the persona he presented to the public. He was Dr. Alfred C. Kinsey, Professor of Zoology, father of three, contentedly married, above suspicion or even rumor. He built a fortress around us, data compacted into stone, stone piled atop stone, and we all climbed up hand-over-hand to man the battlements.

And so, when Violet Corcoran did come to town and she and the girls had had a chance to settle in, Prok made a point of hosting a small gathering at Bryan Park for just the six of us and the children—it was his way, I think, of smoothing over any potential situation that might arise among us and of reinforcing our bond as well. That was one of the things about working with Prok, about being his protégé—he always managed to make each of us feel a vital part of the enterprise, wives included, as if we were members of a secret society, which, in some respect, I suppose we were. And the children were a part of it too—they might not have understood what was going on among the adults, but they did, I'm sure, appreciate that they were bound up in something unique.

There was an easygoing, friendly feel to our outdoor gatherings, a familial current that was prominently, but never artificially, on display. We had children, just like anyone else—Prok's and the Corcorans', and later the Rutledges' and John Jr.—and if our neighbors should see us gathered there in public over a smoking grill, the older children kicking a ball while the younger picked buttercups or climbed trees, we were recognized as performers in the rite of the familiar and all was understood and all forgiven. People might say, *Oh, look there's Dr. Sex with his wife and children and his colleagues and their children too, roasting wieners on a stick like anybody else, and the children have their bicycles with them, look at that, and I'll bet the ants'll have a high old time of it, don't you?* We picnicked a lot in those days.

But back to that particular gathering, at Bryan Park, the first to include the Corcorans *en famille.* Iris didn't want to go. She categorically refused, in fact, at least at first. Prok had guillotined her affair. He'd talked to her behind closed doors—lectured her, berated her—and she'd listened to him only because it meant my job if she didn't, but she was resentful, and though I don't like to think about it even now, she was in love. Still. With Corcoran. I woke up early that Saturday and went to the grocer's while our biggest pot rattled on the stove with the tumbling diced wedges of the potatoes I'd peeled the night before, and another, smaller pot seethed with eggs cooking hard in their shells, and yet I can't say I was looking forward to the picnic myself. I'd been tentative around Iris ever since the confrontation at the office, and I felt we were just beginning to make progress, to appreciate each other again in a tender and loving way, and I didn't want to do anything to threaten it.

When I got back from the store she was still in her dressing gown, the Victrola turned up too loud and Billie Holiday annihilating all hope, phrase by phrase, bar by bar, with her unfathomable lisping sorrow. I heard that voice and I felt like pulling out a gun and shooting myself, but Iris was at the table, slicing egg and chopping onion, and when I came through the door she looked up and gave me a rueful smile. I didn't say anything for fear of breaking the spell, just set the bag on the table—mayonnaise, in the twelve-ounce jar, paprika, apple cider vinegar—and went into the bedroom to dig out an old blanket to spread on the grass. We'd talked the night before about the practical impor-

245

tance of accepting the invitation—Prok wanted us there and we were going to have to go, it was part of the job, part of the commitment—and I could see that Iris was softening. Yes, it would be awkward, we both admitted that, and, yes, Violet Corcoran would be there, but we had to move forward, get it over with, get it out of our systems, didn't we?

I'd been sitting at the foot of the bed, idly plucking at the raised pattern of the bedspread while Iris lay propped against the headboard, her feet splayed before her, beautiful feet, high-arched and bobby-socked, feet that I loved as I loved every part of her. I wanted to make amends, wanted her back, fully, in body and soul both.

"We're above all this, Iris," I argued, "we are. Truly. Sex is one thing and marriage another. Commitment. Love. That's what we have. There's just no room for raw emotion in this business, and you know it as well as I. We're professionals. We have to be." I'd paused then, studying her face, but she was staring down at the book in her lap and wouldn't meet my eyes. "Besides," I said, "if anyone should get, well, emotionally upset, you'd think it would be me—and Violet. What about her? Shouldn't she be the injured party? Because, if—well, you know what I mean."

She'd looked up then, the outflow of her eyes, the faintest ripples of irony at the corners of her mouth. "Yes, John," she said, "you're the injured party, you, always you."

"That's not fair," I said, "and you know it."

She shifted her weight to draw her legs up to her chest, as if to protect herself. She gave me a long look, then dropped her eyes. I could have said more, could have made accusations, but there was no point.

"That's not fair," I repeated.

It took her a moment, and when she spoke her voice was barely audible. "I know it," she said.

But now she was chopping onion and preparing to anoint the diced potatoes with vinegar and mayonnaise, and when that was done and the potato salad crowned with sliced egg and a dusting of paprika, she was going to stride into the bedroom and put on a pair of shorts and a blouse and we were going to heft the picnic basket and amble down the street together, like lovers. From the bedroom, I heard Billie Holiday parsing her misery.

Prok was in a high state of excitement that day—he'd been communicating with a man in his sixties whose serial sexual feats dwarfed even the most prodigious we'd encountered for variety and continuity both and the man had indicated that he might be amenable to an interview—and he radiated his delight all over Iris, giving her his biggest Prok-smile, bending from the waist like a mock courtier to kiss her hand, and he clapped my shoulder and called me John and avowed that we were on to great things now, great things and getting greater. Mac and Iris embraced gingerly, in the way of war veterans, as if they were afraid of tearing open each other's wounds, and then we turned to the fire, which Prok had already built to a controlled inferno, thinking, in his ever-efficient way, of the coals it would furnish when it was time to lay the chops and bratwurst on the grill.

I was watching Iris when the yellow convertible pulled up on the street across from the park. Corcoran was at the wheel, smiling like an ambassador, already waving, Violet regal beside him, and the two girls, Daphne and Lucy, emerging from the car in identical pink dresses and with the perfectly composed faces of the innocent. Iris might have been paler than usual, might have seemed thinner and smaller, as if she'd been reduced inside her clothes, but when Violet had made her way across the expanse of the field, her shoulders thrust back and her breasts pointing the way, Iris took her hand and smiled and made small talk without missing a beat. And Corcoran. She looked him right in the face, gave him her brightest, fullest, most rigidly unwavering smile and small-talked him too, and before long we were all sitting on the blanket listening to Prok and sipping punch while the sun graced us and the Corcorans' girls played decorously in the distance.

Prok, as I've said, was a great camper, and he took delight in squatting before the fire and looking to the slow incineration of the various cuts of meat he'd laid out on the grill (little of which he'd eat himself—he hated any foods he considered dry, and that included steaks and chops which were overcooked, and, I'm sorry to say, when he was at the grill everything was overcooked). The scent of the open fire brought me back to our honeymoon and the first meals Iris and I had prepared together, and back even further, to my boyhood and the woods behind the house, and maybe the others were having similar thoughts, the day lazy and serene and the smoke drifting out over the lawn in running tatters. Any small tensions we might have felt seemed to dissipate, everyone gradually unwinding as the afternoon wore on, and I was able to help there because I'd secreted a bottle of bourbon in the depths of our picnic basket, and when Prok wasn't looking I poured stiff little pick-me-ups into everyone's cups, except his, because he wouldn't have approved of our drinking in public with the family gathered.

Violet, especially, seemed to relax into the day, both hands cradled behind her head as she stretched out her abbreviated but extremely robust body on the blanket, and Corcoran was his usual insouciant self, entertaining us with jokes and quips as he pulled at his cup and sucked the bourbon and fruit juice from his upper lip. Iris didn't get drunk—or not that it showed—but she did seem to climb down the ladder from a kind of edgy animation to an enveloping quiet that might have been interpreted as contentment or surfeit, and she too stretched out in the sun on her own corner of the blanket while Prok chattered on and Corcoran and I bantered in quiet tones and Mac pulled out her knitting and mutely counted stitches in a dapple of shade. As for me, I was beginning to think that the world that had so recently seemed skewed away from its axis had all at once come back into alignment. My colleagues were taking their ease and so was I. I felt the sun like a benediction on my face. All was well.

Until we'd eaten, that is, and the first clouds—both actual and metaphorical—closed over the day. With the cloud cover came a slight chill, and we slipped into sweaters and jackets (all except for Prok, who was bare-chested and -footed and barely contained by his khaki hiking shorts). Violet called her daughters to her to help them into matching knit pullovers while Prok's children said their goodbyes and walked off in the direction of home. The other cloud fell over us after we'd split into two groups on either side of the fire, which Prok had built up again for the sake of warmth and the little girls' delectation in the toasting of marshmallows. Mac, Iris and Corcoran were seated on one side of the fire, their faces distorted by the thermal currents rising from the flames, and Prok, Violet and I were on the other.

The afternoon was getting on, shadows lengthening, the sun tugging itself toward the horizon as if there were something urgent about the process. Prok sat cross-legged, poking at the fire. He was talking about Gilbert Van Tassel Hamilton, the psychiatrist and author of *A Research in Marriage,* and how courageous the man was, but how flawed the results of his sex surveys (too small and selected a sample, results compromised by the researcher's own preconceptions, moralizing, psychologizing, et cetera), when he suddenly fell silent and looked from me to Violet Corcoran and back again, as if he'd just remembered something. Violet was leaning back on her elbows now, her bare legs stretched out before her and crossed neatly at the ankle. I was sitting up, Indian-style, in unconscious imitation of Prok. Birds had begun to settle in the trees. From across the street came the crack of a baseball and the cries of several small boys racing after it.

Prok lowered his voice and leaned forward. "Do you know," he said, "I was hoping you two might become better acquainted, for your own pleasure, of course"—a pause—"but don't you agree that it would bring a kind of symmetry to our inter-relationships, that is, in light of your wife, John, and your husband, Violet, having enjoyed themselves together?"

He looked to me, then let his gaze rest on Violet. My heart began to misfire. I couldn't believe what I'd just heard. My first thought was *Has he gone crazy?* but then almost immediately I began to understand that what he was proposing wasn't crazy at all. Far from it.

Violet's eyes were dark, nearly as dark as her hair, and they dominated her face. She was attractive, as I've said, if not particularly pretty, but there was something carnal in the way she held herself, the way she smiled and continually readjusted the set of her shoulders and breasts, almost as if it were a tic. I thought she might laugh or try to deflect the comment with a joke, but she surprised me. "Are you suggesting a liaison? Is that it, Prok?"

Prok never waffled, never vacillated—nothing embarrassed him, and he was continually pushing the limits so as to break those limits down; that was his crusade and he was a crusader at heart. "Yes," he said, "that's exactly it."

I couldn't look at him, couldn't look at Violet. There was an old, familiar stirring in the crotch of my pants. I wanted to slow things down, hold the moment in abeyance—*Had he actually said that? Was he pimping for me?*—and I got my wish.

The two girls had been off playing tag in the field, their shouts riding high on the cooling air, but all at once they were right on top of us, their faces alive with hope, crying "Mommy, Mommy, can we toast marshmallows now? Can we?"

"Sure, honey," Violet murmured to Lucy, the eldest, "but you'll have to cut two green sticks—and sharpen the ends. Can you do that? And help your sister?"

Lucy's face took on a sober look. "Yes," she said, "I can do that. C'mon," she said, turning to her sister, barely able to suppress the excitement in her voice, "let's go find sticks!"

I stole a glance at Iris. She was smiling at something Mac was saying, and now Corcoran put his two cents in and she turned to him, oblivious, even as the wind shifted and the flames fanned and broke apart in a ragged ascending trail and the two little girls darted off into the trees.

Violet leaned away from the drift of smoke, propping herself up on one elbow to redistribute her weight. Her voice was soft and relaxed, and we might have been talking about a rubber of bridge or a swimming party. "It's nothing to me," she said, looking first to Prok—a long, slow, languid look—and then to me. "But I'm game if John is."

It wasn't long after—and I don't recall when or how this came about exactly—that I was working late at the office on a series of new charts and tables incorporating updated data that Prok was eager to have. This was work that I especially enjoyed. I'd found that I had a talent for drawing, for squaring off the orthogonal angles and gently rising curves of our graphs, and as the new Hollerith calculating machine made tabulating data so much easier and our new secretary had assumed the lion's share of the clerical duties, I had more time to devote to it. It must have been eight or so. The building was deserted. Insects of some sort—Prok would have known in an instant what they were—kept battering at the glass of the window, attracted by my light. I was in a state of suspension, so tightly focused on my work that I'd forgotten all about dinner and about Iris too—but she would have been busy cramming for her final exams in any case. My ruler framed the sheet before me, my pencil ticked off the figures. All was still.

On some level, I suppose, I might have been aware of the footsteps approaching from the far end of the hall, but that's neither here nor there, because the first I knew that I was no longer alone was when I glanced up from my work and saw Violet Corcoran standing there in the doorway. She was wearing a stylish dress—belted, with an off-white front and collar and the back and sleeves a very dark navy—and she'd spent some time in the sun, deepening the color of her legs till it seemed as if she were wearing nylons (this was during the war, remember, and nylons were all but impossible to come by, and so women had taken to baby oil and to drawing that ersatz seam up the backs of their legs, from ankle to hemline, and I'm sure I wasn't the first man to wonder just how much higher along the incline of the thigh that line was meant to reach). Her makeup was designed to accentuate the appeal of her outsized eyes. She was short, Italian, busty. She came into the room without a word and perched herself on the edge of the desk.

"Oh, hello," I said, glancing up from the page before me, expecting Iris, or maybe Prok dashing in for something he'd forgotten, and I had some trouble getting her name out, "hello . . . Violet."

"Hi," she breathed, and she threw her eyes to the ceiling and back again, as if the effort of the greeting had exhausted her. She brought her purse into view, clicked it open, and began fishing for cigarette and lighter, and I almost expected her to present me with a silver cigarette case, as if this were a scene out of the pictures, William Powell and

Myrna Loy, or Bacall warming to Bogart in *To Have and Have Not*. She took her time with the ritual of the tobacco, and I made a stab at small talk—"Going to rain tonight, isn't that what they say?"—but I was hard already, hard instantaneously.

"Want one?" she asked, and I did, and she leaned in to light it for me.

For a moment, we just sat there, inhaling, exhaling, nicotine seeping through our veins and capillaries in the way of a shared secret. I knew what was coming—I'd pictured it since the afternoon of the picnic—but now that it was here, I felt tentative and unsure of myself.

"Listen," she said, "John, I wanted to talk to you." I watched her throw back her head and exhale, just like Bacall, and I realized she was as much aware of rehearsing a role as I was. A pulse of excitement leapt from my eyes to my groin.

"About Purvis," she said. "He's a free spirit, but I guess you already know that." Her voice was pitched low. It had a soft, lulling quality, as if nothing were at stake here, as if we routinely shared the little wooden ship of my desk and sailed it out to sea in every sort of weather. "So am I—we both are. But we *are* married, and we intend to stay that way." A pause, the manipulation of the cigarette, that tic with the shoulders and breasts. "I don't know if Iris—if she fully appreciates that."

"No," I said, "I think she does, I think that's all worked out now."

"Because to be honest with you," she went on as if she hadn't heard me, "Purvis is worried about her—and so is Prok. Which is why I'm here."

I set down the pencil—again, unconsciously—but I suppose it was so I could get a firmer grip on the edge of the desk. She was six years older than I. She had beautiful lips, lips and teeth—I'd never noticed that before—a beautiful smile. Her eyebrows were thick and unplucked, Italian eyebrows, and she was perched on the edge of my desk and the office was deserted. Motives didn't interest me. I wasn't suspicious. I wasn't concerned about Iris or Corcoran or the quid pro quo that was being offered here—all I wanted was to watch her and absorb the soft purr of her voice and I didn't care what the subject was. "So what do you think?" I said finally.

She gave a minute shrug, leaned over to tap the ash from her cigarette in the wastebasket beside the desk. "Oh, I don't know," she said, straightening up now and adjusting her shoulders, "what do you think?"

I gave her a smile. I was nervous—I'd never done anything like this before, my new colleague's wife, Violet Corcoran, the devouring eyes, the lips, the smile, the unholy shape of her—and I was trying to project a kind of casual interest in the event that I was misreading her, that she'd come to talk only and that I was on the verge of embarrassing myself. Now it was my turn to shrug. "I don't know," I said.

"You know what I think?"

"No," I said, leaning closer, the smile frozen to my face.

"I think we should just enjoy ourselves."

The summer came on that year with a tympanic burst of thunderstorms, Iris graduated with honors and worked full-time at the five-and-dime till fall, when she accepted a teaching position in one of the local elementary schools, and then fall gave way to winter and winter to spring and we went on as usual, collecting and tabulating data, Corcoran, Prok and I hurtling down back roads and potholed highways in the stalwart shell of the Buick, our only limitation the rationing coupon—and if it weren't for that, for rationing, you would never know from anything Prok said or did that there was a war going on out there in the wider world. Prok wasn't interested in international affairs or politics either. I suppose he must have deplored the Nazis and the Fascists and the Imperial Japanese as much as anyone, but he certainly kept it private—in fact, if he caught Corcoran and me discussing Midway or Guadalcanal or even the latest scrap drive, he invariably changed the subject. Never, in all my years with him, did he mention current events, not even in passing—we detonated the A-bomb, the war ended, the Korean conflict flared up and died—and Prok talked only of the latest sex diary he'd acquired or his need to duplicate Dickinson's experiments on the gripping power of the levator ani muscles when a wax phallus is inserted in the vagina. He was dedicated, no doubt about it. Perhaps even single-minded to a fault. But you could say that of practically any great man.

It was during this period—it might have been as late as 1944, now that I come to think of it—that we were finally able to induce the sexual champion I mentioned earlier to sit for an interview. Prok had been courting him for some time now, and the man had been cagey, feeding us portions of his sex diaries by mail, but expressing his reluctance to meet because of the criminal nature of so many of his sexual contacts. Certainly, what he'd sent us—photographs, penis measurements, case histories and written records of various sex acts with every sort of partner, male, female, nonhuman, preadolescents and even infants—was provocative, perhaps even offensive, but invaluable to our understanding of human sexuality. And, as Prok put it so well, we were scientists, not moralists—our duty was to observe and record, not to pass judgment.

At any rate, Prok knew instinctively that this subject—let's call him Mr. X, as we have done in our files in order to afford him absolute anonymity—could be cajoled into contributing his history through an appeal to his vanity. Mr. X had devoted his life to sex—he was insatiable—and was, I suppose, a sort of sexologist in his own right, and so Prok from the very beginning treated him as a learned colleague, praising him repeatedly in his correspondence ("Certainly you have very much more material than we have in our records" and "This is one of the most valuable things we have ever gotten, and I want to thank you most abundantly for the time you put into it and for your willingness to co-operate") and wooing him with the prospect of legitimating his findings by recording them for posterity. He even offered to pay Mr. X's expenses if he would come to Bloomington, but Mr. X declined—he would meet with us, he said finally, but only if we came to him and only if we were to rendezvous in a small town some hundred miles from where he lived, so as not to attract any notice.

When Prok received the letter he was overjoyed, practically dancing round the office. "Pack your bags, Milk," he cried, leaping up from his desk and striding past me to poke his head into the inner office, "and you too, Corcoran. We're going on a field trip!"

That night, after dinner, I told Iris I'd be taking an extended trip, and she barely glanced up. "Actually," I said, getting up to help with the dishes, "I'm excited about this one."

She was standing at the sink. I went to her, slipped the dishes into the suds, put an arm round her waist and touched my cheek to hers. "Oh?" she said. "And why is that?"

"It's Mr. X. You know, the one whose diaries take him right off the scale?"

Her hands were lifting and dipping in the sink, the hot tap open full. Her voice was flat. "The pedophile?"

"Yes, but—"

"The one who—let me see if I've got this right—the one who masturbates infants in the cradle and rapes little boys and girls? That Mr. X?"

"Oh, come on, Iris," I said, "get off it, will you? He's an extreme example, that's all, the icing on the cake—and Prok is in heaven over it."

We'd been over some of this ground before. Mac had been transcribing Mr. X's diaries for the files so that we could return the originals to him, and naturally, all of us were excited and had been discussing some of the revelations the diaries contained, and sure, I'm guilty of bringing home my work like so many other men, but my enthusiasm was genuine and it hurt to have Iris belittle it. Mr. X was a real find. A gem. The extreme case that gives the lie to the norm. He'd started his career when he was a child himself, having been initiated into heterosexual activity by his grandmother, and homosexual sex by his father, and, ultimately, he had sexual contact with seventeen members of his extended family. Over the course of his life—he was then sixty-three—he had had sexual relations with six hundred preadolescent males and two hundred preadolescent females, in addition to consummating innumerable sex acts with adults of both sexes and several species of animals. He was a prodigy, no doubt about it, and he had data—and experience—we could make use of. To me, that was all that mattered. Iris felt differently.

"Yes," she said, turning to me as I fumbled to take the dish from her hand and rinse it under the faucet, "but I teach those kids. Second graders, John. They're seven years old. They're like puppies, like lambs, as innocent and sweet as anything you'd ever want to see, you know that. And then you have the gall to stand there and tell me you're excited because you get to talk to some monster who's devoted his life to molesting them? I'm supposed to be happy for you? Tell me. Am I supposed to like that?"

"I'm not condoning his behavior," I said, "it's just that I, well, I feel it's important to document it, because, well, because it's already happened, for one thing, and there's really nothing I or anyone else can do about that—"

"No? How about turning him over to the police? How about locking him up? Huh? That's what you can do. And Prok can too."

"Listen," I said, backing away from her now—just setting the wet plate down in the dish rack and backing away from her before I had a chance to let the resentment come up in me—"that's not the point and you know it."

She'd swung round on me, arms folded over her breast, hands glistening with the beads of wet suds. "When are you leaving?" she asked, holding my eyes.

"Day after tomorrow."

"Is Purvis going?"

I nodded.

"How long? Not that it matters, because being deserted week in and week out is what I've come to expect, haven't I? 'Where's your husband?' everybody asks me. 'Oh,' they say, 'another business trip, then? Don't you miss him?' Well, I do, John, I do miss you."

I dropped my chin, gave a shrug to minimize the idea of it, to show I was listening and empathizing and that it was just one of those things but I'd be back as soon as I could and that I missed her too. In reality, though, I was looking forward to leaving—not because of her, of course, because I loved her and would just as soon have been there with her—but because we were going west, way out west, and to that point in my life I'd never even crossed the Mississippi. "Well, it'll, I'm afraid—because he lives out west, in Albuquerque. New Mexico, that is . . ." I trailed off. Shrugged again. "Two weeks," I said.

"*Two weeks?*"

"Yes, well, we have to drive—and, I don't know, it's a long ways, something like fifteen hundred miles or more. Each way."

"And what am I supposed to do in the meanwhile? You want me to lie in there on the bed and, what do you call it, *stimulate* myself with my finger? You want me to count orgasms for you, John? Would that be helpful?"

"No," I said, "no, I don't think so."

"What then? Violet and me? Should we stimulate each other? And then record it for our sex diaries?"

"Iris," I said.

"What?" she said. "What?"

2

As I try to place it now, I do believe it must have been the summer of 1944 when the three of us—Prok, Corcoran and I—set out on our trip west. It was hot, I remember that much, oppressively so, and it grew hotter as we swung south, toward Memphis and the network of highways and country roads that would take us west through Arkansas, Oklahoma and the Texas Panhandle and on into the pale, bleached mountains of New Mexico. Prok had the windows down—he liked the feel of the air on his face, and any other arrangement would have been impossible in that steam bath of a climate, but the incessant rush of the wind made conversation difficult and brought us into intimate contact with a whole array of angry wasps, dazed moths and partially dismembered leafhoppers, katydids and the like. There were insects down my collar, in my hair, emerging from the creases of my short-sleeved shirt. "If only they were edible!" I shouted from the backseat to Prok, who was shouting over the roar to Corcoran, who was seated beside him and bobbing his head to some internal rhythm. Prok paused to glance over his shoulder and shout back, "They are!" then hit the accelerator.

Fields cantered by, houses and barns and outbuildings in need of paint, billboards exhorting Christian fervor and advocating the consumption of snuff and chewing tobacco. The countryside smelled of silage, of rot and fresh-turned muck. There were mules everywhere, stage-struck cattle, chickens that never could seem to resist running out into the road. We stopped at small-town cafes and stared at plates of eggs and grits and fried sidemeat, barely able to muster the energy to lift the forks to our mouths. Sweetened iced tea—by the pitcherful—saved our lives.

It was an adventure, for all that—the greatest adventure of my life to that point—and as Prok expatiated on the *Kama Sutra,* Swedish pornography, the erotic art of pre-Columbian America and a host of other subjects, and Corcoran and I swapped seats so that we could alternate stealing catnaps and providing an audience for him, I felt as if the whole world were opening up before me. I was heading west, with my colleagues, and every mile that rolled under our tires brought new sights and sensations—*Oklahoma, I thought, I'm in Oklahoma*—and though I wasn't yet twenty-six, I felt like a man of the world, an exotic, a seasoned traveler and explorer nonpareil. Other men were off at war, experiencing the camaraderie of combat, but we were here, comrades in science, watching the plains and the washes and hoodoos roll away before us in the naked glare of the morning and the beholden mystery of the night.

It took us eight days to get there, Prok forever snaking down this irresistible turning or that, collecting galls out of habit, bumping ten miles along a dirt path just to erect our tent by an unmoving brown band of water someone had once called a river. As I've said, I wasn't much for camping—and Corcoran was even worse—but Prok more than made up for us. His energy was explosive. Even after sitting behind the wheel from early morning till late in the afternoon (he insisted on doing all the driving himself), he sprang out of the car to set up camp, collect armloads of scrub oak or mesquite and cook us flapjacks and eggs or even the odd fish he'd managed to pull out of a hidden puddle in the time it took the cookfire to die down to coals. He was indefatigable, as solicitous of our comfort and welfare as a scoutmaster—or better yet, a big brother—and as genial and full of high spirits as I'd ever seen him. He educated us in the fine points of woodcraft, entertained us round the campfire with stories of his gall wasp expeditions in the Sierra Madre, allowed us the solace of my flask and the bottle of brandy Corcoran had brought along against the chill of the night, though there was no chill and Prok himself had little interest in liquor except as an agent in loosening the tongues of his subjects.

There was, as you might expect, nudity as well. Prok cooked in the nude, set up the tent in the nude, hiked and bird-watched and swam in the nude, and encouraged us to do the same. My tan came back. My muscles hardened. And Corcoran, fair-skinned as he was, burned and burned again until he peeled like an egg and showed off the beginnings of his own tan.

And, of course, there was sex. Prok expected it—you couldn't very well hold back or risk being branded prudish or sex shy—and Corcoran and I complied, with varying levels of enthusiasm. I remember one night—we were in a motor court in Las Vegas, New Mexico, flush with the heady triumph of having arrived safe and sound and looking forward to our rendezvous with the exemplary Mr. X in the morning—when I walked in on Prok and Corcoran stretched naked across the bed. Prok glanced up, disengaged himself, and said, "Milk, come join us."

Did I want to? Honestly? No, not then. It was too complicated, what with the auras of Iris, Violet and Mac hovering over the scene and my own limited H-history, but Prok could be extraordinarily charming and persuasive and there were no hidebound moral strictures or antiquated notions of fidelity to hold us back, not here in a New Mexico motel, not anywhere, not in Bloomington or Indianapolis or New York, and so, in the end, I acquiesced. Why? I suppose because it was just easier that way. Certainly that was part of it, but to be honest, there was more to it than that: I loved him. I did. Not in the way I loved Iris, perhaps, or even Mac, but in a deeper way, in the way a patriot loves his country or a zealot his God, and if that love meant molding my needs to his, then so be it.

At any rate, the following morning we took the cold shower Prok always insisted upon when we were traveling, winter or summer, outdoors or in-, toweled ourselves vigorously, sat down to an anticipatory breakfast at the local diner, and went back to the room to await Mr. X's arrival. Sitting there in the unmodulated glare of the morning, our fingers tapping idly at the scuffed furniture while we belched softly over our scrambled eggs and waffles, pencils sharpened and ready, we couldn't help speculating about the man. He was sixty-three, yes, but a sexual giant for all that, and we pictured an individual of imposing build, broad-shouldered, with big, work-hardened hands and catapulting arms, a man with the strength and tenacity to put all our other high raters into another category altogether, a kind of Paul Bunyan of sex, towering over the field. But of course expectations are meant to be defeated and looks can be deceiving.

Mr. X was five feet five inches tall, one hundred twenty-two pounds. He walked with a limp, hunched his shoulders forward and appeared, if anything, older than his years. Anyone over forty seemed ancient to me in those days—aside from Prok, of course—but this man, Mr. X, might have told us he was eighty and I wouldn't have been surprised. The flesh beneath his chin hung in folds, and his hands were maculated with liver spots. He was almost entirely bald (a sign of virility, Prok maintained, if you excepted the three of us present and the legend of Samson and Delilah), and his face was cross-hatched with infinitely fine lines and the deeper gouges of age and experience. When he first came to the door I thought there must be some mistake, but Prok never missed a beat. "Welcome," he said, holding the door open for him, "we've been expecting you."

Our subject stood there expressionless in the doorway, a cordovan suitcase at his feet, his eyes glittering like flecks of glass in a dry riverbed. He looked round the room a moment, took note of Corcoran and me, then lifted his upper lip in the simulacrum of a grin. Something shrewd came into his eyes. "Dr. Kinsey, I presume?" he said with a mock bow, and let out a low, hoarse laugh.

"Yes," Prok returned, taking his hand, "Alfred C. Kinsey. It's a great pleasure. And these are my colleagues, Purvis Corcoran and John Milk. But can I get you anything? Coffee? Juice? Perhaps a rum cocktail, if it's not too early?"

In the suitcase were the remaining volumes of his sex diaries, which included detailed descriptions of all the omnifarious encounters he'd ever had, as well as measurements of the various penises and clitorises with which he'd personally come into contact over the course of his long career; photographs he'd taken of sex acts with a whole variety of individuals, in many of which he himself appeared, first as a young man, then middle-aged and finally elderly; a selection of sex aids and lubricants; and, puzzlingly, a single carpenter's drill fitted with a half-inch bit. After shaking hands with Corcoran and me, Mr. X unceremoniously flung the suitcase on the bed, flipped the twin latches, and began passing the artifacts round the room as if they were holy relics.

The photographs—there were a hundred or more—had the most immediate effect. I remember one in particular, which showed only the hand of an adult, with its outsized fingers, manipulating the genitalia of an infant—a boy, with a tiny, twig-like erection—and the look on the infant's face, its eyes unfocused, mouth open, hands groping at nothing, and the sensation it gave me. I felt myself go cold all over, as if I were still in the bathtub, standing rigid beneath the icy shower. I glanced at Corcoran, whose face showed nothing, and then at Prok, who studied the photograph a moment and pronounced it "Very interesting, very interesting indeed." He leaned in close to me to point out the detail, and said, "You see, Milk, here is definitive proof of infantile sexuality, and whether it's an anomaly or not, of course, is yet to be demonstrated statistically—"

Still bent over the open suitcase, shuffling through his trove, our subject let out a soft whistle. "Believe me," he said, "it's no anomaly."

We let that hang in the air a moment, and then Prok said, "But the drill—what's the significance of that?"

"Oh, this?" the little man murmured, extracting the thing from the suitcase with a bemused grin, and all I could think of was some extreme form of sadomasochism, disfigurement, torture. I felt my stomach sink. Despite myself, I'd begun to feel distinctly uncomfortable, and I glanced at Prok for reassurance, but Prok was fixated on the instrument in the man's hand, utterly absorbed.

Mr. X took his time. He shrugged. Looked at each of us in succession, then dropped his eyes, and you could see he was a man who enjoyed an audience. "It's for drilling."

Prok gave him a look. He was being his most patient self, smiling along with the little man, encouraging and respectful, without the least hint of condescension. He'd revealed to me the night before that he'd felt a real sense of urgency in coming here to collect Mr. X's history because the man was in ill health and could die at any moment and be lost forever to science, and he'd made no bones about it: this was our most significant interview to date. "Yes?" he said. "And to what purpose?"

"Well, of course, you know my work—aside from sex, I mean?"

We did. The man worked for a government agency, which necessitated a great deal of travel and overnight accommodations in various cities around the country.

"I observe," he said.

Prok wasn't following him. "Observe?"

"That's right," he said in his soft, guttural tones, and he moved to the far wall to demonstrate. He put his ear to the paneling for a moment, and then, satisfied that the room was unoccupied—or that the occupants were either asleep or out of the room—he went down on one knee and with a quick noiseless rotation of his right hand and shoulder made a neat peephole just above the baseboard. "Here," he said, "here, have a look"—and we did, each in turn—"because you'd be surprised what you might see, and how much." He paused to collect his breath. "Because people—well, you know, when they're in a hotel room, safe from observation and the routine of their lives, they tend to do things they might not do otherwise. Oh, yeah. I've seen it all. Whores, monkeys, midgets. Everything. You'd be surprised."

What came next was even more startling—we'd been voyeurs ourselves, after all, and the notion of observing a private act unseen was within the realm of our experience—but this man, this dynamo, had much more to offer us. Somehow the conversation turned to masturbation and masturbatory technique, even before we'd formally begun the interview. "You know, Dr. Kinsey," the little man was saying, comfortable now in the armchair by the window, a cigarette in one hand, a mug of coffee in the other, "I am the most highly sexed individual you will ever come across. Number one. Numero uno. There's nobody like me. Nobody."

Prok, accommodating but empirically skeptical: "Is that so?"

"Oh, yes. As for masturbation, even now, at my age, I probably—what term do you like to use? Beat off?—beat off three or four times a day. And I can go from nothing to orgasm in ten seconds flat, and tell me if that isn't a record?"

Corcoran, seated on the bed, one leg crossed at the knee, and his pencil poised over the position sheet—we would be simultaneously recording this interview—said casually, "That's very impressive. But shouldn't we begin now? To get all this for the record, I mean?"

"You don't believe me?"

"Of course we believe you," Prok put in.

"Just watch." And before anyone could demur, Mr. X had his trousers down. "Anyone have a second hand on their watch? You?" he said, pointing to me. "What was your name?"

"Milk," I said. "John Milk."

"Well, do you?" His pubic hair was white and his penis lay shriveled in the nest of it. He was an old man, shrunken and old, and I wanted to look away, but I didn't.

"Yes," I said. "Well, yes. I think so."

"Okay," he said, "you tell me when," and I looked to Prok and Prok nodded and I said, "When," and this dried-up little homunculus of a man actually did it—went from flaccid to hard to orgasm in just ten seconds. It was amazing. Simply amazing. None of us had ever seen anything like it. There was a moment of suspension and release, and I almost thought Corcoran was going to burst into applause.

A few years later, famously, we would film some one thousand men in the process of masturbating in order to reach a determination as to whether the majority spurted or dribbled (seventy-three percent dribbled, incidentally, myself included), but to this point we'd never observed—or requested—a demonstration. It took us a moment to recover ourselves as Mr. X mopped up and wriggled back into his trousers, and then Corcoran lit a cigarette despite a sharp glance from Prok, and we sat down to record the history—all three of us, simultaneously, barely taking time to break for the bathroom, or for food and drink, for that matter.

As it turned out, Mr. X had almost perfect recall. He slouched in the armchair, smoking one cigarette after another, and brought us back to his childhood, to his father and grandmother and his siblings and cousins and aunts and uncles, and then on through his adolescence and adulthood, through boys and girls, women and men, dogs and sheep and even, in one case, a parrot, and it took two and a half days to record it all. I listened to that voice, that soft hitching rasp of breath, the tireless recitation, act after act, partner after partner, and I couldn't help thinking of Iris, of what she'd said, but I put on my professional face nonetheless and bent over the position sheet and did what I'd come halfway across the country to do.

In all, we were gone just short of five weeks. Prok was clearly enjoying himself, exulting in the season and the freedom of the road as he hadn't in a long while, this trip reminiscent for him of the gall wasp expeditions he'd made a decade earlier, fieldwork, getting out from behind the desk, that sort of thing, and he kept coming up with excuses to prolong the journey. He made a point of seeking out college towns along the route, and we would drive in unannounced and park in front of the administration building, Corcoran and I sitting in the car having a surreptitious smoke while Prok chatted up the dean or the provost. As likely as not we would be invited to stay on and collect histories, Prok, in most cases, being called upon to give an impromptu lecture to concerned faculty or a local civics group. We could have traveled like that for the rest of the year if we'd wanted to—for the rest of our lives, I suppose, gypsy scholars, men of science on the prowl—but of course it was problematic, not only for the cohesion of the project and the correlation of our data toward the ultimate goal of publication, but for our domestic lives as well.

I wrote Iris every day for the first week, postcards featuring pastel cowboys in chaps or an oil rig set against a backdrop of tumbleweed and cactus, and though I was full of enthusiasm I tried to keep my tone neutral and even somewhat regretful, playing down the sheer adventure of it so as to avoid stirring up any feelings of jealousy or resentment on her part. By the second week, I was writing her every other day, three-sentence descriptions of a meal—*frijoles* and *tortillas*, with a hot sauce made of chopped green tomatoes and chilies, a wonder of a thing, like nothing I'd ever tasted—or a depiction of a town or landscape. And then it was every third or fourth day, or when I remembered, guiltily, that she was home alone, in the constricted world of the apartment and the grid of repetitive streets and not even her job to sustain her because it was summer recess now and what was she doing with the long unraveling thread of her days? Finally, in the end, I wrote simply to tell her I missed her.

In Tucumcari, I found a shop that sold silver-and-turquoise jewelry, and I bought her a heavy silver bracelet in what the woman behind the counter described as an Aztec flower pattern, and then in Amarillo I found her a basket made of the tanned skin of an armadillo looped tail to snout. She didn't write back, of course. She couldn't. We were in no place longer than a day or two at a time, and our progress was haphazard in any case. There were telephones, but long distance was cripplingly expensive, not to mention unreliable. I could have wired her, I suppose, and she could have wired back. But I didn't. I promised myself I'd make it up to her when we got back.

By the time we did finally pull into Bloomington, I was as homesick as I'd ever been in my life. All the novelty of travel, the excitement of the wide-open spaces and the long-horned steers and all the rest faded during that last week, and I missed my wife, longed for her with an inconsolable ache that kept me awake in the cramped confines of the tent or the anonymous bed in one or another of the string of motor courts and cheap hotels we checked into every third or fourth night, missed the simple routine of going off to work in the morning and coming home to her in the evening, of feeling the reassuring pressure of her hand in mine as we strolled down the leaf-hung avenue for a beer at the tavern or a night out at the picture show. I'd never been away from home, from Indiana, for so long before, and when we crossed the state line at Jeffersonville, I felt my heart soar.

It was late in the afternoon when Prok dropped me off in front of the apartment, and I was out the door with my suitcase before he'd come to a complete stop, yes, thank you, so long, see you at work in the morning, and I remember how intoxicating the smell of the grass was, the dahlias along the walk, the geraniums in the window box. I was perspiring under the arms and the shirt was stuck to my back, but I hardly felt it. The soles of my shoes pulsed with radiant energy as I came up the walk, my heart pounding, no thought but for Iris and how I was going to surprise her and give her the bracelet and the basket and tell her how much I'd missed her and how I was never going to go on a collecting trip again, never, or at least not for a long while to come. A sudden flash of lightning fractured the sky over the elm then, and as I reached the porch the light shaded from copper to silver and a breeze came up out of the south. That was when I heard the music sifting through the screen in the front window, and the sound of laughter, of women's laughter, two voices clenched round the pith of a joke, and I pushed open the door and stepped inside. "Iris?" I called. "Iris, I'm home."

The room was dim, stifling, and Iris was there, seated on the sofa with another woman, the radio turned up loud and a dance band keeping the beat. There was cigarette smoke, there were cocktails, and as I set down the suitcase I saw that the other woman was Violet Corcoran, in a pair of shorts and a blouse that left her midriff bare.

"John?" Iris called, and her voice was slurred with drink, or maybe that was my imagination. "John? Is that you?" She was up out of the couch now, barefooted, in a pair of white shorts, and she ran to me and threw herself into my arms. "My God, I thought you'd never get here!" We kissed, hurriedly, frantically, and I tasted the alcohol on her tongue—gin—and the heat and surprise and exultation. "Violet," she called, swinging away from me, "look who's here!"

I don't know if this is the time to mention it, but I should say that my relationship with Violet Corcoran, begun on that night in the office at Prok's instigation, was never anything more than merely satisfactory. We came together—she had me inside of her practically before I could get my trousers down—and afterward we had a drink and I walked her home, and then we met in a motor court outside of town three or four times, but it all felt scripted and cold, and gradually we both came to understand that there was no need to pursue things further. I liked her. Truly, I did. She was effusive and genuine and I was glad to see her there keeping Iris company.

"The return of the wanderers," Violet said, or something like it. She'd risen from the couch and was already gathering up her things. "I guess this means I'd better hightail it home for Purvis—and oh, God, the babysitter—but hi, John, and goodbye." She gave a wink. "I wouldn't want to get in the way of anything here—"

The screen door slammed behind her and we both turned to watch her skip down the walk even as a flash of lightning lit the room, followed by a dull rumble of thunder. It took me a moment to realize the radio was still on—static crackled from the speaker, followed by three quick incinerating bursts that were like a rudimentary code—and then the program went dead and everything was still. I could smell the edge of the wetness on the air, as if a swamp had been dredged and everything that had lain seething there had been drawn up into the atmosphere, fish, newts, turtles and tadpoles, the muck itself, and every plant left naked to the root. Nothing moved. The light was like poured metal. I turned to Iris, but she seemed strange to me, a dark and pretty stranger with bare feet and painted toenails staring out through the rusted grid of the screen door. The moment lengthened, stretched to the breaking point, and I have to admit I felt awkward there in my own house with my own wife, as if I were a stranger to her too. Finally, she turned to me, hands on her hips now—more body language—and said, "I guess you want a drink, huh? Or dinner. You want dinner?"

"Sure," I said. "A drink would be nice. But we already, well, we stopped along the way, and—well, I missed you. I did. It was—I never expected it would be so long. It was Prok, you know that."

Her eyes were moist—but they were more than moist, they were wet, overflowing. The breeze stirred the trees and rushed the door. "I feel like a war bride," she said, letting her hands drop to her sides. "I might as well be. And you. You might as well be a soldier. On Tarawa or someplace. You might as well be dead."

I said her name, softly, and I drew her to me and put my arms around her. I held her a moment, rocking with her in my arms, and then it all came out of her. She was crying—sobbing, actually—and I could feel the tug and release of emotion running through her like a new kind of heartbeat geared to some other system altogether. "I missed you too," she whispered.

Ten minutes later we were nestled on the couch, watching the rain sweep the street and bow the trees. The smell of rot faded as soon as the storm broke, replaced now with an astringent freshness out of the north, clear pellets dropping down from the troposphere to beat tinnily at the gutters and saturate the patch of lawn out front. Iris had made me a bourbon and water and another gin and tonic for herself. We were celebrating—drinking to my return—but it didn't feel like a celebration. It felt sad and unformed, and I wanted to take her into the bedroom and show her in the most elemental way how much I'd missed her, but that wouldn't have been right, not yet. First we had to talk things out.

"He was disgusting, wasn't he?"

"Who?"

"Your Mr. X."

I had to give her this. I sipped my drink and nodded slowly. She'd put something on the stove for me, out of duty, I suppose, though I'd reiterated that I wasn't hungry—at least not for food—and the lid of the pot rattled as whatever it was came to a boil. "Yeah," I said. "I suppose."

"I'll bet Prok loved him."

"Prok doesn't make those judgments, you know that."

She said nothing, and we both stared out at the rain. "*Tortillas*," she said after a while, enunciating a hard *l* where she should have elided, "they're Mexican, is that it?"

"Tortee-yas," I said. "Yes, that's right. They have them in Texas. New Mexico too."

"What are they like, pancakes?"

"A little, I guess. They're flat. Like unleavened bread. They make them out of flour or cornmeal, pat them with their hands—the Indians and Mexicans—and then they put a filling inside or use them to scoop up beans and rice and whatnot."

She was silent a moment, sipping at her drink. "Pretty exotic, huh? You're not going to turn Mexican on me, are you? With what—a *serape*, isn't that what they call them, and a *sombrero*? What do I call you, Don John? Or Don Juan, would that be better?"

I leaned in to kiss her. "Don Juan will do nicely. But I wish you were there to taste them, and the *frijoles* and *salsa* too. And these things they call *tamales,* wrapped up in corn husks. You'd like them. You would."

She shrugged. "Yeah," she said. "Sure I would. If I ever got to go any-place."

"You will," I said. "I promise."

"When? We can't afford a vacation. It's a joke. And my mother—just to visit her, just the bus fare puts a strain on the budget. No, John, you can keep your tortee-yas."

The rain seemed to intensify then, a crashing fall that silenced every-thing. I didn't want to bicker, didn't want anything to interfere with the unalloyed pleasure of seeing her again and the prospect of sex, marital relations, the two of us in bed together after five long weeks of enforced abstinence, and I was on fire to touch her, undress her, put my tongue in her mouth and lose my fingers in her hair. I leaned forward to light a cigarette, trying to figure what I could do to defuse the situation. She was bitter, I could understand that. She felt deserted, felt that life was passing her by while I was off experiencing it to the full—which wasn't true, not by a long shot, as I think I've made clear here. The problem wasn't unique. Any man who traveled for a living, whether he was in the service or in sales or meteorology or the railroad industry, had of neces-sity to leave his wife behind for long stretches at a time—that was just the nature of certain professions.

Mac had the same problem, and she'd found a way to deal with it. Though she never let it slip in public, I knew she was frustrated—she wanted to be included too, but Prok made a fraternity of his research and she turned to the children and her knitting and the Girl Scouts in compensation. The closest she ever came to criticism, to my knowledge, was a phrase she let slip in one of the women's magazines after the male volume had come out. She'd been asked about Prok and his travels and if his devotion to research didn't make things hard on her, and her an-swer was telling: "I hardly see him at night since he took up sex." Every-one had laughed—Clara Kinsey had come up with a bon mot—but I saw the truth of it.

One time—and this was after Rutledge had joined us and the Kinsey children were grown and out of the house—Mac came along with us on one of our expeditions, just to participate, to do something other than housework for a change. I can't recall now where it was, some uninspiring midwestern college town, no doubt, a place little different from Bloomington, and it was probably winter too, so that even the scenery was unrelieved. We checked into a hotel, the usual arrangement, and got two adjoining rooms, Prok, Mac, Rutledge and I, Corcoran having stayed behind to man the fort at the Institute. Mac entertained herself as best she could while we recorded our interviews—she might have gone to the snowbound park or poked in at the library or a thrift shop, I don't know. Afterward, we had a late supper and went up to the rooms, where I assumed Prok and Mac would retire and leave Rutledge and me to fend for ourselves. But Prok was especially keyed up that night, pacing round the floor and going on about his enemies—their legions had grown over the years—and some of the oddities that had come up in the interviews that day. And films. He was just then pioneering the use of film in recording the mating habits of various species of animal, and I remember he was particularly excited about the work of a Professer Shadle at the University of Buffalo, who had apparently documented the reproductive behavior of captive porcupines. "Porcupines!" Prok kept exclaiming. "Can you imagine that? With all that defensive armor? And yet they still, of course, manage coitus, or where would the species be?"

Mac was right there with him, never shy about expressing her views, and Rutledge was fully engaged too, interjecting opinions, pulling his chin over this thought or that, waving his hands in expostulation; I was content to sit back with a Coca-Cola and listen, though I wished I could have lit up a cigarette. (About Rutledge: he was a Princeton Ph.D. in Cultural Anthropology, thirty-eight years old, a neat, limber man with a slight stoop and a sardonic grin who wore a wire-thin mustache in homage to his Iberian ancestry on his mother's side, and maybe even to Duke Ellington too. For what it's worth, incidentally, Prok detested all facial hair, arguing that only someone with something to hide would

want to mask his features.) After a while, the subject turned from porcupine sex to human sex and Prok's usual gloss on the mores of the
day—we were all too inhibited, he insisted, even those of us in the highest ranks of sex research, those of us right there in that very room. "Oh,
really?" Rutledge put in, rising to the bait. "How so?"

"Take Mac, for instance," Prok said, catching himself up in midstride.
"Here's an engaging, desirable woman sitting right here with us as we
jaw on about sex, and we haven't given a thought to taking advantage of
the situation, now have we?"

"What do you mean?" Rutledge was leaning against the far wall, an
empty soft-drink bottle and a half-eaten hamburger sandwich on the
bureau beside him. Two quick nervous fingers went to his mustache.

"To enjoy ourselves with her, obviously. You're willing, aren't you,
Mac?"

Mac, seated in the armchair with her knitting, glanced up sharply,
then looked away. She murmured something that sounded like assent,
and I felt myself go numb. I couldn't look at her. I wanted to get up out
of the chair, push through the door and go out into the dark streets of a
city I didn't know and didn't care about and just walk till my legs gave
out. It wasn't jealousy I was feeling, but something else altogether,
something I couldn't have put in words if you'd asked me.

"Oh, but that hardly proves anything—that's just convention."

Prok's eyes were glowing. "My point exactly."

There was some further debate, Mac's opinion solicited, mine, the
ball going back and forth between Rutledge and Prok, but ultimately
Prok made a challenge of it: either we expressed ourselves sexually,
without inhibition, or we proved his point. "Actions speak louder than
words, wouldn't you agree?"

Was she enthusiastic? I couldn't read her, but all traces of her girlish-
ness had vanished and she'd put on her objective face—this wasn't what
she'd come for, wasn't what she'd expected. Rutledge—he was married,
the father of two—seemed nonplussed. "But go ahead," Prok insisted,
"enjoy yourselves—Rutledge, you're the new man, why don't you go
first?"

What I'm trying to indicate here is that Iris's feelings were by no means unique, though I understood and wanted only to placate her, to love and support her and give her everything I had to offer, emotionally and physically both. "Iris," I said, "come on. Let's not fight."

"Keep them," she said, even as the thunder rattled the windows and drummed at the walls, "and all the rest of your Mexican delicacies." Her face was featureless in the dimming light. "I can eat meat loaf."

"Are you listening to yourself? That's ridiculous. You don't have to—"

"Or salt pork. Or hardtack," she said, and she was smiling now, her beautiful smile, enriched with softness and sympathy. "Give me hard-tack any day."

I reached out and stroked the back of her hand. "Okay, point taken. I'll never mention *tortillas* again."

Before she could respond there came a plaintive choked cry from the kitchen, something very like a cat's mewing, followed by the thump of a compact body springing from sink to floor, and in the next moment the bead curtains parted and I found myself staring into the unblinking yellow gaze of the biggest tomcat I'd ever seen. "What's that?" I asked stupidly.

"A cat. His name's Addison."

"You're kidding," I said.

She ignored me. "Here, Addison. Come here, boy," she cooed, and the cat, which had frozen at the sight of me, began to inch across the carpet on its abdomen. When it reached the couch it sprang up with a practiced leap and settled down in her lap.

"But we can't have a cat. You know I'm allergic, and its food—it's an expense. I mean, who's going to pay for the food?"

The cat had begun to purr, a ratchety shifting of breath from nostrils to larynx to lungs and back again. She was stroking the thing. "I need company, John."

I said nothing. The rain drooled from the gutters.

"If you're not going to be here, that is—and I don't think you have anything to say about it, not being gone, what, *thirty-four* days? In a row? Without so much as a phone call?"

It would have been fitting for a thunderclap to shake the house then, but it didn't come. Or maybe it did. Maybe I'm misremembering.

"And there's another thing. And I don't care what you say." She brought her face to mine, closing the gap over the cat and the hand that was stroking him instead of me, her eyes hovering, her lips, her teeth, the sweet scent of her breath. "I want a baby, John. I've made up my mind."

And now it came—*Boom!*—and everything rattled, right on down to the dishes in the cupboard and the knives in the drawer.

3

THINGS SETTLED DOWN for a while after that—or settled into a routine, at any rate. We traveled a bit less frequently that fall, as a threesome, that is, Prok and Corcoran going off on two separate jaunts to New York and Philadelphia, making contacts and bagging histories along the way, and in their absence I punched the clock and focused on the affairs of the Institute. I didn't mind. It was good to be home and spending more time with Iris, though of course I was still on the road a great deal and when I wasn't, I have to confess I did miss the excitement of the chase. In some ways, I suppose, a habituation to routine and the quiet, ordered life was suited to my temperament, but there was another part of me altogether that yearned for the road, for adventure, and once Prok had opened up that world to me I could never get enough of it.

As for the Institute, though we wouldn't incorporate for three years yet, we were growing in prestige and autonomy both, and along with our full-time secretary—the formidable Mrs. Bella Matthews—we'd taken on part-time clerical help as well, and this necessitated shifting things around to fit another desk in the offices, Mrs. Matthews going into the anteroom and the part-timers finding space alongside Corcoran. The library, all of it acquired at Prok's personal expense and already running to some five thousand items—books in the field, photographs, artwork, sex diaries and the like—had taken over every available inch of space in the inner office and a locked, windowless spare room down the hall that once had been used to store lab equipment. To say that we were cramped for space would be an understatement. Even more pressing was the need for "more hands," as Prok put it—that is, another researcher to assist in collecting the new and astonishing figure of one hundred thousand histories he was now determined to record.

To that end, we had begun to send out feelers to various academic institutions—and Prok tirelessly canvassed his colleagues around the country in an attempt to attract a candidate who would reflect well on our research. At that point, I had only a baccalaureate to my name, and Corcoran his Master's, and so Prok had his sights set on an older man—in his thirties, that is—with a Ph.D. in the social sciences or psychology, and from a prestigious university. He himself, of course, was a Harvard man, and though he never said as much in an effort to spare our feelings, he was looking for someone whose credentials and affiliation could balance out our rather pedestrian state university degrees. As I recall, we did conduct some interviews through the fall and into the spring of the following year—1945—but the response wasn't what we'd hoped for. The war was still in progress, after all, and the vast majority of the workforce still employed by Uncle Sam.

On the home front—the personal home front, that is, in the kitchen, living room and bedroom of the apartment Iris and I shared at 619 Elm Street—things began to even out as well. Every marriage experiences growing pains, and certainly we'd had ours, but now I was home, or home more frequently than I had been, and I was determined to make up for past mistakes. I made a real effort to be there on time for dinner each night, even if it meant getting to the office earlier in the morning in order to accommodate the workload; I tried to talk more about literature, art, current events, and less about Prok and sex; I gave up going to the tavern after work and attempted to help around the house as much as I could, though I have to admit I was no paragon here—but I was trying, at least I was trying. Over time, I even began to tolerate the cat. And if I balked initially over the issue of having a child (the usual excuses: we were too young, we couldn't afford it, a cat was one thing and a baby another), I recalled my moment of clarity at the Fillmore School, children, children everywhere, and it wasn't long before I began to come round to Iris's way of thinking.

That first night was a trial, though, and I don't mind admitting it. We didn't seem to be communicating, not at all, and I should have been more sympathetic, but I was exhausted, both physically and mentally, and I wasn't at my best. Far from it. Just as she was softening, at the very moment I was about to dig the bracelet out of my suitcase and make everything right again, the cat came between us and somehow the cat managed to metamorphose into a hypothetical child. "I want a baby, John," she said, and I didn't even think, didn't hesitate or bother with the emotional calculus, just said no. And Iris, with the pot rattling on the stove and I don't know how much gin in her, not to mention the residue of an afternoon's gossip with Violet Corcoran, threw it back at me. "Fine," she said, "if that's how you feel you can sleep right here on the couch then, because you're not coming near me, not even for a touch, a kiss, nothing. You hear me?"

And that was it, the end of our joyful reunion. She took the cat into the bedroom and slammed the door and I went out to the nearest bar and drank bourbon in a corner all by myself while people crowded around the radio and listened to news of the war and I seethed and ached and went faint with lust for her, for my own wife, five weeks away from home and no sex, no affection, nothing but rancor and a cat. I was furious. Heartbroken. Disgusted with myself and with her too—with marriage, the whole corrupt and coercive institution. Prok was right: man was pansexual, and it was only convention—law, custom, the church—that kept him from expressing himself with any partner that came along, of whatever sex or species. Marriage was a ball and chain. It was slavery. And it sanctioned nothing but acrimony. I walked home in the rain, haunted by lust, slept on the couch and woke with a hangover. I was gone before she got up.

At work, I tried to solicit Prok's advice, but he was moving at light speed, flying from his desk to mine and Corcoran's and Mrs. Matthews's and back again, five weeks of accumulated correspondence and metastasizing problems to conquer and all in a single day, because with Prok nothing could wait till tomorrow. It was late in the afternoon before I was finally able to corner him. He'd gone to the lavatory—with a file of papers in one hand and his fountain pen in the other—and I waited at the door for him. When he emerged five minutes later, chin down, shoulders squared, in his usual headlong rush, I made as if I were on the way to the lavatory myself and just happened to run into him. "Oh," I said, "Prok, hello. But do you have a minute? I wanted to, well, have a word with you, if that's all right, if you have time, that is—"

As I've said, of all the individuals I've ever known, Prok was the most rigorously attuned to the subconscious signals people give out when they're distressed or angry or simply trying to cover up their feelings. He would have made a master detective. Now he just gave me a look— the sudden blue fastening of the eyes, the flash of the spectacles—and said, "Problems at home?"

"No," I said. "Or, yes, in a way."

A pair of biology professors—a zoologist in a lab coat and a botanist in shirtsleeves—stepped round us on their way to the lavatory and we both paused a moment to greet them. Once the door had closed, Prok turned back to me, his expression mild and receptive. "Yes," he said, "go on."

"Iris wants a baby."

He lifted his eyebrows. The grin—the famous grin—sprang to his lips. "That's marvelous news," he said. "Simply marvelous. Is she pregnant?"

"Oh, no," I said. "No, no. She just—last night, I mean."

"I understand," he said, taking me by the hand. "It's a big step. But it's all part of the natural progression, John, nothing to worry over. Children are a joy, you'll see. And if it's money you're worried about, I'm sure we can make some sort of arrangement when the time comes."

"It's not that. It's more the principle. I slept on the couch last night."

He said nothing to this, just held my eyes, awaiting the sequel, as if I were one of his interviewees.

"It was because of our trip, that we extended it, that is. She got a cat— for company, she claims—and now she brings up this other issue."

"Of a child."

"Yes. But I resent it. I'm not ready to take on the responsibility, Prok, and even if I was, she's making it a demand, and she says she won't, well, she won't *sleep* with me until I give in. That's what she said."

Prok took a moment to remove his spectacles and polish them on his handkerchief, the file tucked under one arm. He let out a sigh. "There's give and take in every marriage," he said, replacing the spectacles on the bridge of his nose and neatly folding up the handkerchief, square by square, "but my advice is to reclaim your rightful place in the marital bed. I'm not going to tell you to rush into anything, but a child might be just what you need at this juncture, as a maturing factor. I've been more than pleased with your work, you know that, but there's always room for improvement and I can't help but think that fatherhood—the direct experience of it, reproduction, John, your genes passed on to another generation—will make you an even more sympathetic interviewer, in the long run, that is. Don't you agree?"

All the way home, I rehearsed a little speech for Iris. I was going to tell her what Prok had said—that he'd all but given his blessing—but not right off. My mind was far from made up, and the first thing I expected from her was an apology. I worked as hard as anyone on this earth and whether she wanted to admit it or not the trip had put a real strain on me and she had no right whatever to deliver an ultimatum like that. Parenthood was a shared decision, something both spouses had to agree on, without resort to threats or blackmail. She didn't really want to bring a child into the world under a cloud of resentment, did she? Would that be good for the kid? Would that be healthy? No, we would just have to wait—think things over, talk it out—until we were both ready.

There was music playing when I came in the door, something muted and tender that put me in mind of the dances we used to go to, the sort of number the band played at the very end of the last set when they brought the tempo down and the couples just stood there and swayed in place. The table was set for dinner—with flowers in a vase and cloth napkins—and on the end table beside the couch a tall bourbon and water stood perspiring on a coaster. I glanced through the bead curtains to the kitchen and saw a pot on the stove and beside it a frying pan with the pink firm slab of a beefsteak stretched across it, and that was something, beefsteak in those days, really something. I just stood there a moment, taking it all in. This is more like it, I was thinking, and I went for the drink, lifted it to my lips and let the alcohol take away the heat of the day and the last lingering vestiges of my hangover from the night before. But where was she? In the bedroom, no doubt, fussing with her lipstick, dressing to please me, to make it up to me—she was wrong and she knew it. I could forget the speeches.

It was then that I noticed that the curtains were drawn. The day had been clear and therapeutically hot, the diligent Indiana sun burning off the residuum of the previous night's storm and saturating the air with humidity till the least movement made you break out in a sweat, and she should have had the curtains open, if only for a little circulation. I was puzzled. And sweating already, just from the effort of lifting the glass from the table. I called out her name: "Iris? Iris, I'm home!"

Her voice came from the back room—"Give me a minute"—and I took another long pull at the drink, set the glass down on the coaster and went to the window to let some air in. Just as I was reaching for the curtains, I became aware of the sudden swish and click of wooden beads behind me and Iris saying, "Don't."

I turned around and there she was, standing just my side of the dark undulating wave of suspended beads, the room half-lit, the music drifting out of the phonograph. She wasn't wearing any clothes. Nothing at all. Her feet were spread and her hands poised on her hips. I saw that she'd made up her eyes and applied lipstick and done her nails, but all that was inconsequential before the single illuminating gesture of her nudity. Iris was private in her habits and modest about her body, nothing like the exhibitionist Violet Corcoran was, and she'd never posed nude for me before, or if she had it was only in the way of foreplay, in the permissive confines of the bed. "Leave them closed," she murmured. "I don't want any of the neighbors to see."

I came to her as if I were on a leash and she allowed me one kiss, my hands on her breasts, her abdomen, the familiar territory, before she pushed me away. "But John," she said, and this was the very definition of coyness, "what are you doing? You know we can't have relations—aren't you afraid I'll get pregnant? Wouldn't that be a tragedy? Wouldn't it? Hmm?"

She was at the stove now, her back to me, lighting the gas under the pan, the beads rattling, the cat nowhere to be seen. I could taste the bourbon in the crook of my throat. The room was hotter than any sauna. And can I tell you that I took her right there on the kitchen floor, without a thought for Mac or Violet Corcoran or any other woman in the world, and that the condoms stayed right where they were, in the back corner of the cheap peeling laminated drawer of the nightstand in the bedroom?

I'D LIKE TO report that John Jr. was conceived that night, but it wasn't to be. Months went by, then the year, the war ended, Prok, Corcoran and I were traveling at an accelerated pace and collecting histories more assiduously than ever, and despite our best efforts—Iris's and mine—her menses came as regularly as before. We consulted the literature, employed the recommended coital positions and dutifully coupled during the most fertile period of the monthly cycle, but all for naught. Iris took hot baths, cold baths, rubbed herself with oleomargarine, consumed nothing but eggs for an entire month. Nothing seemed to work. I talked it over with Prok, who sent me to a specialist he knew in Indianapolis. I had a thoroughgoing physical, and the doctor even invited me into the back room to study my semen under the microscope in order to reassure me that there was nothing amiss. Prok and I began to suspect Iris, and she was examined too—by a gynecologist Prok recommended, the very man who'd helped Mac with her adhesion problem twenty years earlier—and he pronounced her both normal and fit. So what was the problem? What were we doing wrong? Neither of us had a clue, but Prok did, and he was typically blunt about it.

After reviewing the results—we were in the office and he'd been pacing back and forth in front of his desk with a puzzled frown, murmuring to himself—he motioned me to him. It might have been raining that day, I don't remember, but rain would have been appropriate—as a symbol of hope and fertility. I needed something positive, because I'd been down on myself, feeling inadequate, impotent, a failure even at this. We stood together at the window a moment, gazing out on the campus. "You just have to account for the aleatory factor here, that's all," he said finally.

"I'm sorry?"

"Each of the millions of your spermatozoa fighting for purchase in the uterus and Fallopian tubes, an ovum descended or not, as the case may be, natural selection at work, that is, in the microcosm of one woman's womb—"

I gave him a puzzled look.

"Chance, John, chance. Keep trying, that's all I can say."

In the meanwhile, our larger quest—for new blood at the Institute—had begun to turn up a number of qualified candidates now that the war was over, and we started interviewing in earnest. Each man was invited to campus, with his wife and family—the wives, in particular, had to be scrutinized, not only to determine if they were in any measure sex shy, but if they were discreet and reliable as well—and Prok gave them a tour of the facilities, arranged a picnic or musicale in their honor, took their histories and had Corcoran and me vet them for any irregularities. (Typically, Prok would have us take the candidate out on the town afterward, sans wife, in order to loosen him up and catch him off guard, and if that required a certain outpouring of liquor and a given number of Havana cigars drawn on the Institute coffers, it was nothing more than a practical business expenditure by Prok's accounting.) Obviously, nearly all the candidates had one flaw or another, and Prok, perfectionist that he was, rejected them wholesale despite his almost desperate need for another man.

I remember one candidate by the name of Birdbright. He was forty-five, happily married, father of a well-adjusted and grown daughter, just decommissioned from the Navy and in the process of submitting his doctoral thesis at Harvard in the field of Physical Anthropology. He came to campus and Prok quizzed him late into the night. Corcoran and I took him on the rounds of the taverns, and though he seemed a bit stiff—his military bearing, I suppose, or perhaps it was just academic rigor—we could find nothing to disqualify him. He was a scotch man, smoked Camels, hated sports. He wasn't particularly easy to draw out in conversation, but he wasn't sex shy either and seemed to have few biases against any number of sexual behaviors that were, technically speaking, against the law. The day after his visit the three of us sat down to compare notes. "I find nothing objectionable in the man," Prok said, the candidate's file spread open on the desk before him, and Corcoran and I had to agree. There was a pause. "Yet I don't sense any real enthusiasm either." Prok gently closed the folder and let his eyes roll back in his head. "But *Birdbright*—is anybody going to want to disclose sensitive information to a man with a name like that?" He let out a short, chiming laugh. "*Birdbright*, really!"

There was another man disqualified along similar lines. Again, he was unobjectionable, if not particularly exciting, and he did have an acceptable wife and the proper academic background, but he was burdened with a long, hyphenated name—Theodore Lavushkin-Esterhazy—that set Prok to fretting. Prok put it to him directly: Would he consider shortening his name to the less imposing Theodore Esterhazy, or even, for the purposes of interviewing lower-level subjects, simply Ted Esterhazy? The candidate replied that his was a venerable family name of several centuries' standing and that under no condition would he consider editing it. That was the term he used, "editing." Prok tented his hands on the desk before him, gave the candidate a long tunneled look, and thanked him for his time.

Yes. And there was one other man rejected because of his wife, who had a drinking problem, as we learned through inquiries among the staff at his previous place of employ and discovered firsthand at a Bryan Park picnic held in his honor. The wife was loud, sexually showy, with muscular calves and protuberant breasts, and she hung on one man after another, quaffing Planter's Punch as if it were carrot juice. She didn't create a scene, not exactly, but it was enough to warn us off. Prok had no use for drunks because drunks were unreliable and couldn't be trusted to keep their mouths shut (and he was to lecture me about my own alcohol consumption on more than one occasion, but that's not relevant here, or at least not at this juncture). This is not to say, incidentally, that he was ruthless, as the rumormongers might have you believe, nor that he chose the members of his team based on his ability to control and dominate them, but only that he was preternaturally sensitive to the needs of the project. There were secrets to keep. There was work to be done. Who could blame him for being particular?

Rutledge, of course, as the whole world knows, was the man we finally settled on. We all liked him from the start. Despite his Ivy League credentials and a sheaf of laudatory letters from some of the biggest names in the field, Robert M. Yerkes among them, he seemed down to earth, equally at ease with President Wells and Prok's colleagues in the Zoology Department as he was with the waiter who brought us our chops at Murchison's or the barman who mixed us highballs at the tavern, and from the start he treated Corcoran and me as his colleagues and equals. His wife, Hilda, was a tall asthenic blonde who talked out of the corner of her mouth as if everything she said was a wisecrack—and more often than not it was. She was relaxed and informal, a breath of fresh air after the wives of the majority of the other candidates, who might as well have been auditioning for a part in one of those robot pictures that seem to be infesting the theaters these days. Another plus, to my mind, at least: she took to Iris right off. Prok arranged for us all to have drinks with the Rutledges one afternoon—the Corcorans, the Milks and the Kinseys—and before Prok had even handed me my first Zombie cocktail, she and Iris had their heads together. And the children, never forget the children, because as Prok says they're perhaps the best reflection of the parents, in this case two solemn boys of eight and nine, who seemed well-adjusted and polite enough.

After the preliminary round of interviews, Rutledge was the sole candidate we invited back for a follow-up, and if he passed muster this time, it was understood that Prok was prepared to offer him the job. I met him at the bus station and together we walked up to the Institute. It was autumn—the autumn of '46 now, and I remember distinctly for reasons that will soon become apparent—and the day was unseasonably warm, a taste of Indian summer before the cold weather set in and the leaves turned and the Northern Hemisphere tilted away from the sun for yet another long season of contrition. Rutledge was wearing a tweed jacket over a long-sleeved shirt, he'd pushed his hat back to get a little air on his brow and loosened his tie so that it canted away from his open collar like a lolling tongue. He had a briefcase in one hand and a traveling bag in the other, his raincoat thrown carelessly over his shoulder. I asked if I could give him a hand with anything, and he broke into a smile. "Sure, John," he said, "that would be kind of you," and passed me the traveling bag.

We walked on in silence a moment. The sidewalks had been dampened by a fleeting rain, and every yard we passed seemed well tended and tranquil, with picket fences, overspilling flowerbeds and glistening lawns. Butterflies drifted over the blooms, birds soliloquized in the trees. "You know, I really do like this town," he said. "It has character. And charm too. It's not quite Princeton, maybe, but it's got plenty to offer as far as I can see. What do you think? You like it here?"

"Well, yes," I said, "sure. It's quiet, of course, but we make our own society."

"With Dr. Kinsey?"

We were stopped at a corner, waiting for a bus to move off across the intersection. I was conscious of Rutledge's eyes on me. He was sounding me out, and that was all right with me—it wasn't as if he were asking me to reveal anything he didn't already know. It just meant that he was confident Prok would offer him the job—and further, that he was leaning toward taking it. "Prok's a big part of it," I admitted.

"You're very close, aren't you?"

"Yes," I said, "we are."

He let that rest a moment and then the bus moved on and we crossed the street. His gait was easy, the briefcase swinging, tie stirring in the breeze our progress generated, and we fell into step, in rhythm, and I felt a kind of communion with him then, as if we were two athletes moving across the field of play. "You were his student, weren't you?"

I told him that I was, or had been, and then I laughed. "But I guess you'd have to say I still am, because with Prok the learning process goes on every minute of every day."

"He certainly has energy, Prok," Rutledge said.

"Yes, he does. I've never met anyone like him."

"But I like that. I like the whole project, what you and he and Purvis are doing here. It's very exciting. Groundbreaking, really."

We were striding right along, a block from the university now. It felt good to be out of the office and under the sun, if only for half an hour, and I was glad Prok had appointed me to be the one to go to the station. I didn't get out enough. None of us did. I made a mental note to see if Iris might not like to go for a picnic over the weekend before the weather turned.

"I'd like to be part of it, I would," Rutledge went on, as if I'd been contradicting him. "And I love this town, did I mention that? Seems like a terrific place to raise kids."

I had nothing to say to this, but he was just talking to hear himself in any case. There was a proposition on the table—should he or shouldn't he?—and he was trying very hard to convince himself that he should. "By the way," he said, just as we were coming up on the campus, "do you and Iris have any kids?"

"No," I said, "but we'd like to. We're, well, we're trying, that is."

He gave me a grin. "Trying, huh?"

"Yeah," I said, and I grinned back.

"When you come down to it"—two fingers went to his mustache—"it's all just another facet of the research, isn't it?"

PROK SPENT MOST of the day cloistered with him, then we had dinner at a restaurant—just the four of us, spouses not invited—and Prok must have peppered Rutledge with a thousand questions, and this after both he and his wife had given up their histories. There was drinking, though Prok abstained, and Rutledge, either out of temperance or calculation—he knew he was still on trial here—stopped after two highballs and tucked into his dinner with real appetite, Prok's third degree notwithstanding. I had enough to drink so that I could feel myself drifting out of my body for whole seconds at a time, but nothing excessive, nothing that would draw attention to myself, and Corcoran, who could hold his liquor as well as anyone I'd ever met, imbibed pretty steadily throughout the meal, almost as if he were conditioning himself for some test of endurance. Which, as it turned out, he was.

No one had clued me in, but I could guess from Prok's expression that there was to be some further test or demonstration yet to come, and when Corcoran excused himself before dessert with a wink for the company and the promise that he'd see us in just a bit, my suspicions were confirmed. "Well," Prok said, as we spooned up ice cream and sponge cake and the waitress lurked in the background, "it's been quite an evening. Quite a day, in fact, and I hope you've enjoyed it, Oscar"— and here he used Rutledge's given name for the first time, a clue that something was afoot, because he made a point of addressing his team by surname only—"as much as I have. And, I'm sure, Milk has. Haven't you, Milk?"

I answered in the affirmative, as did Rutledge. "It's been grand," he said, "and I have to say I'm impressed, Dr. Kinsey, with everything you've showed me here—"

Prok had set down his spoon and was staring across the table at Rutledge over the bridge of his intertwined fingers. His face showed nothing—Prok the impassive, Prok the interviewer, the open and accessible and nonjudgmental—but his eyes flashed with excitement. "Call me Prok," he said.

Rutledge ducked his head, put a hand to the back of his neck and came up smiling. "Yes, sure," he said. "It'll be a pleasure. Prok."

"Good, good, good," Prok murmured, and he called for the check then and spent the next several minutes looking it over and carefully counting out the exact change plus a three-percent tip, while Rutledge and I exchanged small talk in a collegial way. "All right," Prok said finally, pushing the neat pile of bills and coins away from him, "and now let's just retire to my place for some more talk and some good strong coffee, if you think you can stand it at this hour"—he paused, grinning now— "because I've got something arranged for your benefit, Rutledge, and yours too, Milk, a demonstration, actually, that should prove more than interesting. Shall we?"

When we turned in at the familiar winding path to Prok's house, there were two figures waiting for us on the porch, their silhouettes visible against the glow from within. One of them was Corcoran, quickly withdrawing a cigarette from his mouth and grinding it under his heel; the other was a young woman I'd never seen before. Introductions were made on the porch—"This is Betty, Prok, the girl I was telling you about? Betty, Dr. Kinsey. John Milk. Oscar Rutledge"—and then we were in the vestibule, Prok singing out "Mac, we're here!"

I barely had time to steal a glance at the young woman—she was a tall brunette with girlish features, high cheekbones and dark darting eyes that all but vanished when she smiled, and she was smiling now, nervously, her teeth sharp-edged and vaguely predatory—before Mac was on us. Mac must have been waiting just behind the kitchen door, because there she was, in a plain shift, barefooted, with a tray of coffee accessories and a plate of oatmeal cookies she'd baked fresh for the occasion. She wasn't wearing any lipstick or makeup and though she'd brushed her hair the curl didn't seem to want to hold. She looked tired. Looked old. "But come in, come in," she urged, ushering us into the living room even as Prok excused himself and disappeared through the door to the kitchen. I wondered about that for a moment—he seemed preternaturally excited, like a boy on the eve of his birthday, and what was he up to?—until he came hustling back into the room a moment later with the coffeepot and his tray of liqueurs.

We took seats around the coffee table and chatted about this and that while Mac poured coffee and Prok offered the liqueurs to each of us in turn. Aside from the hesitant murmurs of our conversation—*Care for cream? Yes, thank you*—it was very still. Moths threw themselves at the screens in soft, arthropodal explosions. From the yard, there was the sound of crickets, dense and sustaining. The girl, I noticed, selected one of the least palatable of the liqueurs and downed it in a single gulp as if she were standing at the rail in some back-alley bar, and Prok immediately poured her another. She was wearing a thin silver chain at her throat, and when she threw her head back to drain the second glass, I saw a flash of silver and the miniature cross with its miniature Jesus riding up her breastbone.

Prok took a seat in the armchair beside the girl, his elegant, tapered fingers gripping and releasing the bright black loops of the bentwood as he eased himself down. "Splendid," he said. "Isn't this splendid?" But he was too excited to sit back and relax, and he leaned forward almost immediately, hands splayed across his knees. "Betty," he said, dropping one shoulder and leaning in confidentially, "I can't begin to tell you how pleased we are—pleased and honored—that you've agreed to this."

The girl looked to Corcoran as if she were lost, then bowed her head and offered a demurrer, sotto voce. "It's nothing, really."

"But you *are* discreet—at least that's what Corcoran told me. You are, aren't you?"

She began to say yes in a voice that got lost in her throat, and then she repeated herself, in a firmer tone. "Yes," she said. "I'm discreet."

"We can rely on you, can't we?" Prok was giving her his sternest look. "What happens here in this house is strictly between those of us present, is that understood? And that no gossip, no mention of your assistance here with the research tonight is ever, *ever*, I repeat, to go any further than these rooms?"

"She's all right, Prok," Corcoran put in.

Rutledge, all but forgotten—wasn't he the main attraction here?—sat over his urine-colored liqueur and tried for an anything-goes sort of smile that withered on his lips. He was nervous suddenly. And, frankly, so was I.

"But I want to hear it from Betty's lips. Betty?"

"I understand," she said, and her eyes dodged away from Prok's to fix on Corcoran. "But are we going to sit here and gab all night? Because if we are—" She got to her feet then, a tall girl, anything but frail, the lineaments of her figure discernible in a sudden sweep and release of movement beneath her clothes. She never finished the thought, or threat or whatever it was, but just stood there glaring at us now, as if she'd thrown down a challenge we were loath to accept.

Prok rose now too. "You're quite right, Betty," he said, "and while it's been pleasant to sit here and have a little chat, we do have business to get to, don't we?" And here a look to Corcoran, then to Rutledge (a significant pause) and finally to me. "Well, shall we?" His voice faded into an echoing hollow, and I saw in that moment that he was anxious too. We all got to our feet. "Corcoran, why don't you show Miss—*Betty*—upstairs?"

My heart was hammering. I'd already guessed at what was coming, but then I couldn't be sure because we'd never done anything like this before, or to this degree, that is, not as a demonstration certainly, not live, not in public, and I couldn't believe Prok was prepared to go this far. Watching a prostitute from a closet was one thing, but—but my gaze was fixed on Betty's hips and rump as she ascended the stairs, her calves flexing and releasing as the hem of her dress rose and fell above them. I could smell her perfume, something I didn't recognize, rose water, lilac, and it went right to my groin. "Yes," Prok was saying, "just up at the top there, that door to the left, Corcoran, that's right—we really haven't done much to the attic, a bit warm up there, I'm afraid, but it's cozy. And private. You'll have to admit that."

And then we were all milling round the attic room, all but Mac, that is—she'd elected to stay downstairs, to "tidy up," as she put it. The room was stuffy and there was a smell of sawdust and varnish, as if the carpenters hadn't got round to completing what they'd begun, the ceiling low and unfinished, the walls constructed of pine boards indifferently nailed to the studs. It hadn't changed much from the first time I'd been there, just after Prok took me on—there was the single bed up against the wall under the slant of the roofline, the fishing rod in the corner and the children's outgrown toys and athletic equipment. The only difference, as far as I could see, was that the Ping-Pong table had been removed and replaced by half a dozen wooden chairs arranged in a semicircle facing the bed.

There was an awkward moment, the girl's presence overwhelming us all, even Prok, till Corcoran took charge. He was in a light summer suit, sportily cut, and he'd loosened his tie against the heat. His hair had been bleached by the summer sun—he was a great one for tennis, and, when he could find the time, for golf too—and his face was deeply tanned. He looked good. Very good. Almost as if he'd stepped out of a Hollywood picture about polo-playing swells or playboys cruising the Riviera. "Why don't you all just have a seat and make yourselves comfortable," he said, taking the girl by the hand, "while Betty and I get down to business." And to the girl: "Are you ready?"

Rutledge gave me a look that was meant to convey perplexity, but I could see what his surmise had led him to and that he was excited. There was a scraping of chair legs as we sat—Prok, Rutledge and I—and adjusted the position of our seats and crossed our legs, trying to act casually and failing, all three of us. Corcoran, in the meanwhile, had begun kissing the girl, deep kissing, tongue to tongue, and he let his hands roam over her body, descending to her buttocks and rising again to massage her breasts, and she gave back in kind. Her hands moved like quick white animals over the terrain of his jacket and trousers.

Then they were on the bed, kissing even more passionately now, and Corcoran was unfastening the buttons that ran up the back of her dress, and as soon as her back was exposed he unclipped her brassiere and in a single movement jerked her arms away from the clothes so that she was peeled to the waist and her breasts fell free. Her hands became more animated, tugging at his shirt, tearing loose the buttons, a kind of frenzy building till they were both naked and Corcoran was on his knees, spreading her legs and performing cunnilingus on her while she snatched at his hair and ears and tugged as if she would pull him into her. After a moment they switched positions and she returned the favor, making a Popsicle of him, and then Corcoran lifted her back onto the bed and climbed atop her.

Prok was wearing his mask of impassivity, but Rutledge looked as if he were about to explode. He was aroused—his trousers were tented in the crotch—and though he tried to be surreptitious about it, tried to remain focused and detached, he began to move his hands in his lap. For my part, I fought to act neutral, for Prok's sake and Rutledge's too—no one there, but for Corcoran, seemed to know what was expected, and Prok, Prok, of course—but I don't think it will come as any surprise if I tell you that I'd never yet been so aroused in my life and that the psychological factors and the setting and company certainly played into it.

This was Corcoran—my colleague and friend, Corcoran who'd done just this with Iris, with my wife, this movement of the head and tongue, this sliding in and out of the female orifice with the slick rhythm and balance of a seal riding a wave ashore—and it was a spur to me, I won't deny it, and I won't deny that spurs draw blood either. I felt choked. I could barely breathe.

All at once Prok was out of the chair and he had Rutledge by the arm, dragging him forward till they were hovering over the scene. "You see, Rutledge, how invaluable this is?" he was saying, bending close now as Corcoran pumped and the girl heaved and snatched at his shoulders and sang out. "You see that?" Prok demanded. "Right there, see?" He was pointing an empirical finger to the girl's left breast. "Do you see how the aureole has swollen and enlarged in arousal—and the tumescence of the erectile tissue of the nipples in both female and male? And see here—even the alae, the soft parts of the nose, have become engorged in the female . . ."

Prok was inches away, bent close, using his index finger as a pointer, and in a soft voice he asked Corcoran if he might turn the girl over in order better to study the physiologic metamorphoses in her rectal and genital areas. Corcoran complied. There was a confusion of limbs, a certain awkwardness, and then the girl was on top, the silver cross swaying rhythmically with the drive of her hips, and Prok lecturing and Rutledge hovering and the whole performance coming to its ineluctable climax.

LATER—it must have been past one in the morning—I slipped the key in the lock, pushed open the front door, and found Iris sitting up over a book, waiting for me. She was sunk into the couch, her bare legs tucked neatly beneath the folds of her nightgown, and she set the book down as I came through the door. "You're late," she said.

I came to her and bent for a kiss, then straightened up and gave her a theatrical stretch and a thespian's yawn. And a shrug to show how pedestrian it all was. "Yes," I sighed.

She hadn't moved. "Poor John," she said, "I don't envy you. It's all work, work, work, isn't it?"

I was treading delicate ground here. Was that a sardonic edge to her voice? How much to tell her? "The usual," I said. "The endless dinner, then over to Prok's to sit around and jaw—he really put Rutledge through his paces." I was standing over her still, gazing down into the deep draught of her eyes, studying the weave of her hair, the shadow between her breasts where the collar of her nightgown fell open. "He got the job, by the way. Rutledge, that is."

She didn't say anything for a moment, but her eyes seemed to reach out to me, opening wider and wider, round as globes, worlds unto themselves, that color of the sea and all the mystery and strangeness invested there. Iris. My wife. Something was up, but what was it? "That's good," she said finally. "Good that it's settled, I mean. He seems fine. I'm sure he'll be fine, and you'll have less pressure on you now, don't you think?"

"I don't know," I said. "I guess so."

She was silent again, but she never took her eyes off me. I heard the distant sound of a phonograph, a single faint violin rising up out of the declension of the hour and then fading away again, and I remember being transported in that moment to another place, an apartment down the block, people gathered there, the last cocktail of the night, the low incestuous buzz of voices. "I have news too," she said.

My mouth tried to close round the words, but my mind was already leaping ahead. "You, that's right, you went to the, the—"

"The doctor," she murmured, and she was smiling like all the angels in heaven.

4

P<small>ROK WAS ALREADY</small> at his desk when I got to work the following morning, and he lifted his eyebrows as I came in, ten minutes late. To Prok, every second lost was a second the project was delayed, and if he'd kept us all out till one in the morning, it was hardly an excuse to get lax about our responsibilities. Mrs. Matthews was there in the anteroom, punctual as a banker, her back arched and chin up, typing. Corcoran was at his desk too, and Rutledge, who'd be going back to Princeton that afternoon to begin making his personal arrangements, was in the corner, head down, perusing one of the volumes Prok had given him so that he could keep abreast of the literature in the field. Ten past eight in the morning and the office was humming along as usual. With the exception of me, that is. I wasn't at my best—hungover, depleted, and late on top of it—but I was ringing like a bell with the news.

Iris and I had stayed up to celebrate—I broke out a bottle of I.W. Harper I'd been saving for the occasion and touched glasses with her, though she was confining herself to ginger ale, already concerned for the baby's welfare—and then we went to bed and I let my excitement spill into her, closing my eyes against the shadows playing across the wall and fighting down the image of the brunette and Corcoran, my wife in my arms and nobody but. My fertile wife. My pregnant wife. Two years of trying and I have to admit I was beginning to think it would never happen, that we were cursed somehow, and as I saw the child denied me I wanted it all the more, no matter the cost or the inconvenience or anything else. Prok wanted it too. And Iris's mother— she wanted it—and Tommy wanted it and my own mother and just about everybody else we knew or came into contact with, from the butcher to the greengrocer. *When are you two going to settle down and start a family?*—that was what they wanted to know, what with every woman in America pregnant or pushing an infant in a stroller while an ex-serviceman strutted at her side.

"Sorry I'm late, Prok," I said, snagging my hat and trench coat on the clothes tree behind my desk. The coat was wet—the temperature had dropped twenty degrees overnight and it was spattering rain—and my heel prints left gleaming arcs on the linoleum tiles. "But I had to stop by Iris's school and tell them she wasn't coming in today."

Prok glanced up sharply. We were working on the text of the male volume now, and he was driving himself through sixteen- and seventeen-hour days, puzzling over the figures, pushing through organization to interpretation, and he'd become increasingly rigid under the pressure of it. He'd been up till one himself, and though he must have been feeling elated over the finalizing of the Rutledge situation and the success of the previous night's demonstration, he might have been just the smallest bit under the weather too. "You're holding up the project, Milk," was all he said, and he gave me a sour look.

Normally I would have been mortified—I hated for anyone to question my devotion and loyalty, especially Prok, to whom I owed everything, and he was in the right, of course: I was late, I was irresponsible, I was holding up the project—but I felt an almost otherworldly sense of well-being, as if nothing could touch me, not fear or disease or recrimination. No reply was called for, but I had one at the ready, and I held it a moment to tease out the pleasure of it. I didn't move. Just stood there at my desk, gazing out over the sanctuary of the office, the golden pools of lamplight, the galls, Prok. Iris was home in bed, too sick to go in and minister to her seven-year-olds. I'd listened to her retching over the toilet. I'd held her hand and wrapped her in a quilt and put her back to bed with dry toast and a glass of leftover ginger ale. "I have news, Prok," I said. "Good news, great news."

He'd already dropped his eyes to the page, and now they came up again, searching and hard. The pulsing arrhythmic din of Mrs. Matthews's typewriter choked off on the downstroke. Corcoran looked up from his desk.

"It's Iris," I said, and I felt inflated, bigger than life, the actor, the hero, the marathoner at the tape. I knew what they must have thought of me. I was the youngest, the least-trained, Prok's puppet, unable even to perform the most elemental biological function of them all, but that was all behind me now. Now I was anybody's equal. I was a man, and wasn't this the very definition of it? "She's, well, we're going to have a baby," I said. "She's pregnant."

Prok let out a low whistle. Mrs. Matthews—she was in her fifties, a grandmother and a widow—gave me a melting look. And Corcoran, from his desk in the back room, put two hands together in a smatter of applause, which brought Rutledge's head up out of his book in time to give me a quizzical glance.

"We found out last night. Yesterday, I mean. When I got home, after the, the—"

Prok had already crossed the room, grinning wide. He seized both my arms and held me in his grip till the familiar scent of him—of soap, astringents, the faintest whiff of witch hazel—penetrated me. "But you'll need advice—you'll need Mac," he was saying, looking beyond me to the clock on the wall as if the baby were due in the next fifteen minutes. "And a good obstetrician. Whom did you say she was seeing? Because I have just the man—"

UNFORTUNATELY, as it turned out, I was away with the team much of that fall and winter, and as often as not Iris had to endure her bouts of morning sickness alone. She wasn't due till June, and so we both agreed that she would fulfill her obligations at the elementary school as long as she could—it was the right thing to do, of course, but we were also in need of the money because now we would have to move to a bigger place, and my raise at the Institute had yet to come through, though I was sure it would once the grant situation was ironed out. When I was home I did my best to help out around the house, preparing meals at night, washing up, laying out her clothes for the morning. She was brave about it, never once complaining over my schedule—it was a fact of life at this stage, a fait accompli—and I remember the way she pushed herself up stiffly from the table in the mornings, her face

296

clenched as she tried to keep down half a soft-boiled egg and three sips of coffee.

I felt bad about it. And I would have been happy to stay home with her, to help see her through it, to be with her and share the wonder of the transformation going on inside her, but this was a crucial time for the project. We'd managed to reach a milestone the year before—ten thousand histories in the books—and yet Prok kept pushing frantically for more as he got deeper into the writing up of the results, afraid of having the figures attacked for being skewed in one direction or another ("We have five hundred and five female alcoholics," he would mutter, "but a paltry smattering of upper-level blacks and virtually nothing on ministers, rabbis and the like, not to mention drug addicts and traveling salesmen"). To complicate matters, we were still working shorthanded, as Rutledge wouldn't complete his dissertation and join us till just before the holidays, so while Iris put on weight and felt her breasts grow tender and her feet leaden, we were bouncing from city to city, Prok lecturing nearly every day, and the three of us staying up into the wee hours recording histories. We went to Chicago, Philadelphia and Washington and any number of smaller municipalities along the way, and we were in residence at the Astor Hotel in New York for nearly three weeks in December, interviewing a succession of male hustlers and female prostitutes.

In the meanwhile, I wrote Iris regularly, if only a line or two, and made sure to telephone her at least every other day, no matter the cost. I owed her those phone calls, and before long I found that I needed them as much as she did. The sound of her voice became an itch in my head as I showered, breakfasted, climbed aboard the train or slid into the Buick beside Prok and Corcoran, her soft tentative "hello" whispering to me over the thump of the rails and the measured beat of the tires. She was subdued on the phone, shy of it, and I'm afraid we didn't communicate very effectively. Still, the important thing was that we did talk. I told her I loved her. Couldn't wait to be home with her—and the baby. Was the baby kicking yet? No? Too early? Well, the baby would kick, wouldn't it? Eventually? Yes, she assured me, the baby would kick. Christmas, I told her, Christmas would be our time together.

A word here about the Astor Hotel, incidentally. This was, in its time, an open gathering place for homosexuals—the long black oval bar on the ground floor was packed shoulder-to-shoulder with men till all hours of the night every day of the week—and it was ideal for our purposes in securing H-histories, our chief purpose on that particular trip (though, as I say, we were also interviewing female prostitutes as well as a number of young college and career women, most of whom were brought to us by Vivian Aubrey, a sexually prodigious graduate of Columbia University whose history Corcoran had first taken on our last foray to New York, and more on her later). Most important, at the Astor, no one asked any questions. And this was significant, because we'd been requested to leave the Lincoln Hotel the previous year (that is, we were thrown out), an incident Prok was always able to recount with equanimity, though he was furious at the time.

None of us had seemed to notice anything amiss, but for one reason or another—prudery, antiquated notions of respectability—our activities began to attract notice. We'd been interviewing at the Lincoln for some days, a whole succession of ragtag hustlers, underage boys and effeminates parading through the lobby, where Prok, Corcoran and I would meet them and escort them upstairs to our rooms, when the manager rang Prok and demanded to speak with him. Prok was in the middle of an interview and put the man off till there was a break in the schedule, at which point he summoned Corcoran and me for reinforcements and went down to confront him.

The manager was a very proper-looking character with swept-back hair, silvered sideburns and the trace of an Italian accent—a real swell, as we used to say, pompous and self-important. "We can't have this," he said.

Prok folded his arms and leveled his gaze on him. He knew what was coming. "Have what?"

"All this sex," the man spat. "Fags and streetwalkers. Whores. I can't have you undressing these people in my hotel."

"But I've explained to you—this is a scientific survey we're conducting. You know perfectly well we're not undressing anybody."

"Oh, no? Maybe not their clothes, but you're undressing their *minds,* and I won't have it, not in my hotel."

But this time, at the Astor, there were no such problems. The management looked the other way and everything went smoothly and professionally, except in one instance that still manages to disturb me, though I don't know why. The subject was a young man not long removed from the war and missing the lower portion of his right arm. He was my last interview of a long night, I'd been drinking and smoking with the previous subjects, and I guess I was feeling pretty wrung out. I met him in the lobby, there was a brief contretemps with the handshake—he offered his left and it took me a moment to follow suit—and then we rode the elevator up to the room Prok had reserved for interviews. The subject had been with the Navy, and though his tan had faded he might have been a modern Billy Budd, with his fair hair parted just to the left of center and the cocky gait and rigid musculature of his class. He was nineteen. He'd been educated to the eighth grade, had parents living in Oklahoma City, and he'd been earning his living as a male hustler since he got out of the hospital. I gave him the dollar we'd agreed upon, he took the bed and I the armchair, and we began to chat.

The preliminaries went well enough, but it soon became apparent that he was wound up on something—Benzedrine, as it turned out, which he obtained by dismantling nasal inhalers and swallowing the drug-soaked pads within. He became loquacious, overly so, each question provoking a breathless running interminable response that went so far afield I began to forget what I was doing there with him in the first place. We'd been trained in the rapid-fire technique I described earlier, and to interrupt and interject where necessary in order to steer the subject back to the matter at hand, but this man—this sailor—just wouldn't yield. At one point, in the middle of a reminiscence about the fifty-three varieties of plants in the hothouse where his first homosexual contact, an older man, had worked, I became so exasperated that I got up out of the armchair and began pacing the floor.

He stopped in mid-sentence and gave me a curious look—an aggressive look, actually. "What," he said, "you're not interested? Because I thought you said we agreed you wanted information, right, the story of my life and all like that for a buck? But what? Is it something else?" He held my eyes. "You want more than just a story?"

"No, not at all. I just wish you would—well, don't take this the wrong way because I don't mean to sound impolite or guide your response in any way—but I wish you'd just stick to the format of the interview or we'll be here all night."

"So what's so bad about that?" He'd risen from the couch and he was giving me what I suppose he assumed was a seductive smile, his bathhouse smile, the smile he used at the urinals at Grand Central Station or downstairs at the Astor bar. "You don't want to get rid of me, do you? Already?"

"Of course not," I said. "But the whole survey becomes suspect if we can't finish out an interview, you understand that, don't you?"

He didn't say anything, just crossed the room to me, the right sleeve of his velour shirt dangling empty, and pressed himself to me. His hand went to the crotch of my trousers, and I froze—that was what we were trained to do in such cases, to remain impassive and reject all advances. He tried to kiss me then, but I turned my face away and his lips grazed my cheek. "Come on," he murmured, his voice low and furred with lust or its counterfeit, "you know you want it. Drop the charade, why don't you? Science. You're no more a scientist than I am."

I pushed away from him and sank back into the chair, all business— this was business, after all—and assured him I was there for one purpose only, all the while cursing myself for having left the chair in the first place. It was unprofessional, it had broken the spell and given him the wrong impression. "And your second contact," I said, trying to regain control of my voice. "Do you recall that? How old you were? Was it just after your experience with the hothouse man?"

He didn't answer. For the first time since he'd entered the room he had nothing to say, as if the drug were a freight train driving through his veins and it had hopped a curve and derailed all of a sudden. He stood there a moment, weaving from foot to foot. His good hand clenched and released and I could hear the erosive friction of his teeth grinding, molar to molar. "Listen," he said finally, "don't you find me attractive? Is it because of this?" He held up the arm, with its dangle of empty sleeve.

"That's not what I'm here for."

"Oh, yeah? Well, I just felt you. I just had your prick in my hand."

"What about women?" I said, because you can never let the subject distract you, not if you're going to be a professional. "When was the first time you saw a naked female?"

"I'll suck you for a buck," he said, and he was leaning over the chair now, staring into my eyes.

"I've told you, I'm not here for that. Now answer the question. *Please.*"

He leaned forward and tried to kiss me again, but I pushed him firmly away, or as firmly as I could while remaining seated. He slowly straightened up and stood there over me, swaying his hips and grinding his teeth. "You aren't fooling anybody," he said.

The point of all this, I suppose, is that I got the interview, one more set of data to feed into the Hollerith machine, and that I always got the interview, just as my colleagues did. Unfailingly. We persisted against all odds, and isn't that something to be proud of? At any rate, we were up early the following day, the cold shower, the stale hotel breakfast, and conducted interviews till about noon, after which we packed up and wandered round the city streets in anticipation of boarding the *Spirit of St. Louis* at 6:05 p.m., arriving in Indianapolis at 8:45 the following morning. It was December twentieth, the air was thin with the cold, and there were Santas and bell-ringers on every corner, pigeons bobbing underfoot, the smell of charcoal and chestnuts blowing across the afternoon like the charred odor of history, Christmas in Manhattan, and every storefront shimmering with elaborate seasonal displays, toys, foodstuffs, liquor, lingerie, hats, furs, jewels. Prok had already bought something for Mac, and Corcoran had found a crystal brooch with matching clip earrings for Violet—she loved jeweled pins, wore them over her left breast in the way men wore handkerchiefs or boutonnieres—but I had yet to find anything for Iris.

I went off on my own then, trailing a flurry of admonitions from

Prok (*Don't be late, don't get lost, look both ways and watch out for sharps and con men and keep a firm grip on your wallet*), who strode up Broadway with Corcoran to look into the peep shows and the more circumspect establishments that specialized in erotica, thinking to add to the library's collection. I didn't know the city very well at all—we rarely saw anything of it but Times Square, the four walls of the hotel room and the railway stations—and I don't mind admitting that the whole time I was afraid of getting lost and missing my train. Was I a bit of a rube? I suppose I was, a Hoosier at large in the big polymorphous city, looking for the one article among ten million that would make his wife happy on Christmas Day.

I don't remember much of the trip back, except that Prok sat up late interviewing strangers on the train while I fell into my berth as if I'd been gang-tackled and slept without waking until Prok fetched me for breakfast. What I do remember, though, is what I got Iris for Christmas that year. I found it in an out-of-the-way shop that advertised ANTIQUES & ARTIFACTS behind a dirty pane of glass illuminated by a single fitfully winking strand of red and green bulbs. There were two other customers in the place, both of whom managed to look as if they'd always been there, poised and silent, heads down, hands behind their backs, bending ruefully to inspect the merchandise. Though it was the middle of the afternoon and the sun still palely shining beyond the windows, inside it was crepuscular and nearly as cold as it was out on the street. But everybody has been to this place, or a place just like it: the proprietor a stick figure in a yarmulke, worn carpets of the oriental variety, tortuous paths through walls of heavy carved furniture piled high with the hoarded bric-a-brac of old Europe, a smell of silver polish and death. What I fixed on, finally, with the help of the proprietor, who assured me it was worth twice what I paid, was an ashtray fashioned from a conch shell with a six-inch bronze figurine of a naked Aphrodite, her hair marcelled and her breasts taut, rising from its mouth. I had him gift-wrap it and hurried off to find the train.

WE WERE TO go out again just after the New Year—more lectures, more histories, the pace ever more frenetic—but Christmas was a real occasion, replete with a surprise overnight snowfall and a festive dinner at the house on First Street for all the team and the children too. Mac was her usual gracious self, Iris, Violet and Hilda prepared the entremets at home and brought them in covered dishes, and Prok concocted a hot rum punch and carved a twenty-pound turkey with all the flair of a master chef. The team had chipped in to buy him a gift—a pair of gold cuff links which he proclaimed too lavish—and then Prok handed out gifts to each of us in return.

I should say here that while Prok was regarded in some circles as a bit of a penny-pincher (and he *was* excessively frugal, even miserly at times, because every cent he ever made had to be pumped back into the project), he was never so generous and expansive as he was at Christmas. All his staff—the clerical help, the janitor, even the undergraduate girls he used to employ in cataloguing his gall wasp collection—received holiday bonuses, and I was no exception. In fact, as the first member of the team, as his confidant and aide-de-camp, I was often the recipient of his largesse, but that Christmas was even more extraordinary than I could have hoped for.

After dinner and a mini-musicale, after we'd gone back to the table to feast on mince and pumpkin pies and allow the general conversation to stretch for whole minutes at a time beyond the subject of sex research, Prok motioned for me to follow him into the kitchen. My first thought was that he needed help with the tray of liqueurs or with some further treat for the children, but that wasn't it at all. As soon as the door had shut behind us, he spun round on his heels, took me in his arms and pulled me to him for an embrace. It was awkward, but I held to him, the stiff fabric of his bow tie stabbing at my collar, his cheek a rough bristle against my own. I could feel the electricity of him through his clothes as he patted me across the shoulders with both hands and murmured, "I'm proud of you, John, very proud." Then he released me and turned on his smile. "Fatherhood, eh?" he said. "No problems, I take it? Everything normal?"

I nodded. Gave him back his smile. Inside, I was glowing.

"Well, you're going to need a bit more space now, don't you think? Something permanent, as befits your position?" The smile opened into a grin. "A house, John. I'm talking about a house."

"But I can't, we can't afford—"

He folded his arms across his chest, watching me, grinning wide. "I'm increasing your salary as of today by ten dollars a week, and I'm prepared to make you a personal loan—out of my own pocket and at a fraction of the interest rate you'd expect to pay at any of the banks downtown—in the amount of two thousand dollars. How does that sound?"

For a moment, I was unable to muster a response. I was stunned. Moved. Deeply moved. To think that he was looking out for me still, me, John Milk, nobody really, a former student, the least of his employees, and willing to sacrifice his own finances into the bargain—it was just too much. My father was dead, my mother remote. But Prok, Prok was there for me, anticipating my needs—our needs, Iris's and mine—as if I were his own flesh and blood. I was so overwhelmed I thought I might break down right there in front of him. "That's, well, that's grand," I said, all my emotion caught in the back of my throat, "but you don't have to . . . what about the grants, the NRC? How will we, the project, I mean—?"

He moved toward the sideboard and the enameled tray that was already laden with the little glasses and the varicolored bottles. "The grants are in for the year, have been in for some time now, so don't you worry." (In fact, as I was later to learn, the National Research Council, under the auspices of the Rockefeller Foundation, had ratified the significance of our work with a $40,000 grant for each of the next three years, nearly doubling their previous commitment.) I listened a moment to the music of the little glasses as he rearranged them on the tray. "And there's more on the way, you can be sure of it. So come here, come to me here and say thank you in a proper way—"

I embraced him again, and we kissed, but just for a moment—the quickest brushing of the lips—before I pulled away. I wanted to find Iris, tell her the news, ring up every real-estate agent in the county. "Can I tell Iris?" I said. "Can I give her the good news?"

"Go," he said, and I couldn't read his face. I was halfway to the door when he called me back. "But wait, wait, I didn't tell you the best part," and he'd recovered himself now, all smiles. "I found the prettiest little place, not six blocks from here."

"I've got to tell Iris," I said, so excited I could barely breathe. I was at the door now, no thought of holding it open for him and his liqueurs, only to push through, to find my wife before I burst with the news. "But thank you," I called over my shoulder, "thank you a thousand times over," and then the door swung open and the noise of the party hit me and I heard him cry out, "And it's got a big yard for the boy!"

NEXT MORNING, early, there was a knock at the door. I was sitting at the kitchen table, reading about the upcoming Bowl games in the newspaper and spooning up cornflakes and milk, heavily sugared. It was seven-fifteen by the clock on the stove. Iris was still asleep. I couldn't imagine who it could be—it was the day after Christmas, the world snowbound, nothing moving, no sound anywhere—and I pushed myself up from the table and went to the door. Prok was standing there on the doorstep, blowing steam through his nostrils. He was in his belted winter coat, galoshes, knit gloves and the old drooping southwester he favored in inclement weather. "Glad to see you're up, Milk," he said, "but it's cold, isn't it? The thermometer read minus three Fahrenheit when I left the house." Behind him, at the curb, the Buick sent up discontinuous plumes of blue smoke.

I was in my robe and pajamas still, a pair of new felt-lined slippers— a Christmas present from Iris—on my feet. I don't mind admitting I was a bit befuddled, my head still thick with the residue of all that Christmas cheer. I tried to read his expression. Had I forgotten something? Were we scheduled to leave on a field trip? Was that it? "Yes," I said, "well, yes, very cold, but please come in, because, well—"

"You're going to have to get dressed," he said, pausing to kick the snow off his galoshes before striding through the door. "We've got an eight o'clock appointment. And Iris—where's Iris?"

I don't think Prok had been inside the apartment more than once or twice before, and then only briefly. He glanced round him as if he were entering one of our lusterless hotel rooms, his eyes appraising and keen.

And then he was pacing the undersized front room in his brisk, long-legged way, snatching off his hat and gloves in two quick jerks and pushing through the bead curtains to cast a suspicious glance round the kitchen as if he were a building inspector come to assess the quality of the plumbing. I felt a surge of shame. The place was small, though as I've said Iris had a real knack for interior decoration, and it was—or had been—sufficient to our needs, but with Prok there, looming over the furniture, everything seemed shabby suddenly, and I felt I'd somehow failed him, as if I should have risen to something grander at this stage of my life.

"Interesting piece on the coffee table there—the Aphrodite," he said. "Is that the thing you picked up for Iris in New York?"

"Yes. At that shop I was telling you about."

"Mother of Eros, sexuality unfettered. Nobody could call the Greeks sex shy, now could they?"

"No," I said, "I guess not."

"Very nice. I'd say your taste is improving, Milk, definitely improving."

I was just standing there in my robe, three feet from him, in the confines of the kitchen that might have been cleaner, brighter, grander, and I didn't know what to say or do. I thought of offering him coffee, of settling him down in the armchair for a moment, of waking Iris and getting dressed, but then I found myself numbly echoing what he'd said a moment earlier, as if it had just managed to sink in: "Appointment? What appointment?"

He was frowning at the cupboard, pulling open each door in succession till he found himself a cup, and then he lifted the coffeepot from the stove, giving it an experimental shake. "With the realtor," he said, pouring, "or actually the owner. I spoke with him myself, at half past six this morning. Iris *is* up, isn't she?"

THE HOUSE WAS conveniently located, as advertised, two blocks closer to campus than Prok's own, but in a neighborhood that was struggling to keep up appearances while the grander homes spread in a formal march to the south and east. Which was fine with me. I didn't expect a palace, and if there was a heavy concentration of boardinghouses and student rentals there, that was testimony to the desirability of the location. Iris wasn't so sure. Prok and I had sat at the kitchen table, sipping coffee and nibbling at a fruit cake Hilda Rutledge had given us the day before while we listened to the muted call and response of Iris's gagging and the cascade of the toilet, Prok tapping his foot impatiently and checking his watch every two minutes, but she'd emerged from the bedroom at ten of eight, in her best dress and with the hair brushed back from her brow in a black silken wave. She was pale, though, and didn't have much to say as I eased her into the backseat of the Buick while Prok and I climbed in up front.

The first thing she did say, beyond the usual pleasantries, was when we pulled up at the curb in front of the place. "It looks odd somehow," she said, and I could tell already that she wasn't going to like it. "Out of balance. Too narrow across the front."

Prok shut down the ignition and turned to look over his shoulder. "Built to fit a narrow lot," he said. "But it goes quite a bit deeper, as you'll see, to make up for it."

"And the color," she said, her breath steaming the window, her face drawn down to nothing round the critical oval of her mouth. "Who would ever paint a house mauve—that is mauve, isn't it?"

"Looks more brown to me," Prok put in.

"Or blue," I said.

"I don't know, I was hoping for something older," she said, even as Prok was sliding out of the car to pull open the rear door for her. "Made of stone or brick maybe, and with more of a porch."

"Older? This was built in '24," Prok said, "and that's plenty old enough. Believe me, you do want the modern conveniences. Some of these antique houses, while they may look charming from the street, are nothing but a headache for the homeowner, substandard plumbing, antiquated electric, all sorts of structural problems, buckled floors and the like. No, what you want is something newer, like this. Take my word for it."

But Iris wouldn't take his word for it. She was as strong-willed as he was, and while she'd come to feel a real kinship for Mac she never really warmed to Prok, though she was always, or almost always, polite enough, out of her own innate civility and an awareness of the awkwardness of my position, but deep down I think she resented the influence he had over me. Over us. And, of course, there was Corcoran, the whole sad humiliating affair that lay between them like an open wound, Corcoran, always Corcoran.

The owner was an assistant professor in the Chemistry Department who'd been offered a promotion at DePauw and was pulling up his roots. He met us at the door, along with his wife, exchanged a cryptic look with Prok, and invited us in. I saw a gleaming oak staircase and handsome wallpaper in a floral pattern; Iris saw a cramped vestibule and a house aching in its ribs, with rooms like freight cars and windows that opened up on the place next door like a claustrophobe's nightmare. She wore her disapproving face (eyes sunk back in her head, brow locked in a rigid *V*, teeth and lips poised as if to spit out some bit of refuse) through the entire circuit of the place, including the lecture in the basement during which Prok and the chemistry professor took turns extolling the virtues of the furnace, and the culinary tête-à-tête with the lady of the house at the narrow table in the tunnel of the kitchen. Prok, the professor and I came back from a tour of the yard and potting shed to find her drinking tea and staring blankly at a platter of gingerbread cookies while the professor's wife (late twenties, styleless, childless, her face a scroll of anxiety) nattered on about Iris's condition and what a blessing children were. Or must be.

"Well," Prok said, "what do you think? Milk? Iris? A tight little ship, wouldn't you say? And convenient to campus, never underestimate the value of that."

The chemistry professor, and I suppose I may as well give you an account of him, since I've managed to dredge up his wife from the memory banks (he was ten or twelve years older than his spouse, IV-F from the Army during the late war because of a congenital deformity—club foot—and so turgid in his speech he must have bored insensate a whole legion of aspiring chemists), averred that there was no finer house in the world and that he and his wife were deeply conflicted about having to give it up. "I'd even thought of commuting, but then, what with wear and tear on the car—"

"Not to mention the wear and tear on yourself," the wife put in, glancing up from her teacup with a look of acuity.

"Yes. That's right. And so we've had to put the place up for sale, but reluctantly. It's just one of those things. Life moves on, right?"

Prok was stationed just behind the wife's chair, shifting impatiently from foot to foot. His coat hung open, the gloves and soft hat stuffed bulkily in the pockets on either side so that he looked as if he were expanding out of his clothes. "And the price," he said. "Is that firm?"

I was watching the professor's face as it went through its permutations. "Within reason," he supposed. "But there's always wiggle-room"— that was the term he used, *wiggle-room*—"if the Milks are really interested and not just here to entertain us with their presence." He gave a little laugh. "And we are entertained, aren't we, Dora, to have such a delightful young couple here with us in this festive season and to think that we can be fortunate enough to give them a hand as they start out on the road ahead—?"

"Would you consider ten and a half then?" Prok said. "With fifteen percent down?"

That was when Iris spoke up. "I think I'd like to have a word with my husband," she said, looking at each of us in succession before letting her eyes come to rest on mine. "If no one minds."

Oh, no. No, no. No one minded.

In the vestibule, while the others sat round the table at the far end of the house, she spread her feet for balance and lashed into me. "You're such a fool," she snapped. "Such a sap. You're soft, that's all. Soft."

"You don't like it?"

"I despise it. And they're manipulating you, can't you see that? Prok, your precious Prok, and the professor and his wife, as if they can't wait to unload this, this crackerbox. Do you really think I want to spend the rest of my life here? And you. Do you want to? This place stinks. It has no style, nil, zero, nothing. I'd rather stay where we are. Or what—move back to Michigan City, to my parents' place, and live at the dairy. Milk cows. Anything but this."

"Can you keep your voice down? What if they hear?"

"What if they do?"

There was a moment during which we both just stood there glaring at each other while the small sounds of the house—groans, creaks, the dwindling patter of rodent feet—ticked round us. "I don't know," I said. "I kind of like it."

"Like it? You're out of your mind. I won't even talk to you. Forget it, hear me? Forget it."

The result was that Prok had to tell the professor and his wife that we would get back to them—Iris wasn't feeling well, a difficult pregnancy, her first, and that was why she'd had to go out to the car without saying goodbye and thanking them for their kindness and hospitality—and then the two of us slammed into the front seat and Prok started in on her. She was passing up a golden opportunity. There was real value here. Yes, there were other houses in the world, plenty to look at, or some, at any rate, given the postwar housing shortage, and, yes, he had to account for differences in taste, but really, at our level—and here he gave me a significant look over the expanse of the front seat—we couldn't expect to find anything more practical or economical.

Iris heard him out as we sat there at the curb and Prok preached at her over his shoulder, then finally turned the key in the ignition and brought the Buick to life. And then, in a small but firm voice, she said, "I have an ad here."

Prok gave her his profile, the hat clamped down over the stiff brush of hair. "An ad?"

"I clipped it from the paper. Listen: 'Charming three-bedroom farmhouse, kitchen, dining, stone fireplace, indoor plumbing, built solid, 1887'—and it's less than this place."

"*Eighteen eighty-seven?*" Prok was incredulous. "A farmhouse? What would you want with a farmhouse? But wait a minute—where did you say it was?"

310

She gave the address.

"But that's got to be eight or ten miles out of town. At least. You'd need a car."

"John's wanted a car all his life. Don't you think, at twenty-eight, he deserves one?"

I kept mum. The heat vent beneath the dash began to hiss and the exhaust roped back in the wind and tied itself in knots outside my window.

"That's not at issue, Iris. That's not it at all. You have to think of economy, that's what I'm saying. A car is just one more expense, the gasoline, oil, upkeep. And the project, our collecting trips—do you really want to be left way out there in the country all by yourself? And with a baby to care for, no less?"

Iris's voice, the stubborn little nugget of it: "We can at least look, can't we?"

The farmhouse, by Prok's odometer, turned out to be 5.2 miles beyond the town limits, just off the Harrodsburg road. There was no farm attached to it—the farm had failed during the Depression—but there was the acre of land the house sat on and a small orchard of fruit trees out back, apple, peach and pear. The owner was an old man, bowed in the back and with hands like baseball mitts, a widower who was planning to move in with his son's family in Heltonville. Iris liked the fireplace in the main room, a massive thing that had once been used for cooking, and she liked the scuffed oak floors and the gentle warp underfoot that rolled you down through the glade of the parlor and into the valley of the kitchen. She'd never seen anything sturdier than the stone foundation and the hand-hewn planks of the front porch—or the well, the well was a thing of beauty in itself. Prok hated the place. It was impractical, a headache in the making, and he appealed to me—"Do you really want to spend all your free time at home with a hammer in one hand and a paint brush in the other?"—but I had already begun to see what Iris was talking about, already begun to envision what she could do with the place given her taste and her resourcefulness, and so I said nothing.

On the way back in the car, while Iris and I were buzzing over the possibilities—"That room under the stairs, it's perfect for a study, John, your own study"—Prok pulled his trump card. He'd been uncharacteristically silent as the frozen fields rolled by and the tires snatched at the piebald pavement between humps of ice and compacted snow, and suddenly he raised his voice and said, "I really don't know if I can see my way to making this loan under the circumstances—that is, John," and he snatched his eyes from the road to give me a sidelong look—"if I don't approve of the property, and I most emphatically do not, because I do have to protect my investment, you understand."

Iris came right back at him, more sharply than I would have liked, but she was right, and I had to admit it. "We appreciate everything you've done for us," she said, biting off her words as if she were paying by the syllable, "but you have to understand that *we'll* be living in that house, not you. It's our decision, not yours. And if we have to overextend ourselves, if I have to get a second job, scrub floors, anything, we'll make it, with or without your help."

"I don't think so," he said, fighting to control his voice.

"Iris," I said.

"No, John, let me have my say."

The Buick sailed over the road like a ship at sea, Prok's hands tightening on the wheel as the tires fought for purchase and slipped again on a rolling white patch of ice.

"Listen, Prok," she said, leaning into the front seat now, her hands clamped to the fabric on either side of his head, leaning in close so he wouldn't mistake her, "if you think I'm going to be dictated to or bullied or blackmailed, then you don't know me very well." There was a bump, and then the long soft shush of the ice. "No," she said, "you don't know me at all."

5

Escrow closed at the end of January, and though Prok was a bit brusque when I asked, he gave me the day off and the use of the Nash (veering and uncertain, but still running and still capable of hauling a load) to facilitate the move. Both Corcoran and Rutledge had volunteered to help, but as time was running out on the male volume and Prok growing increasingly edgy, they couldn't be spared, and so I hired a man for the day and together we dismantled the bed, removed the legs from the kitchen table and shouldered the couch and armchair out the door. The Nash, which Prok had modified into a kind of van, took the larger items, and my own car—the 1938 Dodge D8 Coupe I'd gone out and purchased for two hundred fifty dollars the day after we made an offer on the house, because what was the sense of saving for a rainy day when the deluge was already on us—ferried the boxes of clothes, dishes, records, books, cosmetics, silverware, mops, brushes, tools, pots, pans, foodstuffs and all the rest of the accumulated and husbanded necessities of an American household at the midpoint of the twentieth century, and it was amazing to contemplate how much we'd managed to acquire during our five years in the apartment.

Iris was in her glory. I didn't want her fatiguing herself—she was in her fourth month now and just beginning to show, if you looked at her in the right light, that is—but there was no stopping her. She'd been busy packing for weeks, making lists, discarding various objects and procuring others, doubling brown paper bags and reinforcing cardboard boxes with masking tape. On the day of the move, she wrapped a kerchief round her head, vomited for the last time in the old toilet on Elm Street, and had me take her and a full carload out to the new place before the sun was up. While the hired man and I wrestled the furniture out the door of the apartment she was busy lining the shelves at the house, and by the time we'd got down to arranging the couch and chairs in the new place (as per her very explicit directions), every box and brown paper bag was empty, the drawers were filled with neatly folded shirts, socks and underwear, the pantry stocked and the statue of Aphrodite cum ashtray occupying a position of honor on the mantelpiece.

We had hamburger sandwiches and french fries out of a greasy paper sack that night, washed down with Cokes, and for me, two or three hard-earned bourbons and water. I found a heap of scrapwood in a shed out back and got a good blaze going in the fireplace, and we sat on the newly unscrolled carpet and ate in front of it. For a long while we just sat staring into the flames, content to be there together, enjoying our first meal in our new house. "God, I love a fire," she said, looking around for something to wipe her hands on. There was a sheen of hamburger grease on her lips. Behind her, propped against the side of the couch, were the four prints that had graced the wall of the apartment and a much bigger framed reproduction of Modigliani's *Nude on a Blue Cushion,* a housewarming gift from Prok and Mac.

"Me too," I said, and I handed her the empty hamburger sack to use as a napkin, because neither of us felt like getting up.

"The wallpaper has to go though," she said. "We need something lighter, to brighten the place up. The smoke darkens things too, you know—years of it, the little bit that drifts back into the room? But that's why I haven't even thought about hanging the pictures yet—new wallpaper, that's a must. And the furniture. I'm not sure about the furniture yet either. You think the couch looks strange there, out in the middle of the room like that? I thought it would help divide up the space—"

I watched her ball up the grease-spotted bag and toss it into the fire, the flames rising and falling back again, and then I shrugged. "Looks fine to me. But whatever you want. You just tell me when you're ready to pick out the paper."

"I don't know," she said, running her gaze around the room. "I'll look at patterns tomorrow, because I really didn't want to do anything till we were actually in the house—you have to live in a place before you can get a feel for it, my mother always said that, but the walls are too dark, much too dark. We don't want people to think we're living in a cave, do we?" She paused, biting her underlip, looking right through me. "But that nude. I don't know about that nude."

"What? The Modigliani? It's a famous painting, a great work of art. I think it'd look nice, maybe on that wall there, by the staircase. Or maybe over by the window?"

"I don't know. A nude. What kind of statement does that make?"

"It doesn't make any statement. It's just art, that's all. Just a painting."

"Oh, come off it, John—four woodcuts of Emily Brontë scenes and a two-and-a-half-by-three-foot nude?"

"But what about Prok? He'll, well, he'll expect—"

"Yeah," she said, and her eyes were focused now, flaring up and then settling on me like a pair of flamethrowers, "Prok, Prok, Prok."

Outside it was windy, with temperatures in the teens. The windows shook and we listened to the sounds of the house a moment, alien sounds that would grow increasingly familiar, day by day, till they provided the sound track for the rest of our lives. "Let's not spoil this," I said. "Hang it anywhere you want, I don't care."

"That's nice, John," she said. "Very magnanimous. How about the toolshed? Will that do? Think a nude'll liven it up and remind us how we make our bread and butter here every time we need a crosscut saw or a what, a monkey wrench?"

"Don't," I said. "Just don't."

The fire chased shadows across the walls. The cat, which had been padding tirelessly round the place all day long, in search of mice or the scent of mice, trotted across the room and disappeared in the darkened hallway that led to the kitchen. I got up then and poured myself another drink, the bottle shaped perfectly to my hand as if it were the most familiar thing in this new environment, more comforting than the transposed furniture and the Aphrodite or even Iris with her accusatory eyes and tragic underlip. "You know, it's a shame you can't take a drink," I said. "I think a drink would really help loosen you up a bit. You should be happy—aren't you happy? Iris?"

She said nothing, but her eyes had begun to roam the room again.

"He did loan us the money," I said. "You've got to give him credit for that."

THE NEXT DAY was Saturday, and we worked all that day and Sunday too, putting up wallpaper, painting the ceiling in the living room an expansive high-flown white two shades removed from pure and generally scrubbing and rearranging things till we were both exhausted. Our first formal meal in the house had nothing of the celebratory quality of the meat loaf dinner Iris had prepared for me that first day in the apartment (I seem to remember a chicken of questionable age and tenderness, roasted with potatoes and carrots in a single pan, sans stuffing, gravy or greens, in the interest of keeping it simple) but it was a home-cooked meal nonetheless, cooked in our own home. Our son ("Or daughter," as Iris kept reminding me) wouldn't grow up in a rental, and he'd have his own yard in which to play ball and ride high on the swing set we planned to erect and maybe help his mother in the vegetable patch and just amble outside and pick an apple or peach or pear anytime he felt like it. Despite the smell of paste and paint fumes and the twin draughts that seemed to slice across the living room at six inches and six feet respectively, we were in heaven.

But then it was Monday, and I listened to Iris retch in the new toilet (or rather, the old toilet in the new house) and then I drove her to school and went into the office myself, and the routine started in again. Prok looked as if he'd been at work for hours when I got there at eight, his head bowed, skin drained of color under the distorting glare of the lamp. He glanced up and nodded a curt greeting as I came in, and it was as if he were wearing a mask—suddenly, in that moment, from that angle and in that light, he looked ancient, lines of fatigue cut under his eyes and radiating like parentheses from his pursed lips, his forehead scored, a series of vertical trenches delineating the jointure of his upper jaw and ear. There was gray in his hair, gray threaded through the boyish pompadour like blighted stalks in a field of wheat. And how old was he? I did the calculation in my head as I unwound the scarf from my throat and shrugged out of my coat: in June he would be fifty-three, in the prime of life. But the look of him, just then, gave me a stab of alarm. He was pushing himself too hard, I thought, pushing against a weakened heart and an immovable world, and all his power and magnetism and his unflagging energy couldn't save him, couldn't save anybody. I sat there a moment, sobered, and then I called across the room to him. "Prok, can I get you anything? Coffee maybe? A doughnut?"

He lifted his head and gave me a steady look, as if he were trying to place me, and gradually, the old familiar Prok began to settle back into his features. "No thanks, Milk, but I will need those charts on marital intercourse by educational level this morning, and we're going to have to convene a special staff meeting too." He paused, removed his glasses to pinch his eyes shut a moment. "Something's come up."

Corcoran and Rutledge strode in together then, sharing a private joke, and Mrs. Matthews began machine-gunning away at the typewriter. "Morning, Prok, John," my colleagues chimed, Corcoran's lips clamped round the pipe Prok wouldn't let him light in the offices, Rutledge already sliding out of his coat. "How's the house coming, John?" Corcoran wanted to know, and he bent over the desk to take my hand in his own and give my fingernails a mock inspection. "White for the ceilings, I guess, huh? Or is that the picket fence?"

In the confusion, I didn't get a chance to ask Prok what the problem was—he was already gliding into the back room, conferring with Rutledge over something—and I forgot all about it till he rounded us up an hour later and gathered us in the inner office. We didn't yet have a conference table—or room for one—and so we just pulled up chairs and settled in. Prok took a seat too, but he didn't stay seated for long. He had a newspaper in hand, and he fanned it twice and then held it up for us to see: it was a small-town paper, the *Star Gazette* or *Journal Standard* or some such. "Remember this place?" he asked, and he was on his feet now, giving us a withering look.

We did remember it, if only vaguely. It was one of the comatose Midwestern towns we'd invaded sometime in the past six months, and it might have had a factory or foundry, a grain elevator, a small Lutheran college maybe, and Prok had addressed the League of Women Voters or the Lions Club or the Intercollegiate Anthropological Society's Annual Convocation. It hardly mattered to us: we'd got our data and moved on.

"Isn't that that place in Minnesota?" Corcoran was straddling his chair backward, the dead pipe in his mouth. "The one where we went on that wild-goose chase after the farmer with the giant penis? Or the ostensible giant penis?"

I had a glimmer of recognition. Prok had heard of a man in northern Minnesota whose penis reportedly measured an extraordinary twelve and a quarter inches flaccid—the local M.D. had written him an account of it—and we'd arranged a lecture trip in the vicinity in order to record the measurements. And if it sounds faintly ridiculous to go off in search of some random individual's rumored appendage, please remember that this is precisely what a taxonomist does, recording the entire range of variety in a given species, from the smallest features to the largest. And further, if you'd expect such an individual to have a name like "Long John" or some such and be famed throughout his community, then you'd be disappointed: these unusual specimens, whether they exhibited extremes at the top or bottom of the scale, were unassuming and all but unknown. As I recall, in fact, we never were able to verify any measurement greater than nine inches, and this particular individual— the farmer—always seemed to be out in some distant field when we came round to investigate.

"No," Prok said, his mouth tightening, "not actually. This town"—a finger stabbing at the paper's masthead—"is in Ohio, in point of fact. But that's not the issue, whether you remember the venue or not. What matters—what's alarming, actually—is this article here in the lower left-hand corner of the front page." He handed the paper first to Rutledge, who scanned the article, then passed it on to Corcoran, who finally gave it to me. The piece seemed innocuous enough—of the who, where, when variety of Journalism 101, describing Prok's lecture to "a packed house eager to hear the findings of the noted sex researcher" at St. Agnes College—but Prok was incensed by it.

"I've spoken with the president of St. Agnes, with the editor of the newspaper and the journalist involved, and I've let them know in no uncertain terms that this article stands in breach of our verbal agreement that our figures were not to be published, that no specifics whatsoever were to be revealed." His voice was metallic, laminated with a thin layer of outrage, and he was using the precise diction that became ever more honed and formal when he felt himself pushed into a corner. "And that further, I am considering legal action in that such leakages of our material can be expected to adversely affect the reception of our inaugural volume early next year. What I mean is, if our findings are broadcast now, even by some, some—" He paused, searching for the word.

"Podunk," Corcoran offered.

"—inconsequential rag in a town far off the beaten path, then we are in real trouble, and if you think this is a laughing matter, Corcoran—or you, Milk—then you are as much enemies of the project as this so-called *journalist.*"

The smile died on Corcoran's lips. I dropped my eyes.

"If this should get out to the news magazines—to *Time, Newsweek,* any of them—it will bury us before we get started."

There was a silence. I became aware of the heat clanking on somewhere in the depths of the building. Rutledge was the first to speak up. "But, Prok, as far as I can see from a quick scan, there really isn't much in the way of figures here—"

"Oh, no?" Prok waved the paper as if it had caught fire. "What about this then—'Because of the unrealistic and proscriptive nature of existing sex laws, Dr. Kinsey asserted, the general populace is driven to what is now branded criminal activity; in his home state of Indiana, population three million, five hundred thousand, the Indiana University zoologist estimates that there are some ninety million nonmarital sexual acts performed annually'?"

Rutledge was sitting ramrod straight in his chair. He lifted a hand to stroke his mustache, then thought better of it. "Well, yes, Prok, I see what you mean, but that hardly qualifies as tipping our hand, if that's what you're afraid of—this is one statistic out of a thousand. Ten thousand."

"He's right, Prok," Corcoran put in. "Or you're both right. They shouldn't have printed that, shouldn't have printed anything other than maybe a general description of the talk, but I think you're blowing it out of proportion, I mean, this is just some podunk—"

"And that's where you're wrong, Corcoran, categorically. Any slippage weakens us. And you, Rutledge, with your experience in the military, you above all should appreciate this—'loose lips,' eh? Wasn't that the motto?" Prok was pacing now, working himself up, alternately brandishing the paper and balling his fist. "The interest is building out there, you know it is. Once they get a whiff of it, they'll come after us like hounds, and they'll take our figures out of context and make us out to be charlatans or cranks along the order of the Nudists or Vegetarians or the Anti-Vivisection Society. Imagine what they'll do with a table like the one John drew up for us contrasting the peak age of sexual activity for male and female? Or the prevalence of H-activity? Or extramarital relations?"

No one said a word.

"Well you'd better imagine it. And you'd better brace yourselves. Because the invasion is coming."

That was the beginning of paranoia, and throughout the year, as Prok struggled through the writing of the first volume and we punched data cards and produced the calculations and traveled as a team to collect histories while he lectured across the Midwest and in New York, Philadelphia, Boston and Washington, we were never clear of it. Prok had given over a thousand lectures in the past five years, and the ground rules for every last one of them were the same: no publication of specifics, no statistics, no sensationalizing. Since he'd never charged a fee for his public lectures (and wouldn't begin to do so until after the male volume was published and the expenses of the Institute demanded it), at the very least he expected civility, probity and discretion from his auditors and sponsors. For the most part, he got it. But there were leaks, as with the paper from the little town in Ohio, and as *Sexual Behavior in the Human Male* neared completion and was set in (closely guarded) proofs, the press went mad after the scent of it, trying one gambit after another to pry loose information from us. We got letters, wires, telephone calls, people showed up at the door from places as far afield as Oregon, Florida and Maine, and in one case, Lugano, Italy, and Prok was polite but firm with them all: there would be no exclusives, no excerpts, no information whatever dispensed prior to publication for fear of sensationalizing a very sensitive subject. And, of course, the more we denied them, the more eager they were.

Even I was drawn into it. I recall an incident from later that year—it must have been late May or early June, Iris big as a house, the weather turned brooding and muggy. I was overworked, keyed up, feeling the stress of Prok's ceaseless push to produce—and the sting of his temper too, as nothing I nor anyone else did seemed to be quite up to his standards—and after a long day of calculating correlation coefficients, medians, means and standard deviations from the mean, I wasn't ready to go home. I felt—blue, I guess you would call it. The house, as Prok had predicted, was in need of more attention than I could give it—a windstorm had taken the gutters and half the shingles off the roof over the bedroom, for one thing, and the pipes were so rusty our drinking water looked as if it had been distilled and bonded over the state line in Kentucky, and that was just the start of it, termites in the floor joists, mice in the walls, dry rot behind the tub—and the Dodge, my pride and joy, the one possession I truly loved, was up on the lift at Mike Martin's garage with a frozen transmission. Five point two miles each way, a real trek, and Prok had been right there too. Corcoran had swung by for me that morning and Prok had offered to give me a lift home, but I didn't want to impose, and as I say, I wasn't going home. I called Iris and told her I was planning to head over to the garage to see about the car, and then, if it wasn't ready, I'd probably have a couple drinks and catch a ride home later.

"And if it is?" she said, her voice small and distant.

"I don't know," I said. "But don't wait dinner for me."

There was a pause. We hadn't been getting on as well as we might have, and that was my fault, I admit it, what with the pressures of work and her moods—you would have thought no woman had ever been pregnant in the history of the world before. As she put on weight, as she settled into the awkwardness of pregnancy, flat-footed, distended, sloppy in her personal habits, I began to have second thoughts about this baby, this child, and I suppose every father goes through that sort of thing—one day you're ecstatic, and the next you think your life is over. Or maybe I had it worse. Maybe I wasn't ready, after all. Did I resent the child? Did I resent the fact that my wife was in her eighth month and we weren't having marital relations anymore and that just the night before she'd declined to satisfy me with her mouth or even her hand?

"That's all right, John," she said after a moment. "You need a break, don't you? I understand. Go out and have a couple of drinks, but be careful if you do wind up driving home." There was a click over the line, and I thought she'd hung up, but then her voice came back: "Did Mike say how much the car was going to be?"

"I don't know. Fifty dollars, maybe sixty, seventy. Who knows?"

"Oh, John."

"Yeah," I said. "Yeah, I know."

There was no one I recognized at the tavern, a new crop of students, two men my age at the end of the bar who might have been lecturers or assistant lecturers, a smattering of women sitting with men in shirt-sleeves, the jukebox going, the bartender presiding with his swollen, tenderized face. It was hot and the ceiling fan wasn't doing much to improve the situation. I settled in with a beer and bourbon chaser and lost myself in the newspaper. After a while—I might have been on my second round, I suppose—I became aware of movement to my right, of someone hovering there on the periphery, and I looked up absently into the face of Richard Elster. He was smiling, as if he were glad to see me, and there was another man with him—tall, thin-faced, in a dark wool suit that looked expensive and much too heavy for the place and the season—and he was smiling too, as if we were old acquaintances. "Hi, John," Elster said, "nice to see you. This is Fred Skittering. Fred, John."

We shook hands, and then Fred Skittering said something about how hot it was and he reached up to pull his tie loose and unfasten the top button of his shirt collar. "No reason to stand on formality here, is there?" he said. "We are in Indiana, after all, aren't we?"

"Yes," I said, "that we are."

Elster's grin was of the canned variety, and there was something in his eyes I should have been alert to. Years had gone by since I'd worked as his underling and we saw each other almost daily in the corridors of Biology Hall, and yet there had always been a coldness between us. As I've said, he was the petty sort, and though Prok had put him in charge of that part of our library that remained on the shelves—that is, the tamer books in the field—he never forgave me my elevation above him. Generally, he passed me in the hall or on the walk out front of the building without so much as a nod—and now, here he was, elbowing in beside me at the bar, all smiles, with his sliver-faced friend in the big-city suit. Warning bells should have gone off in my head, but I was preoccupied and I was drinking and I just looked from Elster to his friend and back again, chasing round a smile myself. I suppose, in my mood, I was glad for the company.

I watched them order, light cigarettes, watched the bartender move heavily from the tap and set down two beers on the counter before them. Fred Skittering drained his in a gulp, while Elster raised the glass to his lips with both hands, like a priest with the chalice, and took a delicate sip. Both of them set down their glasses with a sigh of satisfaction, and then Elster leaned in confidentially and asked, "Everything going all right with Iris? It's her first, isn't it?"

I didn't know what to say. This was the first I knew that he was even aware I was married, let alone that my wife was pregnant.

"You know, Claudette's expecting too—in three weeks, actually. This'll be our third—we've got one of each now, and she wants a girl, but I'm hoping for another boy." He bent to his beer. Skittering held on to his smile. "They have the same obstetrician," Elster went on, "the one Prok recommended. He did recommend Bergstrom to you, didn't he?"

Again, I was astonished. *Prok?* He was calling Kinsey *Prok?* "You—I didn't know, well, that you—and Prok, that is—"

"Oh, yes, yes. We've been conferring on the library quite a bit, you know. Space, that's what we're looking for, more space."

Skittering flagged down the bartender. "Another round," he said, and what I heard in his voice was New York, cab drivers, alleyways, night-clubs. "And buy one for John here too," he said. "On me."

The beers came, and a shot of bourbon with each of them. I thanked Skittering and we made small talk awhile. What did he do for a living? Oh, he traveled. For a company. Nothing exciting really. "And what about you?" he asked.

I told him I worked with Dr. Kinsey.

"The sex researcher?"

"I'm part of his staff." I drank off the bourbon and chased it with a long pull at the beer. "The first person he took on, actually," I said, and I couldn't help the pride from creeping into my voice. "I've been with him since the beginning."

"Really?" he said. "Well, that's certainly interesting." And he tipped his head back to drain the shot glass while Elster, his grin still in place, toyed with his own. "But uh, *sex* research—how exactly do you go about that, I mean, you can't just burst into people's bedrooms in the middle of the night, can you? Say, barkeep," he called and made a circular motion with one hand to indicate that another round was in order. "What is it, surveys and the like?"

I'm sure you've already anticipated me, of course—I was being played here, and by a past master. Fred Skittering, as it turned out, had been a war correspondent and had made something of a name for himself in the European Theater, a name I might have recognized in another connection. But here, in Bloomington, in the neighborhood tavern I'd been frequenting since my student days, it went right by me. He was working for the Associated Press even as he stood there at the bar, though I didn't yet know it and I'd already taken the bait. "Surveys?" I gave a disdainful shrug. "Surveys are all but useless. Think of it: where's the control? You get a survey in the mail and either you fill it out or you don't, either you're honest and forthcoming or not, and who's to know the difference? No, our methods"—I lowered my voice—"our methods are as scientific and statistically reliable as you could ever hope to get."

A period of time went by. People drifted in and out of the bar. Beyond the windows, at the far end of the street where the trees gave out, lightning snaked across the horizon. I was never particularly loquacious, never one to run off at the mouth, as our lower-level subjects might have put it, but I just couldn't seem to stop talking that night. Maybe it was my mood. The weather. Iris. Maybe it was just shop talk—I was inordinately proud of what we were accomplishing, Prok, Corcoran, Rutledge and I, four against the world, and yet I was frustrated too because to this point we'd kept it all so close. Here was a sympathetic ear. Here was Elster—and this stranger—and who would have guessed?

What saved me was Betty. I was on the verge of compromising the project, undermining Prok's faith in me, embarrassing myself in the deepest, most hopeless way, the way of the apostate, the quisling, the dupe, when Betty appeared. I hadn't laid eyes on her since she'd played the female lead in the previous fall's demonstration in Prok's attic—I didn't even remember her name actually. But there she was, ducking through the door with another young woman, both of them dressed casually, in skirt and blouse, as if they were students—or wanted to be taken for students. I looked up and we exchanged a glance, and then she was slipping into a booth at the far end of the room in a single graceful movement, one hand going to the back of her thighs to smooth out her skirt as she slid over the slick wooden surface of the bench. Skittering was saying something about another sex survey he'd heard of—in Denmark, he thought it was—while Elster (his shill? his Judas?) leaned over his elbows and concentrated on my face.

I saw the girl—*Betty*, and her name came to me in a flash—glance up at me again as the waitress set two martinis down on the table. She gave me a smile when she saw that I'd recognized her, the child's eyes fading into the woman's face, the prominent cheekbones, the sharp teeth, her hair pinned up at the crown and spilling into a complex of curls at her shoulders. I smiled back even as Skittering said, "But Kinsey, the man, I mean, what's it like working with him?" and because I was drunk, I raised my glass and saluted her across the room.

And then I was back in the moment, regarding Elster's face—the face of a saboteur, not a friend or well-wisher—in a whole new light. I took a moment, studying Skittering now, and all at once I understood. Skittering had got to Elster, and Elster had got to me, and what they were after wasn't statistics, but something deeper, more dangerous. I shrugged. "He's a genius," I said. "A great man. The greatest man I've ever known."

"Yes, but"—a cigarette to the lips, a distracted wave at the ashtray—"underneath all that, I mean. The man. The man himself? Certainly he must have some sort of oddities or quirks, irritating habits—I hear he can be pretty short sometimes, isn't that right?"

"Listen," I said, "I don't mean to be rude, but I see a friend over there—an acquaintance, a friend of the research, actually—and really, I have to"—I was pushing myself away from the bar, patting down my pockets for cigarettes—"but thanks for the drinks, thank you, nice meeting you."

The girl—Betty—watched the entire transaction, the nod in her direction, the dual handshakes, the fading expressions of Elster and Skittering, even as her friend turned to look over her shoulder and I weaved my way across the room to her, glass in hand. I didn't know what I was doing really, just that I was extricating myself from an awkward situation, and that, as much as anything, impelled me toward her. "Hello," I said, sweeping the hair away from my forehead with my free hand as I swayed over her, "remember me?"

Her smile was glossy, her lips pulled back tightly over her teeth, and forgive me if I couldn't help picturing those lips as they stretched wide to receive Corcoran, that heroic motion, in and out, and the tissue there glistening with fluids. "Yeah, sure," she said, and she slid over and patted the seat beside her. "Here, take a load off. Come on."

I eased in beside her, a quick glance for Elster and his companion, who were fixed on me like birds of prey, and the olfactory memory of her came back to me in a rush, that perfume, the heat of her body, the smell of her hair.

"This is Marsha," she said, indicating the friend across the narrow table (spaniel eyes, the face of Stan Laurel, a frizz of apricot-colored hair), "and what was your name again?"

My name was John. And I gave it to her. And I gave her her smile back too.

The waitress was there and she asked if we wanted to see a menu. The girls' martini glasses were empty. Betty wanted another drink and she thought looking at the menu might be a good idea. The friend claimed that the one drink had gone to her head, and she didn't know, but sure, what the hey, she'd have another. That was fine by me, though I didn't have a whole lot of cash on me, because I'd planned on a couple of drinks, a bite to eat, and then a five-point-two-mile hike, and nothing more. Iris was at home, big as a house. The house was at home, bigger than a house. I ordered another beer and Betty told the waitress to bring her a porterhouse steak—"rare to bloody"—with fries and a house salad with Thousand Island dressing.

After that the three of us beamed at one another for a while and we talked about Bloomington, how endlessly, hopelessly, stuporifically dull it was, and we talked about movie stars—John Garfield, wasn't he disgusting, or raw or whatever you wanted to call it?—and our travels, such as they were. Both girls were mad for New York, though as it turned out neither had been there, and I suppose it was only natural that I should play up my experiences there and maybe even embroider them a bit. Then the steak came and the friend left—she had to be up early in the morning—and when I glanced over my shoulder Elster and Skittering were gone too.

"So are you married?" the girl said.

"No."

"Then what's that on your finger?"

"This?"

"Yeah, *that*."

"It's a wedding ring."

She dropped her eyes to the plate a moment, the knife, the fork, cut a wedge of steak and looked up again as she tucked it between her lips. "Divorced?"

"Does it matter?"

She shrugged, dropped her eyes to the plate again.

"What about you," I said. "Are you—and please don't take this the wrong way—are you, well, a *professional*?"

She was chewing thoughtfully, slowly, her eyes reemerging now to lock on mine. "What is this—another interview?"

"You mean you already—?" I made a mental note to go to the files in the morning and violate our code of anonymity yet again. "Who was it, Corcoran?"

"Yeah," she said, "Purvis. He's a great friend of mine, you know that, don't you?"

I wasn't very good at this, but the liquor was in my veins and liquor always made me feel unbeatable. "I gathered that," I said. "From the last time I saw you."

She ignored me. Went for the steak again. Picked up a french fry and licked the salt from it with quick pink stabs of her tongue before folding it into her mouth. "No," she said, "in answer to your question. I'm not a professional, whatever that means. I don't take money for it, if that's what you're asking, and that's down on the interview sheet too."

I was getting the defiant look now, the look she'd given us all when we were milling around Prok's living room trying to summon the courage to get on with what we'd come for. "I like men," she said. "Is that a crime?"

"No," I said, "that's no crime at all."

And then we were both laughing, laughing to beat the band, as they say, and in the throes of it she put a hand on my thigh to steady herself. The jukebox—I wasn't even aware to this point that it had fallen silent—roared back to life with something that had plenty of jump to it and we let the laughter trail off even as we began to feel the beat vibrating through the tabletop and the glasses in our hands and the seat of the bench we were sharing. People around us got up to dance and my fingers, independent of thought, began to tap out the rhythm. I was thinking I should ask her to dance, though I wasn't much good at it, but instead I said, "So what do you do—for a living, I mean?"

She turned her face to me, a blue sheen of neon caught in her hair. "I'm a nurse," she said.

"Oh, really? Well, that's—that's terrific. It really is. A nurse, huh? That must be—interesting."

"You'd be surprised," she said, looking out over the room before her eyes came back to mine. "But you know what?"

"What?"

"You know what I really like? After a good meal?" She leaned in close, so that her forehead was nearly touching mine and I could smell the gin and her perfume and the meat on her lips.

"No," I said, "what?"

"You can't guess?"

IRIS WENT INTO labor on June the twentieth, just after dinner. She'd experienced mild contractions the day before, and there had been blood in her vaginal secretions that morning, followed by a discharge of bloody mucus, normal precursors to the rupturing of the amniotic sac and the imminent birth of the child. Though I'd been unconscionably ignorant of the whole process (witness my question about the kicking of the baby, which even the most untutored or oblivious should know doesn't occur until the sixteenth week), Prok had encouraged me to educate myself, not only for "my own benefit in apprehending the life process," as he put it, but in improving my ability to relate to our female subjects as well. And he was right: now I knew what they went through, what they were afraid of, how the pleasure of the act was followed by the pain of disclosure, abortion, the throes of birth. Though he'd never been busier or more harassed, Prok took the time to quiz me each week on Iris's condition—the swelling of her breasts, the appearance of the linea nigra drawn like a dark chalk mark over the hump of her abdomen, the dropping of the fetus, the widening of the cervix—and made a little lecture of it every step of the way. Terms like "blastocyst" and "human chorionic gonadotrophin," "endometrium" and "progesterone," which I'd probably copied into a notebook somewhere in Intro to Biology and promptly forgotten, became as familiar to me as the baseball scores in the morning paper.

We were lucky, really. We had not only the benefit of the literature on the subject (including an excellent and very thorough new book by Benjamin Spock, a Columbia University M.D.) and the experience of

Dr. Bergstrom, but the advice of Iris's mother as whispered through the long-distance lines and all the support Prok and Mac could give us, Mac especially, who spent hours at the house, knitting, baking and just chatting away with Iris in her soft glutinous tones as if Iris were one of her daughters and the baby out of her own bloodline. My own enthusiasm, as I've said, tended to vary day to day, but there was something of the inevitable in the process and I found myself submitting to the pull of it. And I was informed. At least there was that.

As the due date approached, I made sure that the car—with its rebuilt transmission—was in good running order and the gas tank topped off, ready for the dash to the hospital. The twentieth fell on a Friday, and I hadn't wanted to leave Iris to go into work, but she had assured me she'd be fine—I should stick close to the phone, that was all. As it was, I was hardly able to concentrate through the long, tediously unmomentous morning and into the crux of the slow-grinding afternoon, and I left work early—How was she? No change—to make us a light dinner of macaroni salad and canned fruit, and then we'd sat in the living room listening to the radio and waiting. She'd gotten up to rinse her cup in the sink when I noticed that her dressing gown was stuck wet to her legs. I looked at her in alarm. "Iris," I said, "you're wet, do you know that?"

She'd put a hand out to steady herself against the sink, and there was dripping now, and I was up off the couch and taking hold of her under the arms as if she were on the edge of a dark yawning gulf and in danger of slipping away from me. The terminology rang in my head—*amniotic sac, cervical dilation, oxytocin*—but I felt helpless all the same. She gave me a weak smile, dead weight in my arms, and murmured, "Yes, I think it's time."

6

THERE WAS THE usual rush to the hospital, the wife's face drawn and bloodless, the prospective father's hand trembling on the gearshift, a litany of all the things that could go wrong jamming the airwaves in his head—Catherine Barkley dead in the rain and the infant too, the forceps child down the block with the pinched features like an unfinished painting, the crippled, the retarded, the hopeless, the stillborn—and then there was the wheelchair waiting at the emergency entrance and the two of them sitting in Admissions answering inane questions and filling out forms till the prospective father wanted to get the nurse in a stranglehold and force her to reveal the whereabouts of Dr. Bergstrom, the obstetrician, and where was he? Didn't he realize what was going on here?

I didn't say anything, though. Didn't make a move. Just sat there in the crucible of the chair and held Iris's hand while the nurse nattered on and the ink made its way from the pen to the printed forms and the world went maddeningly on as if nothing at all were out of the ordinary. Iris looked bilious, bleached to the roots of her hair, her eyebrows painted stroke by stroke over the void of her eyes. She was sunk down in the chair, slumped under the terrible weight of the ball she was carrying around with her, teeth clenched, limbs dangling. The hands of the wall clock crept round as expected. Clouds bobbed in the sky beyond the window. All at once, Iris let out a sharply aspirated cry and the nurse smiled. Then they finally came for her, two orderlies with a gurney, and took her up to Obstetrics, and nothing happened, absolutely nothing.

After an hour or so they let me in to sit with her, pulling the curtain around the bed to give us some privacy. Her eyelids were closed, her hands prone beside her. There was no color to her, none, and she might have been dead already, laid out on a slab in the funeral parlor. I took her hand then—out of passion and fear and because I felt so reduced and helpless in that moment—and her eyes snapped open. "John?" she said.

"It's me," I said. "I'm right here." It was movie dialogue, and I kept seeing Helen Hayes's face superimposed over hers, and where was the "Liebestod" to carry us away? "What are the contractions like? Coming faster now? Did he say how long it's going to be?"

They'd given her something for the pain and her voice was drowsy with it. "It's going to be a while, John," she murmured. "It's just one of those things, you know? Sometimes, with your first—"

An unseen woman cried out from across the room then—or no, she shrieked, actually, as if a torturer were at work on her with his hot pliers and his electrodes. There was a silence, and then she shrieked again. I felt chastened, helpless, full of remorse and tenderness. The only thing I could think to do was squeeze my wife's hand. "Should I find Bergstrom? Talk to him, I mean?"

Her voice dropped away. "Only if you want to. But don't"—the woman shrieked again, stone on glass—"get yourself in a lather. I'm okay. I am. Everything's going to be fine, you'll see."

In the end, of course, she was right—everything was fine, and John Jr., at seven pounds six ounces and twenty-one inches in length, was the result. But Iris's was a protracted labor, and Friday night became Saturday morning, the progress of the clock as tedious as anything I'd ever endured, Sunday sermons, a visit to the dentist, Prok in the sixth hour of a Buick-bound lecture, and then the sun was up and Bergstrom back on the job advising me to go home and shower and catch some sleep because she was barely dilated and it would be a while yet. I didn't take his advice. I slumped in the chair at Iris's bedside, listened to the furtive comings and goings of the ward, might even have heard the odd wail of a newborn from the delivery room across the hall. Coffee fueled me, and something greasy from the cafeteria—chili con carne, fried chicken and dumplings—till my stomach was a vat of acid. When Saturday afternoon melded into Saturday evening, and still nothing had happened, I turned to my flask for solace.

Sunday morning came, the small hours revisited, and I went out to the car and slept, and when I woke the sun was high overhead and making a furnace of the Dodge, the windows of which I'd rolled up in order to defeat the mosquitoes. I'd sweated through to my underwear, and I'm afraid that I must have been a walking wall of unpleasant odors and secretions. My mouth was dry, but I took the precaution of refilling the flask before I shuffled back through the hospital, looked in on Iris—still nothing—and made my way into the men's room to throw some water on my face and pat down my underarms with hand soap and paper towels. It was past noon by the time I had a sandwich in the cafeteria, and then I sat through the long afternoon and into the evening with my wife, and it was as if we'd never been anyplace else in the world but here, behind the white curtains, while expectant mothers climbed into the beds on either side of us, cried out their pain, and were wheeled into the delivery room to gratify their husbands and their doctors. I was reading to her from the paper when the sun went down for the third time.

Then it was night, ten o'clock, ten-thirty, eleven, and yet still nothing, though the contractions were coming faster now and Dr. Bergstrom was on the case, poking his head between the curtains every few minutes, inspecting Iris's cervix for dilation and making encouraging noises. I should say, incidentally, that I'd been given permission to be with my wife throughout the process and to witness the birth itself, something Prok had encouraged me to do. He'd been present for the delivery of all three of his children, and he spoke very passionately both to me and Dr. Bergstrom about the significance of the experience from a scientific point of view, and I think he himself would have liked to be there with us if it wouldn't have looked odd in the eyes of the community. Odd enough that the husband should be present, let alone another male, no matter how closely connected and how purely objective he might have been. And of course Iris would have refused him in any case. This was her show. Absolutely.

And then it occurred to me, as eleven o'clock slipped by and my stomach broiled and the bourbon lit me from within and all of my fears came rising to the surface like the corpses of the drowned, that there was actually something serendipitous in the delay, that something extraordinary was occurring here—if Iris held out another forty-five minutes by my watch, John Jr. would share a birthday with Prok. I told myself that everything was happening for a reason, that was all it was, and I couldn't imagine anything more perfect. Or auspicious. *John Jr. and Prok.* I saw a succession of birthday parties stretching on over the years, balloons, flowers, the cutting of the cake, Prok lifting my son to his shoulders and parading round the room with him, uncle, godfather, mentor.

I took a pull at the flask and glanced down at Iris. She lay there like a stone. They'd given her an epidural for the pain and Dr. Bergstrom had begun to talk about inducing labor or even operating because there was the danger now of an infection setting in, and the nurses had begun to bustle a bit because one way or the other the moment was coming. "Iris," I said, and I suppose I was half-drunk at the time, the flask doing wonders for my jangled nerves, and I didn't want to think about the delay and the consequences and the fatality that hung over the bed like a palpable nightmare, because I was going to look on the bright side of things, I was going to buck her up as best I could. "Iris, you know what?"

She was exhausted, drained, all her energy and her optimism gone. She barely lifted her eyes.

"Looks like John Jr.—or Madeline—is going to share a famous birthday."

Nothing.

"With *Prok.* In forty-five minutes it's Prok's birthday, June the twenty-third, did you realize that? Isn't it amazing?"

She let out a sudden gasp, as if a bottle of champagne had been unstoppered, and then, seconds later, another, and then another, and the curtains flew back and the nurse was wheeling the gurney into the delivery room, and as I sat there in surgical mask and scrubs and tried to contain the hammering of my heart, I watched my son come into the world at 11:56 p.m. on June 22, 1947.

I'D LIKE TO say that we gave birth to the male volume at the same time—and we should have, according to the schedule Prok had laid out for himself—but the parturition of the text was a bit more difficult and protracted than any of us could have imagined. As the summer broiled around us and we darted off for abbreviated field trips to this venue or that, Prok worked ever more furiously on the manuscript, writing everywhere—in the car, on the train, at home before work and in the office after the doors had been shut, composing the latter chapters even as the early ones came back to us in galleys from W.B. Saunders. He was putting in eighteen-hour days, sleep a luxury, food nothing more than fuel for the engine, Mac, Mrs. Matthews, Corcoran, Rutledge and I coopted into reading proofs, our offices a blizzard of paper, graphs and spread-eagled texts, always another chart to complete or a fact to check. The absolute final date for completed copy was September 15, and as late as the end of August there were five chapters yet to finish.

I'd never been so busy in my life, nor had Prok ever been so demanding—or short-tempered—and when I wasn't at work there was the nonstop turmoil of the house, diapers in the laundry, boiling away on the stove, strung up like miniature flags of surrender on the line out back, bottles everywhere and the smell of formula hanging over the bedroom and kitchen till I began to think the walls themselves were lactating. There were late-night feedings, John Jr.'s symphony of shrieks, yowls and sputters, the aching quiet of the house at three a.m. and Iris's maternal calm. And her mother, her mother, of course. Her mother was there for the first month, a sponge clamped in each hand, wiping down every horizontal surface till it shone, carting in groceries, sweeping like a robot and forever cooking up vats of lamb stew or succotash or four-inch pans of macaroni and cheese with hunks of sliced frankfurter spread like gun emplacements across the top.

I was neutral toward her. She was like Iris, only older, independent-minded, contentious, and she could never bring herself to address me directly, instead referring to me in the third person, as, for instance, "Is *he* hungry? Does *he* sit here?" But she took some of the pressure off me and kept Iris company and that was fine by me, because, as I've indicated, this was the busiest and most critical time the project had ever seen. Once she did leave, though, to go back home to Michigan City, the onus fell on me, and the timing couldn't have been worse. I tried my best. Iris still hadn't recovered her usual level of energy, and I did what I could to help out, picking up groceries, doing a load of laundry, that sort of thing, but naturally things began to slip and I couldn't help feeling overburdened and resentful.

And yet I don't mean to sound negative, because a kind of miracle grew out of it all: I got to know my son. To this point he'd been bundled and diapered and whisked from one room to the other, from my mother-in-law's arms to Iris's, and if I got more than a peek at the reddened amorphous little face that was saying a lot, but as soon as her mother left—as we came up the walk on our way back from the bus station, in fact—Iris just handed him to me as if he were a sack of groceries she was tired of shifting from one hip to the other. "Go ahead, hold him, John," she'd said, and there he was, the surprisingly dense bundle of him, thrust into my arms. I didn't know what to do. I was afraid of dropping him, of failing to properly support his neck, afraid of his weight and his movements and the way he had of effortlessly sucking in air and letting it out again in a maddened inconsolable shriek. He was a time bomb. He was made of lead. He had the lungs of Aeolus. "It's just a baby, John, that's all—he won't bite. He doesn't even have any teeth." She looked at me, at the expression on my face, and burst out laughing.

I wasn't laughing. I was in awe. He was my son. I held him in my arms, felt the weight of him, the vitality, and something moved inside me. John Jr. The wedding of the chromosomes. This was what we'd worked for, the end result, and it was research no longer.

But the book. The project. That was the focus of the summer of 1947, and if our domestic lives intruded on it—Corcoran's, Rutledge's, Iris's and mine, even Mrs. Matthews's—Prok was there to remind us of our priorities. As he became more demanding, he became more anxious as well, and the press did nothing to assuage his fears, the reporters becoming more importunate and ingenious as the summer went on. I'd escaped Skittering, but there were dozens of others hot on the trail of the story, each of them looking to be the first to reveal our findings to the public. We were besieged with letters, wires, telephone calls, and not just from the plebeian ranks, but from editors and editors-in-chief and even, in some cases, the distinguished owners of various media outlets themselves. Never underestimate the power of sex to incite the public. We were interested in science, but the press was interested in commerce and commerce alone. They wanted to sell copies because copies sold ads and ads sold product and product bought more ads, and none of us of the inner circle had any doubt that they would twist our work in any way they saw fit.

Ultimately, it was Prok who came up with the solution. He'd been feeling increasingly harassed, and one reporter in particular—very persistent, wouldn't take no for an answer—provided the catalyst. Every day, for a period of more than a month, we received a wire from this gentleman (or pest, as Prok called him), begging for an interview, Prok firmly refusing him time and again till one morning he showed up in the anteroom, hat in hand, trying to wheedle his way past Mrs. Matthews. We were working away at our desks when at some point we became aware of a duel of voices from the anteroom, the closer's sanguine inflections and Mrs. Matthews's deft parries, and I remember Prok, in exasperation, raising his head from his work. "Who *is* that, Mrs. Matthews?" he snapped.

We all saw him there through the open doorway, a slope-shouldered man of middle age in a humble brown suit, looking wounded and lost. "Ralph Becker," he bleated. "Of the *Magazine of the Year?* I wired you."

"Oh, yes," Prok rumbled, "yes, you've wired us all right, and we've wired you back. Repeatedly." Prok was up from his desk suddenly, curt and angry, striding through the doorway to confront the man in the brown suit while we looked on sheepishly. "But perhaps you have difficulty with the written word?"

The man stammered out an apology, all but melting into his shoes, but he never stopped wheedling. "As long as I'm here, I wonder if you might just—oh, just the smallest tour of the place. That's all I ask. And the tiniest glimmer of what you hope to accomplish. From all I hear you're fantastically dedicated, rigorous, really rigorous"—and here he looked beyond Prok to where we sat riveted at our desks—"and you've got a real crackerjack staff too. A minute? Just a minute of your time?"

Prok was impassive, hiding behind his interviewer's façade, and if you didn't know him you wouldn't have guessed at how close to snapping he was. His voice gave him away, throttled in the back of his throat, a kind of articulate croak: "I've explained all that a hundred times already, explained it till I'm exasperated beyond the point of civility, and I'm afraid I'm going to have to ask you to leave our offices—"

"But I wouldn't be in the way—I'd just want to get a feel for it, for your work."

"—and not set foot on these premises again till you're expressly invited." Prok waved his hand impatiently, as if dissipating a swarm of gnats. "Don't you see? Don't you get it? If you people don't stop pestering me there won't *be* a volume to review."

The journalist must have detected the same despairing crack in Prok's voice I did, because he immediately tried to hammer a piton into it and hoist his way up: "'*Invited*,' did you say? You mean you're going to open up, then? Good, good. But why wait? I'm here now. Think how useful I can be, spreading the word—that's what you want, isn't it? To spread the gospel? Right?"

The light from the hallway liquefied Prok's spectacles. He hesitated. He did want to spread the word, but not piecemeal, and not in a way that would cheapen and undermine everything we were hoping to accomplish. "All right," he said finally, "I appreciate your interest, and this is what I've decided on—what *we've* decided on, my colleagues and I— as a matter of policy." He took a moment to glance over his shoulder at us, and we did our best to support him, though we were as eager as the man in the brown suit to hear what he'd come up with. "We'll be issuing invitations to all the major newspapers and magazines to come here to the Institute, have a tour of the facilities, record your sex histories and receive full access to the page proofs—once those proofs are completed, that is. And I have to emphasize that: Completed. Finished. Ready to go. Now, do you understand?"

"I'll be the first?"

"You'll be one of them."

There was a pause. The man shifted his weight from one scuffed brown shoe to the other. His face was shrewd, narrow, the face of an ex-tortionist, a second-story man. He'd come to rob us, just as surely as Skittering had. "You don't mean you're going to make me traipse all the way out here again—look, here I am. Can't you just make an exception, just in this one case?"

I almost got up—I was on the verge of it—because why should Prok, with so much on his shoulders, have to deal with this too? I could have ushered the man out the door, could have broken him in two if it came to that, but Prok was in charge here, always in charge, and Prok never wavered.

"Both you and I know that wouldn't be fair, now don't we?" he said. From where I was sitting I couldn't see Prok's expression, but I could have guessed at it, Prok looming over the little brown man, in absolute control—the steely look, the mask of indifference—and subtle, so sub-tle. "But I take your point. You *are* here, aren't you, and as long as you are we may as well get your sex history and save us all the trouble when you return." Prok turned to me then, Mrs. Matthews gone back to her typ-ing, Corcoran trying to suppress a grin, Rutledge fidgeting in his chair. "Milk, would you mind doing the honors?"

And so it was. Prok brought the reporters on in two waves, the mag-azine writers first—in August—and then the newspapermen in Sep-tember, even as he was putting the finishing touches to the manuscript. We set up a conference table in the office across the hall, from which we'd evicted one of Prok's colleagues in the Zoology Department (above his protests, but with the blessing—and imprimatur—of President Wells), and Prok packed the reporters in as if they were so many shot-putters and pole-vaulters crowding onto the team bus. First he lectured them on our findings and the boon they represented for mankind, then gave them a tour of the facilities and an opportunity to talk individually with us, his shining and punctilious staff, finally making a plea to each of them to give up his history not simply in the service of the project but for the practical purpose of gaining insight into our methods. Better than fifty percent of the journalists took him up on it, and that kept us busy, all of us, frantically recording sex histories even as the rest of them snooped around town, looking to unveil a little local color. As you might imagine, there was a real run on the bars.

Before they left, Prok gave them each a set of proofs, and then—this was pure genius—had them sign a thirteen-point contract vowing not to publish their stories or release any of our figures prior to the December issue of their respective publications and to submit all articles to us in advance so that we could vet them for errors. Of course, the effect was to stifle any criticism and at the same time harness the press to the service of our own ends—there was an outpouring of highly favorable articles, and all in that crucial period leading up to the book's release. We endured the sensationalized headlines as a matter of course, because there was really nothing to be done there, but by and large the articles themselves were more than we could have hoped for. Suddenly the whole nation—the whole world—was listening.

The rest is history.

ALL WELL AND GOOD. We'd achieved celebrity—or at least Prok had—but if before we'd been able to work in relative obscurity, now everything we did was magnified. And if Prok had been able to relax into his work in the past, into his gardening, his gall collecting, the meandering field trips to seek out taxonomic marvels and acquire histories, now he was driven and manipulated by his own success, pulled in a hundred directions at once. There were mobs of visitors all of a sudden, many of them quite prominent, travel and lecture requests, nonstop interviews, and letters—thousands of them—pouring in from all over the world, each more heartbreaking than the next. Prok was a guru now, and gurus had to sit at their desks from sunrise to sunset, tending to the needs of the faithful.

Dear Dr. Kinsy: My husbend wants to do unnatural things with me in bed like kissing me in my private parts but I think such things are unattracktive and sinful and I was hopping you could write to him or make a call and tell him to leave me alone. Yrs. Sinceerly, Mrs. Hildegard Dolenz

Dear Professor: Twelve years ago I met the woman of my dreams, Martha, and married her on the spot. She is a woman like no other and I am satisfied with her as a good mother to our six sons and a good cook and etc., but for the fact that she is no longer interested in marital relations and I don't know why. Is this natural in a woman of her age (38)? If so, can you tell me what the cure is or if I should look for relief in other quarters, because I have become friendly with a widow of 54 years of age who seems truly more interested in relations than my own wife. Very Truly Yours, Stephen Hawley, Long Beach Island, New Jersey

Dear Dr. Kinsey: Can you tell me why our servicemen, after liberating France and defeating Nazi Germany, have to spend all these months away from home living with the enemy? Because my husband of seventeen years never wrote me once until he came home on leave two weeks ago and told me that he was moving out of our house that we slaved for together because of some if you'll pardon the expression ex-Nazi floozy who's only idea is to pray on lonely servicemen in her foreign country. I love him. I want him back. But he says he loves her. Thank you and God bless. Mrs. Thomas Tuttle, Yuma, Arizona

Dear Doctor: I am a young teenaged girl and I like to play with myself and with two other girls in my class and I don't really think there's anything wrong with that, do you? Anonymous in Chicago.

Dear Dr. Kinsey: My father was my first lovver and he had a brother I never liked and he was my second I am a young Mulatto girl of mixed race because my father is White and my mother from Trinidad (Black) and my ex-husband Horace wants me to turn tricks in a furnished room and I still love him but my boyfriend Naaman says he will kill me first and I don't know what to "do" can you help me please with any advise?—May

Of course, with all the other pressures on him, Prok nonetheless took it upon himself to answer each letter personally, and sometimes in great detail, though after a while even he became inured to this outpouring of heartbreak and ignorance and either referred his correspondents to the relevant chapters of the male volume or advised them to seek counseling from professionals in their own hometowns (*I regret to say that we are not clinicians, and that while we are interested to hear of your dilemma, we can do no more than to point you toward professional help*). Still, the sheer volume of the correspondence, coupled with the travel and interviews and the desire to move forward with the female text, all began to take their toll.

Prok's first collapse had come some three years earlier, in the spring of 1945, after a hectic round of lecturing at the Menninger Clinic and then at a conference for some of the leading lights of the military, during which he bent over backward trying to convince them that no sexual behavior was deviant (H-behavior, specifically, the old martial bugbear) and that even if it were it would pose no threat to military discipline. You can only imagine the sort of reception he must have met with, the hidebound officers and the tight-lipped military bureaucrats, and the energy he must have expended in the process. I was the one who picked him up at the station in Indianapolis, and I remember the look of him, his pallor that extended even to the dulled irises of his eyes, his slouch, the deadness of his voice. "It's just a cold," he told me, but it was more than that. It was his heart, enlarged and arrhythmic, the legacy of his childhood bout with rheumatic fever, the thing that would kill him, though none of us could imagine it then—other people had coronary problems, other people died, but not Prok. Prok was a pillar. He was indefatigable. He was our leader, our mentor, and we couldn't do without him, couldn't even conceive of it.

The doctor called it nervous exhaustion and ordered three weeks' bed rest, but Prok was back in action within the week, taking histories at the Indiana State Penal Farm, and then the whirlwind descended again and I forgot all about it, even in the face of the evidence. And now, under the weight of his sudden celebrity, he'd begun to flag once more, and I tried to protect him—and so did Mac, we all did—but it was impossible. He was wound tight, and there was nothing that could loosen him but for sex, and sex, for all its meliorating effects, only lasted through excitation to orgasm.

It was Professor Shadle who stepped into the breach. He was, as you might recall, one of the pioneers in the recording of animal sexual behavior on film, the man who first photographed coitus in the porcupine and other unlikely creatures. Prok had met him at the University of Buffalo when we'd gone there some years earlier to lecture and collect histories, and ever since had pursued him over the subject of his films, which would be an invaluable addition to our library. Finally, after a lengthy exchange of letters, Shadle had agreed to leave his porcupines for a week and come out to Bloomington with his films. As usual, I was the one delegated to meet the professor at the train, and I brought Iris and the baby along for the ride. It was late summer, the male volume still riding high on the bestseller lists, "The Kinsey Boogie" paralyzing the airwaves, the southern Indiana heat like a living thing attaching itself to your pores in order to suck all the minerals and fluids from your body. We were early for the train and I bought Iris an ice cream and watched her lick the cone round the edges and bend to the baby as he tried to suck and kiss his way through this new medium, this dense stuff that was sweet and wintry at the same time, the idea of it fastening in his infantile brain in the place where the pleasure centers take their stimulus: ice cream. Ice cream. It was an exquisite moment. And what would his first words be, as the gift of language descended on him right there on the platform under the gaze of the Indiana sun?

"Did you hear that?" Iris was bent over the stroller, vanilla ice cream running like white blood over her fingers, our son's hands jerking in clonic display, and the train just pulling into the station with a long attenuated shriek of the brakes.

"What?"

"The baby. He just said 'ice cream' clear as day."

"No," I said, "did he?"

"His first words, John. 'Ice cream.' I heard him."

I have a picture of that moment in my head, Iris squatting over the baby, her hair in a ponytail, shoulders bare and freckled with the sun, her shorts riding up her thighs, her sandals and painted toenails and the shining arches of her feet, and the train standing there like an illusion, a moving wall, abracadabra. I bent to my son, one eye on the passenger cars as the doors wheezed open. "Ice cream," I said. "Ice cream, Johnnie."

A jerk of the fleshy arms, the glutinous hands clapping together in accidental percussion. And the reduced gurgling glissade of sound: "Iiiice," John Jr. said. "Iiiice."

When I looked up, Professor Shadle was standing there with his suitcase in hand. He was in his mid-sixties, short—very short, almost dwarfish—with a pronounced midsection and clumps of white hair that might have been cotton balls stuck randomly to his skull. "Beautiful baby," he murmured.

"Oh, excuse me," I said, rising to my feet to take his damp dwarfish hand in my own. "Professor Shadle, welcome. To, well, to Indiana. We met in Buffalo, you remember?"

"Yes," he said, in a lisping rasp, his eyes ducking away from mine. "Of course."

"And this is my wife, Iris. And our son, John Jr."

"He just said his first words," Iris put in. She was beaming. "Aside from 'mama' and 'dada,' I mean."

The professor lifted his eyebrows. "Really? And what were these momentous words?"

"Ice cream," we said in unison, and then there was the echo of the little voice beneath us, John Jr. mute no more. Two words, thin as wire: *Iiiice keen.*

"Beautiful," the professor breathed. "Just beautiful." And he left it at that.

In the evening there was a dinner in Professor Shadle's honor at the house on First Street, Prok having whipped up one of his goulashes with a side of homemade coleslaw ("For the cooling effect"), after which we retired to the living room to watch the films on equipment Prok had borrowed from the audiovisual department at the university. Shadle had eight films in all, each sequestered in a round tin, and he chattered happily with Prok as he meticulously threaded the first of them through the projector. We were all there, all of us of the inner circle, and the atmosphere was relaxed and convivial—in fact there was a real air of pleasurable anticipation, as if we'd all gone to the picture show and were

344

sitting there in the dark awaiting the first flickers of light to illuminate the screen.

"All we need is popcorn," Hilda Rutledge said out of the corner of her mouth.

"And Jujubes," Iris said, "don't forget Jujubes."

"You like those—Jujubes? Really?" Violet Corcoran was sitting on the floor, on the rag rug, her elbows propped up on the chair behind her. "They practically pull the fillings out of your teeth. Dots," she said. "Give me Dots anytime."

"What about jawbreakers?" This was Corcoran, leaning in, hands clasped over his knees. "That's what we had as kids. Last the whole movie, double feature even."

"Sure," Iris said, "if you don't suck or swallow—or use your teeth. Use your teeth and they're gone in no time. We used to go through a whole bag of jawbreakers in a double feature. Remember that, John—that candy store across from the movie theater? Laura Hutchins and I used to buy the stuff there and smuggle it in."

I gave her a smile. I was happy, feeling relaxed and tranquil, and for once alcohol had nothing to do with it. "At about half the price they charged in the theater."

"Captive audience," Corcoran said with a shrug. "You can't blame them for trying to make a good Yankee dollar."

"No," Iris said, "but you can save a good Yankee nickel if you think ahead, but of course most kids don't."

"Licorice whips," Hilda said.

Iris's eyes went distant. "Oh, yeah," she said, "licorice whips. Yeah. But the red ones, only the red ones—"

The women were in summer dresses, their shoulders bare, their limbs fluid, poured like liquid, bare flesh, the hovering light, and Prok at the shades now, closing down the fading sun while Professor Shadle worked at the projector. We were in shirtsleeves—Rutledge, Corcoran and I, and Corcoran was even sporting a pair of shorts in a bright madras pattern—but Prok was wearing his jacket and bow tie still, and I wondered about that until it occurred to me that he was putting on a show of formality for his colleague from Buffalo. Shadle had no such scruples. He'd come to dinner in a voluminous Hawaiian shirt, through which he sweated steadily as he bent to the projector. "You'll be seeing Dannie—he's a year younger—and Peterkin," he said, in a voice that lifted away from his conversation with Prok to address us all. "They were wed last year, or at least that's the way I like to put it. But you'll see, in just a"—he paused to focus on pulling the last loop of film through the projector and attaching it to the take-up reel—"in just a minute."

Prok said nothing. He'd completed his round of the windows, and the room was illuminated now only by the lamp that stood behind the projector. It was noticeably hotter with the shades drawn, and there was an aggregate smell of us, of the inner circle, the gently perspiring odor of our humanity, friends and colleagues all, casually gathered on yet another social occasion. Prok said nothing, but I knew what he was thinking—he was thinking that "wed" was just a euphemism, a convenience, and that Professor Shadle, despite his training as a biologist, was dangerously close to falling into the category of the sex shy. I wondered if we had his history.

But then, just as Shadle straightened up and flicked on the projector, the door from the kitchen swung open and Mac appeared, her thin white arms bowed before her under the weight of the biggest ceramic bowl in the house, and the scent of fresh-popped corn, invested liberally with butter and salt, filled the room. "Well," she laughed, setting the bowl down on the coffee table, "I thought since we *are* having a picture show," and there was a corresponding whoop from Hilda.

"Perfect," Hilda exclaimed, "perfect." She drew up her legs and leaned forward to dip her hand in the bowl. "Did you know we were just reminiscing about the movies, and here we are, with popcorn and everything?"

And then the lamp snapped off and the projector began to click and groan and the first flickers of substance illuminated the silica granules of the screen Prok had set up at the far end of the room. I saw a patch of grass, wavering and dark, the camera jumping in the next frame to the pocked gray trunks of a grove of pine trees surrounded by a hurricane fence, and then we were in the enclosure and the creatures were there, two dense clots of life rising up out of the backdrop till they filled the screen and the camera drew back. The animals' quills were combed down like the densest of beards, only their eyes and the occasional glimpse of their teeth shining through. They seemed to sniff at each other, nose to nose, like dogs meeting for the first time, and then, to the prompting of Shadle's narration ("Now watch, this is precious"), they rose up simultaneously on their hind legs and embraced, their black-lipped mouths coming together as if for a kiss. The whole operation was slow and stately, a kind of porcupine minuet.

Prok let out a low chuckle of delight. "Foreplay," he said, in a wondering voice, "they're engaging in foreplay."

And so they were. Beasts, mere beasts, and they might have been human, philosophers in their long coats, coming together in the tenderest way, taking their time, enjoying themselves.

Hilda Rutledge made a clicking noise, tongue to palate, and said, "Aren't they cute?"

"Which one's the girl?" Iris wanted to know.

"That's Peterkin on the right," Shadle whispered, and it was as if we were in a church, kneeling in the pews. "She's never been bred before—or Dannie either."

"So this is their first date?" Hilda's voice floated up out of the darkness, making a joke of it.

No one answered her.

Now, up on the screen, the animals slowly descended to all fours and the male began to press on the female's haunches until suddenly she opened up to him, the barbed quills magically unfolding to reveal the place of entry. The male nosed her there a moment, then entered her with a series of rapid thrusts before withdrawing to lick his penis clean. And that was it. It was over. Someone—I think it was Corcoran—began to clap, and then we all applauded, Prok among the loudest, and I remember his laughter too. He took the purest, most uncomplicated delight in these films, and the films that were to come, not only of the lower animals but of the human animal too, and that delight, as much as anything, helped to keep him going.

But already Shadle was hushing us, because the camera was again hovering over the animals, the light different—brighter now, another day—and the courtship went on again and again, through eight full reels.

Later, as we strolled out to the car, I asked Iris what she'd thought of it all. She'd been in a giddy mood all night, girlish and quick to laugh, the business with Corcoran and Violet long behind us now, and I had a sense that she'd enjoyed herself, really enjoyed herself, for the first time in a long while. "I don't know," she said. "It was better than I thought it would be, I guess."

"Yeah, it was really something, wasn't it? I didn't know what to expect really, but it was nice, don't you think? Charming. They were charming. Almost like—"

"People?"

I let out a laugh. "Exactly."

The night was still. Fireflies traced perforated lines over the flowerbeds and up into the trees as if they were all working in concert on some elaborate design we could only guess at. There was a powerful smell of the chicken manure Prok and I had spread on the flowerbeds the previous weekend, and something else too, a scent of the earth itself, worked and reworked under Prok's tireless spade. "But isn't that the point?" she said. "That we're really no better than—what are they, rodents? They mate and so do we, right?"

"Sure," I said, giving a shrug she couldn't see because it was fully dark now. "If that's the way you want to look at it."

We were silent a moment and I opened the car door for her and then leaned in and pressed my lips to hers. My hands found her shoulders, the silken flesh of her upper arms, and I smoothed back her hair and kissed her throat. We held the pose for a long moment because we were young still, still in love, and John Jr. was with the babysitter and this was what couples did when they were free of responsibility and the night opened up above them into the dark avenues of the universe that had no reason or end. "Mmm," she said finally, her lips brushing mine, "maybe we should watch the porcupines going at it more often. You think Professor Shadle would mind coming over to the house for a command performance?"

"No," I whispered, "we don't need the learned professor or his porcupines either," and then the door of the house swung open behind us—a parallelogram of yellow light painted on the walk—and there was the sound of voices, footsteps, high heels rapping at the pavement. I backed out of the car, shut the door on Iris, and circled round to the driver's side. "We don't need anybody," I said, sliding into the seat and laying a hand on her knee before letting it ride up her thigh under the thin summer dress.

"No," she said, "not even Prok."

That was when the Corcorans emerged from the front yard, their voices twined in murmurous oblivion, and we sat in the darkness of the cab and watched them turn up the walk, arm in arm. I reached for the keys then, to start up the car and take us home, but Iris stopped me. Her hand was on mine, and she guided me back to her, to her naked thighs and the pushed-up rumple of her dress. "You don't mean—not here?" I whispered.

"Yes," she said. "Here. Right here."

7

FILM WAS THE new medium, we all saw that, and we understood from the beginning—from that night at Prok's with Professor Shadle and those indelible images of his amorous porcupines—that it would revolutionize the course of our research. Whereas before we'd been able to observe sexual activity in the flesh, first with Ginger and her clients and then, much more transparently, with Betty and Corcoran, now we had a means to record it so that the sequence of events—from passivity to arousal, engorgement and penetration—could be studied over and over for the details that might have escaped notice in the heat of the moment. And it was especially valuable at this juncture because we were now beginning to turn our attention to sexual behavior in the female. Not only did we have to make sense of a mountain of data, we needed to observe and record physiologic reaction as well, so that we could, for instance, determine individual variation in the amount of fluid secreted by the Bartholin's glands or settle once and for all the debate Freud initiated over the question of the vaginal versus clitoral orgasm.

It was almost as if the public anticipated us. If we were inundated with mail—letters seeking advice, hastily scrawled notes criticizing our methods, morals and sanity, offers of every sort of sexual adventure imaginable—we also began to receive films. Some of them, of the mating behavior of rats, pigeons and mink, came from a coterie of animal behaviorists Prok had cultivated over the years (the mink were magnificent, as close to sadomasochists as you could find in a state of nature, both partners rendered bloody by the time the affair was consummated), while others—crudely shot on eight-millimeter black-and-white film—were from friends of the research and they depicted human sex. I remember the first of them quite distinctly. We'd just come out of a staff meeting—it must have been a Friday, our regular meeting day—to find Mrs. Matthews at her desk in the anteroom, sorting through the morning's mail. "Dr. Kinsey," she called as we emerged from the back room, "you might want to have a look at this."

The letter that accompanied the film was from a young couple in Florida who lavishly praised our research efforts ("It's about time someone had the courage to stand up and lead this puritanical society out of the sexual Dark Ages") and expressed, at considerable length (something like twenty-two pages, if memory serves), their own somewhat garbled but libertine philosophy with regard to sex. In essence, they felt that sex was one of the grounding pleasures of life and should be appreciated without constraint, and as they were both highly sexed, they'd enjoyed relations two or three times a day since their marriage six years earlier and claimed to be all the healthier for it, both mentally and physically. The enclosed film, they hoped, would not only demonstrate the unbridled joy they took in the activity, but also provide a valuable addition to our research archives. "Use it freely," they concluded, "and show it widely," and signed themselves "Blissful in West Palm Beach." They included a return address and a telephone number, in the event we'd like to contact them for a live demonstration.

We'd all gravitated to our desks, but we couldn't help keeping an eye on Prok as he read through the letter. At first, there was no reaction, his expression dour and preoccupied, the glasses clamped to the bridge of his nose, but he began to smile and even chuckle to himself as he went on. "Listen to this," he called out, the old enthusiasm firing his voice, and he began to quote from the letter until he wound up reading the whole of the last two pages aloud. When he'd finished, he lifted the film canister from his desk and held it up so that we could all see it, and it might have been an exhibit in a court of law, he the judge and we the jury. He was smiling, grinning wide—it was the old grin, the one that had been missing lately, seductive, boyish, devil-may-care, quintessential Prok. "You know," he said, and even Mrs. Matthews paused in her furious assault on the typewriter keys, "I do think it might just behoove us to stay past five this evening and arrange a private screening here in the offices. What do you say—Corcoran? Rutledge? Milk? Am I stepping on any toes here?"

No one objected.

"Good," he said. "Good. We'll just call our wives and delay dinner a bit, then." The grin was gone now, no hint of it left, even in his eyes. "In the interest of science, that is," he said, and turned back to his work.

I telephoned Iris and told her I'd be late—something had come up, yes, another nature film Prok was hot on—and then watched the clock till the hour struck five and Mrs. Matthews tidied up her desk, pulled the vinyl cover over her typewriter and left for the day. Prok never glanced up. He was busy, head down, charging through an opinion on a court case that had been consuming him lately—a man in Pennsylvania, victim of a barbarously antiquated statute, was being tried for performing oral sex on his own wife—and he didn't want to appear overeager to view the film, though I could see from certain characteristic gestures, the tapping of a pencil on the spine of the text before him, a repetitive running of his fingers through his hair, that he was as anxious over the film as we were.

We worked in silence for another quarter hour, exchanging glances among ourselves, till finally Corcoran pushed himself up from his desk with a sigh and made a conspicuous show of stretching. "Well," he said, "Oscar, John, what do you think—isn't it getting to be that time?"

Prok looked up from his work, then stole a quick glance at his watch.

"Prok? What do you say?"

The film was of surprisingly good quality, and since both participants were present throughout, that brought up the rather interesting question of who might have been behind the camera for what proved to be as unexpurgated and varied a performance as the one we'd all witnessed in the flesh on the night Corcoran introduced us to Betty. But this was different, very different. I'm no student of film and doubtless this has been observed many times before, but there was something about the distance and anonymity of the viewer that made the performance all the more stimulating. In the raw—with Corcoran and Betty, that is, with Ginger and her clients—there was always a sense of uneasiness, of fragility, as in a theater production when a single gesture or comment from the audience could break the spell and bring the whole thing down.

That wasn't the case here. I didn't really discuss it with my colleagues, but for my part the sense of standing outside of the action only heightened my response, which was, to say the least, unprofessional. I was aroused, and no doubt about it. The woman—the female—was slim and dark, with perfectly symmetrical breasts, and she wore her hair the way Iris did, the brushed-out curls balling at her throat and shoulder blades as she went through her repertoire; the male was of medium build, his penis uncircumcised and about average in length and breadth (all those penny postcards came to mind, all those measurements duly recorded and addressed to Professor Alfred C. Kinsey, Zoology Department, University of Indiana) and there was something winning in his face, a sense of naïveté or insouciance, as if he weren't performing a role at all, as if it were the most natural thing in the world to have sex with your wife while a third party ran film through a camera. Both of them were attractive. Very attractive. And I'm sorry, because that shouldn't make an iota of difference to a scientist concerned with individual variation, the homely, overweight and poorly favored every bit as significant as the Venuses and Adonises, but it did. My mouth was dry. My palms were sweating. And the rest—well, the rest of the physiological response should be obvious.

Immediately, as the film began, the couple were naked, no foreplay or teasing as in the peep shows, the female seated atop the male on a couch, both of them facing the camera. His phallus was visible between her thighs, and she was manipulating it in her fingers and at the same time turning back over her shoulder to lap at his tongue. The scene held a moment, and then they shifted position, she going down to fellate him before he entered her and they went through the usual motions until finally rolling over so that she was atop him, her face to the camera, absolutely rapt, the eyes open and glaring, the mouth slack—almost grimacing—even as the shudder of orgasm ran through her.

"There," Prok cried. "See there? That is the expression of female orgasm, precisely, and it cannot be faked. The wife who smiles during coitus or the prostitute with her crying out and all the rest of her theatrics, should see this—every woman should see it."

We sat in silence, listening to the ratcheting of the film, contemplating the proposition.

"Really," Prok said, even as a second scene presented itself—they were in the kitchen now, she on the counter at waist-level, her legs spread, he visible only as a pair of tensed white buttocks until the camera shifted to show his erection—"this is first-rate work. Should we give them a special citation as friends of the research? What do you think, gentlemen?" Prok was making a joke, or coming as close to it as he was constitutionally able.

"But seriously," he added after a moment, "perhaps we should look them up next time we're in—where was it, Florida?" He glanced round at us, the flicker of the film playing off his face. "I can't help thinking how this might be improved with a little direct lighting, that is, and perhaps a more adept cameraman—or -woman."

THINGS MOVED SWIFTLY after that. Prok was already campaigning for more space—new quarters, as befitted our success, with soundproofed interview rooms, individual offices, clerical space, a separate library to house the erotica collection—and the need for a photographic laboratory only added fuel to his argument. Ever since he'd joined the staff, Rutledge, an amateur photographer, had been taking photos of erotic drawings and art objects on loan to us from their owners around the world, and Prok had set up a primitive darkroom in the basement of the house on First Street to assist him here, but now we all saw how inadequate that was. Prok went into high gear. Royalties from the male volume were pouring into the Institute, and he resolved to acquire the finest photographic and cinematic equipment available and to take on a full-time staff photographer as well. That photographer—Ted Aspinall—would become the final member of the inner circle, privy to our deepest secrets and a participant in all that was to come.

Aspinall was in his early thirties at the time, private, unmarried, rating perhaps a 3 on the 0–6 scale, and he was earning his living as a commercial photographer in Manhattan. Physically, he was somewhat imposing, six feet tall and blocky, with big squared-off hands and a massive bone structure, and yet his manner was anything but—he had the reticent, knowing air of the Greenwich Village hipster, he wore dark glasses even at night and never removed his tan trench coat except, presumably, to go to bed. When the male volume came out, he read it through twice, then telephoned Prok out of the blue to tell him how much it had affected him, and the two of them immediately hit it off. We met him when we were in New York, and then he took up Prok on his invitation to visit the Institute and things progressed from there.

His first assignment for us was the aforementioned study of the means of sperm emission in the human male, because this was essential to our understanding of conception in the female. The medical literature of the time maintained that it was necessary for sperm to spurt out under pressure in order for fertilization to occur, but our data showed that the majority of males did not spurt but rather dribbled. And so Prok determined on a trial. We went to New York that fall (of 1948, that is, and I recall the date because the trip caused me to miss John Jr.'s first Halloween celebration—Iris dressed him as Tigger from the *Winnie the Pooh* books, in a costume she'd sewed herself from a pattern, and she was furious with me) and booked rooms, as usual, at the Astor. Aspinall showed up with his business partner, a man around my age whose name escapes me now—let's call him "Roy," for convenience's sake—and Roy, who had extensive H-contacts, assured us he could get us the one thousand volunteers Prok had decided on for a definitive sample.

Prok was skeptical at first. "One thousand?" he repeated. "Are you sure? Quite sure? Because anything less would be a waste of our time." We were in our room on the fifteenth floor, looking out over the crush of humanity in the square below. The curtains were open wide—Prok favored light—and the furnishings were what you'd expect from a hotel in the low- to mid-priced range.

Roy—struck wire, amphetamine-fueled, a little man waving his arms—let his voice ride up the register. "No, no, no," he said, "you don't

355

understand. I know this boy, he's a genius. He's beautiful. Seventeen years old, perfect skin, hair like Karo syrup, he's a German refugee, or Austrian maybe, with just a trace of that accent to spice things up, if you know what I mean. Right now he's the hottest thing on the street, at least in this neighborhood. It's two dollars for each volunteer, right? And two dollars for the kid for every one he brings in?"

Prok, frowning, showed him his wallet.

"Okay," Roy said, "okay," and Aspinall gave us a nod of assurance. "Tomorrow night, five p.m., at our studio, right?"

The following night, Prok, Corcoran and I turned the corner onto the block where Aspinall and his partner ran their photographic business out of the ground floor of a brownstone, and my first thought was that there had been an accident, a fire, people evacuating the building and the hook and ladder on the way. It took me a moment to realize that the line of people stretching the entire block—the line of men, exclusively men—wasn't leaving the building, but entering it. A number of them recognized Prok as we ducked through the crowd, calling out his name, pressing in for autographs, but Prok gave them his dispassionate face and reminded them that they were participants in a scientific experiment, not a radio quiz program. A hundred hands shot out to touch him notwithstanding, and he shook as many as he could, his grin fixed like a politician's, as we climbed the stairs and strode through the open door of the studio.

Everything was ready for us, camera, lights, mise-en-scène and a cast of hundreds, the young blond hustler at the head of the line awaiting the signal even as he chatted up those immediately behind him. "First, first," he kept insisting, as we squeezed our way into the room, "I do first, and then I go out and bring more custom, ja?"

Prok gave him a judicious look. Then he separated two bills from the wad of singles he extracted from his pocket and handed them over. "Yes," he told him, "yes, good thinking," and the eyes of the men in the hallway fastened on us as if to memorialize the transaction: this was for real, and so was the money.

Roy and Aspinall had pushed the furniture back against the wall and created a stage in the center of the room by means of spreading a sheet over the carpet and positioning the lights and camera above it—the idea was for each subject to disrobe, lie on his back on the floor and consummate his business as expeditiously as possible, and the photographers had provided a small mountain of pornographic magazines, both of the homosexual and heterosexual variety, as a stimulus. Aspinall hovered in his trench coat and dark glasses, fidgeting over the equipment, while Roy escorted us to the three chairs he'd set up just out of camera range, and then the filming began.

We'd budgeted five minutes per man, one after the other coming in, removing his clothes and taking his position on the floor even as the man before him vacated it, a kind of assembly line, but it soon became apparent that we would have to find some means of speeding things up because there were the inevitable delays, subjects unable to perform for the camera, those who needed extra time, a trip to the bathroom and so on. After the first couple of hours we came to realize that just the undressing itself was taking too much time—thirty seconds, forty, a minute—and Prok asked Roy if he wouldn't have the next several men in line undress in the hallway, distribute the magazines and prepare themselves, as much as possible, beforehand. Corcoran had maintained that it didn't make much difference whether the men were clothed or not—all that mattered, really, was the penis, the hand and the ejaculation—and I tended to agree, but Prok, accusing us of undermining the project, insisted on full-frontal nudity. "We want everything, technique, facial expression, the works," he said in a tense whisper, even as the fiftieth or sixtieth subject was going at it on the increasingly soiled sheet, "because all of it is relevant—or will be relevant—in the long run. Jackknifing, for instance."

"Jackknifing?" I said aloud, the man before us in the shaft of light pounding at himself as if he meant to tear the organ right out of his body, his expression hateful and cold, hair all over him, bunched on the backs of his knuckles and toes, creeping up over his shoulders and continuous from neck to hairline, an ape of a man, a chimpanzee, a gorilla, and if you think sex research is stimulating, believe me, after the initial

357

jolt—whether it be living sex or captured on film—a debilitating same-
ness sets in. We might as well have been counting salmon going upriver
to spawn. It was past midnight. I stifled a yawn.

"Yes, of course. At orgasm. One percent of our sample reports it, and
I should say, Milk, that you, of all people, should be aware of that fact.
Very common in some of the lower animals. Rabbit, guinea pig." Prok
looked bored himself. Looked testy. He glanced at the man grunting on
the floor, leaned over and said, in a soft voice, "If you could please just
come now—"

WE WERE THERE ten days in all, and toward the end we tried doubling
up the sessions for the sake of expediency, and finally tripling them, Aspinall expertly maneuvering the camera from one subject to the other
without once missing the climactic moment. I don't think any of us, no
matter our degree of dedication, had even the slightest inclination to
observe masturbation in the human male ever again, but Prok did finally get his one thousand subjects on film and was able, on the basis of
it, to settle once and for all the question of the physiology of ejaculation.
It was a job well done, if tedious—and expensive, coming to just over
four thousand dollars in fees to the subjects and the little blond hustler,
who must have been the best-heeled teenager in New York by the time
we left—and we were in a mutually congratulatory mood in the train
on the way back. I remember Prok springing for drinks as the dining car
trawled the night and presented us with fleeting visions of dimly lit
waystations and farmhouses saturated in loneliness. I had the fish, Prok
the macaroni *au fromage,* and Corcoran the porterhouse steak. We
grinned at each other throughout the meal, and Prok retired early to his
berth to write up his observations while Corcoran and I sat up over
cards in the club car, drinking cocktails and smoking cigars. I slept like
one of the dead.

The next morning, after driving down from the station at Indi-
anapolis (we'd taken my car so as to leave the Buick and Cadillac free for
Mac and Violet, respectively), I dropped off Prok at the Institute and
Corcoran at his place, then drove out to the farmhouse. I'd thought of

picking up a little gift for Iris—flowers, a box of candy, perfume—but hadn't got round to it, so I stopped at the market and wandered the aisles till I found something I thought she might like, and it represented a bit of an extravagance for us: a two-pound sack of California pistachios, salted and roasted in the shell. I was all the way up to the counter before I remembered John Jr., and I had to go back and dig a pint of Neapolitan ice cream out of the freezer, and then I wondered if Iris might not have run out of coffee or bread or eggs while I was gone, so I wound up getting some basic supplies too.

I pulled in under the canopy of the weeping willow out front, its remnant of yellowed branches hanging in a skeletal curtain, and already felt my mood sour. It was always this way. As much as I looked forward to seeing Iris and my son, as much as I held their faces before me as a kind of talisman during the tedious hours of travel and history-taking, the minute I pulled into the drive I saw a host of things that had been neglected in my absence, the trashcan overflowing at the rear of the house, the door to the basement left gaping, the tarp blown clear of the firewood. And more: she'd left the porch light burning, no doubt for the whole ten days, and that kind of waste just infuriated me. I bundled the groceries in one arm and took the suitcase in the other, and the first thing I did on mounting the steps was kick the deliquescing remains of a jack-o'-lantern off the corner of the porch. Which made a mess of my shoe. And then I had to fumble with the door, almost dropping the groceries in the process.

Inside, it was worse. She must have had the thermostat set at a hundred—more waste—and the chemical reek of ammonia from the cat's litter pan hit me like a fist in the face, and whose job was it to change *that*? There were toys and infant's clothes scattered round the living room, newspapers, spine-sprung books, knitting—and food, a smear of it, in two shades of apricot, on the new-painted, or recently painted, wall. I didn't say anything, didn't call out her name, just dropped the suitcase at the door, trudged out to the kitchen and set the groceries on the counter. And, of course, the kitchen was a story in itself. I tried to stay calm. I was tired, that was all—irritable, maybe a bit hungry—and Iris had had her hands full, stuck out here all by herself, John Jr. in his roaming phase, getting into everything, needful, always needful. I tried, but even as I mounted the stairs to the bedroom, I could feel a dark knot of irascibility beating at my temples like something shoved under the skin, like a splinter and the hot needle to chase it down.

Iris was in bed, asleep, curled round the prow of her hip and the sharp terminus of her folded knees; John Jr. stood silently in the playpen at the foot of the bed, clutching the bars and staring at me as if I were a visitation out of the universal unconscious. He had Iris's eyes exactly. "Hey, champ," I said, and I squatted down to poke my face in his, "Daddy's home."

My son gave me a smile of sudden stunned recognition, followed by a gurgle of infantile transport, baby joy naked and unfeigned, and I took him under the arms and swung him out of the playpen even as the fecal odor swamped the room: he needed to be changed, had needed to be changed for some time. "Yes," I cooed, "that's the boy," and set him back on his feet behind the wooden slats of his gaudy prison. At which point, he began to wail.

"What?" Iris pushed herself up, struggling to focus. There were two parallel indentations on her cheek where her face had creased the pillow, red stripes that might have been wounds. She was in her nightgown still, though it was nearly noon. "John? Oh, God, you scared me."

"Yeah," I said, "I scare myself sometimes too." I made no move toward her. John Jr. began to outdo himself, each shriek building on its predecessor like waves crashing in a storm.

"Here," she said, holding out her arms, "give him here."

I lifted the squalling bundle of him from the playpen, careful to avoid the wet spot at the crotch of his playsuit. *Playpen, playsuit, playmate, playtime:* more euphemisms. "He needs to be changed," I said.

I watched her fussing over him, the shrieks subsiding into disconnected wails that were like the sound of shingles falling off a roof. The walls closed in on me. Everything was a mess, everything stank. "What," I said, "are you sick?"

No, she wasn't sick, she wasn't sick at all. She'd never felt better—physically, that is.

So what was the problem?

She was depressed.

"*You're* depressed?" I loomed over the bed. Her face was small, a nugget, sidelong and averted. "What about me? I'm the one who had to sit in some rancid overheated room for ten days and watch a thousand men jerk off. You think that's fun? You think I like it?"

A silence. The tragic underlip. "Yes, John," she said finally, her eyes fixed on mine, "I think you do. You do it with Prok, don't you? And Purvis? And half the tramps and male hustlers in, in—go ahead, hit me. Will that make you feel like a big man, huh, will it?"

I didn't hit her. I've never hit her and never will. And when I spoke earlier in pugilistic terms, of bouts and rounds, you have to understand that it was meant metaphorically, strictly metaphorically. Certainly we had our disagreements, like anyone else, but violence had no place in them, at least not physical violence. I just turned my back on her and stalked out the door. I might have kicked something against the wall in the living room, a teddy bear or a toy dump truck, I don't remember, and then I went out in the yard to have a smoke and let the dead gray November sky feed my mood.

Later, when we'd both cooled off, she got up and dressed and changed the baby. She made a real effort to tidy up the place—it just wasn't in her nature to let the housekeeping go, at least not for long—and she went out of her way to make a nice meal that night. I'd gone in to the Institute to put in half a day, and when I got back I must have dozed off, because I remember waking to the smell of something in the oven, and then Iris padded into the room—the living room; I was on the couch—and deposited a bathed and talcum-scented toddler in my lap, along with a glass of beer.

I played with John Jr. a moment, and then he got down and staggered off across the room to rummage among his dump trucks and steam shovels. "Listen, Iris," I said, lifting my eyes to hers, "I'm sorry about this morning. I didn't mean—I was tired, that's all."

Iris had her own glass of beer. She was wearing a gingham house-dress, blue and white, and her hair was up. "You were in a pretty foul mood," she said.

"Yeah," I said. "I'm sorry." I was thinking of the calculus of a relationship, how sex equals love equals babies, mortgages and cellar doors left ajar, and how love itself is nothing more than a hormonal function, purely chemical, like rage and hate. But I had a beer in my hand and a roof over my head, and my son was there, and my wife, and what more could anyone want? Other wives, other sons, other roofs? I felt charitable. Felt content. "But, hey," I suggested, "how about if I build a fire? Would you like that?"

"Sure, that would be nice." She was propped on the arm of the chair, one leg dangling, her pretty leg, her ankle, her foot in its trim felt slipper. "But, John, there's something I wanted to say to you—and don't give me that look because it's nothing like that. It's—well, I want you to teach me how to drive. Violet and Hilda drive everywhere—Violet says she'd be lost without her car—and even Mac, Mac drives, and if you're going to be gone all the time—"

"I'm not, I'm not gone all the time—and I'm not going to be."

"—leaving me alone way out here for how long? Weeks at a time?"

"Ten days."

"Okay, ten days. But I'm stuck here. What if the baby needs something? What if I run out of flour—which I did—or, I don't know, what if I just feel bored? Don't you know I get bored out here—don't you realize that?"

"You're the one who wanted the place."

"You wanted it too."

I stared into the black pit of the hearth. Cold ash there, the butt ends of charred sticks poking through like bones at the crematorium. Across the room, John Jr. was talking to his toy trucks. "Bad boy," he was saying, over and over, "bad!" The ice cream was in the freezer, the pistachios still in the bag on the counter. I looked up at my wife. "When do you want your first lesson?"

IF I WAS reluctant at first—forced into something I had neither the time nor the patience for—it took only one lesson for me to realize my mistake. I can't speak for Iris, but for me the next few weeks were some of the best times we'd ever had, John Jr. in my lap, Iris at my side, focused and intent, her hands locked on the wheel even as she negotiated the perdurable mysteries of clutch and accelerator. We memorized the back roads, watched the hills roll at us, one after another, like waves on a concrete sea, and we went where the mood took us, stopping for a milkshake or a hot dog or just to wander up a streambed and share a sandwich on a fallen log. Then it was back in the car, the clutch, the accelerator, jerk forward and stall, grind the ignition, the clutch, the accelerator, jerk forward and stall again. I don't know what it was, something to do with her fragility, I suppose, with her very narrow and specific need and my ability to direct it—"Turn left," I would say, "stop here; third gear; put it in reverse"—but I cherished that time. I never lost my temper, never raised my voice, not even when she swerved off the road to avoid a hell-bent squirrel and put three long gouges in the right front fender.

Indulge me a moment, because this is important—not to Prok, maybe, but to me. It was the day after Thanksgiving, the sun stripped of color, Iris gaining in confidence, the wheels firm on the road and my attention drifting into another realm altogether, when suddenly the squirrel made his dash across the pavement and my free hand got to the wheel an instant too late. There was the shock of the impact, a screech of stone on metal, and then the car stalled. Startled, John Jr. began to pipe and then the piping grew in fullness and volume till he was bawling at the top of his lungs though there wasn't a mark on him—on any of us. She hadn't been going more than twenty miles an hour.

Iris's voice rode a thin tube of air up out of her constricted throat, even as John Jr. began to hit his stride. "Oh, God, I've ruined it. I wrecked the car, I wrecked it, wrecked it!"

"It's all right," I told her, though I knew it wasn't.

"I don't want to do this, I don't, I can't."

I remember feeling expansive, feeling calm despite myself. I got out of the car, John Jr. still clutched tightly to me, calmly assessed the damage—heartbroken, my first car, my pride and joy—and then leaned in the window to reassure her. "It's nothing," I said. "Just a scratch. Nothing a little rubbing compound won't cure, and maybe a tap or two with the hammer. Really, Iris, it's okay."

She sat there rigid, eyes shut, forehead pressed to the wheel. Her shoulders began to quake. Her fingers trembled. She couldn't seem to breathe. I saw her humbled in that moment, defeated and brought low, and felt everything a man is supposed to feel for a woman. I wanted to protect her, save her, comfort her, and I eased back into the car and took her in my arms, John Jr. reaching out for her at the same time till the three of us just sat there and held the embrace as if there were nothing more to life.

Unfortunately, it couldn't hold. Three days later—on the Monday—Prok, Aspinall, Corcoran, Rutledge and I took the train for Oregon, where we would shoot nearly four thousand feet of film exhibiting H-behavior among bulls at an agricultural station there. "You see," Prok would exclaim excitedly as one animal mounted another, "it's just what I've said all along—all our behaviors have their antecedents in nature."

8

IT WAS A little over a year later, in February of 1950, that we moved into our new quarters in Wylie Hall, another of the venerable old buildings on campus. This time we were given an entire floor to ourselves, albeit the basement, though in all fairness I should say that the basement was partially above ground, so that at least we could stare up into the opaque wire-reinforced glass of the windows and speculate as to whether it was morning, afternoon or evening. Prok oversaw all the details in his usual obsessive way, of course, insisting on the highest standards of fireproofing in order to protect our records and the rapidly accumulating stock of the library, as well as air-conditioning so that we could seal the place off during the hellish Hoosier summers, and sheets of soundproofing to ensure absolute privacy in our interviewing. Each of us had an office to himself now, there was a file room, a darkroom, and for the first time space enough to consolidate the library in one place (with additional room for visiting scholars to consult our holdings without disturbing the workings of the Institute). None of this was particularly grand—we were in a basement, after all, with long, close corridors and exposed pipes running overhead—but Prok would have revolted against anything that smacked in the least of luxury. Still, the university deemed the project enough of a success to sink seventy thousand dollars into the remodeling of the space, and finally, at long last, we had a place of our own, where we could pursue our research as we saw fit, without worry or interference of any kind.

What do I remember most of that time? Boxes. Cardboard boxes stuffed full of books, files and correspondence. For two solid weeks, during the worst an Indiana winter could offer, I traipsed up and down the stairs at Biology Hall, staggered across campus with my arms strain-

ing at the sockets, and deposited said boxes in the commodious basement of Wylie. Anyone else would have hired movers, or at the very
least, students, but not Prok. He insisted that our records were far too
sensitive to entrust to anyone but the senior members of the staff, and
somehow the gall wasp collection, the filing cabinets and even our
desks, chairs and coat racks fell under that designation too. Corcoran,
Rutledge and I packed, moved, unpacked and reordered everything we
possessed, and then we stood back and marveled at all the empty space
yet to fill.

Ted Aspinall had joined us the previous year, but he was excluded from
any of the heavy lifting by virtue of his speciality—he was an artist first, a
technician second, and his province was the film laboratory. He moved
permanently to Bloomington around this time, arriving with a suitcase of
clothes and two trunks of photographic equipment, and immediately set
up shop in our new offices (or "laboratories," as Prok preferred to call
them). He'd never been outside of New York City before in his life, and he
did seem a bit lost at times, wandering the streets of Bloomington in his
dark glasses and trench coat as if he'd gone to sleep on the subway and got
off at the wrong stop, but Prok had made him an attractive offer (he came
in at a higher salary than I was making, but there was nothing new there,
low man on the totem pole as I was and always will be) and his commercial photography—the eternal weddings, bar mitzvahs, graduation cere-
monies, the unvarying frozen portraits of grandparents, uncles, cousins,
even dogs—had begun to grate on him. He came to Bloomington to stay,
and the whole tenor of the project changed to accommodate him. We
were no longer an earnest if underfunded seat-of-the-pants operation
working out of a warren of cramped dismal offices in the biology building, but a shining enterprise with international recognition, a ready influx
of cash and our own full-time staff photographer.

Aspinall didn't waste any time. Prok budgeted some eight thousand
dollars to the purchase of the newest movie-making, processing and editing equipment, and Ted went through the lion's share of it in a week.
Prok was busy everywhere—furiously busy, lecturing, taking histories,
posing for photos and sitting for interviews, overseeing the move and

the reshelving of the library's holdings and at the same time puzzling over the data for what would become the revolutionary female volume—and yet he found time to hide away in the darkroom and consult with Aspinall over every last piece of photographic equipment. Film—the rapid frame-by-frame encryption and exposure of animal behavior, from the porcupine to the erotically charged bull to the uninhibited couple in their Florida apartment—this was Prok's new obsession, and Aspinall was his purveyor.

And, yes, I'm aware of the evolutionary progression here. Aware that the lower animals are one thing, the recording of their habits uncontroversial, educational, salutary even, and the human animal quite another. Perhaps we did go too far. Perhaps some of the critics of what the public was calling *The Kinsey Report* had a valid point, though none of us saw it at the time. What was it Margaret Mead had said of the male volume? Something along the lines of accusing Prok of being a reductionist, too dour, too scientific—all those statistics and not a single mention of fun, and that was the term she used: "fun." As if "fun" could be measured or catalogued. And Lionel Trilling, Lawrence Kubie and the rest, denouncing Prok—and by extension, us, *me*—as championing a mechanistic view of human relations over the spiritual and emotional. I see now what they were getting at, if only narrowly, but still I stand by everything we did—if we hadn't been rigorously scientific, consummately professional, the whole thing would have been a sham. In any case, I saw the criticism as nothing but a goad, narrow-minded, puritanical, antiscientific, and to move forward—to progress—we had to ignore it. And so it was only logical that we began to film human sexual behavior.

But let me backtrack a moment here. It wasn't solely the arrival of Aspinall and the acquisition of all that equipment that pushed us in the direction of live filming, nor simply the evolutionary progression of the project either, but a third factor played into it as well: the ready availability of subjects. For one thing, Betty was in town still, and still willing. I saw her occasionally, driving down the street in a late-model convertible, pushing a basket up the aisles of the supermarket in the starched white nurse's uniform she'd tailored to fit her lush proportions, and occasionally I stopped to chat with her—we were friends. She was a friend of the research and I a friend of—well, friendly relations. And then there was Vivian Aubrey, the former Columbia student who'd been such a prodigious help to us during our early visits to New York. She was in Bloomington increasingly now, attracted by the aura of Prok's fame, as were a number of other women (another Vivian, the multiorgasmic Vivian Brundage, comes to mind, a sixty-year-old Philadelphia gynecologist we were to film a number of times with various partners) and men. Always men. Because more and more, Prok craved men.

The first film we made—of Corcoran and Betty, reprising their earlier roles—was the one I remember best. It was late in the year—the holidays were nearly on us, Prok dusting off his Santa Claus whiskers, Vivian Aubrey preparing to go off and visit her parents in Florida, my own mother appearing out of the blue to spend some time with her grandson—when Prok, with a hint of mystery in his voice, asked us to gather at his house that evening, sans wives, on Institute business. My mother didn't understand. All through dinner she'd quizzed me about the project and Prok—When was she going to see Prok again? Such a nice man. So dedicated. What had I thought of his picture in such-and-such magazine? And Mac. Didn't that photograph flatter her, because God knows she's no beauty. I sliced meat and dipped the tines of my fork into a mound of mashed potatoes and assured her that Prok hadn't changed at all (a lie) and that he talked of her often and fondly (another lie) and we'd see him at the Institute tomorrow, but that tonight's meeting was strictly business and bound to be a bore.

Iris concurred. "You don't want to go, Irene, believe me. It'll just be Prok and his boys, heads down, worrying over the female orgasm."

My mother gave me a look across the table, then turned to Iris. "But you're not being fair, Iris, he's such a—"

"—sweet and generous man?"

"That's not what I was going to say, but, yes, I think he is. And a great man too. And John should feel privileged to be part of the whole undertaking. I'm very proud of you, John, I am."

Iris dabbed at a blackish smear of strained spinach that had somehow migrated from John Jr.'s bib to his forehead. "Oh, yes, I know," she said, her voice weary and saturated with sarcasm. "I count my blessings every day."

And then it was off in the cold, the Dodge wheezing to life on the third try, headlights drilling the road all the way into town and out to Prok's house, where the faerie cottage glittered with Christmas lights. I slammed out of the car, huddled against the cold, and hurried up the path to the house, hardly noticing the dark humps of the frost-killed flowerbeds and the forest of saplings that had begun to take hold in the neglected yard. I stood on the familiar doorstep and rang the bell.

Mac answered the door with a welcoming smile, and she was dressed up—and made up—as if she were going out to a concert or the theater, in a dress I'd never seen before and earrings in the shape of miniature jeweled Christmas trees. Her hair was newly permed. She was wearing lipstick. "John," she breathed, "come in and welcome," and I felt bad that I had nothing to offer her, not flowers or candy, not even a cheese.

"I don't, well, I didn't know this was a formal gathering, or I would have brought a cheese, at least."

This was an old joke between us, and she laughed to show her delight in it. "No need for cheeses tonight. Prok's made a Barbados punch specially for the occasion." A pause. "And your mother—she's well? And Iris? Good. Well, send them my love. And we'll have them out to the house over the weekend, just us, just the girls. Will you tell them?"

She held my hand a moment too long, and I felt the pulse of all that had passed between us, the slow, sweet, soft heartbeat of those times, and then she led me into the living room.

The others were already gathered there, the erratic light of the fire distorting their features so that they looked like strangers in a crowded waiting room till I came close and all was familiar again, *Hello, John. Good evening. Cold out there?* A lamp was lit in the corner. The Christmas lights at the window winked on and off, fixed to a timer. There was a smell of woodsmoke, the oak and apple wood Prok liked to burn, and of the scented white candles Mac had set on the mantelpiece, everything cozy and festive. I greeted everyone in turn, but when I saw that Betty was there, lounging in the far corner and chatting casually with Corco-ran, it gave me a jolt—something was up, and my interest was piqued, no doubt about it—so that I wound up presenting her with an awkward nod and a puzzled little half-formed smile before settling into a chair beside Rutledge and Prok. Betty acknowledged me with a smile that flickered across her lips and vacated her eyes before turning back to Corcoran, and I wondered what that meant. Did I feel a stab of jealousy, as ridiculous as that might seem? What had she said that night at the tavern—*Purvis is a great friend of mine, you know that, don't you?* But wasn't I a great friend of hers too?

"Is this alcoholic?" Aspinall was saying. He was stalled at the punch bowl, his shoulders slumped and head hanging, as if he were afraid of breaking something. "Ted?" Mac glided across the room to him. "Did you need some help? What about you, John?" she called. "Punch? Or something lighter—a soft drink maybe?"

And then I was clutching a cup of warm yuletide cheer, pressing it to the yielding strip of cartilage at the base of my nose until the alcoholic fumes began to soften the passageways there and the distinct voices of the room came clear to me. Prok was talking about San Quentin, the prison in California—we'd been invited to interview the prisoner pop-ulation there, and he'd managed to set up some lectures at Berkeley as well. His voice was straining for modulation, riding up and down the emotional ladder—clearly he was excited at the prospect of going into a maximum-security prison to delve into the histories of some of the most dangerous men our society had to offer, the ne plus ultra of ex-treme cases, but shouldn't we have been investigating the monasteries too? I smiled at the thought. Prok in a monastery. Imagine that. Mac's voice came to me then, fluting and soft—the weather, that was her subject—and the buzz of Aspinall's high-pitched rasp wrapping itself around it. I couldn't hear what Betty and Corcoran were talking about, but I heard Betty's laugh, the whole trajectory of it, rising up to fly out over the room like a dart descending to the bull's-eye painted across my brow. We were going to witness living sex again, and we were going to film it. That was what was going on here. Corcoran and Betty. And why him? Why not me? What was wrong with me?

It was then that the lavatory door swung open and Vivian Aubrey stepped out to join the party. Her hair—blond, with a natural wave—had been freshly brushed, and she'd reapplied her lipstick, a blood-red dab of which was in evidence on one of her incisors when she smiled her way back into the room. She was elegant in the way of my first female subject—the soigné faculty wife who seemed as out of place in Indiana as a tropical bird, and who'd made me blush—and she'd come straight to us from the rarefied atmosphere of the East Coast. She was confident. Shining. Light-years ahead of any of us in terms of sophistication and *savoir-vivre.* "Oh, hi, John," she said, gliding up to me and taking my hand in a firm, frank grip, "I wasn't sure you'd make it, what with the baby and your mother-in-law—your mother-in-law's still in town, isn't that right?"

Every possibility seethed within me. My voice was a croak. "My mother."

She'd bent now to light a cigarette, ignoring Prok's acid look—she was on stage here and she could do what she liked. I watched her throw her head back and exhale. "Oh, yes, right: your *mother.*"

I don't really think I have to go into the details of the filming that night, because, as I've said, the novelty quickly wears off and the process of filming, observing, even participating, loses its initial *frisson* with time and repetition—one act is very like another, whether it's observed in the flesh or preserved on celluloid. What was different about that night, though—what makes me recollect it now even after all the activity, and trials, that have succeeded it—was what Vivian said to me next. She said, "I hear we're going to be partners tonight, you and I."

I probably stammered. Or, no, I certainly stammered. "I, well, nobody's really, I mean, Prok hasn't said—"

She'd eased down on the arm of the chair so that the overlay of her hip was parallel with my face, then leaned in to bring her eyes closer to mine, and I could smell her, perfume, soap, yes, but something else too, something raw and primitive that can't be feigned and will never come in a bottle. "What's the matter," she said, "don't you like me?"

If you haven't guessed, I'd been filmed already—I was one of the one thousand males recorded masturbating on the sheet in Aspinall's studio, as were Corcoran and Rutledge. Prok saved twelve dollars there, and why not? If I'd felt self-conscious about it at first, there were the other 999 men to buck me up, and the thought of that, as much as anything, stimulated me to the point of response: I performed, wiped up and moved off like any of them.

Vivian Aubrey's hair hung loose, the tug of gravity easing it from her shoulders in a thick shimmering panel. I glanced across the room at Betty—she was watching me, something almost mocking in her expression. Or maybe it was hunger, maybe that was it. I turned back to Vivian Aubrey, the light of her eyes, the single flaming slash of color fixed on the ridge of her tooth, and whispered, "Oh, yes, I do. I like you a lot."

She straightened up then, and let a hand drift to my shoulder for balance. One more puff from the cigarette. A short, trilling laugh. "Anything for science, huh?" she said, and I wondered where I'd heard that before.

I DON'T KNOW IF I've got the dates right here, or even the year (the volume of Prok's travels during the five-year period between publication of the male edition in '48 and the female in '53 would have dwarfed any statesman's), but to the best of my recollection it was sometime early in the following year that Prok, Mac, Corcoran and I entrained for the Pacific Coast, that is, for San Quentin and Berkeley both. Mac spent most of her travel time knitting and staring out the window, silently watching the countryside scroll past, but she came to life for meals in the dining car and the occasional late-night game of pinochle, and it was a real pleasure to have her there, just for companionship, just for that. As for Corcoran and me, Prok put us to work, of course, interviewing travelers, computing data, meeting daily with him in the club car to talk over our strategy for history-taking at San Quentin and the volume on sex offenders he was even then projecting as a successor to *Sexual Behavior in the Human Female*. The prospect was exciting, but we were all a little anxious about taking histories in the prison—this wasn't the Indiana State Penal Farm, but a maximum-security lockup replete with a gas chamber and its own Death Row to feed it, and to be confined in a cell one-on-one with a rapist or murderer was daunting, to say the least.

We took a car across the Golden Gate Bridge, the fog seething below us as if the ocean were heated to a rolling boil, none of us saying much, not even Prok. I remember the look of the prison still, humped and low against a battery of treeless hills, a clustered stone beehive of a place with slits for windows and a medieval funk hanging over it, as if it had been there before Columbus, before laws and juries and judges. It was a place of confinement. Of penitence. And if any of the inmates went from penitence to resentment to rage and violence, we would be on our own. As the guard searched our car at the gate and my palms sweated and my throat went dry, I couldn't help wishing I'd chosen another profession. Or at the very least begged off just this once to stay home with Iris and the baby.

As it turned out, the warden was as concerned for our safety as we were (as I was, that is: once we got there, once we were actually inside the walls, Prok seemed unfazed, one subject no different from another as far as he was concerned), and he'd arranged for us to interview the elite prisoners first. These were the heads of the various gangs and cabals, the foremost Mexican, the leading Negro, the champion boxer, and so on. If we could establish our legitimacy with the inmate leaders, then we would find it relatively easy going with the others—that was the thinking. Of course, we needed absolute privacy, and to conduct interviews in the warden's office or even the chaplain's, where intimacies might be overheard, was out of the question. Prok finally decided on a series of disused cells dating back to the last century, deep in the prison's subchambers. The walls were of stone, two feet thick, the doors each fashioned from a single slab of steel and with nothing but a peephole to break their lines; even so, Prok wound up draping blankets over them to be sure of muffling even the slightest sound.

My first subject was a Negro who was entirely innocent of the crime for which he'd been convicted, viz., lying in wait in the alley behind a bar after an altercation with two of the establishment's patrons, after which he was falsely accused of battering the two men to death with the use only of his hands and a brick wall that presented itself as a conve-nient, if immobile, weapon. Or so he claimed. Nearly all the prisoners we interviewed, particularly the sex offenders, harped continually on the subject of their innocence. At any rate, he was led into the cell by a guard with a disapproving face (universally, the guards thought our locking ourselves in with their charges was a bad idea, even suggesting that we wear whistles round our necks in the event we needed to sum-mon aid), and I offered him a chair, cigarettes and a Coca-Cola out of the eight-ounce bottle, a real luxury in prison, since, for reasons that should be obvious, glass was strictly verboten.

The Negro was thirty-one years old, short but powerfully built, with a cast in one eye and a habit of ducking his head and mumbling his re-sponses so that I often had to stop the interview and ask him to repeat himself. As for his sex history, it was surprisingly unremarkable, very little consensual activity with the opposite sex and a burgeoning list of activities of the H-variety, owing to his long incarceration. He talked freely, seemed even to enjoy himself, the novelty of the situation ap-pealing to him, I think, as well as the special consideration with which I treated him, the Cokes (he consumed three) and the largesse of the cigarettes (he smoked half a pack, then pocketed two others). At the very end of the interview, he leaned across the table and said, "You know, I don't know if I should be telling you this, but I want to be straight with you, because you been straight with me, know what I mean?"

"Yes," I said, holding fast to my clipboard. "We try to be—that is, we pride ourselves on our, how do you say it?—our hep. Or hepness, that is."

"Well, listen: I'm not really as innocent as I might have made out." A pause, a tap at the fresh cigarette he'd stuck for safekeeping behind the lobe of one ear. "The two of them outside in that back alley? That night?"

I nodded.

"Well, I did croak them. My hands—know what I mean?—my hands were like when you get a piece of meat out of the butcher before he wraps it up, just like that. That was their brains, Jack, squeezing through my fingers."

I had no response to this. This wasn't what we'd come to hear—this was a different kind of science altogether. My eyes were fastened on his, on the one that wasn't rolling. There was no sound but the dry wheeze of our internal furnaces, of our lungs pumping in and out. We were in a tomb, deep down, buried deep. Was I frightened? Yes. Absolutely. I mastered myself long enough to say, "Yes? Go on."

He took his time, the undisciplined eye rolling like a porthole in a storm, and then he reached across the table and took hold of my wrist. "That fat fuck," he spat.

"Who?" *Do not react,* I kept telling myself. *Let nothing show.*

"McGahee."

I was puzzled. "Who's McGahee?"

A look of incredulity. "The guard!" he shouted. "The fat fuck of a guard."

Another long pause. If I'd screamed through a megaphone no one would have heard me.

"I'm going to croak him. Tonight." He glanced once over his shoulder at the door and the olive-drab blanket hanging like an arras over the peephole and then pulled a sliver of honed blue steel from the waistband of his trousers, and what was it, a spoon worked to a point, the fragment of an iron bed frame, the blistered head of a meteor flung down out of the heavens? Metal, steel. He had it—here, in prison. The man held it there in the light of the freestanding lamp I'd set up along with the desk and chairs. There was an edge to that steel, and it caught the light in a quick sharp gleam of menace.

"Going to shank him," he breathed, and now I was in on it too, complicit, one of his soldiers, one of his gang. "The fat fuck," he added, for emphasis, even as he rose from the table, pocketed the two unopened packs of cigarettes, and moved to the door so he could hammer the cold slab of steel with the underside of his fist and roar out to the guard at the end of the hall: "Open up down there! This here innerview is quit!"

Of course, I bring this up because of the moral dilemma with which it presented us. I was numb through the next two interviews—I got the boxer next, and then the chief Mexican—and the minute we climbed back into the car, I opened myself up to Prok and Corcoran. The fog had closed in on us, and we sat there in the cab of our rental car as if we were prisoners ourselves, confined forever, confined to this, to these questions and this procedure, and the confidences that weighed on us like a judgment. I wanted to scream. Wanted to turn to Prok and bawl till there was no air left in my body.

Prok sat stiffly beside me, so close our thighs were touching; Corcoran was on the other side of me, gazing out the window into the opacity of the atomized light. Prok had been about to start up the car, all business, all hurry, but he paused now, his hand arrested on the key he'd inserted in the slot of the ignition. "I see your dilemma, Milk," he said after a moment. "But it could be a test, you realize that, don't you? If word should get back that we've broken confidentiality, then we'll be washed up here—or in any other correctional facility, for that matter."

"But a man's life could be at stake—the guard." I named him, and it was like reading a name off a tombstone: "McGahee."

Prok had dropped his hand from the ignition. The fog breathed at the windows. "No," he said finally, "we can't do it, no matter whose life might be at stake. It's regrettable, no doubt about it, and I wish it hadn't come up at all, but we just cannot compromise the project. And, too, it may well be a test, never lose sight of that. Corcoran, you're in agreement? Milk?"

As it turned out, no one was murdered that night. Or the next night either. To the best of my knowledge, none of the guards was assaulted in all the time we were connected with San Quentin, during that visit and subsequent ones as well. I thought of that Negro, with his dirty shaft of steel and the eye that wouldn't hold—I think of him now—and wonder if Prok wasn't right after all. It was a test. That's all it was. A test.

BUT THEN WE were on to Berkeley and what has to have been the single defining moment of all my years with Prok: the grand lecture in the field house, attended by no less than nine thousand souls. We were fresh from our confinement at San Quentin—one-on-one in the silent sweating depths, at a remove from everything life has to offer—and now we were on the familiar turf of a university campus, exposed to all the world, nine thousand of the unincarcerated and free-breathing, students and faculty alike hurtling over one another to have a chance to hear the world's leading authority speak on the one subject that held more fascination than anything their books and philosophies could ever hope to reveal.

I don't recall the weather. It might have been raining, that sheer relentless outpouring typical of the wet season in California, but that might have been another time and another place altogether. I do remember the hall, though. Or rather the field house. This was more usually the scene of intercollegiate basketball games, but now, because of the uncontainable enthusiasm for Prok, Prok the author, the celebrity, the annihilator of sexual taboos, it had been given over to us for the afternoon. All seven thousand seats had been taken some two hours before the lecture was scheduled to begin, and even as we arrived university officials were scrambling to set up an additional two thousand folding chairs in the aisles and on the floor of the basketball court itself. Can I say that excitement was high, and leave it at that?

We were escorted to one of the coaches' offices, in a side door and down a cordoned-off hallway, where the man who was to introduce Prok—the vice president of the university, no less—urged us to make ourselves comfortable while he went off to see to the final details. "We'll need ten minutes or so," he said, and I have no recollection of him whatever, so I'll assign him the shrewd narrow features and evasive eyes of the congenital bureaucrat, "and please, if there's anything I can do for you, just holler." And then he shut the door and left us to ourselves.

"Quite the elegant dressing room, eh?" Prok said, turning to us—to Corcoran, Mac and me. We looked round us. The room was cramped, piled high with athletic equipment, mismatched sneakers, yellowing volleyballs, bats, spikes, mitts, rackets, helmets and the like, the walls all but obscured by team photos and two towering bookcases sagging under the weight of their collective trophies. The smell—of the adjoining locker room, of the distilled and rancid sweat of the generations—brought me back to high school and a reverie I'd had after my concussion on the football field. They'd brought me into the locker room on a stretcher, my mother's voice floating round the door like a bird battering its wings against a pane of glass, my consciousness fading and then looping back on itself till the world opened up on me like a woman's smile, though there was no woman there, only the grim bald-headed team physician, administering smelling salts.

"Yes," Mac said, "and you see what your celebrity gets you? Next thing they'll be putting us up at the Ritz, Prok. Just you wait."

We laughed, all of us, though Prok's laugh was more of a whinny and his eyes jumped from one of us to another, as if we'd all collectively spoken. Was he nervous? Was that it?

At that moment, as if in response to my question, the building seemed to shake with the vast stirring of the crowd just beyond the door and down the corridor. Thousands of undergraduates had simultaneously stifled a yawn, shifted in their seats, elevated their voices so as to be heard over the building expectant hum of the crowd.

Mac had moved to Prok's side, the two of them poised there in the center of the room as if listening to the rumble of distant thunder. "Can I get you anything?" she asked, her voice muted. "Coffee? A glass of water? Cola?"

He seemed to hesitate—Prok, who never hesitated, never wasted words or motion—and then, so softly I could barely hear him, he said: "Water."

"Good," Mac murmured. "I thought you'd be dry, Prok—you've got to keep your throat lubricated, you know. I hate to say it, but you're almost like a star tenor at the Metropolitan—or a radio host." She turned and gave Corcoran and me a look.

"I'll go," Corcoran said. "Just water, right? Plain water?"

The crowd shifted again, a great and vast soughing of bench, chair, muscle and sinew. It was as if all the air had been squeezed out of the field house, the corridor, the coach's office, and then it came back again, on a wave of echoing sound. I tried for the light touch because my heart was going as if I were the one about to mount the podium: "Sounds like the natives are restless."

Prok was standing there rigid, the fingers of his right hand arrested in the act of running through his hair. He gave me an acerbic look, a look that pinned and measured me as if I were one of his errant gall wasps. "Don't be childish," he said. "This isn't the time for levity, nor the place either."

Mac was at his side, one hand on his arm, just above the joint. "Prok," she murmured, "now calm yourself," but he snatched his arm away.

He was still focused on me, his jaws clamped in fury, and there was a minute twitching of his lips, as if he'd tasted something bitter. "That is precisely the sort of thoughtless remark that undermines the entire project—that has been undermining the project for as long as I've known you. Your work is retrograde, Milk—is, was, and always will be. Do you hear me?"

The crowd breathed as one. The building quaked. I bowed my head. "I was just, I, that is—it was only a joke."

"And stop stuttering, for God's sake. Speak up like a man!"

"Prok," Mac said, interceding for me. "Prok, please. He was only trying to—"

"I don't give two figs for what he was trying! He should know, of all people, that I don't need his assistance"—and now a look for Mac—"or anybody else's, for that matter, when I prepare to address a gathering . . ."

Mac's voice was reduced. "Perhaps you'd like us to leave, then?"

It was at that moment that Corcoran, the fair-haired boy, appeared in the doorway with a glass of water, the vast percolating intensity of the crowd arriving with him in a wave that rolled through the room and crested against the trophy-laden bookcases. "Yes," Prok snapped, stepping forward briskly to snatch the glass from Corcoran's hand, "yes, I'd like you to leave. Most emphatically. And take him"—the accusatory finger pointed at Corcoran now—"with you."

By the time we'd found the seats reserved for us in the front row, I'd already forgotten—and forgiven—the incident. It was nerves, that was all. Prok was under intense pressure to perform, and though I'd never seen him waver in any of the hundreds of lectures for which I'd been present, this one was special. There had never been a crowd like this, and he would have been less than human if he didn't have a case of nerves. At any rate, the vice president—that generic face and figure, the academic, the bureaucrat—made his own stab at levity in his introductory remarks, and the students in the audience let out a collective titter. Shuffling through his notes and gazing up myopically at that mass of humanity, he cleared his throat and said, "I'm pleased to see so many faculty here today, and faculty wives, in attendance at a university meeting. Of course, most of us must view the subject to be discussed largely in retrospect." There was a pause, as if the audience hadn't heard him right, and then the titters ran through the stacked tiers of chairs and benches like a motif out of *Die Walküre*.

Then there was Prok. He strode out of the wings, chest thrust forward, spectacles flinging light, and mounted the podium to an avalanche of applause, which suddenly died to nothing as he raised a hand to adjust the microphone. As usual he began speaking extemporaneously, without notes or props of any kind, his voice low and unmodulated, adopting the matter-of-fact tone that had served him so well through the years. He started off with variation and how the extremes at both ends of a given behavior define the norm, an old theme. Listing the various outlets available to the human animal from puberty on— masturbation, petting, coitus, the oral component—he went on to discuss frequency, and here the crowd, which had been slowly awakening to what he was saying, nearly got away from him. "There are those, for instance, who require no more than a single orgasm a month or even a year, and others who require several per week, or even per day."

At this, there was a low sustained whistle from the row behind me, what was known to us then as a "wolf whistle." The crowd jumped on it as if it were a rallying cry, the whole interconnected organism stirring again with that sound as of the wind in the trees, but Prok came right back with a barb that stopped them dead. "And then there are some," he went on, unfazed, "whose output is as low as that of the man who just whistled."

Nervous laughter, and then silence. He had them. And he never let go of them for the next sixty minutes, every last one of those nine thousand souls intent and focused on Prok, that erect figure on the podium, the celebrity of sex, the reformer, the pioneer, the preacher and spellbinder. I watched him from the front row, Mac on one side, Corcoran on the other, and though I'd heard the speech so often I could have recited it verbatim, right on down to the statistics and the pregnant pauses, the intensity of it in that setting on that afternoon gave me a chill. This was the apex, the moment of glory, Prok at his height. The students held their breath, the professors' wives leaned forward. There wasn't a sound, not a cough or murmur. No one stirred, no one left early. He concluded with his usual plea for tolerance, then took a step back and ducked his head in acknowledgment of the audience—it wasn't a bow, exactly, but it had that effect.

And oh, they roared. They roared.

9

WHEN WE GOT back I found that Elster had been named official librarian of the Institute and that Iris had taken up the clarinet again, the hollow doleful sound of it greeting me even as I came up the drive and assessed the state of disrepair in the house and yard. The car (I'd left it for her, Corcoran having given me a lift home) was listing over a flat tire on the driver's side front, and there was a raw new crease in the rear bumper. Because it was very still and clear and cold, the sound of the clarinet carried to me from deep inside the house, and it took me a moment to realize what it was—at first I'd thought some wounded animal was moaning out its final agony behind the toolshed. But no, it was Iris. Playing her instrument, the instrument in the little black velvet-lined case she'd kept untouched in the lower right-hand drawer of the dresser all these years.

Imagine that, I thought, and that was the extent of my thinking. The car was undrivable, half a dozen other failures leapt to my attention as I came up the front steps, and it didn't really affect me one way or the other. I was beyond caring. The place could fall down for all it mattered to me, the car could go up in flames—I was tired, deeply tired, and there was no way in the world I could continue to travel with Prok and fit neatly into the role of house-husband like one of those cool unflappable fathers grinning out at us from the television these days.

As I stepped through the door, John Jr. leapt up from the welter of his toys and bolted across the room to throw his arms round my knees, and I set down my suitcase to lift him high and greet him with a kiss. Iris had her back to me. She was seated on the sofa before the fire (she had a fire going, at least, but I saw that she'd used the wrong wood, the stuff I'd reserved for kindling only and had begged her at least a hundred times to use sparingly), her legs splayed in front of her, the instrument at her lips. The sound it produced was pitched low and mournful, a groaning, creaking reverberation that put me in mind of the freighters plying the fog on Lake Michigan. I felt depressed suddenly, seeing her there with her distended cheeks and splayed legs, her hair in disarray, her eyes shut tight in concentration, Iris, my Iris, and she might have been anybody, a girl in the marching band, a prodigy of practice and desire working toward something I couldn't begin to imagine. For just a moment, before I set down my son (gently, gently, the miniature grasping limbs, the uprush of the carpet) and called her name, I felt I was losing her. Or, no: that I'd already lost her.

"Iris," I said, "Iris, it's me," and she started, her eyes flashing wide, the instrument pulling away from her lips with a long filament of saliva still attached. It took her a moment, and then she smiled, and I said, "Playing the clarinet again, huh?"

"Come here," she said, and I sat beside her and we kissed, John Jr. scrambling up into my lap and the cat appearing from nowhere to adhere to the arm of the chair. It was a sudden joyful moment, the return of the hero, and I felt my depression begin to lift. We let the moment stretch out a bit, and we said the usual things to each other, and I filled her in on the highlights of the trip, the scare at San Quentin and Prok's mastery at Berkeley, and we had a drink together and I gave John Jr. the box of Crackerjack I'd brought back for him and dug out the lacquered nautilus shell I'd got at a seashore gift shop for Iris, and then, after a silence, I came back to the subject of the clarinet.

"So what prompted you to start playing again?"

Iris gazed up at me over the rim of her glass. She'd made herself a gin and tonic, though it was cold still and would be for some time yet. The instrument lay tucked in against her shoulder, the reed and mouthpiece wet and glistening, the keys shining, the long black tube cutting like a shadow across her arm.

"I don't know," she said, shrugging, "something to do, I guess. You know, to pass the time."

There was the hint of an accusation here, the old argument, and the anger came up in me. "You left the car out there with a flat. You didn't drive on it, did you? Tell me you didn't drive on it."

She ignored me. The glass went to her lips and came away again. "And Hilda. She encouraged me—she plays herself, you know, and we're planning on getting up a duet for the picnic this spring, on Memorial Day, maybe, just Hilda and me. I didn't think I'd get my embouchure back, but I have." The fire gave a sigh, then subsided, because it was built of twigs instead of the painstakingly split oak that was stacked up in the woodshed perhaps fifty feet from where we sat. "I wanted to surprise you."

"I didn't know Hilda played." I tried to picture Rutledge's wife, angular and airily blond, with her stingy lips and small high breasts, perched at the edge of a chair with the sheet music spread before her, taking the instrument into her mouth.

"All through college. Like me." She smoothed her thumb over the pale glistening surface of the reed. "We've got to do something, what with our men gone all the time."

"Oscar was here."

"Yes," she said, "that's right. But you weren't."

At this point, John Jr., who'd gone back to his toys, looked up and announced that he was hungry. "Mommy, I'm hungry," he piped, as if he'd just discovered some essential truth about the nature of existence and himself in particular.

"Maybe we should just go out," I said.

Iris gave me a look. "Can we afford it?"

"Something cheap. Hamburgers. A pizza."

"Pizza!" John Jr. cried, taking up the refrain. "Pizza!"

"Hush," she said, and he'd flung himself at her legs now, burying his head in her lap. "There's no reason why I can't whip something up, because we really don't have to make a celebration of it, do we? I mean, you go away and you come back. Isn't that the way it always is?"

I had nothing to say to this, and we sat there a moment in silence, even as John Jr. tugged at her blouse and keened, "Please, Mom, please?"

"I'd have to change," she said. "And put on some makeup. And I do want to get right back—"

I tipped my glass to her. "For what—more practice?"

She was smiling now, John Jr. all over her—*Please, please*—something playful in her eyes, as in all is forgiven and why wrangle when love,

384

the love between us, between two young healthy male and female human *beings,* was so much more than the sum of its losses and hesitations. "No," she said, "it was something else. A statistic you could maybe help me with because it's been a while."

"Yes?"

"What was the average frequency of s-e-x"—spelling it out so that our son wouldn't make a pet word of it, as he had with "bra" and "jock"—"for couples married at least five years? Once a week, wasn't it?"

"Oh, no," I said, wagging my head in a professorial way, "it's at least twice that."

THE NEXT DAY, at work, Rutledge and I took a coffee break together, and that was when I learned about Elster. We'd started out on the subject of the clarinet—I'd said something like, "I hear Hilda's rediscovered her musical inspiration"—and then we'd gone on to discuss the Pacific Coast trip and how happy he'd been to stay behind this time because he really was getting tired of conducting interviews like a hired hand ("No offense, John") when he thought he'd been taken on to do original research. As Prok's equal, or at least his partner. And then, casually, as if it didn't matter a whit, he dropped the news about Elster.

I was dumbstruck. "Elster?" I repeated. "But he's, well, he's no friend of the research. He—did I ever tell you about Fred Skittering, that whole incident?" And I told him, at length.

Rutledge was imperturbable. That was his chief characteristic. The building could be on fire—his hair could be on fire—and he wouldn't raise his voice or move any more precipitately than he would at a funeral. I remembered the night in the hotel room with Mac and how he'd squared his shoulders and strolled into the bedroom with her as if it were a military matter, orders given, orders received. But now, as I revealed Elster's perfidy—or his potential for it—his face took on a new look altogether. Finally he said, "You don't think he can be trusted then?"

"No," I said. "I don't."

He stroked his mustache, glanced down the hall to see if Prok were in sight, and lit up a cigarette. I watched him shake out the match, drop it to the floor and grind it underfoot. "Well, we'll just have to be careful, that's all, make a note of it, be sure Prok's aware of the situation, because really, nobody's in on anything here except for us, and I don't have to tell you how the shit would hit the fan if anything, even the least tidbit, got out to the public. But look at Mrs. Matthews and the other women we've taken on, Laura Peterson and what's her name. They haven't got a clue, have they? And they're right there with us every day in the office."

I wasn't convinced. Maybe I was overreacting, maybe I'd misread the man—but then there was that night at the tavern when he tried to get me to talk, and it wasn't even for his own sake, but for some third party's, for a journalist's. Had he been paid off? Or was he just constitutionally a snake?

"By the way," Rutledge said, squinting against the smoke of his cigarette and taking a sip from his coffee mug at the same time, "did you hear about the musicale Sunday?"

I held out my palms in response, and I suppose I must have looked bleak over the prospect. "Uh-uh," I said finally. "No." It wasn't that I didn't enjoy the opportunity to learn about classical music—as I say, I've really come to appreciate it, even opera—but that the musicales seemed just another extension of work, of the Institute's tentacles. And Iris hated them. "I don't know," I said. "I'm tired. I've had it up to here with musicales, if you want to know the truth."

Rutledge was watching me steadily, his lips composed round the butt of his cigarette and the thin tracery of his mustache. "Yeah," he said, "I know what you mean. But something's up—it's going to be just us. And the wives."

"Just us? That *is* odd. Because Prok, not to my knowledge anyway, has never given a musicale with fewer than twenty or thirty guests—that's the whole point, to educate people."

"And to show off."

This seemed to suck the wind out of the conversation. I wouldn't hear any criticism of Prok, and especially not from one of my own coworkers and colleagues, and I gave him a look to warn him off.

Rutledge shrugged, threw a furtive glance up the hall, then came back to me. "Listen, John, loyalty is one thing, don't get me wrong, but he's not above criticism, you know. He can be a real pompous ass at times, with his *obbligato* and his *menuetto* and *largo e cantabile* and all the rest of it, and then there's that look he gets on his face, the same look he gets when he comes, like a penitent nailed to the cross."

I felt as if I'd been slapped across the face. "Listen, Rutledge—Oscar—" I said, and my voice went cold, "I have to tell you I don't feel comfortable with any sort of criticism or bad-mouthing of Prok, I just don't, I'm sorry, so please, in future, if you would just keep it to yourself—"

"But you've seen it. You've seen that look on his face. You've been on the receiving end of it, haven't you? Well so have I. It's part of the job, isn't it?"

"No," I said. "No, I don't want to talk about this."

He was still watching me, holding my eyes as if he were taking my history. "And Ted, of course. Ted'll be there," he said. "With his camera."

THE SUNDAY CAME, wind-whipped and bathed in a tentative March sunshine that hinted at better times ahead. Crocuses were blooming, pussy willows, azaleas. Townspeople were out in their yards, raking the grass, thinking about where to string the hammock, and the students were everywhere, crowding the sidewalks in clusters of three and four, their jackets open to the waist, grinning and frolicking and shouting to one another as if it were May already, as if it were June and finals were over. It was kite-flying weather, and though I hadn't flown a kite in twenty years, Iris and I bought a cheap paper version at a novelty shop and took John Jr. to the park to launch it. All well and fine. But before we'd gone to the park we'd done something even more out of the ordinary, and I didn't know how I felt about it or what it meant exactly. We went to church. It was Sunday, and we went to church.

As I've said, Iris was raised in the Roman church, but she'd given it up in college, and certainly I myself had neither the faith nor reason to enter any ecclesiastical structure of any denomination. But Iris had awakened that morning with an idea fixed in her head—we were going to church because it was Lent and because she missed the ritual of it, the mumble of Latin, the immemorial fragrance of the censers—and I couldn't argue with her. I wouldn't want to say that she was reverting to childish things because that wouldn't be fair to her, and yet she'd begun to write long missives to her mother almost daily, about what I couldn't imagine, and she *had* taken up the clarinet again . . . and baking. She told me she'd loved to bake as a girl. And now, over breakfast—eggs poached just the way I like them, lean strips of bacon, crude crumbling hunks of a homemade bread that hadn't risen—she'd announced that we were going to church. The whole family.

"Church?" I'd said.

"That's right."

"But why? What are you thinking? You know that I don't, well—I've got better things to do with my day off, don't you think?"

"Because I miss it, that's why. Shouldn't that be enough? Can't you do anything for me, just for me, just once? And for John Jr.?" We were at the kitchen table, the aforementioned boy nearly four years old now and perched on the edge of his booster seat, making an improvisatory scramble out of his own eggs. She paused to wipe his chin, the cheerful yellow splotch there, and then came back to me. "He's growing up a pagan. Doesn't that bother you?"

"No," I said, "not at all."

"You know what the other mothers say? The other children?"

It would have been useless to point out that I didn't care in the least what the other mothers might say or that Prok would have a fit if he knew that I'd been within fifty feet of a church, temple, tabernacle or mosque—he hated them all, all religions, with equal fervor. Religion was antithetical to science. The religious simply couldn't face the facts. They were living in the Dark Ages, et cetera. I couldn't have agreed with him more, but Iris wanted to go to church, and that was all that mattered.

I will say that the experience was at least mildly interesting from a sociological perspective. The women had their heads covered, most with spring hats, but a good number with simple black or white scarves knotted under the chin, and the men—and the children too—were turned out in their best in deference to the God they'd come to worship. There was the smell Iris had spoken of—some sort of herb or aromatic gum reduced over hot coals, a holdover no doubt from the days when the devotees went largely unwashed and it was thought that contagion was bred spontaneously out of the miasma of foul air—and a whole panoply of ritual that Iris performed with a simple grace that stirred me more deeply than I wanted to admit. I watched her kneel, cross herself, dip her fingers in the holy water and let her lips move along with the priest's in the ventriloquism of rapture, even while John Jr. gurgled and writhed at her side and she turned to hush him. In a way, the whole thing was quite beautiful, not that it meant anything and not that we've been back since—or not that I've been back—but it was like being at a concert, I suppose, when you're free to let your mind empty itself and wander where it will.

Yes, and then we went to the park and John Jr. ran wild with the release of it, like a puppy let off the leash, and we had a picnic, though the wind made its presence felt whenever the clouds obscured the sun, which they did, off and on, all afternoon. We'd bought a box kite and assembled it at home, despite the fact that studying directions on a sheet of paper and translating them into action wasn't my strong suit, and when I ran with it twirling and twisting above my head, my son let out a whoop of the purest, elemental joy. I paid out the line and felt the tug of nature on the other end, and it goes without saying that the sensation brought me back to my own childhood. "I want," my son said. "Give me, Daddy. Me, me!" And I sat myself down in the naked grass with John Jr. in my lap and together we held tight to the string.

It might have been that day when he lost hold of the kite, or maybe it was another occasion, another day, another year. But I remember being confident enough to let him take it himself, to feel that mysterious suspensory tug all on his own and master it, and he ran with the thing, giggling like a maniac, paying out string, getting cockier by the minute—and that was good, all to the good—until there was no string left. Before I could reach him, before I could leap forward and snatch at it, the thing was gone, receding in the sky on its bellying tether as if we'd never had hold of it at all.

Then there was dinner, a roast turkey Iris had put in the oven before we went out, the smell of it heavy on the air as we came in the door, and the fire I made to take the chill out of our fingers and toes. We dropped John Jr. at the sitter's—Were we going to be late? she wanted to know. No, we didn't think so, not too late—and then drove over to Prok's.

As it turned out, we were the first to arrive, which was unusual in itself. Mac took our coats, and Prok, absorbed in mixing cocktails—we were having Zombies, I saw—called out a brusque greeting from the chair he'd pulled up to the coffee table in the inner room. There was no fire that night, and yet the house was warm, bearing the faint olfactory traces of radiated heat, of the furnace in the basement and its conduit of pipes and radiators, and that was odd, given Prok's Spartan tastes. He rose to greet us as we came into the room, a peck to the cheek for Iris and a handclasp and his famous smile for me, and it was like coming home all over again, arriving at a foreordained destination, the place I was meant to inhabit in my fatherless transit of the planet. Prok's house. Prok and Mac's. A wave of emotion swept through me, and I can't say why or what it was about that particular moment that moved me so, though it had to do with continuity, I think, and with my sudden apprehension of it. I suppose Prok would have classified it as a chemical reaction, a fluctuation in the hormonal levels originating in the endocrine glands. Just that, and nothing more.

"Zombie cocktail?" he offered, thrusting the tall cold glasses into our hands before we'd had a chance to respond.

I noticed then that there were no chairs set up for the musicale, that the light over the phonograph was switched off and the records were still in their jackets on the shelves. Iris must have noticed it too, because she took a long pull at her drink and then asked about it in a voice that might have sounded just a shade too conciliatory: "Do you need any help with the chairs, Prok? For the musicale, I mean? We *are* having a musicale, aren't we?"

Prok was finished with the cocktails now—or the first batch of them, four frosted glasses standing on the tray atop the low table, awaiting the remaining guests. He rose from his seat, warming his hands together as if at the conclusion of a job well done. "No," he said, focusing on Iris, "I'm afraid we've decided to do something else altogether tonight—"

That was when Aspinall slammed the door that led to the attic and came clumping down the stairs. We all turned to watch him as he slouched across the room in his dark glasses and belted coat. The heat seemed stifling suddenly—I had to reach up and jerk loose the knot of my tie—and I wondered how he could stand it.

"Everything all set up there?" Prok asked, and I felt the first faint quickening of my blood.

Aspinall shuffled up to us and ducked his head to peer over his glasses and give Iris and me a nod of greeting before answering. "Oh, yeah, we're good to go. But the lights, of course—"

"Right," Prok said.

"No sense in wasting electricity—"

"Right."

I'd never noticed before how pale Aspinall was, how bloodless and colorless, as if all those hours in the darkroom had bled him dry, and I couldn't help asking if he felt all right—"Ted, are you coming down with something?"—instead of turning to Prok and demanding an answer to the question that was kicking and twitching like a newborn in my brain: *What were we planning to film, and if we were filming, then why had the wives been invited?*

Ted let out a little laugh and nodded to Iris again. His face was neutral, but the corners of his mouth turned up slightly, so that even in repose he looked as if he were smiling over some private joke. "My mother used to ask me that all the time," he said. "Teddy, you need to get out and play with the other boys, play ball, get some sun, but I'm just a night owl, I guess. Hell, in the Village nobody gets up before noon—and those are the early risers."

"I could sleep all day myself," Iris said, and we all three looked at her. "And I think I would if it wasn't for John Jr. But then you know how it is with a three-year-old, going on four—"

Aspinall didn't know. His eyes were faintly visible behind the smoked lenses, half circles rinsed of light, like lunar bodies in eclipse. I noticed that Prok didn't offer him a drink.

But then there was a knock at the door, and the Rutledges and Corcorans arrived together, Violet in a fur coat over a low-cut dress that showed off her breasts, Hilda in a pink spring jacket and beltless frock that might have been a nightgown but for the Jacquard pattern of it, Rutledge his usual sleek self, and Corcoran in a camel coat and his snappy shoes. Their faces were flushed with the chill and they stamped around the entryway a moment, divesting themselves of their outer garments, their voices intertwining excitedly in a recitative of arrival. Prok hurried everyone in, all business suddenly, dispensed the drinks in the tropical fug of the front room, and immediately set to making a second batch. Iris was already showing the effects of the first drink, her eyes shining and her lips ever so slightly parted as if she were trying to catch her breath or remember the words to a tune no one else could hear. I heard her say something to Hilda, something about the clarinet, and her words dragged in a stately adagio. She was standing with her legs spread for balance, and when I caught her eye she gave me a conspiratorial smile—we'd escaped the onus of a musicale, and here we were, in the midst of a party. With friends. Good friends. Our best friends. I should have taken her arm then, should have led her out the door and into the car, should have taken her home, but I didn't.

For those who don't know it, incidentally, I should say that the Zombie is an especially potent drink. It's served in a tall glass—and the glass needs to be tall in order to incorporate all the booze the concoction contains, that is, two ounces of light rum, an ounce each of dark rum and apricot brandy, with pineapple juice and simple syrup to meliorate the bite of the spirits, and a float of one-hundred-fifty-one-proof rum to top it off—and just a single one of them was enough to make me feel that familiar tingling in my extremities that lets me know I've already begun to descend the long glassy slope of inebriation. And what was Prok doing? He was getting us drunk, his inner circle, his intimates, and once we were drunk and our inhibitions were down, we were going to go upstairs. To the attic.

We were all watching one another, at least the men were, because we knew what was coming, and we were frightened of it and exhilarated too. Rutledge was sitting in one of the hickory chairs at the far end of the table, leaning in over his knees to banter with Violet Corcoran and Mac as if nothing in the world were the matter, his Portuguese eyes glittering at me even while Corcoran flashed me a triumphant look and led the room in a short sharp explosion of laughter. The cocktail shaker went round. I heard the clock in the hallway strike the hour—what hour I didn't know. And then Prok was tapping the long silver cocktail spoon against the side of the shaker. "May I have your attention, please?" he said, and the conversation trailed off with a whinnying laugh from Hilda Rutledge in response to something Violet had said.

Prok was dressed as usual in his standard dark suit, white shirt and bow tie, though I couldn't help thinking the flesh-colored shorts would have been more appropriate to the occasion. His head—the massiveness of it, the solidity, the shock of hair, immitigable features, the hard cold empirical eyes—seemed like a sculpture cast in bronze. He was a giant among pygmies. I would have followed him anywhere. "We have a surprise for you, Mac, Aspinall and I, a surprise that's long overdue, and if you would just go along with Ted here"—a gesture for Aspinall, who slouched against the near wall, shoulders slumped, dark glasses drinking up the light—"all will be revealed."

I don't know what I was thinking, but I followed the group up the stairs like a child on a field trip, Iris just ahead of me, the women's perfume concentrated in the stairwell till it was like an intoxicant, as if I needed anything more. The steps creaked and shifted under our weight. Prok said something I didn't catch, and Mac was there too, right at his side, an interplay of shadows, Corcoran two steps above him and joking in a low voice even as Ted Aspinall led us into the room and flicked on the lights. My heart was pounding, blowing out of my body. It was as hot as midsummer. I was sweating through my clothes. And what did I expect—that Iris would enjoy it? That it was time she saw what my real work was? That watching Corcoran and who—Violet?—go at it would somehow stimulate her, disarm her, at the very least make her an ally in all this? Or maybe I was getting ahead of myself. Maybe Prok had something entirely different in mind, another animal film, beavers, hamsters, chinchillas. But there was no projector. And the lights were fierce.

"All right," Prok said, sidling round to shut the door behind us with a definitive *click*, "this is good. Very good. Now, if you would all please make yourselves comfortable—"

The bed in the corner was lit like a stage, as it had been the last time we'd filmed in the attic, but the chairs had been removed and a number of mattresses laid out on the floor in their stead. I was thinking of gym class in high school, the way the coach would have us unfurl the mats for wrestling and make us sit up against the walls, tense as wire, until he selected two boys at random and had them grapple for three interminable minutes, from the initial takedown to the writhing, sweaty denouement. We eased ourselves down, silent now, unconsciously pairing off as couples, aside from Mac, who settled in beside Iris and me with a soft smile on her lips. Rutledge gave me a look, and it was the same look he'd worn on the night Corcoran and Betty had performed for us the very first time—he was aroused, and so, despite myself, was I.

"I say this is long overdue," Prok began. He was standing just outside the curtain of light, bent stiffly toward us, one hand gesturing, and the effect was to darken his face even as his silhouette burned with a crackling electrical radiance, as with an actor stepping out of the scene to deliver a soliloquy. And who would he have been in that moment? Iago? Richard III? Prospero? "Because the foundation of what we're accomplishing here relies on our commitment to the project—it relies on us, on my staff and the wives who stand behind them. None of us can afford to be the least bit sex shy—or even accused of it—because of the irreparable damage it would do not only to the project, but to the principles behind it."

He paused to look round the room, the light gathering and bunching as he swung his head to take us in. "I'm sorry to say it, but we're nothing better than hypocrites if we can't practice what we preach—if we can't be uninhibited with one another, all of us, because we are the pioneers here and make no mistake about it. Of course, a survey, no matter how scrupulous, can never get at the facts in the way of direct observation, so as most of you know we have for some time now been engaged in observing and filming sexual activity right here in this room, and I see no reason"—and here he looked directly at Iris—"for any of you to be kept in the dark about it. This is science. It is objective and impersonal. And necessary, never forget that."

Iris's hand felt for mine and I squeezed it and leaned in to touch her ear with my lips. She was sweating too—the room was like a furnace—and I could smell it on her, her own individual odor, private and furtive, the smell of Iris and Iris alone.

"Now," Prok was saying, "what I'd like you all to do, initially, is to remove your clothing"—there was a titter from Hilda Rutledge, who was seated on the mattress across from me, beside her husband—"without constraint or self-consciousness. We are all adults here," he said, his voice dipping as he bent to remove his shoes and socks, "and what's more, unlike so many of the sad, repressed cases we hear from daily, we're enlightened and fully attuned to the enjoyment of what we were made for—that is, sexual relations, of every kind and without inhibition or prohibition."

In a moment he was naked, looming over us with his veiny muscular legs, the slight stoop and the revelation of a middle-aged pot, the breath whistling through his teeth as he spoke. "Come on," he said, "off with your clothes, all of you—that's right, good."

There was a rustling as we stretched our limbs, leaned this way or that to release zippers and work at buttons, and I was aware of Mac beside me slipping out of her clothes as easily as she might have shed water after a bath. Iris looked to me then, the light like a shield hammered round the bed in the corner, and I had my jacket off, my shirt unbuttoned. Her eyes were luminous, cat's eyes, fixed unwaveringly on me, and for a moment she didn't react, just watched me as I unbuckled my belt and worked the trousers down my legs. Then she reached behind her for the buttons to her dress—she was wearing black, her color, the color she'd worn to the musicale all those years before when Corcoran came into our lives, a simple black dress with white trim and puffed sleeves, pearls in a single strand, flat shoes, stockings, white brassiere, white panties. I was naked before she was and she could see the state I was in, the state all of us were in—the men—but she never hesitated. She dropped the brassiere behind her and leaned back against the wall on the fulcrum of her hips to slip the panties down her legs.

Prok was working at himself—masturbating, proud of his technique and his endowment, a bit of a show-off, really—and I should say here, because there's no point in holding anything back and there's nothing to be ashamed of, nothing at all, that ever since puberty he had often incorporated the pleasure-pain principle in his sexual activity. He enjoyed urethral insertions, enlarging himself over the years to employ an object as big as a toothbrush to this end, and now he did just that—inserted the toothbrush—as if he were a magician performing a trick. The lights caught him in profile as he worked it in, and he even managed a mini-lecture on the subject as we all watched in rapt silence, maybe even in awe.

He didn't come to climax, though—he was saving that for the filming. After a moment he removed the insertion, and, in a low voice, invited me to join him on the bed. "Milk, would you like to be first in the filming tonight, to show the others some of the techniques we've acquired?"

Iris sat against the wall beside me, naked and hunched over her knees, and Mac was on the other side of me, sitting Indian style, her spine erect over the carriage of her small pretty breasts. All eyes were on me. I didn't know what to say, Iris on one side, Mac on the other, my H-history dwindling over time—dwindling right then and there—till I doubt I was even a 1 on the scale anymore.

"Milk?" Prok said. "John?"

Aspinall was at the camera, the skirts of his trench coat drooping like wings so that he was like a big carrion bird hunkered over an object of supreme interest. The film was ready to roll, the lights burned. "No," I heard myself say, "I can't. Or not now. Not first."

There was a moment of silence, then Corcoran—the exhibitionist—spoke up. "I'll go," he said, as if this were a team sport after all, and then he and Prok broke the curtain of light and went to the bed together. Aspinall began to run the film and I felt Iris shrink beside me. Then it was the Rutledges, then Corcoran and Mac, and then—we'd been there for what seemed like hours, sweating as if we were in a sauna, afraid to speak because there was nothing to say, no words to express what we were feeling, what *I* was feeling—Prok rose from where he'd been sitting with Violet Corcoran and crossed the room to squat down at the edge of the mattress Iris and I were sharing. He was erect again, heavy in the gut, the cords of his knees and lower legs pulled taut over flesh that was tough as jerked meat. His head loomed. His face. "Now, Milk," he said, "are you ready now? You and your own wife."

I said nothing. I couldn't look at Iris.

"You're not getting sex shy on me, are you, Milk? Iris?"

That was when Iris spoke for the first time since we'd entered the room. She said one word only, and it went right to my heart. She said, "Purvis."

"What was that?" Prok asked, his voice low and ominous.

She turned her head away. "I'll do it with Purvis."

There was a long pause, everything in freefall, the whole project— files, the interview sheets, dog-eared proofs and thick-bound volumes— poised to drop down out of the sky as if dumped from the hold of an airliner, and I could picture it, clumps of papers thick on the hedges and lawns and rooftops of America and the housewives and their harried husbands plucking at the strings of one anonymous heartbreaking secret after another till they collapsed in one another's arms and wept for us all, us poor suffering human animals with our lusts and our hurts and our needs. And then Prok dropped his voice to a whisper and said, "No, not with Purvis. With me."

I remember his legs, his massive hardened arterial legs, as he rose then and tugged at her wrist till she was standing too, her breasts exposed, all of her, and how she pulled back against him, how she said, "I would die first," and then I was in motion and it was just like that wrestling match, like the football field. I don't know what came over me—or I do, I do—but Prok was on his back in the middle of the floor and everybody was rising now, even as Iris bent to snatch up her clothes and run.

We were very late with the babysitter that night—or at least I was, because Iris wasn't in the car and she wasn't at home or on any of the dark windswept streets I roamed till the sky went light and the sitter thrust her furious face at me through the gap of the door and John Jr. went heavy in my waiting arms.

10

I DIDN'T GO INTO work the next day. I saw to the needs of my son and sat by the phone, waiting for it to ring. After lunch—I boiled franks and opened a can of pork and beans—I put John Jr. in the car and drove the streets in a slow repetitive pattern, as if I were one of those geriatric cases looking for something I couldn't name. But I could name it: *Iris*. And what did I expect—that she'd be bouncing down the sidewalk somewhere, her hair flying in the wind, going shopping? I stopped in at the elementary school where she'd worked till our son was born, on the off-chance that she was filling in for an absent teacher, but, no, she wasn't there—in fact, the secretary in the main office, a new employee apparently, couldn't quite grasp who I was talking about. John Jr. chattered away at me for the first half hour or so, and he fooled with the buttons on the radio till he fell asleep in a haze of static, the car creeping along on its own while I stared through the windshield and let my mind race. At one point, desperate, I drove out to the quarry where in more innocent times we used to park and neck, and found myself scrambling over the stepped white rock and peering down into the darkening waters as if I could detect the slow wheeling drift of a suicide there.

After dinner—more franks, more beans—I sat numbed in the armchair in front of the cold fire and read *The House at Pooh Corner* aloud till I had it memorized and still John Jr. wanted me to go on. Couldn't we listen to the radio? I wondered. "No, read," he said. And he interrupted me in the middle of the windy-day episode to ask, in his half-formed tones, "What's *blusterous*?" "You know, like yesterday," I told him, "when we were flying the kite?" He sat there beside me, the foreshortened limbs, the recalcitrant thatch of his hair that was a replica of my own (unbrushed, just as his face was unwashed, because I wasn't much at that sort of thing either), and after a moment, he said, "Where's Mommy?" for what must have been the sixtieth time. "She went out," I told him, and then I told him it was time for bed.

No one had called, not Mrs. Matthews to inquire if I was ill or Prok to apologize (or rather to accept my apology), not Rutledge or Corcoran or Mac. Finally, around eight, I dialed Corcoran's number, and Violet answered.

"Violet, it's John. Is Purvis there?"

Her voice was muted, all the familiarity washed out of it. "John," she said, as if trying the name out. "Sure. Sure. I'll get him."

"Hello, John?" Corcoran came on the line, and before I could respond, he was onto me. "What was that all about last night? You can't be—John, listen, we're all in this together, you know that. Nothing personal, right? You don't go shoving Prok around, nobody does. And then you don't show up for work—?"

"Is Iris there?"

"Iris? What are you talking about?"

"My wife. Iris."

"Isn't she with you?"

"No," I said, all the blood rushing to my face. "Isn't she with you?"

"John, listen, you're just upset right now, and it's foolish, it really is. Don't let this break us down, don't throw away your whole career over, over—"

"Love?"

He came right back at me, his voice cracking with exasperation. "No," he said, "this isn't about love. Love has nothing to do with it. Nothing. Nothing at all."

I put John Jr. to bed as best I could, with a cursory brushing of the teeth and a minimal face-scrubbing—he objected to the washcloth for some reason, it was too rough or it wasn't warm enough or there was too much soap on it or too little—and the next thing I knew I awoke to the sound of the car turning over in the driveway. By the time I got out the door and into the still-blustering night, the car was at the end of the drive, receding taillights, a quick angry flare of the brakes, no signal, and then the twin beams of the headlights swinging out onto the highway, and by the time I got back in the house, back to John Jr.'s room, it was too late to realize that he wasn't there anymore.

For the next two days I was drunk. Not a pretty thing, not a rational thing, a weakness of mine, inherited in the genes from my dead father and his father before him—the Milches, from Verden, on the Aller River south of Bremen—and for all I knew there were a dozen Milch lushes there still, cousins and grand-uncles listening to tinny postwar jazz on second-rate radios and drowning their sorrows in Dinkelacker and schnapps. The first day I lay prostrate on the couch and drank what we had in the house, which consisted of a quart of beer gone flat in the refrigerator, my reserve fifth of bourbon, and finally, the contents of my flask (half-full of something that tasted like Geritol but was actually, I realized, the dregs of a pint of Southern Comfort with which I'd last filled it when Iris and I went to an IU football game the previous fall). I brought the flask to my lips—JAM, my graduation present, from Tommy, from Iris's brother—and stared at the ceiling. Earlier, I'd called Iris's mother in Michigan City. Was Iris there? A pause. The deep-freeze of my mother-in-law's voice. Yes, Iris was there. Could she come to the phone? No, she couldn't.

The second day I woke with a headache and made a shaky mess of the eggs and bacon and the rock-hard remains of Iris's loaf. I wasn't going into work, I wasn't calling my wife—let her call me—and above all I wasn't allowing myself to think about anything, not Prok, not the project or my colleagues or what had come over me in the attic three nights ago. We'd drunk Zombie cocktails, hadn't we? Well, all right: now I was a zombie, without affect or will. Around noon, still shaky, I walked into town in the burnished sunshine of an early spring day and made for the tavern, where they would have beer in abundance and a cornucopia of backlit bottles of hard liquor to steady it on the way down. I kept my head low and my eyes on the pavement, because the last thing I wanted was to see anybody I knew.

I don't remember having had anything to eat that afternoon. I drank, read the newspapers, went to the restroom, drank some more. It must have been about six or so when I felt a tap on my shoulder and looked up to see Elster standing there beside me. Richard Elster, that is, newly appointed librarian of the Institute, the man in charge of what would soon become the biggest sexology—and erotica—collection in the world, bigger even than those of the British Museum and the Vatican. "Hey," he said, "John, where've you been?"

I didn't answer.

"I asked Bella, she said you were sick."

I felt the irritation rising in me. "Who?"

"Bella. Mrs. Matthews. She said you had the flu."

"I don't have the flu."

The barman intervened to ask Elster what he was having and Elster ordered a beer before turning back to me. "Everything all right? Are you sure? Because I heard a rumor, about the other night—something about you and your wife?"

He was fishing. He didn't know a thing. None of us would have leaked a word, not on pain of death. I was sure of it. Absolutely. Still, I felt something clench inside of me.

"How is she, by the way? Because I wanted to tell you to tell her how well Claudette's doing, and Sally, our little one. Did you know Claudette's expecting again?"

"She's fine," I said.

There was movement at the door, comings and goings, the jukebox lurched to life with some brainless female vocalist cooing something about love nests, and I lifted a finger for the barman. "What do I owe you?" I said.

"You're not leaving, are you?" Elster's mouth tightened around a look of disappointment and something more, belligerence. His voice went up a notch. "Because I just got here, and we're colleagues now, right? We're going to work together, share things, aren't we?" He was leaning over my shoulder as I gathered up my change, too close to me, invading my space, pushing—pushing, and I didn't know why. Then he said it: "Secrets, right? What goes on behind closed doors? I won't breathe a word, I swear it."

I'd been drinking all day, and now all of a sudden I was sober. I stood—he was a small man, his head at the level of my shoulders—and I think I might have jostled him, just a bit, and if I did it was purely accidental. "I've got to go," I said.

"Where? To an empty house? Where's the fire, John?"

I stood there at the bar looking down into his prodding eyes. Elster, a little man in every way, but dangerous for all that. My voice was thick. "Nowhere," I said, and I shoved by him.

"I know you!" he called at my back. "I know what you do!"

I'm not a violent person. Just the opposite—Iris is forever saying I let people walk all over me, and I suppose she has a point. But not that night. That night was different. It was as if everything I'd ever wanted or had was suddenly at stake—Prok, Iris, my career, my son—and I couldn't control myself. I was on my way to the door, faces gaping up at me, students, locals, women with their drinks arrested at their lips, when I swung round and grabbed Elster by the lapels of his jacket. His face whitened, his eyes sank into his head. "Hey," the barman shouted. "Hey, cut that out!"

I could feel Elster coming up out of his shoes. My hands were trembling. "You don't know me," I said, my voice steady now. "And you never will."

THE NEXT MORNING I went into work. Mrs. Matthews tried not to show anything, but she couldn't help giving me a look caught midway between puzzlement and relief, and as I passed Prok's office he glanced up and leveled a steady gaze on me for a moment, then cleared his throat and said, "I'm going to need those charts, Milk. As soon as it's convenient."

I might have said, *You can stuff your charts.* I might have said, *I've had it. I've had enough. I quit.* But all I did was return his stare just long enough so that he got the meaning of all I was feeling, and then I said, "Yes," with a long propitiatory release of air, "I'll get right to them."

I worked without pause all morning. I focused on the rectilinear lines and shadings of the graphs I was drawing, the correlated figures, the means and incidences that never lied. Both Rutledge and Corcoran stuck their heads in the door to welcome me back while Prok stayed put in his office and Elster twice marched down the corridor with his shoulders thrust back and his gaze fixed on a point in the distance. The first chance I got—when I heard the telltale sounds of Prok rattling the paper bag in which he kept his lunchtime repast of sunflower seeds, nuts and chocolate bits—I went straight to his office and shut the door behind me.

"Prok," I said, "I just wanted to, well, I wanted to—"

His elbows were splayed over his work, his eternal work. He looked worn and vitiated. His head hung there a moment as if on a tether, his shoulders slumped forward, and there was something in his eyes I'd never seen before—it wasn't weakness, never that, but something very near to it, a mildness, an acceptance, a plea. "No need, John," he said, and then he repeated himself in a softer, gentler tone, "no need. But sit please. I need to talk to you—*we* need to talk."

I pulled up the chair reserved for interviewees and eased myself down on the cushion. Something clanked in the pipes overhead. A thin restless light roamed over the windows, clouds chasing after the sunlight and then giving it up again.

"Where do I start?" he mused, sitting back now to run a hand through his hair. "With women, I suppose. With marriage. We are studying the female of the species, after all, aren't we, John?"

I nodded.

"Interesting how the X chromosome prevails, isn't it—over time, that is?" He picked up a pen, set it down. "But what I mean to say is that marriage is the great and governing institution of our society, and we're devoted to it, you and I both, devoted to our wives, to Mac and Iris. And what you did the other night—no, now just hear me out—was understandable in its context, even if it shows how little you've learned here all these years." He let out a long, slow breath. "But really, I do think that as my colleague, as my co-researcher—almost my son, John, my *son*—you have to realize that emotions, and emotional outbursts, have no place in our research. Let it go, John. Please."

I never took my eyes from him, that much I'd learned. I could put up a front as well as he could. I said, "I can't."

"You can. You will."

"Iris—" I began, and I didn't know what he'd heard or how much he knew. I wanted to tell him she was gone and that nothing, not the project, not him or Mac or all the charts and tables in the world, was worth that. But I couldn't get the words out, the whole business complicated by that image of him, naked and erect and hanging over her like an animal—not a human animal, just an animal—an image that bludgeoned my sleep and festered through the waking hours. What right did he have? What right?

"She'll come back."

"How can you be so sure?"

He sighed, broke his own rule and gazed up at the pipes a moment before shooting me a quick sharp look of impatience. "Women have the same physiological needs as men, and our figures will show that, as you're well aware. Especially with regard to the physiology of arousal and orgasm, the correspondence of organs and glands—the fact is, females need and respond to sex as much as males. Every bit as much. And it's a crime to deny them or put them on some Victorian pedestal as blushing virginal brides who tolerate sex once a month in the dark in order to reproduce the species—how many interviews have you conducted, John?"

"I don't know. Seventeen or eighteen hundred, I suppose."

Now it was the old look, the grappling eyes, the triumphant set of the mouth: "Exactly."

I felt myself calming, the engine slowing, and it wasn't hypnotism—there were no tricks or carnival acts necessary, nor psychoanalysis either. It was just Prok, Prok himself, Prok in the flesh. My wife had left me, Elster was a cancer, I'd toppled my God, if only for a moment, and here I was sinking into the cushion as if I didn't have a concern in the world.

"By the same token, and again you already know this, intuitively if not empirically," he said, "there's another side to the female altogether, and this is where things become problematic for so many males—for you, John. For you." Prok was settling into his lecture mode now, getting into the rhythm of it, relishing it, and I let myself go. There was nothing

I could do, nothing I could say. I embraced the chair. I listened. I suppose I should have taken notes.

"Women are not the initiators of sexual activity, as you know, but rather the reactors. Once they are embraced, arousal begins. But men, on the other hand—the average man from puberty to senescence, or the climacteric, in any case—are aroused any number of times throughout each and every day of their lives. Mentally aroused. Aroused by the sight of the female form, by paintings, music, art, by the fantasies they indulge, while women, the females, are all too rarely aroused by anything other than contact itself and in most cases regard the male genitalia as ugly and loathsome. Given that, it should come as no surprise that they've been forced into their roles as inhibitors, as prudes, as the watchdogs of what society calls morality." He paused, let his eyes bore into me. "Do you see? Do you see what I'm saying?"

I didn't. But then this wasn't a conversation, not anymore.

"John. I'm saying that you have to allow for your wife—if she remains sex shy, then that is certainly a part of her nature, but more, her acculturation, and that can be changed only if she'll open herself up to what we're trying to accomplish here. Like Violet Corcoran, for instance. Or Hilda, Vivian Brundage or that young woman friend of Corcoran's—Betty, isn't it? These things aren't written in stone. Think of *physiological* response, John. *Physiological.*"

I was reminded of what Prok had said privately to a woman after a lecture one night in which the term "nymphomania" had come up. *A nymphomaniac*, he explained, *is someone who has more sex than you do. Period.*

I took a moment and then I told him that he was right and that I would consider it, absolutely, because Iris needed more experience, more variety, more physicality. For a moment, I was back in that attic, the women's breasts shining with their sweat, the men hard and anxious, all my hopes and fears and inadequacies on display for everyone to see. "You're right," I repeated, "you are." But then my voice cracked and I very nearly broke down right there in front of him. "Prok," I said, miserable, absolutely miserable, as miserable as I've ever been in my life, "Prok, I *love* her."

The word seemed to bounce off him like a pinball hitting a baffle, *love*, such an unlikely term to incorporate in the scientific lexicon, but give him credit: he bowed to it. "Yes," he said dryly, "and I love Mac. And my children. And you too, John."

He pushed himself back in his chair then and let his gaze wander, the pipes rattling overhead, the sun gracing the windows a moment and then vanishing. The interview was over. But there was something more; I could read it in his expression. He refocused his eyes on me and let just the hint of self-satisfaction creep over his features. "You know, I've arranged two lectures in Michigan City," he said, "on very short notice. We'll be taking some histories in conjunction, of course, two nights at the hotel there." He paused, moved the pen from one corner of his desk to the other. "I thought you might like to come along."

THE DRIVE UP to Michigan City was uneventful, no different from a thousand other drives Prok and I had taken together, he at the wheel and I in the seat beside him, staring through the windshield and calling out directions because he tended to get involved in what he was saying and cruise right on by the crucial left-hand turn or miss the junction we were looking for and have to swing a U-turn a hundred yards up—at the risk of both our lives. Prok was getting older, less attentive to detail, and his driving had suffered. Of course, he would never consider asking me to get behind the wheel, not unless he'd been knocked unconscious. What else? It was spring again, another spring. The sun was unimpeded and the shoots of green things were springing up everywhere. We kept the windows down to feed on the glory of it.

We didn't talk about Iris, but she was there with us the whole way, one more hurdle for Prok, the beginning and end of everything for me. I'd called, again and again, but she wasn't coming to the phone and her mother's voice could have crushed the hulls of icebreakers. I didn't know what she expected from me. Didn't know if this was the end or not, if we would divorce and my son would be taken from me—and my job. Because Prok wouldn't have a divorced man on his staff—or even a remarried one. That was the rule, simple and final.

What we did talk about was Elster. "I don't mean to say things behind anybody's back," I said, "but I think, well, I think it's a mistake to hire the man. In any capacity. But especially not as our librarian, where he has access to our—well, you know what I mean."

Prok didn't know, and he interrogated me nearly the whole way there, his eyes gone cold and hard. He made me go over the details six times—"Fred Skittering? The reporter? And Elster put him on to you? How long ago was this?"—and he was still questioning me, still brooding over this treachery in his midst, when he pulled up to Iris's girlhood home. It was a modest house on a street of modest houses, two stories, with rust streaks under the gutters and a battered Pontiac in the driveway. "This is it, then?" he asked, waiting for a car to pass before he backed in at the curb.

"Yes," I said, my stomach sinking, "the white house, right here, number fourteen."

He shut off the car and turned to face me. "What was the name of Iris's mother again?"

"Deirdre. They're Irish."

"Irish. Yes. Right. And the father?"

I glanced at my watch. "Frank," I said. "But he'll be at work still."

And then we were at the door, Prok running a hand through his hair while I rang the bell and the dog—a sheltie named Bug, which Iris's father delighted in calling Bugger every chance he got—began barking at the rear of the house. There was the sound of footsteps, the scrabbling of the dog's nails on the bare floor, more barking, and I tried to compose myself even as Iris's mother pulled back the door and gave me a look of iron while the dog whined and leapt at my legs. "Um, well, hello," I said, and I tried out her name, "Deirdre. Oh, yes, and this is Dr. Kinsey, my, well, my boss—"

Everything changed in that instant. Iris's mother let her face bloom with a Kilkenny smile and the door swung wide. "Oh, yes, of course," she said, "I would have recognized you anywhere, and please, please come in."

I stepped through the door and froze: *Iris. Where was Iris? And my son?* I thought I heard the piping of a child's voice from upstairs, from Iris's old room, and I had to force myself to put one foot in front of the other. The dog whined and flapped about the floor and I stooped mechanically to stroke it.

I hadn't been to the house in six months or more—we visited when we could, both Iris's parents and my mother, but my work didn't allow much time off, of course, as I think I've made clear here. At any rate, the place didn't seem to have changed much, the same coats on the coat tree, the same umbrellas in the umbrella stand, even a pair of galoshes that looked vaguely familiar set aside in the corner. I noticed all these things with a kind of heightened perception—the dog looked shabbier, Iris's mother older, the carpet was worn in the living room—because I was snarled up inside, twisted like wire. All I could think of was Iris. Would she talk to me? Would she see me even?

"Here, please, have a seat," my mother-in-law was saying, "but you must be exhausted—did you drive all the way up today?"

"Yes," Prok said, easing himself down on the sofa, "but John and I are used to it, isn't that right, John?"

I stood there hovering over him, incapable of decision—I didn't even know if I could sit, if the muscles would respond or the factory of my brain issue the command. "Yes," I murmured.

Iris's mother was transformed, as inflated as I'd ever seen her—there was a celebrity in the house, the great man himself, parked on the sofa in her living room at 14 Albion Drive. "Tea," she said, extending her smile even to me, "would you like some tea? And sweet buns, I have sweet buns—"

Prok, at his most courtly, in the voice that had mesmerized how many thousands I couldn't even begin to guess, said that that would be very nice indeed, a real treat, and my mother-in-law practically fell at his feet. I wondered, even in my distracted state, how long it would take before she volunteered to give up her history.

I was on the verge of breaking in, of demanding to know where my wife and son were and why she hadn't gone to get them, first thing, when suddenly the sound of the clarinet came drifting down from above, something hesitant, broken, infinitely sad, as if all the sorrows of humankind had been distilled to the single failing breath of that melody. "That's Wagner," Prok said. "The 'Liebestod,' isn't it? From *Tristan and Isolde?*"

"Honestly, I don't know," Iris's mother said, throwing up her hands. "With Iris, it could be anything—"

And then I was gone, through the door and up the steps two at a time, and I didn't care about Prok or the project or anything on this earth but her, Iris, my wife, the woman I loved and needed and wanted. I flung open the door and there was my son, sprawled out asleep in the middle of the bed as if he'd dropped down from the sky, and Iris at the window with her clarinet. She was wearing a pair of child's slippers, fluffy and oversized, and a blouse that fed off the color of her eyes. She played two notes more, *sostenuto e diminuendo,* and then, very slowly, with infinite care, she laid the instrument aside and held out her arms. And can I tell you this?—I never let go of her, never once, never again.

EPILOGUE

Bloomington, Indiana

August 27, 1956

I'D LIKE TO be able to report that everything continued on an even keel, that Iris and I were able to make the necessary adjustments and live in harmony ever after—or until the present, at any rate—and that the project came to fruition and Prok received the recognition he deserved as one of the great original geniuses of the twentieth century, but in life, as distinct from fiction, things don't always tie up so neatly. Iris never attended a musicale again, and she never again mounted the stairs to the attic at the house on First Street. She was present for the social occasions, the picnics, the occasional staff dinners at Prok's, the holiday celebrations, but she saw them as an obligation, nothing more, and gradually she began to withhold her friendship from Mac and Violet Corcoran and Hilda Rutledge and take up with a new circle of people she'd known from her days at school, even talking about going back to teaching once John Jr. matriculates from the lower grades. In the interval, I've continued with the business of the Institute, with the interviews and the travels and the filming, sometimes as an observer, sometimes a participant. Iris and I don't discuss it. I try to leave my work at the office, as they say. And Elster—Prok had him transferred back to the biology library the day we returned from Michigan City and he's been persona non grata in Wylie Hall ever since. Good riddance, is what I say.

As for Prok, his life was too short. Dead at sixty-two, buried this morning. He wanted to record one hundred thousand histories—that was his grand ambition, the definitive sample—but at last count we had something less than twenty percent of that figure. And he projected another several volumes in the series to take advantage of all that raw data, a volume on sex offenders to follow the female, but everything is in flux now. His last words to me, as they bundled him off to the hospital, were: "Don't do anything till I get back." I don't know. I'm too distraught right now to see things clearly, but if there was a catalyst in all this—in his exhaustion and the wear and tear on his heart that ultimately killed him—it was the female volume. Less than three years after its publication, he was dead.

Publishers are forever using the cliché "eagerly anticipated" to describe ordinary and humdrum volumes of which no one is even remotely aware, but I can say, without doubt, that *Sexual Behavior in the Human Female* was the most feverishly awaited and explosive title of the century. Everything that worked so spectacularly for the male volume—the marshalling of the press, the close-guarding of the proofs, the secrecy and vigilance—was redoubled for the female. During the months leading up to publication, Prok brought the press in for a series of lectures, meetings with the inner circle, long exhaustive face-to-face talks until late in the night, and, of course, a first look at the proofs and the signing of his standard contract limiting their articles to five thousand words and a proscription against publishing before August 20—1953, that is—which one wag had already dubbed "K-Day." Excitement was so high, in fact, that we had to reschedule the publication date from the fourteenth of September to the ninth, because the retail outlets began putting the book on the shelves the minute they received their shipments, no matter the prohibitions and pleas from the Saunders Company. Predictably, sales were spectacular, outstripping those of the male volume by something like two to one in the first weeks.

But then, as I'm sure you're aware, the adverse reaction set in. It's not as if we didn't expect it—Prok had warned us from the outset that the public would react very differently to revelations about female sexuality than to those regarding the male of the species, but that it was absolutely necessary that we publish our findings in any case, because, as he liked to say, people just had to learn to face reality. If the male volume was shocking, especially in regard to the statistics relating to pre- and extramarital relations and the prevalence of H-behavior, at least the general public had always viewed men's sexual mores with some degree of skepticism, but to put women in the same category was something else altogether.

Whether Prok liked it or not, women *had* been placed on a pedestal—they were our wives, daughters, mothers—and people came to see the book less as a scientific survey than as an attack on American womanhood. They objected to hearing women called "human animals," a phrase that recurs some forty-eight times in the text, and to Prok's bias toward premarital sex as well (our statistics, as I informed Iris in the backseat of the Nash so long ago, showed that women who engaged in premarital sex were more likely to make a satisfactory adjustment to marriage than those who did not). In fact, they hated all our statistics and what they implied—that women were sexual beings too, 62 percent of whom had masturbated, while 90 percent had engaged in petting, 50 percent had had premarital intercourse and 3.6 percent reported sexual contacts with lower animals. Mothers and daughters having sex with animals (and never mind that only one of our subjects had experienced full coitus with her pet, a German shepherd, as I recall, and that our single highest rater had achieved no more than perhaps six hundred orgasms through oral-genital contact with her cat)—the notion alone was enough to inflame the public to almost universal condemnation of us, our methods, our objectives, personalities and characters. There were even stirrings among the legislators on Capitol Hill to the effect that *Sexual Behavior in the Human Female* played into the hands of the Communist menace that sought to destroy the moral fiber of the country.

Prok was called variously "an advocate for free love," "a peddler of obscene literature and smut," and a "deranged Nebuchadnezzar" whose agenda was to drag women down to the level of "the beasts of the jungle." Old adversaries like Margaret Mead and Lawrence Kubie arose to denounce him, as well as new ones like the Reverend Billy Graham,

Reinhold Niebuhr and Karl Menninger, the latter of whom had praised the male volume and now wounded Prok deeply and insupportably with his apostasy. The criticism? At first it was strictly on moral grounds, taking Prok to task for suggesting that all sexual outlets were equally unobjectionable and that frequency and numbers somehow legitimized certain behaviors, asserting instead that in fact such behaviors *should* make people feel guilty because guilt was essential to the establishment and preservation of basic morality, but then the scientific community weighed in to undermine our statistical analysis, and that was truly devastating.

Of course, Prok was shrewd enough to escape the initial furor—all of us, Mac, Corcoran, Rutledge, Aspinall and myself, piled onto the train on publication day and made a three-week excursion to the Pacific Coast, where we locked ourselves up with the inmates in San Quentin, as out of reach as anyone could ever hope to be. But then it was back to Bloomington, where the phone never stopped ringing, and Prok began his counterattack. If anything, he pushed himself even harder now, seeking justification, fighting for the very existence of the Institute, but the Rockefeller Foundation, feeling the heat, dropped our funding and even President Wells's defense of academic freedom began to ring hollow in the face of assaults from outraged alumni, the Board of Trustees and the Indiana Provincial Council of Catholic Women. Prok slipped. He faltered. The more he drove himself, the greater the strain on his recalcitrant heart. He began to suffer a series of small strokes. His physicians recommended bed rest, but there was no keeping Prok in bed. Even his vacation, a trip to Europe with Mac designed to slow the pace and distract him from his work, proved exhausting, as he couldn't help but stay out till all hours interviewing prostitutes and male hustlers in the streets of London, Copenhagen and Rome. Finally, inevitably, he gave out.

But I don't want to remember him like that, I don't want to remember the drawn and confused-looking shell of a man who began to convene daily meetings because he no longer had the focus and mental capacity for work, the imposter Prok who we all felt would throw off the mask at any moment and roar out, "Milk, Corcoran, Rutledge, you're obfuscating the facts and delaying the project!" The dead Prok. The Prok in the casket that felt as if it were filled with rock, with lead, with hot lava, because no mere mortal could weigh anywhere near that much—

I don't know what I'm going to do. I don't even know if I'll have a job come tomorrow. And I can't drink another Zombie cocktail because they no longer have an effect on me, and this one before me is the last I'll ever have, in honor of Prok, out of respect to him. Bourbon, I'll drink bourbon, but not rum. Never again. Just the smell of it brings him back, *Fifteen men on a dead man's chest.* But here I am, locked in my study, the recording tape moving through the sprockets and across the heads, a fleeting tan strip of magnetized tape imprinted with the thinnest layer of everything I've ever felt in my life. It's hot. Blistering. Not a breath of air. Iris is in the living room, in her black dress, drinking iced tea and leafing through a magazine, and John Jr., released from the onus of mourning, is out in the yard—or the neighbor's yard—playing ball or running through the sprinkler with his playmates. If I concentrate, I can hear their shouts and cries carrying out over the lawn.

But Prok. This is how I remember him, how I want to remember him:

I see Corcoran and me pulling up to the curb outside Wylie Hall, a winter's day, five or six years ago. We are in Corcoran's Cadillac and both of us are exhausted after the long drive out from New York City on roads slick with ice and fraught with potholes and a hundred other hazards. We've driven straight through, relieving each other at the wheel, and my stomach is queasy from too many cups of coffee and the blue-plate special at some anonymous diner in a town I've already forgotten. What we're carrying is precious cargo—a group of outsized clay models left to the Institute by the late Robert Latou Dickinson, along with his library, the histories he'd taken, his sex diaries and erotica collection. The models are of human genitalia, depicted in the act of coitus, in a scale of roughly five to one, so that the phallus is nearly a yard long and the clay vagina meant to receive it proportional in every way. In all, we've transported seven of these models, and given their various angles and ex-crescences, it was no mean feat to maneuver them into the trunk and back-seat of the car on the frigid streets of New York while a not-inconsiderable crowd of kibitzers looked on, and now, exhausted, we are faced with the task of removing them safely from the car and hustling them down the steps of the building, through the corridor and into the library without attracting undue attention.

We've had Prok's advice, by both letter and telephone—his very ex-acting advice as to routes, padding to protect the models, the ideal speed we should maintain, how much rest we should need and where we should stop for meals, et cetera—and we can both hear his voice in our heads as we throw open the door and begin fumbling with the first of the models, the one with the fragile outsized phallus. It is windy. A cold rain has begun to fall. One misstep and the model is forever destroyed. I want only to be done with this, to be home with Iris and my son, sitting by the fire with a glass of bourbon and something warm and wholesome in my stomach, and my attention has wandered. I'm bushed. I tug in one direction, Corcoran in the other.

Then I hear Prok behind me. "I'm sorry, Milk," he says, "but I can see that you don't know the first thing about unloading an automobile. Here," he says, "let me," and I feel him take the load from me as if it had never been there at all.